"STARTING DATA RECORDING NOW, POV."

Katrinya smiled into the monitor as she began her report. "We've got the dust wall north of us with a density you won't believe, and Josef is cruising us alongside it."

She turned to look at the large wall-window above Josef's console. "That's odd. Josef, why don't you . . . oh, never mind. Who says gravity waves have to be regular?"

She stopped talking, frowning as she glanced up at a light-scan screen. "Now, that *is* odd. Josef, will you polarize the window into infrared?"

The next instant a brilliant red glare swept across her face, flashing through the pilot's window into the small cabin. Josef threw his arms across his eyes and cried out, then tumbled sideways out of the pilot chair.

"Get down!" he shouted at Katrinya.

THE CLOUDSHIPS OF ORION
by P. K. McAllister

SIDURI'S NET

When an unstable comet severely damages *Siduri's Net's* mothership, the once unified gypsies become a people divided. Only the siren call of even rarer molecular treasures can save both ships—if the crew survives. Can Pov Janusz, cloudship Sailmaster, guide *Siduri's Net* through the dangers of comet dust and newborn stars to harvest the rich minerals of deep space?   (453190—$4.99)

MAIA'S VEIL

What should have been a triumphant return for Sailmaster Pov and the crew of the cloudship *Siduri's Net* quickly escalated into a dangerous confrontation. For Net's mother ship, *Siduri's Dance*, had done the unthinkable in exchange for its own survival. Now Rom, Slav, and Greek must each choose between virtual enslavement and a perilous flight to the unknowns of the Pleiades. (453204—$4.99)

from ROC

*Prices slightly higher in Canada.

THE CLOUDSHIPS OF ORION

Orion's Dagger

▼

P. K. McAllister

A ROC BOOK

ROC
Published by the Penguin Group
Penguin Books USA Inc., 375 Hudson Street,
New York, New York 10014, U.S.A.
Penguin Books Ltd, 27 Wrights Lane,
London W8 5TZ, England
Penguin Books Australia Ltd, Ringwood,
Victoria, Australia
Penguin Books Canada Ltd, 10 Alcorn Avenue,
Toronto, Ontario, Canada M4V 3B2
Penguin Books (N.Z.) Ltd, 182–190 Wairau Road,
Auckland 10, New Zealand

Penguin Books Ltd, Registered Offices:
Harmondsworth, Middlesex, England

First published by Roc, an imprint of Dutton Signet,
a division of Penguin Books USA Inc.

First Printing, March, 1996
10 9 8 7 6 5 4 3 2 1

Copyright © Paula King, 1996
All rights reserved

 REGISTERED TRADEMARK—MARCA REGISTRADA

Printed in the United States of America

Chapter 1

Pov Janusz woke early in TriPower's morning and heard one of the twins fretting in the nearby nursery, a baby's pleasant babble that meant matters weren't too serious yet but Da had better get up soon. He slid out of bed, taking care to not wake Avi, then padded on bare feet into the apartment living room and on into the small adjoining kitchen. Above the kitchen sink, an exterior window looked out onto a star-strewn sky and the drifting gas veils of the Pleiades, the view moving slowly sideways with the space station's rotation. The window filtered to deep violet as the local sun came into view, its slanting light filling the kitchen with dusky golden shadows.

He blinked sleepily and yawned, then leaned over the sink to look down at his cloudship in her construction cradle below TriPower Station. He always checked every morning and *Siduri's Isle* was always there, but it was an easy habit he had enjoyed during the new cloudship's five months of construction. The golden sunlight gleamed on *Isle*'s triangular prow and sail structures, with long shadows aft of the holds and lab modules, residential pods, and the large engine assembly. *Siduri's Isle* would be larger than her mothership, *Siduri's Net*, and built for strength and speed, strong enough to challenge the Orion Nebula itself. And she was his as shipmaster. His.

During *Isle*'s construction, he and Avi had transferred from *Net* to TriPower Station, joined by Pov's gypsy family and several of *Isle*'s key staffpeople as TriPower's shipwrights built two cloudships, *Siduri's Isle* and *Diana's Mirror,* a new class of cloudship that blended the best of *Arrow*'s ship designs and *Net*'s new engine technology. Two other cloudships, *Net* herself and *Ishtar's Jewel,* would join the Nebula venture; TriPower had earlier refitted the two older cloudships, strengthening the hull shielding, rebuilding the engines, and modifying computer systems and sails. A few more days, perhaps another week, once *Net* and *Diana's Arrow* had returned from T Tauri with a new harvest of the superheavy particles that would make such a journey possible, and four cloudships would launch across the gulf to Orion's Great Nebula. It would be the first attempt by any cloudship to reach the Nebula, the first ever.

They would go in search of a new future. *Net*'s new ship-drive had given her a windfall in consortium fees from her partners, paying the cost of *Isle*'s building and *Net*'s refit, with enough left over for a capital reserve. But the drive secret could not be kept forever, and Earth was doing her damnedest to shorten the wait—by every means the mother planet had in her formidable powers. It was an uneven war, one lone ship's stubborn insistence on her rights of discovery against the combined industrial, political, and popular forces of collective humanity.

By long-established treaty, *Net* was entitled to a one percent franchise fee for her trade secrets, payable by every ship and colony that used the technology. When *Net* had suggested to Earth that Earth simply pay for the drive, Earth had added up one percent of the entire interstellar economy and sternly lectured Captain Andreos about *Net*'s unseemly greed. Greed is good, Andreos had retorted, and one percent is one percent: read your laws. Ridiculous, Earth sputtered. One percent, *Net* replied, and so the assault had begun.

For months now, the Earth senate had tried to pass a law to force *Net* to reveal her secret, with its effort blocked only by EuroCom's shaky alliance with other interstellar corporations, each of which had its own secrets to protect but also lusted for the new drive. In the interim, half a dozen Earth ships had destroyed themselves at T Tauri while trying to repeat *Net*'s discovery, an effort that would continue, ship after ship after ship, until it succeeded or *Net* handed over the drive. While the public and scientific assaults stalled, Earth opened another front in civil litigation, quietly encouraging public interest groups to file lawsuits against *Net* "in the interests of humanity," one lawsuit after another, each joining the dogged effort by Tania's Ring to bludgeon *Net* into submission, the more long-winded and expensive the legalities the better.

And all the while, egged on by government and corporations both, the News-Net on Earth had gone crazy, talking constantly about the drive and *Net* and cloudships and Pov the Gypsy and the dauntless Thaddeus Gray and the wise and canny Captain Andreos, breathless with excitement, open-mouthed with wonder, thrilled and awed and endlessly loud. Whenever another ship wasted itself at T Tauri, the News-Net gasped in horror and shock, blaming *Net* personally for each disaster, totting the names and numbers for each new death toll, lecturing, berating, pontificating, endlessly loud, loud, loud. The media frenzy simply would not stop, and indeed could not stop until *Net* surrendered and gave the drive to Earth for free. Earth would see to that.

Until then, *Net* chose to be stubborn, standing on contract and virtue and her property rights—in the hope that *Net* and her sister cloudships might find a better future at the Nebula, a venue that only cloudships could sail, a future that would last. If they could find it there, before time ran out on the secret. If.

If. Below his window, *Siduri's Isle* drifted in her cradle, gleaming brightly in the golden sunlight. You are lovely, Pov thought. No matter how often he looked at *Isle* these several months, his pleasure and joy and satisfaction in *Isle* remained ever fresh. Somehow his new cloudship made the other worries less demanding, just by the looking. Loving Avi was the same: they both seemed a part of each other, *Isle* and Avi, and all other things new.

I won't worry today, he decided firmly. I have work to do.

He washed his hands in the sink and yawned again, still trying to wake up properly, then got two small bottles of milk from the refrigerator and snapped the seals to let them warm. He waited, yawning, until the bottle caps beeped at him, then picked up the warm bottles and headed for the nursery.

In the nursery off the bedroom, he glanced into Anushka's small crib, but his baby daughter was still fast asleep, her dark eyelashes shadowing her plump cheeks. In the other crib, his son Garridan was wide awake, old enough at four mouths to smile in recognition when Pov bent over him.

"Hullo, son," Pov said in Romany. "It's morning and a good road ahead. The sun's up. So are you."

Garridan waved his arms happily, ready for anything.

"That's the spirit," Pov approved.

He checked his son's comforts and repositioned the soft blanket that Garridan had kicked off, then offered one of the bottles. Garridan opened wide and fastened his mouth contentedly, his dark eyes watching Pov's face as he drank. Pov leaned an elbow on the crib railing and fingered the ribboned gypsy token that dangled over the crib, making it bounce and spin. Garridan's eyes tried to track on the dancing movement, not very deftly. Garridan was still learning how to connect to his environment, with uneven results: it was a problem that would lessen with age.

"Pretty?" Pov asked. The silvery token spun brightly over the crib, catching the sun's gleam from the window. His son kicked joyously. "I think so, too." Garridan kicked harder at the blanket, his lips curving upward as he sucked on the nipple. "That's the man."

The coin was a saint's protection against any jealous spirit of the night, part of the gypsy ritual that guarded Rom children in their earliest months, one that Avi had liked. Pov's Russki wife had found the other Rom rules for babies and new mothers less attractive, especially Avi's traditional seclusion from the other Rom during childbirth and the following six weeks. Avi had not expected Pov to be excluded from the twins' birth, and had wanted him there. Avi had wanted to show off the twins to Pov's gypsy family, proud and happy in her accomplishment, and a brief surreptitious visit by Pov's younger relatives had not satisfied her—nor the custom's implicit comment about new mothers and Avi's personal purity. Later, Avi had watched silently as Pov's mother threw away the possessions Avi had touched during her seclusion, including a silken baby blanket Avi had embroidered during the last few months of her pregnancy. Avi had forgotten and had touched the blanket and Patia had seen, and so the blanket was lost, "polluted" by Avi's ritual impurity. They were old rules dating back to the Rom's South Asian origins, and Avi found them hard to accept, however she had tried to adapt to a culture quite different from her own Russki heritage.

During those six weeks, Pov had taken her often to *Isle* and involved her in Tully Haralpos's work on *Isle*'s Sail Deck—Avi would be Third Sail on Tully's staff—but Avi still felt she had missed something important, something more than a blanket or even Pov's sharing of the twins' birth. Likely she had, and it troubled Pov that Avi lost any wish because she had married him. He had given her his Rom family, a family connection she had always wanted, and he had given her the twins, a source of pride in herself that balanced much of her bleak life before she had joined *Siduri's Net*. It was something, but he always wanted everything, no exceptions, for Avi.

I should try harder, he thought. He scowled in frustration, worried for her. The same pressures that had created unexpected trouble for *Net* had affected the Siduri Rom as well, and his family could not currently be as flexible as it might have been for Avi's sake. For some unknown reason, the Earth News-Net had found itself utterly fascinated with Pov Janusz, *Net*'s gypsy sailmaster, and had put his face and story across the airwaves for months. Gaje reporters had harassed Pov's relatives on Perikles, getting usually nowhere, and had published all kinds of nonsense about Pov and his family and their doings, most of which the Perikles Rom eventually heard. And so the family *voi-*

voide, the tribal chieftain, had sent a delegate to Tri-Power to inquire about the stories.

It had been a nasty visit, for the *voivoide* had sent Uncle Simen, his mother's sour and unpleasant elder brother who thought any digression from Rom law, however minor, disgraced the family and insulted the wider Rom as a race. He had scowled at Pov's Russki wife, large in her pregnancy, and then ignored Avi carefully, refusing to touch anything she had touched, refusing to eat anything she had helped prepare. Avi had fled to the other apartment in tears, and had refused to return until Simen left, a favor Margareta firmly granted. The second day of his visit, Simen had tried to persuade Karoly against accepting his ranking as *Isle*'s Second Hold, and had advised Kate and Patia to give up their ship trades altogether, and had listened attentively to Bavol's whining complaints about the family's gaje attachments, and had disapproved, disapproved, disapproved.

Simen had looked especially hard at Kate's marriage to a gaje husband, a fact only rumored on Perikles and now unfortunately confirmed by himself. When he'd arrived, Simen had glanced once at Sergei, just once, then had never looked at him willingly again, an ostracism exceeding even his rudeness to Avi. Then, during the final loud argument, Simen had called Kate a whore in Margareta's hearing, and had threatened the entire family with explusion from the Rom if Margareta did not order immediate divorce—not that divorce, he added snidely, could ever repair Kate's honor. She was tainted beyond any forgiving, he declared, and her daughter Chavi with her. No self-respecting Rom would ever marry Chavi, a polluted gaje half-breed girl—better to give her to the gaje to raise, if they'd take her, of course. Personally, Simen doubted it.

Margareta had thrown Simen bodily out of the apartment, and not a Rom soul had seen Uncle Simen off when he reboarded the Perikles freighter a few hours later. And so it sat, for now, with the ball in the *voivoide*'s court.

Rom law was not as harsh as Simen wished, and Simen's threats far exceeded his authority as the *voivoide*'s delegate, but the worry had lingered like a drifting odor after Simen's departure. Years ago the Perikles *voivoide* had approved Margareta's request to join *Fan* and had never complained since; the family had the value of the precedent. A Rom elder only reluctantly reversed a decision, and other Rom had made a few untraditional choices within Perikles society, though not as extreme. The matter was arguable, and even Kate's marriage was arguable. And the *voivoide* was a wiser and more tolerant man than Simen, very old now but still hale, and a man that his mother had known all her life and still trusted.

Even so, it was not a good time for the family to relax its traditions, not even for Avi. It was not a good time, yet it was a joyous time, an odd and uneasy blend of old and new, troubles and happiness. Ahead lay a bright possible future at the Nebula, if they could find it there, and a surer legacy for all of *Net*'s children. He looked down at Garridan in his crib, healthy and vigorous and growing fast. His son. Pov the Gypsy. Fame. They could keep their fame, all of it.

By the time Garridan finished his bottle, Anushka was awake and wanted hers, a courtesy in timing that the twins had recently worked out somehow. Pov picked her up in her blanket and sat down in Avi's nursing chair by the window, then cradled his daughter as he fed her the other bottle of milk. Anushka watched his face solemnly with Avi's dark eyes, her tiny hand patting softly at his arm. In the nearby crib Garridan burbled to himself, kicking vigorously at his blanket, full and dry and warm with a parent nearby, a baby's paradise.

Da's paradise, too, Pov thought happily, now that the routine with the twins had settled down. He had thought he knew what to expect when the twins were born, a fine event, surely, and a fatherhood he had delayed overlong for a Rom male. He had expected Avi's joy, the late-night wails, the anxieties of new parents. He had not expected his feelings when he held his child's small weight and saw that first smile made not at random, but at him.

You're a dote, Avi had told him, and claimed she'd known all along he would be. Suits, he thought happily and smiled at his solemn little daughter. So I'm a dote. "Baby girl," he murmured. "Pretty girl."

Anushka patted his arm softly, content, and they sighed in unison. Pov laughed softly and leaned back in the chair, Anushka cradled snugly in his arms as she nursed, then looked out the window.

Most of TriPower's exterior windows were set into the floor instead of the walls, a natural result of the station's ring design and gravity by rotation, but Pov found walking across an apparent open pit unnerving, especially when half-asleep late at night. Most of the station inhabitants agreed, and so TriPower put different window arrangements in the residential quarters, building a long lower edge of apartments with a single window per apartment on an exterior wall. Pov's apartment had an extra window in the nursery, courtesy of its vantage on a projecting extension from the station's inner ring. It gave him a view to watch without sitting in the sink, which he appreciated. During the past five months, he had missed a cloudship's many windows more than he had expected, but not enough to disrupt TriPower's busy traffic patterns by moving *Isle* into visual range of his morning routine.

Even a shipmaster has his pinches, he thought cheerfully, not minding at all.

Beyond the strong polymer barrier of the window, *Ishtar's Jewel* drifted out of TriPower's detached ship-dock, her engine refit completed and her shipmaster obviously restless for action. Captain Janofsi had no good reason to undock today, and Pov suspected his reasons for doing so. When Earth's siege had begun in earnest, Captain Andreos had been forced to withhold certain essentials of the drive secret from his consortium partners, not from concern about their principals, but because a secret available to several hundred more people had several hundred more chances to leak away. It took only one person to forget loyalty and listen to the bribes or threats or promises for *Net* to lose it all. Sigrid Thorsen, TriPower's stationmaster, had accepted the decision with grace, and Thaddeus Gray of *Diana's Arrow* had shrugged, knowing he would get it all in time. *Jewel* had chosen to feel insulted, and had remained insulted, quarrelsome and sour.

As Pov watched, *Arrow*'s daughter ship, *Diana's Moon*, undocked from the ship-bay too, and began drifting away to nowhere particular. A few minutes later, *Arrow*'s other daughter, *Diana's Hound*, also undocked and floated randomly away, joining the display. The three cloudships migrated around local space for a while, touring slowly, until *Jewel* drifted back toward the ship dock, followed reluctantly by *Moon* herself. One by one, the cloudships redocked, their tall prows just visible above the large metal structure of the docking bays.

And there was silence, Pov thought sourly.

Skyrider strut, Athena Mikelos called it. Pov hadn't decided if Janofsi's troublemaking was mere show, as Athena thought, or intentional politicking in the hope of nudging *Net* to *Jewel*'s side of things. Whatever the truth of it, Athena had the perfect metaphor in her crew of rowdy skyrider pilots. Who needs adult behavior?

"Watch my jets," Pov murmured to Anushka. Anushka thought about it, and solemnly agreed.

When Anushka had drained the bottle empty, he set it on the table beside the chair. As he looked down at his daughter, Anushka curved her lips in one of her rare smiles, her dark eyes warming. Exuberant Garridan smiled at everyone who came near him, eager for contact with all the world and its parts, but Anushka's was the smile Pov always waited for. Avi's smile could be as shy, and perhaps Anushka would grow into the same quiet worries that Avi kept too much inside, her mother's daughter in several ways. For now, thankfully, Anushka's worries were few: Pov would see to that.

"Pretty girl," he murmured and got up from the chair, patted Anushka's back until she burped softly, then laid her down in her crib. He turned to the other crib and pulled Garridan's blanket back up again. His son went right back to kicking. Pov left him to it, but he moved the thermostat up a fraction as he left the nursery.

Avi was still sleeping, her long dark hair tumbled over her face and moving with each long slow breath. One slender foot poked out from the bottom of the bedcovers, showing which parent had handed Garridan that bit of heredity. Pov glanced at the wall clock and considered mercy, then decided not. He bent to tickle Avi's bare foot. She stirred and jerked her foot out of range under the covers, then rolled over on her back and sighed, still fast asleep. Pov took hold of the bottom edge of the bedcover and yanked.

Avi's eyes flew open. "Hey! Stop that!" she said, and grabbed at the sliding coverlet.

"No," he said and tussled with her for the covers. "Up!"

With another yank, he jerked the bedcovers out of her hands, then grandly tossed the covers into the far corner of the bedroom. Avi came swarming off the bed, intent on mayhem, and Pov ran into the living room with Avi in quick pursuit. As Avi grabbed at him, he dodged around a chair.

"Maybe if you move faster," he said smugly, "you might catch me."

"You just watch what happens when I do," Avi warned, her dark hair swinging as she grabbed again. She missed badly, giggling too hard to get efficient. Pov danced sideways across her path, taunting her, then dodged behind the chair when she lunged at him.

"Move it, Avi," he told her severely as she circled to cut him off. "You have to do better than this."

She grabbed again, and he darted past her into the bedroom, not quite fast enough. A well-timed shove in the back sent him flying, and he landed hard, nose-down on the bed. He was trying to right himself when Avi pounced on him, flipped him neatly on the rebound, and pinned him flat.

"Umph," Pov said in surprise, then relaxed bonelessly as Avi kissed him. She chuckled against his mouth, then lifted her head.

He smiled back at her. "Good morning," he said.

"You lost," she boasted.

"I did not. I woke you up, didn't I?"

"I won't comment on that." Avi yawned and craned her neck to look at the clock, then wrinkled her nose. "I think they've got the gravity set too high here," she said irritably. "I'm still sleeping longer than I should, then go dragging around all day, one foot after the other." She rolled on her back and yawned again. "How do you file a complaint? I think I'll complain."

"I fed the twins," Pov said.

Avi had closed her eyes and smiled vaguely.

He poked her hip. "We can do the bedcover bit again," he warned.

"Don't you dare."

"And maybe next time," he added, "I'll let you catch me."

Avi opened her eyes and turned her head to look at him. "What d'you mean, 'next time'? I caught you *this* time."

"Did not." Pov stretched out his legs comfortably and took her hand into his.

"Did too."

"Did not. I fed the twins. Did you hear that before?"

"Oh, you did? Good." Avi yawned again, then closed her mouth with a snap and sat up, fluffing her hair with her other hand as she yawned again. She turned her head to smile as he squeezed her fingers.

"Did too," she said. "You didn't used to play as much before," she added, tipping her head as she looked at him. "Serious Pov, dutiful Pov, and all that. I think I'm good for you."

"I decided you were good for me a long time ago."

Avi leaned back on an elbow and moved her hand

slowly down his chest, caressing him, then stilted her fingers down his abdomen toward his pajama trousers.

"And dutiful Pov has to go over to *Isle* for a meeting," he said as her hand sneaked inside. "So do you." He firmly shifted her hand back to his chest, then tugged on her hair to bring her mouth down to his again. "Sorry, love."

"Meetings, meetings." Avi swung her legs off the bed to sit on the edge, then sighed dramatically.

"Endless meetings," he agreed. "That's the way it was when *Net* was new." He sat up and kissed Avi's shoulder, then her neck. When she raised her hands to untangle her long hair, he slipped his hands around her and cupped her heavy breasts.

"Really?" she asked drolly. "You keep this going, and I could make you late." He shifted his hands suggestively, not minding at all if he was late, though he shouldn't be, not two days in a row. On the other hand, he was the shipmaster, wasn't he? He could be late if he wanted to. Sort of.

"Ouch," Avi said as he pressed too hard. "Careful with those."

"Sorry. You made me late yesterday, you'll remember, and I got comments from Tully and Athena both. Let's space this out."

"Why?"

"There's probably some reason, but I haven't a clue." He slid his legs over the edge of the bed and stood up, then held out his hand. "Come take a shower with me. You can grope and I can grope and then I can sigh dutifully and tell you no way."

"That's a deal. And we'll see about 'no way,' Povinko."

Avi took his hand and came into his arms. He kissed her lingeringly, her body pressed warmly against his. As the kiss went onward, Avi leaned slowly backward, and laughed as Pov cooperated in sinking back onto the bed. "Shower later, maybe?" she asked.

"I think I'm going to be late again."

"Too bad," Avi murmured, with no sympathy. "You had your chance."

As the water streamed down on them in the shower stall, Avi pressed close to Pov, her arms wrapped around his waist, and stepped them around in a slow circle dance. He kissed her wet face, then tangled his fingers in her long hair and arranged the curls on her shoulders, taking care with the arrangement. She caressed him, stepping them slowly around, then laughed softly as she looked up at him.

"I never knew," she said, "what joy really was. Until you. Then I knew."

"I want you to be happy, Avi."

"I am happy, Pov—of course I am. You worry too much about that. Take it from a Russki: we know everything that counts. What we don't know isn't worth knowing."

"That's a nice reality." He let his hands wander down her back, then up again.

"I think so." She sighed and laid her head on his shoulder.

"We're late," he reminded her. She chuckled low in her throat. "Don't gloat. One of these days I'm going to get some moral spine and fend you off when I should."

"Oh, sure you will," Avi scoffed. "Ho, ho. You are nicely accommodating, Povinko, and I'll gloat all I want. It's my privilege."

Avi turned off the water and clicked open the

shower door, then looked back and smiled before stepping on out. It was a moment he wanted to remember forever, he knew suddenly, when Avi had turned and smiled at him over her shoulder, all her love in her eyes. He leaned against the shower wall, willing himself never to forget.

"Pov?" Avi said.

"I'm coming." He followed her out of the shower. Avi slipped on a robe and went out to check on the twins, then rejoined him in the bathroom.

"Your mother's talking at me again," she said. She nudged him sideways a step with her hip and ran water into the sink, then bent down to bathe her face. "Give up Sail Deck, be a proper mother, she says. Don't go to the Nebula with Pov, think of the children."

"Sergei says she's after Kate, too, same subject. I think she's been thinking about Uncle Simen and setting up a few preemptive moves."

"Good luck on that," Avi snorted. "Kate told me she's thinking of moving out again after the family moves aboard *Isle*. Patia keeps interfering with how she's raising Chavi, and asks these snide questions about why Chavi's a blond, as if that's all a mystery."

Pov sighed. "Patia is hardly an example of perfect wife."

"Oh, she *thinks* she is, and Bavol backs her up all the way. He's insufferable now, preening himself about how he's been right all along, blah, blah, blah. Pov darling, I have trouble liking one or two of my new relatives." Avi splashed her face vigorously.

"I can't promise it'll get better, Avi. It could get worse." He grimaced. "That's not a new comment, is it?"

"It's okay. I'll survive it, whatever it is."

"Want to move over to *Isle* today?" Pov asked. "Tawnie's been waiting for you to say the word."

Avi thought about it. "Yes, I think I would." Then she shrugged, looking tired, too wan. "Running away won't solve anything."

"Nuts to that. It's all going to follow you to *Isle,* right?"

Avi made a face. "I suppose." She sighed.

Pov opened the over-sink cabinet and rummaged for his beard depilatory, then started taking off his stubble, wondering if his Rom family would ever settle down into any real peace. Probably not. After the three-year fight about Kate's choice of a gaje outsider as husband and then Pov's own marriage to Avi, his family wanted a reprieve from the troubles that had plagued them for too long. Margareta Janusz had discovered limits to her power as *puri dai,* and now sometimes chose, instead of delivering direct commands, to drift a few ideas and watch the family's reactions: it helped. For a similar reason, he and Avi had delayed moving aboard *Isle,* as they could have done by now, to give his family the extra time together on TriPower.

But Simen's visit had not helped; it had stirred up the old conflicts again that his mother had recently tried to settle, then added a new worry that the Perikles Rom, pressured by gaje reporters and newly alarmed by the gaje threat to the temptable young, might force the *voivoide* to make an example of Pov's family. It was not likely, not at all, but until now it hadn't even been a possibility.

Why are people so difficult? Pov thought in frustration as he toweled his face dry. It'd be much easier if I could say "do it" and they do, even Uncle Simen. I think I need to be a king, he decided. King Pov.

"She also wants us to move in with the other Rom on *Isle*," Avi was saying. "It's about the seventeenth time she's brought that up. She says I need training to be a proper *bori*. What's a *bori*, Pov?"

"Bottom-ranked daughter-in-law," Pov said. "You get to do all the housework while the other women loll on cushions."

"Indeed?" Avi turned her head and raised an eyebrow.

"That's the theory. Later, when the *bori* is older and has four or five kids, she can be more of an equal, do only *most* of the housework."

Avi straightened abruptly. "Are you suggesting we—?"

"Not at all." He clucked, chiding her gently. "There's a reason for Rom *bori*, Avi. Back when Rom girls married at twelve, that young a girl still had to learn almost everything about keeping a house and caring for her children, so her mother-in-law did the teaching. It's the same for youngest daughter. Tawnie genuinely likes keeping house for Damek and Narilla; ask her. It's her gift to them, younger to older: it's one of the strengths of the Rom, why we have the strong family ties that we have. So stop wiggling your eyebrows and thinking it's all social domination."

Avi pursed her lips and looked dubious. "Your balance again, I suppose."

"True. Somehow I don't think I'm persuading you."

"But why give up Sail Deck?" Avi said, frowning. "Why is that a rule? I can be a good mother *and* a sail officer."

"Of course you can. And it's not a rule, never has been. It's just my mother's idea of things she'd like— or Bavol's niggling. Just watch: Bavol will make Patia give up her ship job and stay at home as Judit does.

Three down, you and Kate to go, Bavol thinks, though Tawnie won't stay stuck as he thinks she will. But, still, they've got Kate at home; now they're after you, I think."

"For sitting duck? Avi around all the time to criticize?" Avi was scowling seriously now. Ordinarily, Avi tried to hide her irritation with his family's not-so-subtle pressures, not wanting to worry him. He wondered what Patia had said the other morning to set this off, and could guess at a suitable comment or two.

"I admit the opportunity," he said dryly, "all those mistakes you can make, the raised eyebrows, the aghast comments when you goof on the purity rules. Don't listen to them. Rom women have always worked, just like the men, though at different things. And just because Mother says things doesn't mean she ought to get what she wants, elder or not." He frowned back at her distractedly.

"Should we take the twins to the Nebula?" Avi asked softly, voicing the worry that had troubled them both.

Pov sighed. "No, we probably shouldn't." He looked at her bleakly. "Infants are too vulnerable to x-ray radiation, and we're bound to catch some hard x-rays, especially if we attempt the Core. You know that. Kate should leave Chavi behind, too." His sister's baby daughter had just started to walk, getting into everything.

"Is Tully taking his kids?"

"Yes. So is Athena—but they're older, Avi, old enough to be safe in the shielded sections. A baby isn't. And that means the twins will have to stay here."

"With your mother, I suppose." Avi wrinkled her nose.

"Or Aunt Narilla. Somebody would have to stay

behind. But I doubt either could turn their hearts and minds before we get back, true?" Pov found a comb in the cabinet for other straightening.

"True." Avi hesitated, watching his face. "Do you want me to give up Sail Deck?"

"No. How can you even ask that?" Pov turned to Avi and studied her expression. Avi hid so much from him, wanting to spare him, that sometimes he lacked a database on how hard she had to try. He saw his beloved's unhappy face and wished he had a magic wand, wished lots of things he somehow couldn't manage to give her. "Listen," he said softly, "anytime you want to back off on the culture adapting, it's okay. You want to be Russki, I'll love you as Russki. You want to keep trying to turn into Rom, I'll love you as Rom. It doesn't change what you are—and even if you *do* decide to change what you are, I'll still love you. Call it a constant, right?"

"So tell me what you want on this *bori* item."

"Why is what I want the main factor?" he asked her. "Why should you make all the changes? Why should you give up what feels comfortable to you, just so I can feel comfortable?"

"I *want* you to 'feel comfortable,'" Avi said stubbornly.

"We have a problem, I think. I want you to have everything, and you want me to have everything, and so we go toe-dancing around every time we have another of our culture-shock discussions. There's got to be a better way. How about trading off each time? First the Rom wins, then the Russki, then turnabout again. It'll average out."

"Humph."

"Indeed."

"I don't want to move in with your family," Avi said. "Not with Bavol and Patia there."

"Neither do I."

"And I don't want to leave the twins behind."

Pov sighed. "But—"

"It's part of being a cloudship, taking the twins wherever we go," Avi said in a low voice. "It's part of being a family, too, both Rom *and* cloudship. Kate says Rom children always travel with their parents, whatever the dangers. So it's part of *our* road together, Russki and Rom, of not being separated, ever. And it's part of me, never leaving my children." She firmed her jaw and looked at him squarely.

"They could be hurt, Avi," he protested. "It's too dangerous, especially at their age."

"You or I could be hurt at the Nebula. Everybody could be hurt. But that's part of our road, the road I want the twins to have and never to lose, not even now. So I'm telling you what I want, part of the everything." She quirked her mouth and looked away. "God, what a hard choice this is. But I don't think it's just my selfishness, wanting them by me. I think it's important for other reasons. Can you understand?"

"Yes, I do," he said slowly. "And I think you're right."

"Well, we still have a few days to decide."

"Haven't we decided already?" He saw her lift her chin, and she took a shaky breath.

"Yes," she said. They both gusted their breath at the same moment, then laughed softly at each other. "Love you," Avi said.

He leaned to kiss her. "Thank you for being patient, Avi," he said. "Thank you for trying."

"Surely, Pov. Though I'd thought it'd be easier by now."

"Bavol and Patia aren't helping, I agree. I suppose it's not much comfort to tell you my mother is actually being quite moderate, compared to what she could do."

"You're right. It's not." Avi plucked a towel from the rack and covered her head, then walked out of the bathroom, drying her hair.

Chapter 2

At TriPower's skyrider port, Josef Novak waited patiently in his skyrider's cabin, checking over his instruments. As Pov and Avi stepped through the hatch, he looked around and smiled.

"Morning, sir," he said cheerfully. Quick and lean, dark-haired like his Greek mother, Josef had his own version of Athena's pilot flair. Nothing daunted Josef, and he met everything head-on with the same good humor and determination. Those qualities had led Athena to choose Josef as *Isle*'s chief pilot, a decision Pov had fully seconded. Josef was the best of *Net*'s blending of Slav and Greek, an asset to their new ship.

"Morning, Josef," Pov said. "Sorry we're late."

"No problem, sir."

Pov sat down by Avi and buckled himself in, then watched as Josef smoothly lifted them from dock and set course for *Isle*. As they crossed the several hundred meters of open space, Pov studied *Isle*'s sleek lines, looking for any irregularity, any lack in her grace. Complete except for some interior finishing, some last computer checks, *Isle* gleamed in the sunlight, brand-new, with *Arrow*'s own grace and size in her overall design, a dozen other ideas in the finer points added by Sailmaster Ceverny and *Net*'s engineers. A thousand meters beyond her, now coming into view just under the other curve of TriPower's outer ring, her twin, *Diana's Mirror*, drifted inside her construction cradle, an inspection craft hovering above her sail assembly.

Avi clucked her tongue softly as *Mirror* reminded her. "Oh, I forgot, Pov. I invited Rachel to dinner tonight."

"Dinner is where you have it, right? Rachel won't mind. No reason not to move aboard *Isle*."

Avi shrugged humorously. "I suppose. I'll go back and start packing after alpha watch. I'll expect you to show up later to help," she added with a Rom wife's firm command.

"Yes, Avi," he said patiently. Avi snickered at his tone. Pov had eight million other things to do on *Isle* and Avi knew it.

"You'd better show up," she warned. "No excuses. You're in trouble if you don't."

"I'll show up."

"Good."

The skyrider swept easily under *Isle*'s starboard wing and climbed toward the skydeck port in the rear of the prow. As the clearance lights began flickering, the port ahead irised open into the outer airlock. Josef set the skyrider down neatly on the exterior landing platform, then rolled the ship into the lock. When the interior door opened, the skyrider continued onward across the skydeck into a small docking bay on the right.

"Safely delivered, sir," Josef said, when they had stopped.

"Thank you." Pov unbuckled his belts.

Pov handed Avi down the short skyrider ladder and got a nose wrinkling for his trouble—Avi always felt she could hand herself down just fine, thank you—

then he thanked Josef again. The young man nodded and loped off toward *Traveler* in the adjoining skydeck bay, where a crew of TriPower technicians were working busily on the cutter's exterior hull plates, carefully fitting an array of sensors into the nose assembly. The large skyrider, eight times the size of the standard pilot-ship, gleamed palely under the deck lights, smooth white and blue metal with a stepped-back raked profile.

Traveler was another design idea *Net* and *Arrow* had adopted for *Isle*'s prototype class, one with good possibilities for the Nebula. With the cutter's jump capacity, the cloudships could extend their light-ranging baseline across several light-years, rather than limit themselves to a single point for data-gathering or a series of jumps along a baseline. As *Isle*'s lead pilot, Josef had a say in assignments, and he had promptly assigned himself as *Traveler*'s pilot, with Athena's amused indulgence. Pov smiled as he watched the young man vault up the cutter's steps, vanishing inside. If only he and Athena could somehow prod Josef into more interest in Helm Deck, an interest so far largely absent in favor of Josef's beloved piloting, Josef had good promise for the future.

Look at me, he thought, amused by his own plots. Thinking like a shipmaster. He smiled more widely, tempted to be far too pleased with himself, as he probably was already. Avi glanced at his face and tipped up the corners of her mouth, then slipped her hand into his. They strolled off skydeck into the connecting companionway to the elevators, taking their time. Late was late. What the hell.

He dropped Avi off at Sail Deck and rode the elevator upward another two levels to Admin level. As Pov stepped out of the elevator, a blond TriPower tech dressed in a utility coverall looked around and straightened from his work on an environmental duct. The man smiled and nodded pleasantly.

"How's it coming, Axel?" Pov asked, walking up to peer into the open control panel. Inside, a maze of crystalline chips and power rods gleamed in orderly disorder.

"We'll be done with this ducting tomorrow, sir—or at least we TriPower gnomes won't be quite as visible in corridors. Some of the interior wall systems still have to be brought online with the computers."

"Sounds good." Pov looked around at the pale white and pastel decor of walls and carpeting that Tri-Power's designers had borrowed so artfully from their own station. Everything metal gleamed. "She's beautiful," he said enthusiastically.

"That she is, sir." They smiled at each other in total accord.

Axel Bergstrom, one of Sigrid's station engineers, had asked to transfer to *Isle*'s engineering department, once the contract details could be arranged with Euro-Com. Sigrid was still fighting gamely, not at all inclined to give up one of her best station techs, but she'd likely lose the argument for all her guile. Axel had that look.

Pov left Axel to his work and walked past two other techs farther down the hallway, each busy with final details, then turned into his office. A litter of data printouts from yesterday still spilled across his side table, and Irisa Haralpos was busily getting them into order. Tully's wife had decided to come out of her semiretirement, now that their youngest was four and old enough for day school, and had volunteered to work as Pov's admin aide. The offer had pleased Pov—he hadn't known that Irisa might be interested until she actually offered—and so far they'd enjoyed their different relationship. Irisa had a nimble mind and wasn't at all impressed by his shipmaster loftiness, or so she had told him. She had promised Tully within Pov's hearing to keep him in line, which had led to other comments. She and Pov were still amicably debating the finer points.

"Morning," he said absently as he sat down at his desk and shuffled some of the paper there. More computer reports. Somehow lately, his office paper had multiplied like rodents whenever he left his office untenanted. A new scientific principle, perhaps. Pov's version of spontaneous generation, like little animalcula springing to life in pond water. Or dark matter creating itself in deep space when telescopes weren't looking. Or gnome magic. TriPower had gnomes; Axil said so. "Where does all this stuff come from?" he complained.

"Don't you love paperwork?" Irisa asked, not looking around.

"No," he said, then grabbed hastily when a stack of reports started unzipping itself off the edge of his desk.

"I do, too." They both shuffled papers in silence for a time, then compared papers, trading this for that. "My sons' guinea pigs do this," she commented, handing him another report. "Each paper curl in its proper spot makes a pigly home."

"Pigly forever, I'm sure. Does Chief Putakin *have* to print out all this stuff?"

"Well, he says we'd better until he's sure the computer system works."

"Isn't it working?" Pov asked, alarmed, raising his head.

"Of course it's working. All of this is just *in case*."

Irisa rolled her eyes, then leaned a hip against his desk and crossed her arms. She regarded the stacks on Pov's desk for a long moment, looked at the side table, then pursed her lips judiciously. "I feel secure, I think. Don't you feel secure?"

Pov shoved the tallest pile of reports toward her across the desk. "Co-opt a side room and pile most of it in there, will you? I can't think with all this stuff staring at me."

"It's going to get worse," Irisa warned. "Today he's running a total system download, and he wants you to have a copy of *everything*. I expect the stack will run a meter high." Irisa grinned as Pov pretended to clutch his head. "Maybe more," she added blithely, rubbing it in. "Maybe two meters high, maybe even three. When the first stack gets to the ceiling, we can start a new stack alongside. In fact—"

"Put it *all* in the other room," Pov told her firmly.

Chief Yuri Putakin, the brilliant computer specialist *Net* had lured away from the Russkis at Tania's Ring, was the chief architect of *Isle*'s new computer systems, a genius at his trade, an unquestioned treasure to *Siduri's Isle*—but he carried caution too far.

"Yes, sir." Irisa gathered up the nearest stack of reports from the table and sauntered gracefully out of the room.

While Irisa finished clearing most of the paper out of his office, Pov turned on his computer and ran through a brief check of the various tech reports on screen, a medium he far preferred to paper. *Isle*'s main systems were now fully installed, with only some minor hold installations left to complete. Tully had begun actual sail drills with *Isle*'s sailset, and the engine chief had twice taken *Isle* out of her cradle to test-run her new engines. Soon. When *Net* returned from T Tauri in a few days, she would offship a third of her crew to *Isle,* filling up her new daughter ship's ranks with other transfers from *Jewel* and TriPower.

Even with the multiple transfers, *Isle* would still be somewhat undercrewed, but would compensate with increased computer control. Most of Athena's Helm Map programming, for instance, would be capable of piloting the ship by itself through a range of possible crises, and could continue that piloting for hours without actual human direction. Most of the sailset would be controlled by computer, too, and TriPower had lent several of its sorting programs from its own gas processors for *Isle's* Hold Deck programs. *Net's* ship engineers had thought about such changes for several years, and one idea had contributed to another when *Isle* presented her blank slate. With the aid of her computers, *Isle* would function as a smooth machine, one entity.

Different to think of the ship as a whole, he mused. On Sail Deck, his preoccupation had always been his sails, and how they intersected with Athena's piloting through plasma. Elsewhere, he had known vaguely, Janina had been catching atoms, and still other places other ship people were experimenting in labs, teaching the children in schools, inventorying supplies near the holds, quietly disputing contract interpretations on chaffer's level. Now he saw *Isle* as an integrated ship, her many parts working together. It was a new way to look at a cloudship he already loved, a larger way that pleased him. As sailmaster, he had often watched *Net's* exterior beauty through any available window, what part of her he could see: now he saw another beauty in *Isle,* the elegance of design and purpose that lay within, and within her the people who shared that purpose, made the ship theirs in her essential ways.

Irisa glanced at him as she carried the last stack toward the door. "Need me for anything?"

"Not especially," he said absently. "Go do whatever you want to do."

"Yes, sir." She sauntered out of his office.

As he did first every morning, Pov windowed into the extensive operations plan for the Nebula and clicked quickly through TriPower's latest observatory scans of the Nebula, checking the newest data.

Astronomers had studied the Orion Nebula for three centuries, and still did not understand its most fundamental processes. Perhaps controlled by galaxy-wide magnetics or density waves, the galaxy's ever-present hydrogen sometimes collected in massive dense clouds a hundred or more light-years in breadth, and the Orion Molecular Complex was one of the galaxy's largest, stretching from Orion's sword through his tri-starred jeweled belt, with a spray of older stars mounting his left shoulder, an accumulation of matter equal to the mass of half a million suns. At its heart, the multiple O-stars of the Trapezium illuminated a vast fan-shaped region of gas and dust twenty light-years across, forming the visible Nebula, but an even larger collection of dark and cold hydrogen bulked behind it. The Nebula was a treasure trove in hydrogen and other molecules, if the cloudships could handle the conditions. If.

The Nebula would be a beautiful and perilous sea to sail. Over the years Thaddeus Gray had sponsored extensive research of the Pleiades blues in the hope of a chance at the Nebula that might never have come. The blue stars of the Pleiades were the nearest equivalent to the massive Trapezium stars that powered the Orion Nebula—but the blues were not O-class stars like the Trapezium's stars, and the Pleiades' remmant gas veils were not the Nebula: somewhere in the gap, the cloudships might find a desperate discrepancy. A gulf of fifteen hundred light-years hid the smaller detail, obscured fact, continued the mysteries. Like the mariners of Earth's old-time sailing ships probing Africa and the Far East, or Jason's *Argo* in her wild adventures in the Aegean, the cloudships would discover the Orion seas mainly by sailing them.

The Pleiades had completed their star formation millions of years before: aside from a few dim dwarfs still assembling their planets, the local star cluster no longer had any protostars. The Orion Nebula was busily building hundreds of stars from the dark molecular clouds behind it, a process involving a complex of turbulent masses of gas, complicated gas phasing, and odd phenomena found only in an active star nursery. In the right conditions, existing only at a certain stage of a protostar's birth in a high-density nebula, molecules of nearby gas—water, silicon dioxide, or hydroxyl—could phase with certain frequencies of the young star's light emission to produce a cosmic maser, a winking flash of coherent microwaves with enormous penetrating power. Earth had detected masers in the Orion Nebula two centuries before, discrete microwave sources like winking fireflies that endured a few months and then disappeared, perhaps reforming nearby, perhaps not. Often the masers were the only clues to the actual existence of a protostar embedded in nebular gas, an object usually invisible among the infrared of surrounding dust.

And a cloudship had many windows, a vulnerability that had worried them all. Even if they opaqued their windows to microwave, the external sensors remained vulnerable. If they opaqued the sensors, shielding them from an unexpected maser burst, they lost half their relevant light-data. Molecules and dust resonated in microwave and far infrared, as did several key atomic emissions, data they needed to understand the Nebula. It was one of the trade-offs that could kill them: the Nebula had several such trade-offs.

At T Tauri, *Siduri's Net* had dared to sail a proto-star's gas-jet and had reaped a wild fortune she had never expected. The Orion Nebula held scores of pro-tostars, waiting for the harvest. At the Nebula, *Net* and her sister cloudships would try to repeat the luck, hoping the fortune in still newer discoveries would match the risks. And so they had tried to cover as many advance points of the bet as they could, even as Earth nipped at their heels, wanting the drive se-cret. They were in a race now, with a narrow window of time in which they might win a long-term future with riches only a cloudship could harvest.

Two months earlier, TriPower had launched four probes to the Nebula during *Net*'s final test of the new engines. All the robots had returned successfully with some data, though the size limit on their instrument package had proved frustrating. The Nebula was too big and complicated for a simple robot to plumb its secrets; and so part of the initial operations plan called for two full days of light-ranging, just looking to see what they might see. If the Nebula allowed them the time to look, of course, another of the trade-offs.

If. They had ships strong enough for the Nebula. They had the reason to go, one that balanced the cost and risks, and the ship-drive to get there. When Ma-gellan and Cook had set out in their tiny wooden ships, daring the waves, when the Chinese junks had ranged throughout Asia, when the Polynesians had boarded their outriggers and launched into the un-known, they had trusted to luck and divinity's favor and their own raw courage. The cloudships would go with more deliberation, but the daring would be the same.

Pov leaned forward and clicked quickly through the rest of the Nebula program, his heart beating faster as he thought of daring the Nebula. It was the wild fortune of his own life that in his generation, by his ship, he would be one of the new mariners. In future decades, his children might find new ventures deeper in the Nebula complex, perhaps more spectacular wonders not even suspected now, if Pov and the other parents could give them this first foothold. It would be a gypsy road of challenge and danger, a frontier worth any effort to win. Soon. *Isle* was nearly ready. The careful plans now required the trial.

Soon. With a sigh, Pov shut down the Nebula program and turned to the more immediate tasks of readying his ship.

He spent a quiet morning with his reports and a series of brief meetings with a few of the subchiefs, then got up to stretch his legs with a tour around the ship, putting his nose into several departments and visiting with the skeleton crew of chiefs and techs, then went back uplevel for lunch with his fellow captains. In the lounge, Athena Mikelos was comfortably sprawled in one of the chairs, flipping through some diagrams in her lap. She looked up as he came in.

" 'Lo, Pov." She waved casually.

"How was your morning, Athena?"

"Papered," Athena said sourly. "How about yours?"

Pov sat down in a chair across the table and stretched out his legs. "You should see the room next

to my office. Or rather, don't. It'll blight your hope
for humanity."

Athena turned the diagram in her hands sideways
and frowned as she looked at it. "You were late
again," he said. She tried her picture upside down.
"I heard."

"Soar off, Helm."

"I'm going to tell Captain Andreos," she promised.

"Soar off." Athena snickered. Pov rocked his chair,
watching her as she turned the diagram around again.
"I've heard," he said casually, "that there are some
trick diagrams floating around. No matter how you
turn one, it doesn't make sense."

Athena handed him a mild glare. "Watch out. I am
mean today. I am covered with spines."

"Good to hear," Pov retorted. Although Athena
had recovered most of her strength since her radiation
illness a year ago, she still looked frail when she tired.
Pov had warned her he would nag, got snippy comments when he did, but each time Athena had backed
down and gone off to rest. It was enough. "Why
mean?"

"Nothing in particular, just spiny. Helm Deck is settling down very nicely, and Lang is bringing over his
latest version of a Helm Map update this afternoon.
Wants to play with our computers to see if it works."

"Sounds good."

Tully strolled in, followed by Katrinya and Miska
Ceverny. To Pov's surprised pleasure, Katrinya Ceverny had agreed to take Hold Deck as *Isle*'s holdmaster, bringing her expertise of twenty years as senior
chemist on a cloudship's hold deck, though this would
be her first posting at captain's rank. Her husband
would be Pov's chief technical expert, refusing to take
a command position that might rival Pov's own au-

thority. It was a deference Pov didn't think necessary, but on which Ceverny had insisted. A few minutes later, Danil Tomasik walked in, looking harried.

"Pov," the Slav chaffer said in an absent greeting, nodded generally at the others, and sat down. He folded his hands on the table and frowned at them.

"Want to look at my diagrams?" Athena asked him. "It might clear your mind."

"Pardon?" Danil looked up and blinked.

"Don't mind her, Danil," Pov said. "She's mean today."

An admin aide brought in sandwiches and salads, and *Isle*'s captains traded casual conversation and a few technical updates over lunch. When most of the plates were cleared away, Pov asked for formal reports, if any. Danil, who was still picking at his salad, sighed and put down his fork, then looked at Tully.

Tully wiggled his eyebrows back. "You first, Danil."

Danil grimaced. "Thanks a lot. Sirs, we still don't have a final contract for the *Jewel* transferees. Ludek insists that any retransfer by *Jewel*'s people back to *Jewel* be no-cause, no-penalty."

"That's not unusual," Athena said. "*Net* had the same clause for her first six months."

"He doesn't want a time limit, Athena," Danil said, scowling. "He wants it to be a permanent provision for any transfer between *Jewel* and *Isle*."

"Permanent!" Ceverny swore. "Those damn Slavs! Here it comes again, all of that First-Ship idiocy about special privi—" He stopped as he got nudged by his wife. "Yes, dear," he muttered. He scowled blackly at his hands.

"Speaking as Slavs, of course," Katrinya said. She smiled at Danil.

"I refuse the label," Ceverny declared vigorously. "I do."

"Yes, dear," Katrinya said and patted his hand.

Danil tried to smile, but hesitated tiredly for a moment before he continued. The grandson of a First-Ship Slav stockholder on *Ishtar's Fan,* Danil Tomasik had grown up surrounded by the self-assumed superiority and privilege of *Fan*'s Slav elite, a social arrogance of wealth and preferred stock that had continued on *Fan*'s daughter ship, *Siduri's Dance.* When *Net* had absconded to the Pleiades, *Dance* had angrily confiscated Danil's inherited stock, erased his name from the First-Ship rolls, and otherwise cast Danil and *Net*'s other Slavs into First-Ship hell. *Net*'s Slavs honestly hadn't cared a whit, satisfied with their different choice for *Net,* but *Jewel*'s similar behavior steadily embarrassed them, reminding them of too many years on earlier ships.

Danil straightened and pulled a sheet of paper from his tunic pocket and unfolded it slowly. He spread it on the table in front of him, smoothing the creases with a dogged attention that Pov noticed with concern. Danil looked exhausted, as pale as Athena when she was ill.

I should order him to rest, Pov thought, but knew that Danil would probably ignore him, order or not. Danil had his own style of polite Slav reserve, his own careful judgments and coolness, but they came from his quiet passion for the law, its elegant logic and its firm protection of the interests Danil wished to guard. Danil tried to weigh every factor objectively, without emotion or bias, believing sincerely that cautious and clear-minded judgment was his best service to his ship—even if, he said dryly, it made him a cold-minded, frigid-souled, bloodless lawyer that nobody liked. Danil really believed that last bit of drift-gas.

A stubborn man, Pov thought as Danil fiddled with his list. Maybe I should put the order in writing, he decided, as Danil got his list smoothed just right. Danil revered paper beyond reason, like all lawyers. It might work.

"Unfortunately," the blond chaffer said, "there's more." He looked down at his paper and frowned. "Ludek wants their profit-shares segregated for easier accounting upon retransfer. He wants a special category of stock modeled on *Jewel*'s valuation methods, not ours. He wants their shares listed as temporary stock, not includible in *Isle*'s working capital, and he wants full buyout upon retransfer by direct cash payment to *Jewel*. He also wants delay of any payment by *Jewel* for converted stock, pending exercise of retransfer rights."

"I'm hearing 'retransfer' a little too much," Pov said.

"Exactly. We can't agree to the last clause, of course: with permanent retransfer rights, *Jewel* never has to pay us their converted shares, but we have to buy out those same shares if they go back to *Jewel*. At least Ludek had the grace to look embarrassed, but he's still pushing it."

"Is it going to delay the *Jewel* transfers?" Pov asked, concerned. "We don't have enough people for *Isle* without them."

"No." Danil gave him a slight smile. "We did manage to agree on an arbitration clause, with the arbitrator choice ultimately landing on *Arrow*. How will you like *Arrow* mediating our personnel disputes with *Jewel*? That's the drift, I think. *Jewel* wants some maneuvering room in her alliances. I think Captain Janofsi is jealous of Pov and Rachel's friendship, of all things." He looked at Pov ironically. "Thinks he's missing out."

"That's stupid." Pov sighed, and wondered how many ways a pattern could change—and how things one trusted could come unstuck. *Net* had handed *Jewel* her survival and a small fortune as *Net*'s sister ship in the consortium, then had seen the alliance slowly unravel ever since for reasons that made little sense. Last week Janofsi had unexpectedly refused to go to T Tauri with Andreos and Gray, claiming practice runs in the veils were enough and that his crew was tired and needed a rest—and he would not be budged, no matter how the others argued at him. Why choose such an issue to make a point? And what point? Why? It made no sense—and now this.

He shook his head, bewildered. "Why would *Jewel* risk her senior status by giving *Arrow* that kind of advantage?"

"Maybe *Jewel* doesn't feel senior," Katrinya suggested. "This could be Natalya pushing Ludek, I think. She's angry that Janofsi isn't leading the Nebula group. He's the senior Slav captain, after all."

Athena made a rude noise and shook her curls indignantly. "*Isle* is *Net*'s daughter ship," she said, "not *Jewel*'s." She waved her hands. "What do they want? Title to *everything*? Sigrid and *Arrow* built *Isle* to buy in with *Net*, not *Jewel*."

"Natalya knows that," Danil said. "It just doesn't make any difference." He spread his fingers expressively, and both the Cevernys sighed.

"We need four ships at the Nebula," Pov said slowly. "Four ships cooperating, not dusting each other whenever possible. The Nebula doesn't care about Natalya's loyalty to Janofsi or Slav jealousies."

He frowned, irritated with *Jewel,* a too familiar feeling lately. "Tell Ludek no special clauses, Danil. They get the standard six-month provision, or we'll staff from *Arrow*'s ships. Wind it up today, or they don't transfer."

Danil raised an eyebrow. "Should I mention *Arrow* specifically?"

"No. Let's not menace. And don't approach Gray's chaffers quite yet. Let's see if *Jewel* will back down." He rubbed his temples as he felt a headache settle in, a poor companion that now occurred all too frequently. "God," he muttered, as the pain lanced through his eyes.

"It might take years to build a true consortium," Danil offered, "with the fussing we've got."

"I really needed to hear that, Danil," Pov said ironically. "Thanks a lot. What else don't I want to hear?" He looked at Tully and raised an eyebrow.

Tully scowled. "It's a question of what do we do about it," he said. "Chief Putakin *thinks* they didn't get anything before he caught them at it, and he *is* sure the data-worm didn't damage our computers. He's got the beastie corralled in one of the educational programs, listening to Sammy Cloudship sing a song to the kids." Tully smiled. "God, I'd love to see their faces if we sent back Sammy Cloudship instead. Can we, Pov?"

"Send Sammy instead of *what*?" Ceverny rumbled, then answered his own question as the light dawned. "They were after the ship-drive data?"

"Exactly," Tully said.

"Who?" Pov demanded.

Tully shrugged contemptuously. "The dauntless Christopher Talbot of *Diana's Moon,* the man we love to admire and emulate. Captain Gray ought to hang him out to dry, maybe outside the ship airlock. It'd improve his personality, I'm sure."

"Tully came to me," Danil said, "to ask the contract details, all those clauses about sabotage, mayhem, and general misbehavior. It's a clear breach. If we want to kick *Arrow*'s group out of the consortium, we can. How in the devil did he get access to *Isle*'s computer, Tully?"

Tully shrugged. "Standard data-sharing. As in sail data, as in their sailmaster to our sailmaster. As in me. They give me theirs, I give them mine, and it's consortium forever. Only *theirs* had a little trick built in. Putakin earned his profit-share today, captains. Now what do we do about it?"

"What can we do?" Katrinya asked.

"Send them Sammy," Tully said emphatically, "then kick them *all* back to GradyBol. This is too much."

"Are you sure it was *Moon*?" Pov asked.

"Positive," Tully declared. "It rode in on the carrier beam as we traded data this morning. Right after that little cloudship parade around TriPower, by the way. Apparently Janofsi sent a little message afterward commenting on Talbot's piloting, and Talbot sent one back just as nasty, and then I called up just about that time and said, hey, how about that data-sharing, *Moon*? Sure, they said. Glad to oblige, Tully old pal. And blitzo." He spread his hands.

"He must have prepared the data-worm in advance," Athena said slowly. "Our new system isn't that easy to slip into."

"Oh, he had it ready," Tully said. His eyes glinted with barely suppressed anger. "After all, Talbot made that map virus we picked up at Tania's Ring."

"We don't *know* it was Talbot, Tully," Pov objected. "We just think it was." He looked around the table. "What do you recommend? Full comment, though I advise you I'll take the decision upline to *Net.*"

"What do *you* think, Pov?" Katrinya asked suddenly. "Gut reaction."

He shrugged. "I think we should ignore it."

"What?" Tully exclaimed. "After the way Talbot has—"

"Calm down, Tully. I'll bet you Captain Andreos agrees. We need Gray."

"In a hog's eye!" Tully said. Athena stirred uncomfortably in her chair, then glanced at the Cevernys. "This was sabotage!"

"No, it wasn't," Pov replied. "It didn't threaten essential systems, am I right? All he wanted was access to our data storage, access to the intermix formula we haven't given to them yet. It's not like the other virus. Talbot made that map virus, thinking it was crafty and smooth, just to impress Gray, then chickened out on admitting it when he realized too late it might mutate and kill a ship. Today he got provoked by Janofsi, and there he is again, trying to act crafty and smooth." Pov shrugged. "Talbot is a pompous fool, and God knows why Gray keeps him in command, but it's not a crime to be an idiot."

Tully stared at him. "You're defending *Talbot*?" he asked incredulously. "I can't believe this!"

Pov looked at him evenly. "Is a captains' meeting the right forum to say so?" he asked quietly. "And in that tone of voice?"

Tully paled, and abruptly looked uncertain. Pov tightened his lips, then looked down, breaking their stare, and sighed. Tully had been Pov's best friend since boyhood, had shared years with him on Sail Deck, a constant advocate, a true brother. But sometimes Tully just didn't see what he should. Pov rubbed his face with his hands, not looking at any of them.

"I pride myself on my spies," Tully said finally, his voice low. "So I think I know everything. I'm sorry, sir."

"I didn't mean it that way, Tully."

"It was deserved." Pov looked up and saw Tully grimace uncomfortably. "I forget things I shouldn't. I'm truly sorry, captain."

"Oh, hell, Tully," Pov muttered, embarrassed himself now.

Tully shrugged, markedly subdued. "I'm missing a fact, I think. Why do we need Thaddeus Gray?"

"Because," Pov said heavily, "if Captain Janofsi finds out we have cause to expel Gray, he'll insist we do. And if we don't, *Jewel* will storm off in a huff. If *Arrow* then commits a second ship to make up the four we need for our safety margin, it'd be our two ships and *Arrow*'s two ships, and *Arrow* could rightfully claim a larger interest in the consortium. That makes Sigrid minority partner and breaches our contract with TriPower. EuroCom would shriek to high heaven and sue, cancel its political support, Earth gets her new law, and we're suddenly illegal. Does this register, Tully?"

Tully blinked. "Personally, I'd have called me names, Pov, the more scurrilous the better. I'll give you an option list for next time, some of the better ones."

"Do that," Pov said, still irritated with Tully for barging. Katrinya smiled and glanced at her husband.

"Can I add to your list, Tully?" Athena asked aggressively. "I know some good ones, too, maybe some you don't."

"No." Tully swiveled his chair at her. "It was *my* mistake. Don't muscle in and take advantage."

"So how often do you make mistakes?" she retorted. "Give me a break, Sail."

"Rarely, I admit. And no way, Helm."

Danil looked thoughtful, his eyes flicking from Pov to the other captains. "Are you going to tell Sigrid? She's the most neutral party in this warfare, and we've missed having her advice."

"Probably not," Pov admitted. "Sigrid is trying to juggle the loyalties, but she still works for EuroCom. Captain Andreos should decide that, too." He frowned. "So I'm asking you all to store it on confidential and let Andreos decide how to use it, if we do." All five nodded immediately. "In the meantime, we'll let Talbot's data-worm listen to Sammy Cloudship and get some education. Maybe it'll buy us some time while Talbot tries to figure out what happened to it."

"We might educate it another way," Ceverny suggested, "then send it back with bad data, something that looks like the drive but isn't." He grimaced. "No. It'd be the map virus all over again. A ship might try to jump with it."

"I might, if I were them," Athena said quietly. "Pov's right, I think. Let's keep it corralled right where it is." There was a rumble of agreement.

Pov looked around at their faces. "Anything else? That's it, then, until tomorrow. Oh, and by the way," he added, remembering as they stood up, "Avi and I are moving over to *Isle* this afternoon, so we'll be here from now on."

"Want some help in moving?" Tully offered.

"Sure," Pov said easily. After the others had filed

out, Pov put his hands in his pocekts and slouched, then shrugged at Tully.

"Sorry," Tully said and shrugged back. "I barged."

"You've got to remember better, Tully. This isn't Sail Deck anymore. Especially with that kind of stuff in front of the Cevernys and Danil."

"Danil's okay."

"So are the Cevernys, of course. But it affects things in subtle ways. You remember how Andreos always kept it under control, whatever happened. It's important."

"I'll carry all the heavy cartons," Tully said briskly. "Make it up to you."

"Tully . . ." Pov began, then threw up his hands. "What am I supposed to *do* with you?"

Tully smiled oddly and rocked on his heels, his blue eyes alight with open affection and something else Pov couldn't scan. "I'll remember better, coz," Tully said softly in Romany. "I promise." He sketched the gypsy gesture, vowing it solemnly, then softly clicked his heels together, all sobriety now, and bowed.

Pov stared at him, wondering if Tully had finally lost his mind. "Greeks," he muttered. "God save me from Greeks."

"Too late for that, I'm afraid." Tully laughed. "Come on, Pov. Let's get you moved to where you belong."

Chapter 3

Rachel Gray arrived for dinner in the midst of the kitchen unpacking, and cheerfully lent a hand in disemboweling the kitchen boxes. Tall and leggy, with a heart-shaped face framed by soft curves of brown hair, Rachel wore her trim uniform well, a stylized mirror in gold weave winking on her sleeve cuffs, her three shipmaster's slashes above at the elbow. Her companion for the evening, a *Mirror* subchaffer named Ricardo Grant, hesitated in the living room, eyed the cartons with visible alarm, then sidled to the wallwindow for a long look at *Isle*'s midstructures. Pov offered him a drink, but the man refused with a tight smile and went back to watching lights twinkle. Pov left him to it and joined the women in the kitchen.

"Zachary's away with Dad at T Tauri," Rachel was telling Avi. She nodded through the doorway at the tall man in *Mirror*'s ship brown. "So I brought in my chaffer reserves—at Ric's insisting. Where do you want these, Avi?" she asked, holding up a set of plastic bowls.

Pov sighed to himself, knowing he'd have to remind Avi later that Rachel's touching their dishes shouldn't be mentioned to the family. After Simen's visit, if Patia and Bavol were loud enough, his mother might make them throw the dishes away, and he would *not* explain that to Rachel later.

"Anywhere," Avi replied with a smile, oblivious. "I'll find everything later when I make up some sandwiches. Simple dinner okay?"

"Suits," Rachel said. "Will we be talking business, Pov?"

"Not unless you want to," Pov said. He leaned against a counter and crossed his arms, then pointed his chin at the living room. "Another suitor, Rachel?"

"Sadly, yes." Rachel rolled her eyes. "Don't mind Ric. He can't help lacking a personality."

"Chaffers aren't that bad," Pov objected. "Not all the time."

"Your Danil is different. So is Dad's Zachary." She sighed, and lowered her voice so it wouldn't carry. "But I'm afraid Ric fits the usual lawyer parameters—intense, stubborn, well-meaning, and boring. He'll probably insult you during dinner, thinking he'll prompt some amazing revelation of your inner thoughts. Then he'll patronize Avi with what-a-nice-wife flattery, and I'll have to tell him to go home early, which will make him sulk all day tomorrow." She dimpled and rolled her eyes again. "Don't I sound simply awful?"

"You sound tired," Avi commented.

"Of lots of things. Did you see the cloudship parade this morning, Pov?"

"Yes, I did."

"I'm glad Janofsi's *your* problem, Pov, not mine. I have problems enough." She shook her head vigorously.

Her smile tilted up, then sagged down again like a balloon slowly losing air. Avi glanced at her with concern. Normally good-tempered and nicely practical when it counted, Rachel seemed brittle tonight, too nervous in her jokes and mannerisms, her smiles forced. During the months of their cloudships' building, Pov and Rachel had found extra occasions to visit back and forth, far more than was really needed, and Pov valued her now as a solid friend. Rachel shared the liking, and openly approved of Avi and the twins and all things remotely related to Pov. He suspected Rachel was lonelier than she would admit, too much the titled princess on her father's ships to find a good place as ship officer, too pursued by multiple young men with visions of married wealth to trust easily. Ric was not the first target of Rachel's sardonic commentary about her suitors.

"Want to come over to *Isle* tomorrow to play with sail diagrams?" Pov offered. "We can load the Nebula parameters and destroy our ships a few times, doing the wrong thing."

"I would *love* to do that," Rachel declared. "I would love to focus on the purity of science, not murky declarations, bent feelings, backstabbing, snide comments, hovering suitors protecting their turf." She made a face. "Oh, I shouldn't say that. Ric isn't that bad; neither are the others. What can you do, after all, when the babe is loaded?"

"True."

"Sometimes I wish Dad would disinherit me," Rachel said, a little savagely. "Then maybe Colleen Ingram would talk to me again. Dad should have given *Mirror* to her: she's earned it. But I'm the princess. I get the pretty jewel."

She slammed down another plastic bowl on the counter in ragged frustration. "I just *love* being in the middle. When I was fifteen, Dad wanted me to be a skyrider like he was and Colleen wanted sail tech like she was, and while they were arguing about it I picked what I wanted. Surprise, Dad." She winked at Avi and put dishes on a shelf. "Then Dad wanted to get married and make it official, but Colleen didn't; now she wants to get married and he's changed his mind. They've been together so long they might as well be married, but you know how that goes."

Rachel waved her hand, and Avi put a plate into it. Rachel looked down at the plate and blinked in confusion, and Avi said, "Oh," and tried to take it back, and while they were getting that straightened out, Pov checked around the doorsill at Ric. Still watching lights, his narrow face tense with complex thought.

"Anyway," Rachel said, rattling her story onward, "Dad decided to put Colleen on *Mirror*'s Sail Deck, best people and all that, and she *is* the best of everybody. He was assuming she'd want *Hound* back later like he wants *Arrow* back, but *she* was assuming he'd give her *Mirror*. So she got mad before he could explain, and now he's mad because she didn't wait for an explanation, and she's mad because what's the difference between mistress and daughter, if we're talking your basic nepotism, and he's mad because she's being unfair. So they aren't talking to each other unless they have to, with me in the middle." She sighed gustily.

Rachel had been talking too fast, pretending she wasn't really bothered when it was obvious she was, very much so. As Avi turned away from Rachel to put some dishes in the side cupboard, she traded a glance with Pov.

Pov unleaned himself and slipped an arm around Rachel's slim waist, then gave her a hug. "So send Ric home now and we'll put our feet up. I'll tell you my problems, you tell me more of yours. We can focus on the topics we're not supposed to discuss, get ourselves in trouble for telling secrets."

Rachel laughed. "I'd like that. Let's do."

Ric was stubborn, insisting on a private consultation or two with Rachel in the room corner to offer better advice, but finally took himself off, looking unhappy. Rachel smiled wryly and sat down in a chair, then unbuttoned her uniform collar and put her feet up on the table. "He insisted on uniforms. It's proper, he said. After all, Captain Janusz is Captain Janusz."

"I am, indeed, Captain Janusz. Ask News-Net." Pov sat down in the other chair, handed her a glass of vodka, then nudged her boot over for room and propped his feet, too. "Aren't you going to join us, Avi?" he asked as Avi headed back for the kitchen.

"No," she said. "I'm going to labor onward while you two loll. Sandwiches in a bit."

"Sounds good to me." Avi flipped her hand at him, then smiled and disappeared into the other room.

Rachel slouched lower on the couch, then blew out a breath. "I'd rather work on your Sail Deck," she said, then took a long swallow from her shot glass. "It doesn't do any good to wish, of course. I'm stuck. Even Dad admits that now." She shrugged elaborately. "Oh, he meant well, of course. Colleen will come around, however she's fussing now, and they both know she will, even if they're not talking. But it just didn't occur to Dad that the other captains had expectations of their own, too. This is *Arrow*'s first new daughter ship in twenty years: some people had plans. He thought they'd be as loyal to me as they are to him."

"Don't let it get you down, Rachel." Pov saw the glimmer of sudden tears, which she tried to hide behind her sleeve.

"They don't like me, Pov," Rachel said in a low voice. "None of them do. All I get at captains' meetings, when Dad isn't there, is resistance and blank stares and resentment. No real backstabbing yet, thank God, not the kind that might hurt the ship. I guess they figure it wouldn't work with Dad, setting me up somehow by sabotage. I guess they figure it's hopeless, and so they just show their dislike when they can. How did you ever manage with your own kind of prejudice, the gypsy labels?"

"It's easier when it's not really personal—and it was never that bad, even on *Dance.* I could ignore it, get away from it."

"Well, I can't. I don't know what to do."

"Maybe it's just a question of waiting it out."

"Yeah, great." Rachel made a face. "We've got a good crew, the best. They'd follow Dad to Hades itself. It's always been that way. He just has this *presence,* this way about him that brings out the best in people. He can trick and manipulate with the best of them when it comes to GradyBol or another cloudship or the other outsiders, but never with our ship people. They know that. They trust him."

Pov nodded. "After all these years in command—and his successes—they should."

"No, it was that way in the beginning, when he first took command of *Diana's Arrow.* I remember how it was. I adored him, too: still do." She managed a crooked smile. "Larger than life—that's my dad. Super-pilot, super-Helm, super-everything. It's a hard act to follow."

"And you're what—twenty-five? What was he at that age?"

"Larger than life." She took another swallow of her drink. "You know, I'd like to get nicely drunk and sing bawdy songs, cry in your cups some more, and then go back to *Mirror*. Maybe I'll hunt up one of the nicer suitors and seduce him so he can brag to the others and strut, make them turn green. And tomorrow they can all talk about Rachel's hangover as I blear around, stumbling over my feet." She twisted her mouth. "And make comparisons."

"God, Rachel, you *are* depressed," he said, concerned. She wasn't listening, her face abstracted and unhappy. He tipped his boot into hers with a soft *thok*, getting her attention again. She looked up. "It can't be that bad, Rachel," he said firmly.

"Sorry, but it is." She smiled at him, already a little smashed. "You're such a nice man, Pov Janusz. You listen well."

"And your friend. I always will be."

"Thanks, friend." Rachel tried another smile, not her best skill tonight, then stared down gloomily into the vodka glass cradled in her hands. "I sit here and snivel about how they don't like me, and you smile and say comforting things. A good friend. You don't even mind when I roll in the self-pity." She was silent for a moment. "It just got to me today, the way they behaved at the captains' meeting. Any reports? I ask brightly. Nobody says a word. Sailmaster? No problems, captain, Colleen says. Well, uh, good, I say. Holdmaster? Nothing to report, captain. I see, thank you. Helm? Blank stare. Well, fine, sirs. That's all for today, chirp, chirp. And they troop out." She sipped at her glass. "They're waiting for Dad to come back. You just feel it resonating on the air. I finally asked Dad, before he left, to disrank me back to Sail Deck, let Colleen take *Mirror*, but he won't do it."

Pov shook his head. "It wouldn't work, Rachel. It just shows them they can block you from command."

"I know, I know. Bad precedent. It would affect not only me, but him. They've never tried to block him before, not even when he put Talbot in command of *Moon*. He can't let it happen a first time, for his sake as well as mine. I know all this, endlessly. I'm stuck." She looked up and tried another crooked smile. "So what are *your* problems, Pov?"

Pov took a sip of his vodka. "Well, my cousin is harassing Avi about being a proper Rom wife."

"Really? I bet Avi loves that."

"Not much, I agree. And I keep getting headaches and get to take these pills that don't work."

"Pills are good," Rachel said firmly, shaking her head at him. "Take your pills, Pov."

"I do." Pov recrossed his ankles comfortably. "And Captain Janofsi is angling his crew transfers to get some advantage with *Arrow*."

"Really? More squabbling among the Slavs?" She clucked her tongue, teasing a little too hard. Though Rachel sympathized, she thought certain Slav attitudes were a problem Pov didn't need, and sometimes told him so. "Tsk," she said again and shook her head.

Pov brought her back down to ground with a clunk. "And today," he said casually, "your Captain Talbot tried a data-snatch on *Isle*'s computer."

Rachel's jaw dropped open in shock. *"What?"*

Pov winced a little, wondering if he should have told her that. It was supposed to be a secret, but he and Rachel got tangled up sometimes on where to draw the lines. "That could get me in trouble, Rachel. Keep it stored."

Rachel was still busy sputtering and didn't hear him. She threw up her hands in outrage. "That idiot man! Are you sure it was *Moon*?"

"Positive," Pov said. "It looks like Talbot has a

short fuse on getting called names by Karol Janofsi. Squabbling gets contagious, I think."

"Oh." Rachel stared at him, more aghast as she thought through the rest of it. "And I thought the cloudship parade wasn't my problem. Great stars! If Janofsi finds out—"

"Exactly."

Rachel got up to pace, the shot glass jiggling dangerously in her hand. She looked down distractedly when her glass splashed, then set it down on the table before pacing some more. Finally she stopped and put her hands in her pockets, then gave Pov a keen glance.

"I assume because you're telling me this," she said carefully, "*Arrow* is still in the consortium."

Pov smiled. "Now who's an idiot? Of course you are."

She narrowed her eyes, just as her father did. Thaddeus Gray's daughter, larger than life. He smiled back at her fondly. "If only to keep our consortium share just where it is," Rachel suggested.

"More than that, *Mirror.*" Pov gestured expansively.

"You're sure?"

"Positive." Rachel relaxed and started pacing again, and ended up by Pov's Rom shrine near the wallwindow. She leaned forward to look at the golden statuette and its tiny votive light, careful not to touch.

"Why did your father ever make Talbot a shipmaster?" Pov asked curiously.

"Because Gunter Weigand is Gunter Weigand," Rachel replied, turning around to face him. She put her hands in her pockets again, tall and leggy and graceful, with a skyrider's unself-conscious poise. Pov wondered why Rachel had chosen Sail Deck when she was so obviously suited to follow her father into skyriding, and then thought of a few good reasons why not. Even a princess had her imperatives, maybe even more than most.

"We've done most of our harvesting for GradyBol," Rachel said with a shrug, "and Dad wanted a shill to fool Weigand. It isn't hard." She made a pose of the arrogance, looking suspiciously like Christopher Talbot at his worst. *Moon*'s shipmaster had copied less admirable facets of Thaddeus Gray's character, perfecting them to a shine while ignoring the rest; Rachel had chosen differently.

"Weigand's the same type of idiot as Chris," she said, "and Weigand felt they understood each other, unquote. So Weigand would try to outfox Talbot, thinking he was winning big points over *Arrow* when he did, and all the while Dad was out robbing Euro-Com blind behind his back." She grinned. "It's one of the dozen or so reasons why we're rich. I didn't mind Talbot until Dad put me on his Sail Deck, but Dad said that bureaucrats like Weigand litter the universe and I needed some practice in dealing with them. Better *Arrow*'s bureaucrat than EuroCom's." She made a rude noise. "Dad's reasons always *sound* good. He's practiced."

"I *have* wondered about Talbot," Pov said casually. He leaned back in his chair and crossed his ankles comfortably, then made a show of a yawn.

Rachel chuckled and made a face at him, then strolled back to sit down on the couch. "So put on an act, you crumb. I can take it. When Dad hears about this, Talbot's in big trouble. If Dad had had a smidgeon more of proof, he'd have pasted him good for that map virus." She darted a sudden glance at Pov, as Rachel got tripped flat, too. It was tricky, Pov agreed.

"We know Talbot did that, Rachel. It's not a surprise."

"And still you invited us into the consortium? You're a forgiving man." Rachel suddenly leaned forward and took his hand tightly. "Alliance, *Isle*. Dad meant it. *Arrow* will keep her promises, just as Dad keeps faith with our own people. You can count on that. It won't *all* come unglued." She hesitated, and the color rose in her face. "I apologize for Captain Talbot," she said awkwardly, flushing still more. "So will Dad, when he gets back."

"It's all right," Pov said heavily, and saw Rachel's face fill with open concern, not for their alliance—she trusted enough for that—but for him. "God, the worries we've got," he said, trying to lighten the mood.

Rachel winked at him. "Hey, Pov," she said, "when we get rich in Nebula, let's build a ship together and go exploring somewhere. Let's take a crew of half us, half you, and make it work. The others can come if they want, and if they don't, it's their loss. We'll flip a coin for who gets to be shipmaster, use the right coin with double heads. You call heads; I'll call tails."

"We'll do that."

She smiled more widely, then saluted him with her glass. "To solutions, when we can find them."

"That's a deal."

Rachel left after supper, half smashed but happier, and by midnight, Pov and Avi had worked through most of the cartons and had the closets in a tentative order, though Avi would rearrange for a few days and Pov still had to tackle the datafile offprints stacked next to his computer in the small side office. The printed set of the Nebula plans stacked a full meter high, diagrams and charts, light-readings, maps, operation plans, projections, alternatives. He knew all of it by heart, and knew also if he sorted it now, he'd be up all night reading it through again. He managed to get himself out of the office, even turned out the light.

Out in the living room, Pov knelt down by one of the cartons and rummaged, then lifted out Avi's set of nested Russian dolls. Brightly red and blue, wearing a painted babushka scarf, a peasant's dress, and a big smile, each wooden doll had a smaller doll inside it, one after another. The nested dolls had been a Russki girl's toy for centuries, and he knew Avi treasured hers. "Where do you want these?" he asked her. Avi straightened from a dish box and looked around.

"Where do you want them to go?" she asked.

"Avi, they're your dolls. You say where they go."

"How about the shelves in the nursery? I want to give them to Anushka, anyway, when she's old enough."

"Okay." Pov walked into the nursery and put the nested dolls on a middle shelf, then rearranged a toy goose, a bear, a clown, and some alphabet blocks. He and Avi had bought the toys in a TriPower shop before they thought of proper age groups, but the brightly colored toys made a nice decoration for the shelves until the twins were old enough to mangle them. On the shelf above, Lasho's tiny gypsy wagon and horse glinted in mellow brown and gold trim, its wheels bright red, the horse properly spirited and prancing. His cousin had a gift for making things, and he had given the toy freely as a christening present, thinking Pov and Avi would like it, not hinting at anything about proper priorities like the others, just making this lovely miniature with his skills to celebrate the family's joy.

He picked it up and moved the wheels around, remembering his own toys when he was young. They hadn't had much money to spare, even before his father had died, but his mother had always managed one special toy for each of her children, his Blue Ranger spaceship, Kate's frilly-skirted doll, his silver puzzle rings, Kate's brightly colored picture book. When Pov had moved on to data tapes and boys' corridor games, Kate had taken over his toy spaceship and raygun, zapping everybody in sight as she imagined them the awful evils and horrendous horrors in her imagined galaxy, always winning, always triumphant and un-bowed. He smiled, remembering how she had been. The succession of their toys marked the years, the icons of being a child. Now the cycle began again, with new toys, new years.

I thought I knew all about it, he mused. I thought I knew how a father feels, but I didn't even guess at this part, the way children answer a question I didn't even know I was asking.

He replaced the wagon carefully on the shelf, de-cided to push the two cribs farther apart for a wider walkway between them, then spent some time untan-gling the strings of the play mobiles that dangled over the cribs. For the night, the twins would stay on Tri-Power with their grandmother while he and Avi un-packed, a concession Avi had graciously granted and Margareta had graciously accepted.

As he sat cross-legged on the floor, fiddling with the strings that had somehow managed to make an utter tangle of themselves, he smiled again, pleased that his mother could be gracious to Avi, that she forwent the snide comments, the little digs, the disdain she could so freely substitute for an occasional kindness, the small statement of praise, the mildness of a shared joke. He suspected his wife and mother actually liked each other, though neither would yet admit they might. Somehow in her many ways, Avi had pleased

his mother, bringing a new kind of peace into the
family, something that endured quietly despite Patia's
misbehavior. And somehow Avi had found in her
mother-in-law an older woman who assuaged an emptiness Avi had found in her own mother, that stark
and rigid pioneer who had little time for a sensitive
and vulnerable daughter, who thought emotion a
weakness, Avi's sweet yieldingness a vapid lack of
character. Pov's mother might never fully accept
Kate's gaje husband, not with her ambitions for Kate
as her Rom heir, but Pov thought his mother and Avi
might become friends. He hoped so. Another grand-
child might clinch it, it seemed that close.

"Where have you disappeared to, Pov?" Avi called
from the other room. A moment later, she appeared
in the nursery doorway, her hands on her lips. "Oh,
there you are."

"I'm figuring out the key to the universe," he told
her, holding up the tangled mobile. "It's in these
strings somewhere. Once I get it solved, we'll be rich."

"Really?" she asked skeptically.

"Absolutely. Trust me."

Avi sat down in the nursery doorway, folding her
long legs comfortably beneath her, and watched him
as he fiddled, unwrapping one plastic block on its long
string, only to find he had somehow rewrapped another block. He sighed and studied the strings, then
tried another solution program. After a few minutes
of absorbed silence, he looked up again at Avi. She
had her hands in her lap, sitting comfortably against
the doorjamb. Her dark hair tumbled around her
shoulders, framing her pale face, a counterpoint to her
lovely eyes. She was smiling slightly.

"Don't I look domestic?" he joked, then looked
down at the tangle in frustration. "At this rate,

though, it could take weeks to finish unpacking. The whole ship will talk about it, wondering if we'll ever be done."

Avi leaned her head on the doorway jamb. "At least you have a distraction, which I'm glad to see. Is your headache better?"

"How do you always know when I've got one?" he complained. "Do I wear signs or something?"

"Plus a marching band tootling the news, I'm afraid. You can't fool me. Pov, I want you to see Dr. Karras again. This medication isn't working any better than the last one."

"It was a hard day," he said, dodging. "I'm all right."

"Dr. Karras," she insisted.

"Yes, dear." Pov frowned at the strings in his lap.

"So tell me, love," Avi said softly. "What do I have to do to lock myself tight with your family, just to get that item off your worry list?"

"Get pregnant," he replied succinctly. He chuckled when she made a face.

Avi sighed. "I thought as much. Oh, well. At least the first step is great fun." She winked at him. "And so are the later steps, after the end product is duly produced. I'll have to think up a way for you to pick up your share of what's in between, let you throw up for two months straight, let you be fat, let you pitch in on the labor bit."

"When you figure out how to arrange that," he said smugly, "let me know."

"I'll do that." She leaned her chin in her hand and narrowed her eyes, studying him. "I'm sure there's a way."

Pov eyed his wife with alarm.

*   *   *

Later Pov woke suddenly in the darkness of their bedroom. Beside him, Avi slept deeply, her body warm against his, her breaths a slow whisper against his shoulder. He gently eased away from her, not wanting to wake her, then got up and navigated by feel through the darkness, not quite remembering where everything had been put and very aware that a few remaining cartons lay in wait in the probable traffic patterns. He managed to get to his office, a small room off the living room near the bedroom doorway, without causing a racket. He closed the office door behind him, then turned on the light.

On the wall, the clock informed him he had slept a whole two hours. He frowned at it with some disgust, knowing that tomorrow afternoon could be very bad if he did not go back to bed and get some decent sleep. He pulled out his desk chair and sat down stubbornly, knowing he'd regret this, then tugged over the box of Nebula plans.

You know these, he told himself. You can recite them, chart by chart.

So? he retorted. It doesn't hurt to look at them again.

You zero, he told himself back. Get some sense.

Pov scowled as the slow beat of a headache resumed in his temples. He leaned his elbows on his desk and rubbed his eyes, then told himself to go back to bed. No such luck. He got up and navigated back through the darkness to a closet and got some better clothes than pajama bottoms and bare feet, then left the apartment to wander through *Isle*.

Isle's corridors were darkened during the night watch as the ship still kept its skeleton watch. Only a few dozen people lived aboard her at night, though that would change immediately when *Net* returned and the new crew began coming aboard. *Mirror* had transferred her crewpeople aboard as soon as her residential sections were habitable, but *Net* had delayed *Isle*'s transfers until everyone could transfer at once, perhaps too wary of repeating first-ship problems in a new guise. They would be his crew to manage, his to weld into a single people: that and all the other tasks, some of them unnecessary in tedious shipmasters' frets, some of them critical in an unforgiving Nebula.

It might be better to wait and go later, he thought, though he winced at the thought of more delay. He had waited patiently through the months: now his restlessness had better hold of him, eroding away his patience like water undermining a dam, a laser steadily melting through a slab. Soon, he promised himself, as he had promised himself for months now.

Pov stopped on the companionway and looked at the stars through the wide windows that lined the central bridge. Thousands and thousands of stars within reach, thousands of roads, a nomad's frontier when Earth's ships had the ship-drive to reach that extra distance in all directions. He smiled, comforted for reasons he couldn't quite define, and looked a while at the distant gray patch of the Nebula among Orion's bright stars, then walked onward toward the elevators.

On Admin level, he walked down the silent and dark central hallway, then turned into *Isle*'s interlink room. *Net* had borrowed heavily from *Arrow*'s longer experience with the interlink to design a new system that had worked well in trials. On one wall a large console handled the intraship operations of *Isle* herself; one of the other captains, usually Miska Ceverny, would sit there to assist. On the opposite wall was his own console, the interlink reaching out to the other ships, coordinating maneuvers with discrete light-pulses that maintained a precise distance between the ships, keeping an open channel to each of the other shipmasters, allowing the usual computer displays of useful data.

Between the captain stations a wall-sized screen allowed other displays, giving the two interlink captains as much data as they could handle, organized and windowed for the most efficient scans. Putakin had come into his element in designing the new software, delighted to share ideas with the computer chief on *Arrow* who had invented the interlink years ago. The Grays were openly enthusiastic, but Captain Janofsi had shown obvious disinterest in the new command tool, preferring his manner of operations tested by the years, so he said.

Why can't he see? Pov thought in frustration. Why can't he see what lies there for us all?

He sat down before his console and keyed up the central wallscreen to an outside view of the Pleiades veils, a beautiful view of drifting blue gas and brilliant suns, but a depleted nursery for the cloudships' future, another fact Janofsi could not see—or chose not to see. The interstellar economy was powered by tritium, the rarer isotope of hydrogen used in ships and power plants everywhere, but the small amounts needed for power production usually made it more cost-effective for Earth and the colonies to buy tritium from cloudships instead of funding their own collecting fleet. And so the cloudships had found a niche, independent ships on contract, beholden to no one. *Net*'s new fuel would upend that equation: *Net*'s secret promised a revolution in humanity's power technology, sweeping across the board into every significant industry and starflight itself. Whole economies had changed when wind and sail gave way to steam engines, and later steam to petroleum and atomics. The new drive and the fuel upon which it was based had the same potential impact.

It would be a boon to humanity, a wonder for humanity's farther exploration of the stars, but a technological change that might easily make the cloudships obsolete. And so Captain Andreos had decided to seek a new niche, one of their own choosing. If it was there, at the Nebula.

It would be a glorious sea to sail, Pov thought with sudden longing. A sea that glowed with the moving light, alive with new stars and the storms of creation, a sea no one had sailed before and one exquisitely suited to his beloved cloudships. It could be a future— a road, in gypsy terms. Garridan and Anushka's road and, perhaps, if the Rom were willing, a road other gypsies might follow. He stirred restlessly.

I'm tired of waiting, he thought. I am so heartily tired of waiting. I'm tired of "soon." He slouched lower in his chair, watching the veils drift softly against a black sky, and listened to his headache pound at his temples.

"Pov?" a voice said behind him, high with surprise. "What are you doing here?"

The voice jerked Pov awake in his chair, fast enough to hear his last rattling snore. In the doorway of the interlink room, Irisa stood with her hands on her hips, staring at him. Behind her, the corridor lights were brightly lit for day watch, with a low murmur of other voices in the distance.

Pov groaned and shifted himself straight in the chair, then blinked at her. "Oh, please don't comment," he said and decided to rub his face. It probably needed the rearrangement. He heard the soft padding of her boots on the carpet, then felt her hands on his shoulders. She slowly kneaded his muscles with her strong fingers, getting deep into the knots.

"We've had a message capsule from *Net*," Irisa said. "They're on their way back, probably get here tonight."

"That's good news," Pov said with relief.

"And then we can up and go to the Nebula, and stop all this stupid waiting around."

"I'd like that, most sincerely." Pov closed his eyes and relaxed as her fingers continued their work. "That feels good," he added after another minute, "but you'll put me back to sleep if you keep it up." He covered a yawn with his hand.

Irisa chuckled, then bent and lightly kissed his cheek. "You're a fine man, Pov Janusz, one of the best. And *I* think we're going to do it all, the entire venture. Take it from an expert: we Greeks know everything."

"Avi says the Russkis know everything."

"They're deluded, I'm afraid. I'll talk to her, get her straight." She winked.

"Thanks, Irisa."

Irisa paused in the doorway, then lightly touched her heels in salute. "Thank *you,* sir."

And then she was gone, leaving Pov to blink at the empty doorway.

Irisa had no way to know, whatever her Cassandra fancies about Greek know-it-all, but somehow he felt more optimistic just because Irisa thought he ought to. Odd, but then the Greeks in his life often turned things sideways, a nice event when it happened. He stood up and stretched hugely, unkinking his muscles, then walked out to meet the new day.

Chapter 4

After alpha watch, Pov and Avi stopped by the family's new apartment to pick up the twins. Margareta had chosen a comfortable apartment on C Deck near Pov and Avi's own quarters for the twelve adults and eight children who made up the rest of Pov's Rom family. After the crowding in the Rom's cramped apartment on *Net*, his mother had chosen large and had knocked down an interior wall to boot, though she'd had the courtesy to inform Pov before she did it. The Janusz were still a crowd, despite the extra space.

Pov and Avi walked into the ordered chaos of a Rom family at lunch, now complicated by the final stages of the family's own unpacking. The men and older boys sat eating on cushions in the front seating area of the larger room, with the boys noisy as they poked and joshed their brothers and the older men. In the kitchen, the wives bustled with pots and dishwater, ignoring *Isle*'s modern conveniences, their own soft conversation a pleasant countertone to the deeper male voices in the front room. The smaller children played underfoot in the kitchen, indulged with an occasional pat or small push by the women while the kids hit spoons on a saucepan or poured their milk on the floor to see it puddle. As Pov walked in, Kate bent and picked up Chavi, who was crying lustily, then shook her finger at two-year-old Cappi for applying his spoon on more than a saucepan.

Children were universally indulged by the Rom, treasured, pampered to excess, and rarely disciplined by more than a light scolding. Most misbehavior was simply ignored, and the child with it, until the behavior improved, a system of child-rearing that worked rather well, if somewhat chaotically in the interim. And, indeed, a Rom child had few of an adult's restraints in what he or she was permitted to do. Until puberty, Rom children were excused from *marime,* the purity rules that Rom adults observed, a complex of gypsy observances about parts of the body, floors, clothing, and food preparation that defined Rom culture.

Avi had learned the *marime* rules, as had Kate's gaje husband, but both Avi and Sergei thought the rules arbitrary, as they in fact were, and Avi still did not like the implicit commentary about women in several of the older rules. A woman could not walk in front of a seated man, lest her skirts accidentally touch the man's head or shoulders, polluting him. A menstruating woman could not touch food that would be served to the men, nor sit with the men at dinner until her impurity had ended. Those same rules had isolated Avi after the twins were born, a restriction lifted only slightly for their christening. Avi fretted quietly about *marime,* rarely admitting her discomfort even to Pov, and stubbornly kept the rules in her effort to please his family. With a few exceptions, and those not Avi's fault, she had succeeded.

His cousin Karoly looked up as they came in and smiled broadly at Avi, and she stopped by him and Sergei to say hello, a careful two steps away, then nodded shyly at Uncle Damek, who nodded back. Pov walked onward to the cribs in the back of the room, where Garridan lay in his warm coverall and blanket on the small mattress, his sister beside him.

He picked up his son, then moved aside as Avi caught up to collect Anushka. Pov shifted Garridan to a left-arm hold and offered his right elbow to Avi. Avi neatly shifted Anushka sideways and took his arm. Practice. In the beginning, they had both so feared dropping a twin that they'd have preferred a few extra arms each. As they turned around, Patia came bustling out of the kitchen toward them, her mouth stretched into an artificial smile.

Avi's fingers tightened convulsively on Pov's forearm as she braced himself. If Avi had not been gaje, Patia would be junior to Avi in age and ranking among the wives, an inapplicable fact that rankled Patia beyond reason. And, perhaps, Patia thought she pleased Margareta in her behavior, though Pov's mother rarely openly objected to Avi, and was often kind, whatever her other nagging. Whatever the reasons, his young cousin took every opportunity possible to remind the family of the *gaji romni*, the non-Rom wife, in their midst, and Avi had tired of it the first time it had happened.

"Pov!" Patia caroled loudly as she bustled forward, drawing every male eye in the room. "And Avi, too!" she added, blinking at Avi, as if Avi's presence were a total surprise.

"Hello, Patia," Avi greeted her in Romany, though her fingers tightened again on Pov's arm.

"Yes, indeed, it certainly is," Patia answered brightly in ship-Czech, as if she kindly ignored Avi's social blunder in daring to speak the Rom's own language. Her thin face was filled with a sly malice against Avi, a malice that had grown in the months since Pov's marriage. Pov almost said something he shouldn't—what's the harm in wishing hello, after all? Patia would say, looking hurt, then ask all nearby for their opinions, endlessly spinning it on—but saw Kate and Tawnie issuing fast from the kitchen, beetling to Avi's defense. Patia sensed them coming and promptly shifted orbit to Pov, another fine way to dig at Avi.

"My, you're looking formal," Patia declared, just as loudly, as she looked Pov's uniform up and down. As if Pov didn't wear his ship grays every day, as if that were all a surprise, too.

"I'm trying to impress people," he said lightly, refusing the bait.

Patia snorted and waved her hand. "It takes more than a uniform to impress the Rom, coz," she said snidely. "I thought you'd know that by now." Patia's tone nicely totted the idiocy of wanting to impress anybody gaje else.

Pov checked Avi as she started forward instinctively, stopping whatever Patia was about to get, but Kate had reached them with her long-legged strides, Tawnie close on her heels.

Kate stopped, put her hands on her hips, and inspected Patia, a slow up, then down. "My, you're in good form, Patia," she drawled. "I'm always amazed how you manage to put so much into a few choice words." Kate's voice carried nicely, and the men all looked around from their meal, though they weren't supposed to notice when the women started pulling rank on each other. As Kate and Patia squared off, Pov had a sudden male urge to fade, maybe over to lunch with the other men.

"Silly Pov, silly Shipmaster Pov," Kate mocked onward in a singsong voice, shaking back her wiry dark hair. "We Rom don't care about that, we Rom don't care about what you want, we Rom just don't care. And all in a sentence or two. It's simply amazing."

"Shut up, Kate," Patia said irritably, then flushed as Bavol frowned at her from his cushion.

"When the skies fall down, I might," Kate retorted angrily. "Start holding your breath while you wait, Patia. I'd appreciate it."

Before Patia could retort to *that*, Tawnie took over and gave Avi one of her sweetest smiles. "Good *morning*, Avi," she caroled prettily, copying Patia's voice tones to the last decimal. Patia went stark white, but Tawnie only batted her long eyelashes, piling it on. "You're looking *so* beautiful again. How *ever* do you manage *so* wonderfully?"

Patia opened her mouth, thought better of it, then whirled and stamped back to the kitchen. Kate's sardonic laugh and Tawnie's high giggle trailed after her. "The right side wins again," Kate gloated.

"Good grief," Pov said weakly.

"Oh, Kate, you shouldn't have," Avi tried to reprove, then covered her mouth as she giggled too, her eyes dancing.

"I should, and I will," Kate declared. "Oh, don't look that way, Pov. The world is fine and Patia will survive. But she'll keep this up until we other wives make her back down." Kate tossed her head. "Besides, she deserved it after what she said the other day."

"Said what?" Pov demanded, looking at Avi.

"Never mind that." Kate flashed a grin. "We just balanced it nicely, believe me." Chavi let out another yowl in the kitchen, and Kate swiveled her head to look, then sighed. "Tawnie, sweet coz, I am going to do something dire to your son if he hits Chavi just once more with that spoon."

"He has *another* spoon?" Tawnie blurted in horror. She rushed away.

"A born engineer, that boy," Pov commented. "Already pounding on things."

"Not on Chavi, he won't," Kate said darkly. "Not if he wants to live to grow up." Kate strode off.

"Oh, my," Avi said.

"Welcome to the Rom," Pov agreed. "We'll all survive, I think."

Pov's mother stuck her head out of the kitchen doorway, frowning distractedly at the scene. Everybody looked back, as innocently as each could manage, and Margareta did not look satisfied as she turned back to Patia. The voices rose in the kitchen, Kate's and Patia's the loudest, and Pov took Avi's elbow, deftly steered them past the men, and got them all out into the corridor.

As they walked onward, Avi sighed and shifted Anushka to her other shoulder, saying nothing.

"Avi?" he said softly.

"It's like a gauntlet, Pov," she said reluctantly. "It's not fair. Every single morning she starts something and I have to stand there and take it or they'll just call me typical gaje, don't know my place. Why do I have to be perfect and she can do what she wants? Why do I end up the cause of it all when I don't do a thing? I'm really tired of it, Pov, especially when she loops in Kate."

"Well, at least you won't have to listen to Patia tomorrow or even the next day. With the moving-in, she'll have other things to do." Avi did not look reassured. "And we could dispense with most of the purity rules for a while if you want to," he offered, watching her closely. "Patia will be too busy to lurk around our apartment all the time: there'll be gaps. Russki choice. Would you like that? Just for a break?"

"You're sweet." Avi smiled at him, and her face finally lightened a little. "I'll think about it. Maybe."

"I told you we can trade, if you want. I want you to be comfortable."

"I'm not going to be comfortable," Avi said, frowning. They turned up the corridor to their own apartment. "I don't mind all the rules, the food and the laundry and the floor. They're just stupid rules that don't mean anything." She heard what she'd said and darted her eyes at him guiltily, then tried to apologize. "Oh, Pov, I didn't mean—"

"Relax, Avi. I've never thought the rules make sense. They're just what gypsies do."

Avi snorted. "And *marime* binds the gypsies together and has a certain rationale and all the other stuff you've told me. But I don't like its commentary on women. I've never liked it, and I never will. I don't pollute other people just because I'm a woman." She set her jaw stubbornly, and her dark eyes flashed with quiet anger. "Women have value. Women are not polluted people."

"The rules don't mean that, Avi. I've told you ..." Avi tightened her lips and looked away.

Pov sighed. "I'm sorry, Avi," he said inadequately, not knowing what else to say that he hadn't said already too many times, and saw her eyes come back to him.

"I'm sorry, too," she said softly, and blinked at tears. "I shouldn't bring it up, never, never."

"Don't say that. Of course you should. It's too important, for both of us."

"It doesn't do any good when I do."

"Not yet, at least." He juggled Garridan to his other

arm, then took her hand and smiled. "There's always the future, true? How's that for a fatuous comment?"

"Pretty fair, Povinko," Avi decided, wrinkling her nose. "Not bad at all, actually. Personally, I'd rather hit Patia hard, not too hard, but enough to get her attention and cause a total family uproar. Take that, sweet coz." Avi feigned a neat left uppercut into the open air, demonstrating, and leveled an invisible Patia with a single blow. "Avi's version of gypsy balance," Avi said with satisfaction, admiring her result, "with *me* diverting my frustration onto an innocent target. How's that for a comment?" She kissed Anushka's forehead and cuddled her.

"Kate'll love to help," Pov said. "Be sure to ask her before you do."

"I'll be sure to do that." Avi smiled tightly, still angrier than she wanted to show.

Pov repressed a sigh. "How'd the sail drill go today?" he asked, changing the subject.

Avi slipped her hand back into his. "Fine. It'll be different taking night watch later, with me in command." Avi's expression lightened still more and she lifted her chin, posing a little for him. "Of course, nothing much happens on night watch," she added.

"You'd be surprised," Pov warned. "I have some instructive stories I could offer about my years as Third Sail. And the Nebula operations run around the clock, remember."

"True." They reached their apartment door, and Avi maneuvered an elbow to the doorplate, keeping his hand firmly in hers as the door opened. "I look forward to it," she said fiercely. "I look forward to everything."

They took the twins into the nursery and deposited them in their cribs, and Avi slipped her tunic over her head and found a loose robe, then sat down in her chair to nurse Anushka. Pov watched her for a minute from the nursery doorway, and smiled when she looked up at him.

"Love you," he said.

"That makes everything worthwhile," she said, her expression easing. "Sorry to get mad."

"It's okay." She still frowned slightly. "Really okay."

He raised his hand and gestured a gypsy oath, one of great solemnity, and one he knew she would recognize. "I swear."

"You worry too much," she advised him, her smile more genuine.

"So do you. We're even. I don't know what war it is, but so far it's a draw." Avi chuckled.

Pov was halfway through fixing lunch when his mother showed up. Margareta inspected his meal preparations, sniffed her guarded approval, and then vanished into the nursery. Pov dried his hands and followed hastily. He found his mother bending over Anushka's crib, tucking her blankets, while Avi watched her, Garridan nursing at her other breast. When Pov appeared in the doorway, his mother turned around and tsked at him.

"You are too obvious," she said. "I haven't ragged Avi for weeks."

"Oh? What about giving up Sail Deck?"

"A suggestion only. I have dropped the matter." Margareta leaned comfortably against the crib railing and crossed her arms across her breasts. She was dressed in her hold uniform and was badly late for beta watch, but his mother had always set her own priorities. It helped that her eldest nephew was now

Hold Deck's second-in-charge, Pov supposed. Margareta eyed him.

"What?" he demanded.

"Oh, very well," she said impatiently. "Intrude if
you must. Avi, I know it is hard for you, learning our
ways, and Patia is not fair." Avi looked up and
blinked in surprise. "You do not complain enough.
You can fight back. It is appropriate."

"Not as a *gaji romni*," Avi said and looked down
at Garridan again. "I can't."

"*Gaji romni* is a matter of pride," Margareta declared, "not a shame. Perhaps in some families,
younger wives are oppressed, but not in ours. I have
spoken to Patia, but you can guess it won't do much
good, not now. If I sanction her, she'll only divert it
into subtler methods—and those you won't like at all."
Margareta quirked her mouth. "Believe me, you
won't."

Avi bit her lip, her head still bowed over Garridan,
and Margareta clucked her tongue, a little exasper-
ated. She shot a glance at Pov, willing him away, but
he stayed put. His mother scowled at him, but then
turned back to Avi. "When I was a young bride," she
said, "my mother-in-law did not like me. No particular
reason, aside from having married her son. I came
from a proud family, my bride price was respectable,
and Garridan loved me—but what does that matter?
She had another bride in mind, and knew her wishes
would prevail once she arranged the divorce."

Avi looked up. Margareta's mouth had become a
rigid line. Pov rarely heard his mother talk about those
early years, though he had seen Grandmam's stiff behavior to his mother throughout his boyhood. To her
grandchildren, Grandmam Janusz was warm and understanding and loving, a great tease and always indul-

gent, but to their mother she had never relented. It was a part of her past life Margareta firmly ignored whenever she could, and probably a large part of the reason she had taken her brother and children aboard *Ishtar's Fan* all those years ago.

"I endured three years in that family," Margareta said, "until we could afford our own wagon, and even then we traveled with them most of the time. The other women followed her lead, and I was ostracized." Margareta shrugged, pretending indifference. "Tradition can be used in many ways, some of them not kind. After I failed twice at bearing a child, I finally produced a son, and she relented a little—not much, but a little. Then I lost the next three and matters were much worse." Margareta shifted her weight, her mouth still tight. "They never improved later, even after Kate was born, and then Garridan had died, of course."

"Miscarriage isn't a failure, Margareta," Avi protested. "It's a natural process. There's no shame in it."

His mother smiled gently. "A woman is known by her children, Avi. It is the Rom way." She pointed at Avi imperiously. "But you do not understand why it is so, and the misunderstanding is hurting you more than it should. Patia uses that against you."

"I can't help it if I don't understand." Avi looked down again rebelliously. "And I can't help what Patia does."

"And where is the fault in needing to learn?" his mother asked reasonably. "Patia is unhappy, but that is not an excuse. But I have constraints right now in what I can do about it. Do you understand that?"

Avi tightened her lips, still not looking at her, and Margareta looked at Pov, her frustration obvious. "When *she* was young," Pov offered, "her mother tended to list her faults regularly, probably just like this. We get stuck in old patterns." Avi shot a glance at him. "Avi, she's trying to be kind," he said, answering the look. "She's apologizing, in a way, as much as my mother ever apologizes for either herself or the Rom." Pov walked forward and leaned himself comfortably beside his mother. "Thank you, Mother."

"But she doesn't understand," Margareta said to him in distress.

"We're working on all that. And since you're softened up," he added, "I'd like a favor." His mother's dark eyes went wary in an instant, and Pov chuckled at her reaction. In some things, his mother would never change, not a bit. "I want to relax *marime* here at our apartment for a while—and I don't want Patia sneaking over here to check up and running back to Bavol to tattle. I don't want comments about Tully and Irisa coming to visit, or Rachel Gray, or any other gaje we have over. I don't want comparisons and comments and advice about proper wifely behavior, just for a while and at least over here. It's too hard on Avi."

Avi shook her head. "No, it's not," she murmured. Margareta's eyes shifted back to her daughter-in-law.

"Yes, it is," Pov said firmly. "This is our apartment, Mother, and if Avi wants it half-gaje until she prefers otherwise, that's what I want, too."

His mother sighed feelingly, but she thought about it, her eyes flicking from Pov back to Avi. "Half-gaje," she said slowly, "is our problem with Simen and the *voivoide.*"

Pov felt a flicker of hope: his mother was really considering it seriously. Avi's charm, he thought, and felt a burden begin to lift from his shoulders. He hoped she would agree, and he was glad he had asked.

"Uncle Simen isn't here," he pointed out. "Neither is the *voivoide.*"

"A blessing to us all," his mother said tartly. "But do not tell the *voivoide* I ever said so." She thought a moment more, and then nodded her permission. "I worry for my daughter-in-law," she said softly, and Avi's eyes lifted to her. "It is the right thing to do," Margareta said, nodding more briskly, more to herself than to them. "Since I cannot constrain Patia, not right now, Avi should use her own judgment in these matters, how the household should be kept and children tended." She pointed at Avi again. "And I expect her judgment to be wise, as befits a *romni.* Wise for herself as much as for her husband and her children."

"I hear you, *puri dai,*" Avi said solemnly. Then she smiled, her face lighting with relief. And she sighed despite herself.

Margareta tsked at her. "I hope so." She glanced at her wristband. "I am late for watch."

"You just noticed that?" Pov asked dryly.

Margareta flipped her hand, not impressed. "A skeleton watch with nothing important to do, but Karoly will be sure to reprove me, as is proper." She held up her cheek for Pov to kiss, then smiled at Avi. "I think I am proud of my daughter-in-law," she announced to the open air. "I am still considering the details, but she has the benefit of her mother-in-law's history, a notable advantage. And I am late." Margareta touched Avi's hair briefly in blessing, then bustled out of the room. A few seconds later, the outer apartment door hissed open and shut.

Pov and Avi stared at each other for a moment, both a little stunned.

"What *marime* rule are you going to break first, Avi?" Pov asked curiously.

Avi grinned. "I've got a wide selection, don't I? I'll have to think about it." She hesitated, her smile softening. "That's awfully nice of her. She likes me." Avi's tone sounded almost startled, as if such events rarely happened in life, that one might be liked for oneself, without preconditions or tests or qualifiers. Perhaps in Avi's past they rarely had, but that had now changed. His gift to her, a part of the everything, because she had married him. In his mind, Margareta had balanced several of their troubled years in this one kindness to Avi.

"No 'think' about it," he said firmly. "It must be your Russki charm: after all, it toppled me long ago." Pov walked over and kissed her soundly, then went back to lunch in the kitchen.

Siduri's Net returned from T Tauri early in the night watch, the American cloudship *Diana's Arrow* in her wake. As soon as *Net* had docked in TriPower's ship-bay, Pov took a skyrider over to see Captain Andreos. *Net*'s shipmaster looked tired but pleased, and grandly waved Pov into his office, then shut the door behind them. A litter of data reports stretched across Andreos's desk and the floor beyond, with several large charts fastened to the walls. One showed a detailed course-track schematic of the latest harvest runs at T Tauri; others showed energy plots of the gas-jet and several atomic models of the new catch. Pov glanced with interest at the large diagrams as he sat down, then smiled at Andreos.

"Good to have you back, sir," he said, making it loud.

Captain Andreos sat down and leaned back in his

chair. He grimaced. "I'd rather not hear about it, but I know I have to ask eventually. Let's talk about something else first. How's *Isle* coming along?"

"Final checks. So's *Mirror*. How'd it go at T Tauri?"

"Well, the gas-jet was still there." Andreos ran his fingers through his graying hair and sighed. "So was a OkiSeki observer ship, unfortunately. Apparently the corporations have T Tauri staked out, if only to see what the competition does wrong, and they picked up a bonus when we showed up. The freighter practically sat up and gawked when they realized who we were."

Pov clucked his tongue in dismay. "They watched the run maneuvers?"

Andreos shrugged. "Yes. I considered adding a few fake moves, just to mix things up, but they're bound to try whatever we did, decimal by decimal. I'd rather not deserve the blame the next time a ship gets wasted." He scowled. "Dammit."

"The key is the fuel intermix, sir, not the catching."

Andreos looked sardonic. "I believe in fairies, too, Pov. I give our secret maybe four months of remaining life, if that. *Ceti Rose* actually caught some particles before she blew herself up trying to mix them, and the Japanese will use a test chamber for the next step, not a spaceship. After that, it's all engineering." He rocked his chair and sighed. "Well, I didn't expect it to last forever."

"Talbot tried a data-snatch on our computer yesterday," Pov said, knowing he was putting a perfect cap on Andreos's day. "Karol provoked him into it, and I've told Rachel."

Andreos's jaw dropped for a moment. "Thanks for getting all that out quickly, Pov," he said when he could talk. "What did Rachel say? Does Karol know yet?"

"She thought we might kick *Arrow* out of the consortium, and no, he doesn't. I'm sorry, sir."

Andreos leaned his elbows on his desk and rubbed his long face up and down, then dropped his hands abruptly, looking old. Captain Andreos's face was heavily lined now, his hair nearly grayed through. Though he moved with his same lanky vigor and recuperated quickly from any effort, Pov knew that Andreos felt himself running out of time, with only a limited window of opportunity to pass on his knowledge and skills to the younger captains, especially to Pov. Since Pov's formal appointment as *Isle*'s shipmaster, Andreos had intensified his direct tutelage, spending as much time with Pov as possible. Their discussions often ranged into different channels now as Captain Andreos tried to articulate, not always successfully, his full experience of twenty years in a captain's posting.

It was a legacy Pov valued, and it had brought them still closer, had made them father and son in a very real sense. Pov thought Andreos's fear of his own mortality was not justified and tried to tell him so, but Captain Andreos still dreaded that his work might not be finished as it ought, that he might fail to pass on some crucial knowledge that would be needed.

Andreos sighed again. "Thaddeus Gray set the pattern here, and it's not an easy one to dislodge. Everyone is too used to ships alone, doing your rival dust, fighting for every inch of veils light-years wide." He rocked his chair back and forth, narrowing his eyes. "I keep telling myself the answer to *Jewel* is patience. Ditto Gray. I hope to God I'm right."

"You look tired, sir. Try to rest."

"I will, son. Don't worry about me." Andreos smiled. "The gas-jet runs went well, easier than last time. I've gained a new respect for *Arrow*'s ship designs—and for Thaddeus Gray's better gifts. Once a skyrider, always a skyrider, of course, but the flair gets tempered by the years in command. He's damned good at ship handling. You could learn from him. I expect you to do so."

"Yes, sir."

Andreos rocked his chair and looked thoughtful. "Speaking of skyrider captains, I've been thinking along another line. Our shipmasters have all come from Hold or Sail Deck; maybe it's time for a change. I think I'll resume pushing at Athena, get her to thinking about our next daughter ship."

"Athena's mine," Pov objected promptly. "Go steal somebody else."

"It's not stealing," Andreos retorted. "It's putting quality junior captains where they belong. Recognizing potential, rewarding command skills, the good of the ship, et cetera. Read your ship manual."

"Theft," Pov accused.

Andreos shrugged humorously, conceding the point. "And theft. Keep our war mild, Pov. I intend to win. I'll let you win something else for the trade." Andreos sat up straighter. "And speaking of trades, when are we starting our personnel transfer?"

"Whenever you say, sir."

Andreos pushed a button on his desk console, and his aide Temya opened the outer door briskly. "*Isle* is open for transfer, Temya. Post the word on the all-ship."

"Yes, sir!" Temya disappeared in a flash.

"She's been getting calls all morning," Andreos said dryly. "Constantly, before we even got here. 'Is *Isle* ready?' 'When can we go over?' 'What does Captain Janusz say?' You'll notice they don't ask what *I* say anymore, just you. I hope you're prepared for the horde."

"Most of them have already picked out their apartments. I allowed some sneakover trips before *Net* left for T Tauri."

"Oh, you did?" Andreos raised an eyebrow, then pretended vast offense, looking suspiciously like *Dance*'s Captain Rybak, *Net*'s own ever-useful icon. "I don't remember you asking me about that. *They* can ask you, Pov, but you still have to ask *me*. Let's get that clear."

"If you steal Athena from me," Pov warned, "it can get very bad."

"I hear you—but I'm still going to steal Athena. Get prepared, as she says." Andreos got to his feet. "Come along and say goodbye to *Net.* I suppose it's official today, more than paper."

"My pleasure, sir."

Pov got to his feet and followed Andreos out of the office, catching up with him in the corridor with a quick stride. Captain Andreos walked along with a comfortable slouch, his quick eyes seeing everything, and took them on a detour from the central companionway into the residential areas of the ship. Pov enjoyed the glad-handing among *Net*'s crew, since Andreos was so obviously bent on arranging a walkthrough for both their benefits. Pov paced down the familiar hallways of his former ship, remembering the years aboard her under *Net*'s clever shipmaster. A large number of the people now bustling in and out of the apartments would transfer to *Isle,* and they walked through a noisy, happy crowd, a few tears here and there over the partings, but most excited and pleased.

They stopped to chat several times as children raced excitedly up and down the halls and their parents struggled with the last-minute packing. As they continued their tour, Pov let Andreos take the lead, realizing that Captain Andreos was offering him a special last look at *Net* while she was still partly, in some ways, Pov's ship. When *Isle* left her construction cradle for good, a certain marker would pass by, a milepost in Pov's own road. He put his hands in his pockets and smiled at everyone, watching the excitement and bustle as *Isle*'s new crewpeople from *Net* prepared to move aboard her, giving farewells and gaining fervent hugs, Greek and Slav, Slav and Greek, *Net*'s special mix that gave her part of her character as a ship, and as much a tribe as the Rom understood that binding.

The mixed nationalities from *Net* would help build a core on *Isle* that could assimilate the Slavs from *Jewel*, the smattering of Scandis from TriPower. It would be Pov's task as her shipmaster, as Andreos had crafted for *Net*, to weld another ship's crew into a special people, a people who belonged to and owned *Siduri's Isle*.

His people, his ship—as he was their shipmaster. Theirs.

He smiled and chatted with *Net*'s crewpeople, both those who would transfer and those who would stay, knowing that Andreos watched him as he did so. He hoped that, in the watching, Andreos could find some comfort for his fear that he had not given enough to Pov, that he had overlooked some essential, and that his constant worry about their cloudships' future could be eased. Andreos began to smile wryly as it continued, alert as always to the subtleties, and near the end their eyes met in a flash of total understanding.

They stood in front of *Net*'s Admin window high on her prow, and looked out at *Isle*, sleek and lovely in the golden sunlight.

"A beautiful ship," Andreos murmured admiringly, a half-smile on his face.

"So is *Net*. She always was, and always will be." Pov turned to Andreos. "I'll miss her, sir."

"*Net* is a road I wish to continue traveling, I agree," Andreos said, "a gypsy road of great value." He smiled at Pov benevolently. "See? The teaching goes both ways, son." Still smiling, he put his arm around Pov's shoulders and walked with him back to the elevator.

Chapter 5

During the hours of night watch, the skyrider crews fueled the four cloudships with the superheavy fuel harvested at T Tauri, and *Isle* completed her crew transfers, taking on her new people from TriPower and *Jewel*, and *Mirror* filling out her few remaining crew rankings with last-minute transfers from *Arrow*. *Isle* and *Mirror* then detached from their cradles for the last time, and now drifted in a loose tandem near the station's ship-dock. All was ready. If the captains agreed, they would launch this afternoon.

During alpha watch Captain Andreos called a consortium meeting at TriPower to discuss the final details, and the principals brought several of their key aides to the meeting. Pov sat between Miska Ceverny and Danil at Sigrid's large conference table as they waited for the others to arrive. Pov's excitement was a steady boiling under a hard-won calm exterior, and he did his damnedest to hold himself still in his chair, as if today didn't matter much, as if launching to the Nebula happened every day. Beside him Sailmaster Ceverny was pretending to be asleep, the old fraud, and Danil had brought some diversionary legal papers to read, which he wasn't doing. Across the room, Captain Andreos and Sigrid talked quietly in a corner, probably the only genuine calm in the room.

Pov smiled at Stefania Bartos across the table, as *Net*'s blond pilotmaster made a better act out of lounging in her chair. Skyriders always do it better, he reminded himself. Ask any skyrider.

"You look relaxed, Stef," he commented.

"I'm *always* relaxed," Stefania replied, then busily patted her hair, fiddled with her sleeves, and jiggled a few times, piling it on. Her grin was wide and comfortable as she poked fun at her own mannerisms. After six months as *Net*'s pilotmaster, Stefania's warmth in personality and her excellence at Helm had earned her nearly as much loyalty from *Net*'s skyriders as Athena had enjoyed during Athena's years on *Net*. Captain Andreos made a frequent point of showing his open approval. The youngest skyriders now copied Stefania's long walk, not Athena's, as they strode here and there on skydeck, doing their pilot strut, and Stefania didn't bother to hide her joy in her new rank. Pov grinned at her, and got another raking grin back, and a teasing pat, and a jiggle.

"Soar off," he advised and watched her chortle, full of herself.

Bjorn Nilsson, Sigrid's second-in-command at Tri-Power, had copied Stefania's slouch in another chair, and was waiting for her to notice. She did and they launched a genial war in the one-upping: as they were working into the second fusillade, Thaddeus Gray walked briskly into the room, flanked by Rachel and Colleen Ingram, a tall and striking redhead in her forties.

Gray's eyes flicked around the room, taking in the scene in a single glance, and showed a barely suppressed elation. His tall muscular body seemed coiled in springs as they paused in the doorway, lithe in his eagerness for action at last. Pov had fretted through the long wait of several months, but Captain Gray had literally waited years. Although Gray's three cloudships had dominated the Pleiades for two decades, their senior captain had long yearned for another horizon for his many talents, not content with the comfortable satisfactions of an unquestioned merchant prince.

In an earlier time, Thaddeus Gray might have captained a four-masted wind-driven ship, battling the ice-clogged seas to hunt whale or tuna or the unending cod of the Grand Bank, or else scrutinized his oblivious surface-bound opponents through his submarine's periscope, stalking them silently through the deep. Such men, who must win to survive, had had the same unconscious arrogance as Thaddeus Gray—for a captain who did not win consistently did not survive. And Gray was used to winning.

In a still earlier and less civilized time, such captains had terrorized the European coasts, ferocious in their piracy as Elizabeth's freebooter, Knut's Viking pilot, or a wild Celtic chieftain bent on booty, fire, and gold. Gray had that same potential, and saw no reason to apologize for his past manuevers against *Jewel* at GradyBol, Gray's personal turf. Blocked from trade with EuroCom's principal space station, *Jewel*'s fortunes had turned far worse. Even so, and despite Janofsi's vociferous objection, Captain Andreos had invited Gray into the consortium, valuing him for other and more admirable gifts. Andreos intended to tame him, if he could, an objective of which Gray had not been informed.

As Rachel stopped by her father in the doorway, her eyes met Pov's across the room, and suddenly they both laughed out loud, together. Rachel flung her arms wide, and Pov surged to his feet, and they war-danced toward each other, meeting halfway around the table.

"Isle!" she declaimed dramatically, plucked out the sides of her trousers, and curtsied.

"Mirror!" he declaimed back and gave her his best bow, the best ever. And then they waltzed.

The room broke up in loud guffaws of laughter. Pov twirled Rachel around and looked over at Captain Andreos. "Today," he demanded. "We go today!"

"Today," Captain Andreos agreed, smiling.

Thaddeus Gray put his hands in his pockets, then looked at Colleen Ingram behind him. They shared a tentative grin and, after another moment, Colleen stepped forward and slipped her hand around his elbow, then stood beside him, tall and smiling as they watched Rachel dance.

After a few minutes more, Pov and Rachel stopped the waltz and laughed at each other. "And I was going to be so calm and aloof," Rachel said, rolling her eyes.

"No use," Pov said. "I can tell you. At least we woke up Sailmaster Ceverny." He swung around and Ceverny shut his eyes, not quite fast enough. Pov chuckled.

"Well," Sigrid said, and put her hands on her hips, "once *Jewel* gets here, we can make it unanimous."

"Have you decided to come with us, Sigrid?" Rachel asked courteously. "You'd be more than welcome on *Mirror,* if you want to be wheedled elsewhere."

TriPower's tiny stationmaster sighed and glanced at Bjorn, then bit her lip. Bjorn made a face at her, and waved his hand lazily, boneless in his chair. "It's called executive power, I think, how to make a decision."

"I'll decision you," Sigrid threatened. "Don't you think I won't."

"I can handle LeClerq, Sigrid," Bjorn said. He

looked at the others. "We have a EuroCom bigshot coming on next week's freighter, with Gunter Weigand in tow. They want things, especially Gunter."

Sigrid smiled evilly, thinking of Gunter and what Gunter hadn't got when Sigrid had.

"I'll play dumb," Bjorn offered, seeing the look. "Gunter never could handle me when I'm dumb. Uh, what ship-drive?" He put on a vacuous look, dropping half of his IQ in a crash. "Particles?"

"Not too dumb, Bjorn," Sigrid told him. "You get LeClerq too alarmed about my choice of staffing, meaning you, and I'm dished. He's got pull back at headquarters. When I come back, I'd want TriPower still mine."

"So you'll go." Bjorn looked pleased.

Sigrid glanced at Captain Andreos as she hesitated a moment longer. "Yes," she said slowly, and her small face lit up with a glow. "Yes, I will." She playfully held out her arms to Pov. "Dance with me, sir."

"Enough dancing, I think," Andreos said, preempting firmly. "Pov and Rachel made their point." He strode over to the conference-room doorway and looked out impatiently into the hall, then turned back to the room.

"We've already got a majority on the vote," Gray commented, his expression carefully neutral.

"Don't start that, Thaddeus," Andreos growled and walked back to the table. After a few earlier sharp reproofs from Andreos when he had tried, Gray had learned to keep silence about *Jewel*'s continued misbehavior and *Net*'s eerie tolerance of anything Janofsi chose to do. It was an effort, but Gray had learned to manage. A captain of many gifts.

Pov sat down and stretched out his legs, then laced his fingers on his stomach. Everyone took a seat, and they passed the next ten minutes in comfortable conversation, waiting, until *Jewel* finally arrived.

Natalya Tesar, *Jewel*'s sailmaster, strode in first, her face pale and severe. Her black hair was pulled back to coil tightly at her nape, framing her thin face, and her body had a catlike leanness, as if Natalya still skipped meals regularly, going hungry for the sake of *Jewel*'s survival. For years, Natalya had skimped and improvised with *Jewel*'s antiquated sails, scrabbling for the next harvest, however lean, that might keep *Jewel* going onward. It had toughened her, those hard years, but the inner woman had suffered, making her too bleak in her expectations, too fanatically loyal to her captain, whatever the further cost to herself.

She nodded to the people present and found a chair near the other end of the table, leaving a space between herself and Stefania. "Sorry we're late," she said gruffly as she sat down.

"No problem," Andreos said smoothly.

Natalya's glance flicked across Pov and moved onward quickly, avoiding his eyes. If Katrinya was right, and she had the Slav connections with *Jewel* to know, much of *Jewel*'s worsening behavior recently had been prompted by Natalya's resentment. Pov watched the older Slav woman with regret, remembering the early connection of Sail Deck they had shared, but a bond which had steadily unraveled since *Net* formally announced Pov's appointment as *Isle*'s shipmaster. Had she really hoped *Net* would give *Isle* to Janofsi? Or had it been a thought afterward, now festering these many months?

How do I reach out to her again? he wondered sadly, sensing that Natalya's formidable will to shut out the unwanted easily rivaled the Rom's own gift in building cultural walls. He admired Natalya for her strength and devotion, and sincerely regretted their divisions, for more than the trouble it had created for the consortium, but for the aching gap between them personally.

Karol Janofsi strolled in a few minutes later, his black eyes flicking around the room as he walked down the table to join Natalya. "Sorry we're late," he said.

"No problem," Andreos repeated carefully.

Janofsi sat down with a grunt and laced his fingers on his stout middle, his aging face lined with long discontent. He had gained weight in the past year, developing some blood pressure problems and suspicious heart sounds that had worried *Jewel*'s doctors. Janofsi had shrugged it all off, declaring that his rages had never killed him before and he would do what he damned pleased, but had, in the end, grumpily consented to a change in diet, a mild medication for the occasional angina. He did not look well, and Pov wondered if Janofsi had other health problems he chose to ignore.

"Well, Karol?" Andreos said. "Shall we go to the Nebula? How does *Jewel* vote?"

Janofsi narrowed his eyes. "I imagine you've already had your vote," he challenged, testing the waters.

"It should be a unanimous decision," Andreos replied. Janofsi smiled.

Captain Gray shifted in automatic protest, then flushed as he nearly strangled in the effort not to talk. Beside him Colleen scowled quickly, then erased it just as fast; Rachel sighed and decided to watch the ceiling. It's easier, Pov thought, eyeing the Americans with sympathy, when you're never *been* a king, as Gray had been in all the essentials. *Jewel* was not going to "do it" as a matter of course: she'd proved that, and probably would keep on proving it. *Net* and Sigrid understood that, but *Arrow* did not, and so *Jewel* would keep on teaching until everybody got the point.

He looked at Jewel's two stubborn captains with a mixture of dismay and amusement as Janofsi continued his ostentatious thinking, needling Gray. After a few more moments, when Janofsi started stroking his short beard to think some more, he got nudged hard by Natalya.

"We agree," she said loudly, and gave Karol an unreadable look. He bared his teeth at her.

"Do we?" he asked.

"Well, as I remember our captains' meeting last night, we did," Natalya said irritably. "You were there, too, Karol. Or am I delusional?" Janofsi snorted, amused, and Natalya sat back and crossed her arms, a smile tugging unwillingly at her own mouth. "Today," she said softly, and her eyes met Pov's for just a moment.

"Today," Pov answered, for all of them.

Three hours later, *Siduri's Isle* moved away from TriPower under slow sail, *Diana's Mirror* following just off her port beam. Pov stepped into his interlink room on Admin level and looked around at the multiple consoles and screens, half of them dark, then sat down at the intraship console and began keying in the links to *Isle*'s other decks, as if it were all routine, just practice.

As Pov linked to her deck, Athena popped into view from a monitor camera mounted over Helm Deck's main screens. She was lounging in her central Helm chair behind a wide console, one hand dangling loosely over her chair arm. The monitor light caught her attention, and she winked at him gaily.

"Hey there, sir," she said, her smile stretching from ear to ear. "We're on the green."

"Let's go, Helm," Pov said. "Let's stick out the oars and row."

"That *is* a deal." She flashed him another grin, then leaned forward and tapped one-fingered at her console. "Hey there, *Mirror*," she said in English. "Where'd you come from? I thought you'd sleep all day."

Mirror's pilotmaster retorted a single-word reply, not polite at all.

"My, oh my," Athena said and snickered behind her hand. "Aren't we rude?" She got another word, even ruder. "I don't know that word," Athena retorted, her tone changing abruptly to an icy disdain. "Is it in a dictionary? I'd like to look it up."

Pov raised his head, surprised by the nasty exchange.

"Do that, Athena," *Mirror* growled. "You smart-ass."

"That I am," Athena said, tossing it back. "Same to you, nullzero." Pov winced, and Athena started chuckling wickedly, promptly answered by a bark of laughter over Athena's comm channel to *Mirror*.

"Did he wince?" *Mirror* asked.

"Of course," Athena said, and tsked as she shook her curls. "And his sister is a skyrider, too: you'd think he'd understand by now. I just can't track it."

"Soar off," Pov retorted, aware now that he had been set up by a Helm conspiracy. Athena laughed and waggled her fingers. Got you, Pov. Got you, got you. "Both of you soar off," he said, raising his voice to include *Mirror*'s Helm. "And take it away."

P. K. McAllister

"Yes, captain," Athena said demurely. "We are indeed soaring off."

She gestured grandly at the course track on her Helm screens, where *Isle* continued her smooth spiral away from TriPower, *Mirror* tracking neatly in her wake. Behind them, *Jewel* and *Net* undocked in sequence and moved into the train, following *Isle* outward.

Miska Ceverny walked into the interlink room and put his hands on his hips, repeating Pov's own inspection of the equipment. Pov moved aside and Ceverny sat down at the intraship board.

"I hope this works," Ceverny muttered, and began tapping at the computer board, completing the intraship links.

"Well, we've practiced enough." Pov moved across the small room to the outship console and sat down. As he began making comm connections to the other ships, the wide screen above his console began windowing into segments. In *Mirror*'s interlink room, Thaddeus Gray sat at the outship board, Rachel seated behind him as his co-captain. *Mirror* had a duplicate system of *Isle*'s double interlink, intended only as backup if needed, and both the Grays would sit the interlink watch throughout the voyage. Rachel turned and smiled at Pov, her face flushed with excitement.

"Morning, Pov," Gray said comfortably, echoed by Rachel's lighter voice. "Today the adventure!" His handsome face broke out in a smile. Pov grinned back, and Gray laughed with genuine delight. He spread his hands. "*Years* I've waited for this."

"A common dream, sir."

"One we must proselytize, a bit more than we'd like—" Gray broke off as *Net* came into the link. Captain Andreos smiled.

"Exulting, Thaddeus?" he asked.

"My privilege, *Net*," Gray said unperturbed. "And thank you for providing it."

Andreos shrugged, his face still tired, but the eyes were keen, clever and aware and intent. "God save us," Captain Andreos said ironically, and draped an arm over the back of his interlink chair. "We're fools, the whole lot of us."

"Better than listening to lawyers talk," Gray suggested. "They're suing *me* now."

"Chaffers have their purposes," Captain Andreos said. He looked around and winked at somebody. "Mine is lurking behind me. Rolf, go do something useful. Think of some good threats we can use. We'll lend a few to *Arrow*."

"Maybe when we're on our way back, sir," Rolf's voice said impudently. "I'm busy."

When Pov completed the connection to *Jewel*, Janofsi's interlink room was empty. Captain Andreos tightened his lips, but said nothing.

Pov decided in an instant to ignore Janofsi's absence. Whether from his often-muttered disdain for the interlink or genuine tasks elsewhere on *Jewel* that delayed him, Janofsi was late again, and Pov would not embarrass the older Slav captain by pointing out the obvious. "Sirs, we are continuing on the planned trajectory. Please maintain your stations."

Andreos and Gray nodded. Behind them TriPower had dwindled to a small dot in the distance, then vanished into the glare of the local sun and its whirling planetary cloud. By the time they had cleared the cometary margins and had reached fully empty space, Janofsi still had not come to his interlink room. Pov nodded genially to the other shipmasters and got up from his chair, then headed out into the Admin level to talk to Andreos on a more private channel.

"I'll be right back, Miska." Ceverny rolled his eyes.

Pov found Sigrid Thorsen first in a side room, where she had been chatting with one of the admin chiefs, then took her into his office. Of all the consortium partners, Janofsi tended to listen most to Sigrid. She was good at wheedling—and wasn't a cloudship captain. Probably both had equal weight.

Net's patience with her Slav sister ship baffled Gray, though the American captain did not comment. Even Sigrid had sometimes wondered, though she personally liked Janofsi, despite his tantrums. At times, Pov had earnestly wished that *Jewel* would find a destiny elsewhere, out of his life. But *Jewel* was another of *Fan*'s daughters, and was a connection to the past *Net* did not want to lose. There had been too much division, too much pain, among the Slav ships: with her patience, *Net* hoped to achieve a peace that the Slav ships had rarely enjoyed. So far the results had been mixed, complicated by *Jewel*'s difficult captain and his fiercely loyal crew.

This latest trick of being late would not work well at the Nebula, not at all. Their safety would depend on finely timed coordination and sticking to plans. *Jewel* would have to choose other ways to make her points.

"What's the matter?" Sigrid asked as she saw his face.

"*Jewel* again." He put in the radio call to *Net* and Captain Andreos responded promptly from his office monitor. "Will we have to leave *Jewel* behind, sir?"

Sigrid threw up her hands. "Of all the times! He *told* me he'd cooperate, Leonidas. He promised me."

"Obviously Janofsi still wants to score points," Andreos said tiredly.

"Is he waiting for me to beg?" Pov asked.

Andreos grunted. "Probably—but don't." He pursed his lips. "Leave the position for *Jewel* in the phalanx when we launch. Even if Janofsi skips the entire maneuver, the computer pulse-bounce can keep *Jewel* in configuration. After all, it's *supposed* to be automatic." Andreos shook his head. "Damnation," he said. "Sigrid, I don't expect miracles, but do try when you have another chance. He's obviously not listening to me."

Sigrid nodded. Andreos scowled as he broke the connection.

Pov walked back to the interlink room, and Sigrid followed him, then hovered outside the doorway out of line of sight, not wanting to send signals they didn't need. Janofsi still had not come to his interlink room. Pov sat down and put on a bland expression, as bland as he could make it. "Sirs, prepare for launch." Pov moved his hands over his boards, setting up the light-beam pulses that would keep the ships in alignment. "Take your positions, please."

With *Isle* at the apex, *Net* and *Mirror* aligned themselves off her port and starboard beams, creating a wedge shape that would be the phalanx's principal ship configuration during acceleration. A little belatedly, *Jewel* moved, too, settling in behind *Mirror* on starboard. Pov traded a resigned glance with Andreos, then turned around to Miska Ceverny.

"Miska?"

"It's all yours, Helm," Ceverny said to Athena. "We are ready to launch."

"Sirs, I am taking position," Athena said, her voice ringing clearly over the interlink. "Please align your ships. Pulse-beam activated." Between the ships, a near-invisible web of light beams pulsed into existence, growing stronger as *Isle*'s Helm computer wove its ship-web. "Sirs, we are linked."

"Helm is yours," the *Mirror* pilotmaster responded, echoed an instant later by Stefania on *Net*, then, again belatedly, by *Jewel*'s pilotmaster. As one, the four ships swung slightly in space, pointing their wedge at the distant blur of Orion's Nebula. Athena fed the starfield into the interlink, the distant glowing patch of Orion's Nebula directly in screen center.

"Activating Helm Map," Athena said, her head turning slightly to look at a side wallscreen. "Locking down. Link-up complete. Sirs, prepare for launch."

"We are prepared for launch," *Mirror*'s Helm responded for everyone.

"Beginning engine flow." Athena waited until her console showed all four ships at ready. *Net*'s engineers had tinkered with the new engines for months, hoping to make a brand-new idea into a smooth technology. "Sirs, I read ninety percent capacity. I am assuming control of all ship engines."

"Acknowledged," came a rumbled response from the other Helm Decks. Pov could not tell if one of the voices came from *Jewel*.

"And launch," Athena declared firmly.

Pov clutched tighter at his chair arms as he felt the first surge of acceleration, but the gravfield compensated almost immediately. As one, the phalanx surged forward as the new fuel flowed smoothly into the ship engines, accelerating them toward lightspeed.

Athena turned her head to look at a monitor. "No drift in alignment," she said. "Sirs, we are at one-quarter lightspeed."

In *Jewel*'s interlink room, Captain Janofsi strolled in

and sat down, looking self-satisfied. He said nothing, though his black eyes shifted across his screen, checking reactions. To a man, Andreos and Gray and Pov looked back blandly, not commenting, not a chance. Undented, Janofsi laced his fingers on his stomach and smugly rocked his chair. Pov looked away.

Of all the times to prove a point, he thought. Of all the times. Unfortunately, he suspected Janofsi would choose other times to pose. The man was incorrigible. During *Jewel*'s years at Aldebaran, *Fan* had struggled to cope with her junior ship and her tempestuous shipmaster: now some of those same Slav problems had come to a new roost with *Isle*, persistently, inevitably. Captain Andreos had talked to Janofsi, Pov had talked, Sigrid had talked, and each time Karol would agree to behave himself—only to misbehave a day or a week or a month later, as if nothing had ever been said, nothing promised.

Perhaps Janofsi thought he gained some advantage by keeping his partners continually off balance. Perhaps, too, Janofsi knew that *Net* would not act drastically and expel *Jewel* from the consortium, based on the same ties that had drawn *Net* into partnership with *Jewel* in the first place. Perhaps, after so many years, now aging and sometimes unwell, Janofsi sincerely could not change. Perhaps. Pov doubted that even Janofsi knew. Pov certainly did not.

Patience, he reminded himself. It'll help your moral force. Or something.

Gray started an idle technical discussion with Andreos as the launch continued, the ships steadily gaining speed through a series of microjumps. Janofsi rocked his chair, smiling faintly, and did not bother to join in. After ten minutes, Pov felt his chair vibrate with another surge of the drive's acceleration.

"Acceleration continuing," Athena said on the interlink. "We are at half lightspeed."

"Acknowledged," the Helm voices rumbled again. The stars in the starfield ahead began to shimmer, then crawled slowly off the screen as their ship speed began distorting light reception. Pov watched as their ships raced toward jump-point, turning the stars into streamers of light. His heart beat faster and he felt a sudden wave of exhilaration. After all the quarreling and worries for months, the gateway had opened. In the center of the screen a distant glow of nebular gas brightened to a lovely glare.

The vibration became a steady hum. "We are three-quarters lightspeed, sirs," Athena said at last. "Prepare for jump."

Pov tried not to hold his breath as the ships edged closer and closer to the singularity created by their own speed, taken there in barely an hour's time by *Net*'s marvelous new fuel, a fuel that had made the Nebula possible. On the top margin of Athena's window of the wallscreen, a display from Helm Map ticked off the final percents. Nearly at lightspeed, the visual contact with the other ships, even at such close range, disappeared in a blur of static, with only one sure contact remaining in *Isle*'s coherent laser pulse that bound the group together.

"And jump!" Athena shouted.

As one, the ships leaped convulsively into no-time, linked by their pulse computers, leaping fifteen hundred light-years into the unknown. As *Isle* jumped, Pov felt the familiar odd lurch, gone in an instant, and his heartbeat increased its rapid pounding. All the screens were a gray and painful glare, their view distorted by their speed. Had they arrived? Were they now in the Nebula? Taking a deep breath, he distracted himself by adjusting the screens to better comfort for everyone who watched all over the ship. Had they arrived?

"We are turning ship," Athena said, watching Helm Map's automatic displays. In this kind of coordinated jump, the computer would handle more than the exquisitely delicate push at the instant of jump; it would guide the four ships through their initial turn and deceleration, at speeds far higher than usually attempted with standard drive.

"On the mark," she said. "Initiating turn."

Isle rotated quickly, bringing her blazing engines into retro-fire. They counted on the shock-front of a ship's entry into normal space to shield their turn, a minute or two of safety to turn a ship, whatever medium lay around her. Theory, half proved by the robots and field tests in the Pleiades, but fully proved at the Nebula only by doing it.

"Well, the sails weren't ripped off," Athena announced. "It's working.'"

"I feel relieved," Pov said dryly. "Thank you, Helm." Again the ship's gravfields shifted subtly as they compensated for the changing forces of the turn, then steadied.

"Ninety percent of lightspeed," Athena told Pov a few minutes later. "We should reestablish interlink soon." As if timed to her words, the interlink screens rippled into ghosted shadows. Pov keyed his interlink board, trying to adjust the frequencies through the lightspeed distortion, then clucked his tongue in satisfaction as one windowed screen steadied to show Thaddeus Gray sitting calmly at his station on *Mirror*.

"Later we might try some other lasering frequencies," Gray said absently as his eyes flicked across his own panels. "Enough to support the outship link during jump. The laser-pulse works perfectly for the slaved drive, but we could use the other." He nodded in satisfaction, his hands working his board. "I have partial contact with *Net.*"

"So do I. Still hunting *Jewel,*" Pov replied, copying Gray's smooth calm. "Soft x-rays might work better, Thaddeus. Shorter wavelength, less expansion."

"Maybe. We can fiddle with it." Gray smiled, then turned his head suddenly to his daughter. "*Ad Orionem,* Rachel," he murmured, his voice intense. "For you, all of you." Rachel looked back, her beautiful face lit by mute exaltation.

"Eighty percent of lightspeed," Athena reported, promptly echoed by *Mirror*'s pilotmaster's deep voice.

"Acknowledged," he said. "I read eighty percent." There was a pause, then a fervent mutter came from *Mirror*'s Helm Deck: "Man, oh, man, *what* a drive! Sir, request permission to sell my soul."

"Denied," Gray said dryly. "Your soul belongs to me." A ghost of a chuckle slipped between the two ships.

A few minutes later, another of the interlink connections cleared of its static, and Janofsi's face frankly showed his relief. Jumping blind with another ship controlling your helm would try the nerves of any doughty spirit.

"Welcome back, *Jewel,*" Pov said.

"Thank you," Janofsi grumbled, then turned his head to look out his interlink door.

A few more minutes, and both *Isle* and *Mirror* reestablished full connections to *Net.* All had jumped safely, then had held into the wedge by the sureness of *Isle*'s computers through the mutual turn. Their engines raged steadily to slow their speed, with all four ships in exquisite synchronicity, percent by percent.

Putakin could stack paper to the ceiling if he wanted, Pov decided: he deserved it. He pulled a real-time graph into another window and matched it to Putakin's launch projections: the curves matched perfectly, decimal by decimal. Amazing.

"Sixty percent lightspeed and decelerating," Athena said. "Our exterior wing scanners should clear soon. Prepare for the view, people. It ought to be spectacular."

Pov gave up any pretense of doing anything useful and turned his chair toward the gray glare in their wallscreen.

The cloudships' projected course would exit in the southern fringes of the nebular fan, twenty light-years from the Trapezium and well within the ionized Nebula. Together they waited, all the crewpeople of all the ships, watching the distorted glare of the telescopic screens for the Nebula to reveal itself, the first time ever to human eyes at this close a range. Then, as the cloudships slowed to half lightspeed, then to quarter lightspeed, the viewscreens filled with a sea of glowing light, sparked by the red fireflies of hundreds of protostars, with the blazon of the Trapezium at its heart.

"The colors!" Gray exclaimed in awe.

In their screens, the Nebula glowed in hundreds of shades, red and greens, blues and violets, the flash of gold, a sudden gleam of copperish red. As the computer extended the filtering of *Isle*'s aft scanners into infrared and ultraviolet, the colors fractured into even greater complexity. The sky blazed with color, moving, scintillating color, more colors than they had ever imagined existed here.

Directly ahead, the Trapezium stars burned brilliant blue-white, surrounded by the oranges and reds and yellows of three hundred smaller protostars, all packed within a few cubic light-years. Flowing west from the central Core, the gas excited by the O-stars' ultraviolet illumination moved outward from the dark clouds behind, colored a dozen sullen reds by gas-borne dust that flickered and roiled in an intricate web of gas-currents. To the east of the Core, one finger of the dark cloud curled around the Trapezium, masking part of its brilliant glow, impenetrable black against the jeweled blaze of hundreds of suns. And beyond the Trapezium on all sides, barely visible as a vaguely shifting darkness that blotted out all more distant stars, lay the enormous depths of Orion's dark molecular clouds.

"Magnificent," Pov whispered. He stood and lifted his hands to the wallscreen between the interlink consoles, mesmerized by the shimmering colors of the Nebula. "Yes!" he cried aloud.

From the interlink he heard Rachel's hoarse shout echo his, then Ceverny's fist thumping his console in delight.

"Yes!" Pov shouted, throwing up his arms in exultation.

From *Isle*'s decks and the faint filter of the interlink came the shouts from Helm Deck, the cheering from Hold and Sail Decks, as the ships' twelve hundred voices joined in a rolling wave of sound. They had reached the Nebula—and had found glory waiting for them.

Chapter 6

Athena slowed *Isle*'s rate of deceleration into the Nebula as they dropped speed, the other cloudships in close coordination, but the ships kept retro-fire positioning for its protection against the Nebula's heavy dust. Pov watched as hull sensor temperatures started to rise. Even protected by the engine exhaust's destruction of the dust ahead, *Isle*'s aft wing edges had fluxed into significant infrared—not enough to damage metal, not yet, but enough to trip every sensor along the wing edge. They had modeled for various densities of dust, then tested the hull metal in acceleration chambers: the temperatures that now showed were comfortably within the median, but higher than the long-range scans had indicated.

Dust ratios in the outer Orion Nebula exceeded the galactic average by almost 400 percent, far heavier than the Pleiades veils and often heavier even than comet dust. Some of the Nebula's dust drifted in opaque walls as much as half a light-year deep; other dust rocketed along with outflowing gas at immense speeds. Near the protostars, dust gathered in dense circumstellar shells, or hurtled outward in the protostar's jets, or drifted vaguely away under light pressure in ragged curtains until some other phenomena of the Nebula caught it for a new transformation.

"Dust," Ceverny muttered to himself, and shook his head in dismay at the sensor readings.

"Courage, darling," Katrinya said from Hold Deck. "At least all that isn't hitting us in the face."

"Not yet," he said, unappeased. "That will come in due time." Ceverny scowled ferociously. Miska Ceverny hated dust, and would never change his opinion an iota, whatever the surrounding wonders.

"Down to a thousand klicks per second, sirs," Athena said. "Shall we turn the ships?"

Pov looked at Andreos and Thaddeus Gray.

"Thaddeus?" Andreos said. "Your call." Gray had the Helm experience: they had agreed he should lead the primary maneuvers, especially in the beginning.

"Dust," Gray muttered as he scowled at similar readings on *Mirror.* "Well, we knew it'd probably be this high in the fringes. I suggest we power up our sails before we turn, not afterward. It might ionize some of that dust into our sails instead of our faces. I also suggest that the two dreadnoughts take overlap position in front of *Net* and *Jewel.* We have the extra sail capacity and hull strength for full dust impact."

"We could handle it," Janofsi said quickly.

"That's true," Gray replied evenly, "but later we may want you two to shield *us.* We may learn some unsuspected limits to our hull alloys if we try launch velocities through a dust wall."

"Surely you're joking," Janofsi said with obvious alarm. "At launch velocity? You can't be serious, Gray."

Gray shrugged. "I prefer to use robots for that kind of hull testing, I agree. But this heavy a dust extinguishes light as much as it reradiates in infrared. We may not see a wall before we hit it. Never mind, captain," Gray added impatiently, as Janofsi opened his mouth again. "We'll sample and test and look earnestly before we leap, I assure you. All of us intend to keep well within the set parameters."

Janofsi did not look reassured.

"Orders, sir?" Athena prompted. "We have slowed to eight hundred."

Gray turned to talk to his pilotmaster on Rachel's inship screen. "What do you think, Isaac?"

"I say," Isaac answered after a moment, "that we just coast to a stop backwards."

"Awww," Athena said playfully.

"Hush up over there, Helm," Isaac advised. "*Mirror*'s wing infrared is over a hundred degrees. Try the power sailing later, sir—try *everything* later, I suggest. We have to coast to a dead stop for the light-ranging, anyway. Let's do it backwards."

"Awww," Gray said lightly, mimicking Athena. "Oh, well. It's great scenery while we do." He turned back to the outship link. "Let's coast in backwards, people."

"We are at six hundred klicks, sirs," Athena reported, taking it in stride.

Ceverny cleared his throat. "I suggest some radial velocity readings to make sure we're not in a local dust current—and not going the wrong way if we are. Carbon monoxide readings should show the gas moving with it."

"Good idea," Gray approved. "Rachel? Would you ask Colleen to light-range for CO? Sample array only, forward course, out to a light-year or so."

"Yes, sir."

"And let's disperse our wedge a little," Andreos added judiciously. "Say by twenty percent. We may be eddying dust into each other in this tight a formation."

"It's called reverse drafting," Pov suggested lightly.

"Good a term as any," Andreos grunted. "I can't see any possible useful function besides the label."

"Sail Deck reports no unusual currents ahead, sirs," Rachel said. "Our course is convergent with the local rotational flow, but is angled at twenty degrees cross-current."

"I suggest we shift course by that amount, Pov," Gray said. "Easier to just flow along with the gas. How fast is it going, Rachel?"

"A little faster than nebular average, about twenty-three kilometers per second."

"Then let's stop at that velocity, sirs."

"Athena?" Pov said, turning his head. "Your lead."

"Thank you, captain. Sirs, please increase ship separation to two kilometers. We will shift course when separation is complete."

Pov watched as Athena deftly inserted the phalanx into the local gas current, bringing their ships to a near dead stop relative to the moving gas and dust all around them. Right on the numbers, he thought admiringly. The four ships now turned on their axes to pace the direction of the gas current, then increased speed slightly to activate a flow into their sails. On Tully's Sail Deck screens, the glowing smoke of the local nebular gas fluoresced even brighter as it struck the sail gridlines and spiraled inward into Katrinya's holds. They sailed a local sea of light, with easy weather. Storms might rage elsewhere in the Nebula, whipping ionized gas and dust to greater speeds, but they had chosen their entry place well.

Pov took a deep breath, filling his lungs to the bottom, then rotated his chair to face the wallscreen between the interlink consoles. Glory everywhere, in a thousand colors. Glory.

"We have arrived, sirs," Athena said, quite unnecessarily, a big grin on her face. "We are *here*!" She thumped her fist on her Helm console in delight.

He laughed, and Athena laughed with him.

"Okay, people," Andreos said eagerly, "let's get to work!"

They had planned their first studies for months, discussing the sequencing, the division of tasks among the ships, the possible findings and alternatives, then training their crews with simulated data drawn from TriPower's long-range studies. In conjunction with the other sail decks, Tully and Colleen would make a tentative map of local space, using a scaled-down search program from the longer light-ranging program that would come later, then offload the results to the physics lab for more detailed analysis of the first light-readings. Ceverny took supervision of that two-ship project, supplementing Tully's skills with his own decades as sailmaster. Katrinya and the other holdmasters would sample the local medium to weigh and measure and analyze. Through those clues embedded in the bits of matter drifting nearby, they could amplify to the Nebula processes which had produced them. Pov windowed into Hold Deck to watch Katrinya start her "cooking," as she always called it.

As the first samples swirled into Hold's counters, Pov rearranged the windows in his outship screen to tap into Katrinya's Hold displays. With some satisfaction, he pasted the molecular weighting graphs over Janofsi's bored expression—maybe feigned, maybe real—then erased the Grays with the spectrograph displays. If only it were so easy, he thought, amused by the silent mayhem, perfectly scientific, on his fellow captains. To scoot Andreos politely offscreen, he enlarged the picture of Katrinya Ceverny sitting at her Hold console, a nice improvement on scenery. Several meters beyond her, Karoly stood at the sampling controls, ready to sort the catch as Katrinya decreed.

" 'Lo, Pov," Katrinya said as she noticed him. "Beginning composition sampling. First sample for hydrogen, of which I see lots," she added impishly, as if that were a surprise. The spectrograph bar display appeared in Pov's screen, a display wall-size on Hold Deck, and highlighted in visual red and near-ultraviolet. "Standard Lyman and Balmer lines, as well as the virtual continuum between the first and fifth quantum shells. It's active, but not high-energy, about what we'd expect this distance from the Core. No helium lines." She turned her head toward Karoly. "Let's weight this sample, Karoly, hydrogen and helium only."

"Yes, ma'am." Karoly shifted his shoulders comfortably and calmly tapped in the computer commands.

"Hmm," Katrinya said, as the sample spun through Hold Deck's magnetic sampler, sorting by atomic weight. "Eight percent helium, compared to hydrogen, a little less than nebular average. We'll pulse the sample with hard UV to confirm." The spectrograph display pulsed a few moments later near the borderline between ultraviolet and x-ray. The extraordinary stability of helium's four-proton atomic structure set its first ionization level high into hard ultraviolet, making interstellar helium invisible everywhere except near the hotter stars. "Confirming at eight. It's supposed to be ten, Pov."

"Mystery to me," Pov said. "Maybe some of it's still invisible, lurking around your sample edges."

"Not to *mass* counters, Pov," Katrinya retorted. "Wake up a few more of your neurons, please. Be useful."

"Yes, ma'am," Pov said dutifully. "Eight's still within averages, Katrinya."

Katrinya smiled. "Well, I suppose. Let's pull a larger sample, Karoly, and start on the trace elements.

Thank you. Irradiate." On the spectrograph, a dozen
lines pulsed, several in visual light, a few fainter lines
in low ultraviolet. Pov immediately recognized the
twin green lines for oxygen, the reds and two blues
for neon, another set of reds for silicon.

"Sorting for line intensity," Katrinya said. She
waited for the computer displays as the Hold Deck
computer resorted the sample's emission frequencies.
"For singly ionized oxygen, we read fifteen parts per
million, compared to hydrogen, about what we expected. About half that much for the double ion.
About two parts per million for neon, about five for
ionized carbon. I see traces of silicon, chlorine, magne-
sium, some iron, argon, enough to count a few in this
size a sample." She pursed her lips, her eyes flicking
across the wallscreen displays. "About what we read
long-range. Either we are visiting an amazingly typical
nebula neighborhood or the element distribution is re-
markably even in the Nebula. Except for helium," she
added darkly, and frowned.

"Mystery to me," Pov teased her.

"I freely admit, captain, I prefer a universe that
follows my rules." She flashed him a grin. "Once I
arrange that, I'll let you know." She watched as Karoly shifted a third sample into the Hold counters.
"Let's double that and count some molecules, Karoly.
Changing sort to infrared and millimeter lengths.
Hmm." The spectrograph display had suddenly enlarged nearly off Katrinya's wall. In its attempt to display hundreds of spectral lines in readable detail, it
managed one wall-size millimeter line, very largely la-
beled "formaldehyde."

"Wrong move," Katrinya decided. She pursed her
lips and fiddled with the wall display controls, then
blinked in startlement as the entire radio spectrum

flash-shrunk into a single bar length, utterly obscured by unreadable notations. It looked like an ant factory.

"All right!" Pov said. Karoly laughed out loud.

Katrinya muttered to herself and fiddled some more. The bar display zoomed outward again, replaced by three brilliant single lines in infrared, wall-high and wall-wide. Katrinya glared at the display. "Damned computers! Putakin, if you're listening, I want your hide. This used to scale on a single sample, and I *liked* that way." She fumed a moment, looking utterly fierce. "I think we're catching both the free float and the molecules still attached to dust. Dump the sample, Karoly, then weight the next one to dump the grains. Dump the larger molecules, too."

"Oh, please don't!" a voice exclaimed from offscreen.

Katrinya swiveled her head to look. "Sigrid, I will count your PAHs later."

"Count them now," Sigrid demanded. "I want to see the PAHs!"

Earth astronomers had been counting molecule types in interstellar clouds since the twentieth century, a list now in the hundreds, and many found only in the near vacuum of interstellar gas. A few were simple fragments of more common substances—half an ammonia molecule, a fragment of water, half- and quarter-chain hydrocarbons—but others hinted at an entirely new form of hydrocarbon chemistry based on the aromatic hydrocarbon rings, called "PAHs" in chemicalese.

Sigrid openly admitted that she lusted for PAHs—usable as solvents, catalysts, and inciters that could function in Sigrid's station processors much as enzymes functioned in the human body—if only she could catch enough pure types to play with. The PAHs were her primary interest in the Nebula, and the over-whelming focus of her future hopes for her station. The cloudships usually harvested ionized gases and free radicals, easily sorted by Hold Deck's magnetic fields, but Sigrid wanted PAHs, as many as the cloudships could catch. She had plans.

Sigrid sidled into view of Pov's interlink pickup, lurking around Hold Deck as she lusted, though she kept a wary eye on Katrinya.

"PAHs later," Katrinya stated flatly. "It's *my* Hold Deck, after all."

"A debatable point," Sigrid tossed back, "when I've got an exclusive production contract, which I do. True?" Sigrid grinned and sat down in a chair closer to Katrinya's station. "But I can wait, I suppose."

"You do that," Katrinya told her. "You wait, maybe read your contract for what it really says. Dump it, Karoly."

"Dump it, Karoly," Sigrid echoed, copying her exact tone, then laughed as Katrinya reacted.

Every time Sigrid had come aboard *Isle* to watch Katrinya on Hold Deck, or vice versa at Sigrid's pro-cessing plant on TriPower, the two older women got into uppity games, honing their wits on the other's target-in-range. It was a good partnership of two bril-liant chemists, both self-confident and assertive women who liked the qualities in each other, despite the inevitable noise. Their staffs kept their collective heads down, but everyone enjoyed it immensely, espe-cially Katrinya and Sigrid.

"I'll make you a hold officer yet," Katrinya de-clared, tossing her chin.

"I get better money from EuroCom," Sigrid re-torted, tossing back. "Try away."

Katrinya finished the Hold Deck sort her way, assisted by Sigrid's comments on better procedure that Katrinya chose to ingore. TriPower's stationmaster quieted down when the sort reached the complicated procedures for PAHs and larger molecules. Sigrid watched it all with a beatific smile on her face, occasionally vocally cheering as the first benzene or styrene or phenol line appeared in the spectra. It would be a long process, and after a while Pov windowed over to Sail Deck to watch the initial light-ranging.

On a far larger scale than Katrinya's irradiation of samples, the cloudships would scan a full sky hemisphere, a simultaneous light-scan in several frequencies to map meticulously the Nebula ahead of them. With the sky divided into arc-seconds on a horizontal and vertical grid, the full light-ranging would range eight million data-points. Even with four ships dividing the load and shifting an arc point twice a second, the full scan would require two days. But when they were done, they would have the detail they wanted. It was an unparalleled opportunity for knowledge, supported by the very practical information they would need to penetrate deeper into the Nebula. First, however, Athena had mapped their immediate neighborhood, looking for two useful jump destinations for the cutters.

A light-ranging baseline was a necessity for mapping in cubic. The limited capacity of the cutters' light-ranging equipment could not repeat the phalanx's entire program, but their light-readings near the middle of the scan, done on a targeted grid and a precise timeline, would give the study two other parallax points for comparison, and thus a hint at depth-ranging. They would do similar point scans wherever else the cloudships jumped in the Nebula, repeating *Net*'s early point-by-point mapping in the Pleiades until

Jewel had shared her maps. They would not have a complete model, but enough to navigate with some surety.

Here no one had the master map, at least no one accessible to ask, and one of the pilotmasters' chief preoccupations was hunting other tools to assist Helm Map. One option might lie in masers, in the curious ways the phenomena displayed their radial velocity and magnetics; another lay in their store of robot probes, awaiting deployment for future explorations.

Captain Gray had tapped into the discussions on Helm and Sail Deck, too, and welcomed Pov as he came back into the linkage. "We found a dust wall for *Traveler* to explore," he said, without much preamble. "Could Katrinya go with your cutter? I'd like her expertise on site, if we can—Captain Andreos said it was up to you."

"Dust wall rather than a red dwarf?" Pov asked.

"We could send our cutter for that," Gray replied. "We've found a baby red in roughly the other direction."

Pov hesitated, not sure he wished to vary from the Nebula planning this early. They had scheduled a twin study of the tiniest M-class stars in the protostar stage using both cutters. T Tauri had given them a median baseline in star formation data, key data for any further research into the heavy particles they had discovered in T Tauri's gas-jet. If they attempted the Core, a decision still open, their course would pass the larger protostars in O, B, and A class. Red dwarf readings would be useful in completing the data range.

"We don't *have* to double up on the red dwarf study, after all," Gray said, pushing at it. "*Traveler* could go look at a dust wall."

"Well, dust is going to be a constant issue here,"

Pov conceded. "Katrinya's found a lot more molecule variance than the long-range scans suggested, and she's not much past simple molecules in her sort. It'll probably take a couple of days to sort up to the larger dust."

"Dust is *always* a constant issue," Ceverny growled. "And Karoly can supervise the routine stuff. I think it's a good idea."

Pov looked over at Ceverny, still hesitating, then gave in. "All right. Would you ask her, Miska?" He looked up at the wall clock. "She'll have to hurry. It's almost time to launch."

Sigrid and Katrinya were still arguing amiably as the Hold sort continued alongside them. Katrinya agreed to Gray's suggestion immediately, her face lighting eagerly. She got up and traipsed past Sigrid's chair as she left the deck, walking her fingers over Sigrid's shoulder. "All together now," she teased. "PAHs!"

Sigrid pretended vast indifference. "What are those? Have fun out there, friend."

"Oh, I will." Katrinya glanced over her shoulder at her Hold Deck second-in-command. "Karoly, maybe we could do the remaining PAHs a *little* earlier than planned. That's to save you the effort, Sigrid, of suborning my staff after I leave."

"A *lot* earlier," Sigrid suggested, "not a little."

"Split the difference?"

"Suits." Sigrid shrugged.

"Middle little, Karoly," Katrinya ordered. "Heading for skydeck, captain." Katrinya waved as she disappeared from view.

A few minutes later, Ceverny's inship screen windowed to add a view from the cutter cabin on skydeck. "Ready to launch *Traveler*," Katrinya said, and gave them a quick smile. *Traveler*'s sister cutter, *Spirit*, had just launched eastward from *Diana's Mirror*, her diminishing engine flare still visible in the Helm Deck telescope.

"On the green, Hold," Pov said. "You're free to launch. Good luck."

Ceverny scowled at his wife. "Don't get lost, Katinka," he warned in a growly voice.

Katrinya flipped her fingers at him. "Nag, nag, nag. What a life I've got, hearing such things." Her husband lowered his brows another centimeter, with no visible effect on Katrinya. She had lived with Miska Ceverny for too many years. "That's Josef's problem, dear," she said airily, waving her hand again, "not mine. I'll be too busy counting atomic frequencies."

Ceverny sniffed and wisely shifted course to an easier target. "Josef, don't get lost," he repeated, raising his voice so *Traveler*'s pilot would be sure to hear.

Josef turned his head and grinned confidently at the monitor. "Not a chance, sir."

" 'Bye, dears," Katrinya said. "Don't get lost now," she added, zinging it back. "I like a destination to return to. Let's go, Josef. We've got photons to count."

The screen changed to an exterior shot of the cutter as it rolled across its launch bay, heading for the irising lock door. A few minutes later, *Traveler* soared into space and made a graceful arc onto its course westward, its engines blazing.

Ceverny sighed as he watched it go. "Does Avi do this to you?" he asked plaintively, pretending to snivel. Miska Ceverny adored his wife, and everyone knew it.

"Not much, at least not yet. I expect she will eventually. It's a *romni* thing, too, after all."

"It's a *female* thing." Ceverny put on an air of indig-
nation and waved his hand. "Where's the respect that
I deserve?" he asked the open air. "Where, I ask you?
Doesn't being a man count for *anything* anymore?"
He posed, putting out his chest.

"Of course it counts, Mr. Ceverny," Rachel offered
from *Mirror.* "Take it from the ladies." She smiled
broadly. "All of us."

"Thank you, my dear," Ceverny said, and smiled.

"Have we finished your mapwork, Athena?" Pov
asked.

"Yes. Shall we align for the full light-ranging?"

Pov nodded. "We're ready."

Athena accessed the outlink to the other three ships
and coordinated with the other pilotmasters to realign
the ships' positions within the phalanx. Using a few
deft maneuvers with chemical-powered side-jets, the
cloudships swung into a line, slightly curved, that
would aim their sensors at the breadth of the Nebula.

"Initiate light-ranging," Pov said, and the photon
counting began in earnest.

Though they might lack immediate accuracy in
depth, they would sample the Nebula's light eight million times, with each photon a clue, a place, a density
and mass they could quantify. From Earth, the beam
widths used for light-ranging encompassed a half light-
year, consumed hours of patient counting of single
photons by a CCD recorder. Distance and dust attenuated light, and little of the Nebula's light managed the
distance. Within the edges of the Nebula itself, the
cloudships would scan along the beam of a single
cloudship course-track, a few thousand kilometers.

A few thousand kilometers of safety to cushion a
jump inward, a place to go when they leaped again.

*   *   *

Pov watched the scan count until the end of alpha watch, then went downlevel with Ceverny to lunch in the skyside lounge. A number of *Isle*'s crewpeople had the same idea, especially near the windowed wall onto the companionway with its view of the Nebula. He and Ceverny sat down at a side table several rows from the windows—the room had filled quickly after watch—and ordered from the table menu display. It was an occasion when Pov chose to dispense with his Rom food rules, as he usually did when eating with his gaje senior staff in the ship's cafeterias. He had adopted the compromise when he took command of *Net*'s Sail Deck, and it seemed a good policy to continue when commanding *Isle*.

Ceverny craned his neck from side to side, inspecting the occupants at nearby tables, then smiled as the lounge proprietor brought glasses of cider to their table. "Personal service," Ceverny said to him. "This is new."

"Leave me alone, Miska," the man growled. "I'm too busy today." Bluff and stout, Jano Wielka was one of Miska's oldest friends from *Dance,* and a dire rival at Miska's weekly poker games. Jano lowered his voice as he swept the table with his cloth. "Nice of you to sit with *Jewel*'s people. That'll get around. Do some good."

"Excuse me?" Ceverny blinked, then looked at Pov.

"You're in the *Jewel* section," Jano said, looking surprised in turn. "Didn't you know they asked for one? Insisted, actually, at the first meal I served yesterday."

"They wanted a separate restaurant section?" Pov asked.

"Reserved for *Jewel* people, all meals. There's no ship rule against it, sir, none that I could find, and I

need their business. I hear Markos did the same with
the aftside restaurant." He looked uncertainly from
Pov to Ceverny. "Was that wrong, sir?"

"Jano—" Pov began, then changed his mind. "No,
it's all right for now. Who specifically asked you?"

"Antos Dobry. I think he's a subchief in engineering." He shrugged. "Heavyset man, beard, a little
short, don't know him more than that. I don't have
everybody from *Jewel* sorted out yet. It's only been
one day, after all." He tapped his forehead. "Takes a
while to fill the databanks."

"That it does," Ceverny rumbled. "When you get
them filled up with more data and clog your mind,
come play poker with me and lose money."

"Last time you lost, Miska, as I remember," Jano
retorted. "Let's repeat." He turned and strolled back
to his bar.

"Jewel," Pov muttered, then glanced surreptitiously
at the nearby tables, seeing face after face he only
vaguely recognized, if at all.

"Trouble?" Ceverny asked quietly.

"Do you know this Dobry?" Pov asked. Ceverny
shook his head. "Neither do I. I don't know most of
them. Maybe if we had transferred staff earlier—"

"Isle wasn't finished and ready for transfer," Ceverny interrupted. "And staff transitions are easier
when it's all at once. Otherwise you get cliques and I-
was-here-first and I-wanted-your-apartment and other
juvenile behavior. I should know: I'm a First-Ship
Slav. I lived inside that nonsense for years."

"Mirror staffed as they finished each residential section," Pov noted.

"Mirror had a homogeneous cadre from *Arrow*'s
three ships, all of it devoted to Thaddeus Gray. We

don't. Don't second-guess yourself, at least not on this issue. My advice."

"Which is always good, I admit." Pov smiled. "After we're done here, how about finding two comfortable chairs in front of a good window?"

"Sounds delightful. We'll do it."

Jano brought over their plates and served them with a flourish, then went back to get a plate for himself and returned to sit with them for a companionable meal. He sat down with a fat man's wheeze. Pov watched him spar good-naturedly with Miska, and enjoyed the man's running gossip, even about Pov himself, which Jano delivered with a sly smile.

"Young for the job, aren't you?" Jano elaborated. "And Andreos's protégé, gets the special favors. The other captains didn't even get to vote."

"They did, too," Ceverny objected. "I was there."

Jano shrugged. "He's awfully young, though," he said again, and tsked. "Janofsi's a *lot* older."

"But I'm sincere, Jano," Pov said. "Don't forget the sincere."

"Well, of course," Jano replied. "Actually, sir, I think I'll seat people where I wish, no fighting about it, but I get crowded at meals and have to make do sometimes."

"Do you?" Pov asked with a smile.

"In a few weeks, I could have the entire restaurant blended smooth as a soufflé." Jano winked at him broadly, and turned the talk to other subjects.

That evening Avi had the night shift on Sail Deck, taking over from Celka Matousek's beta shift to watch sail techs watch the computers watch photons. Watching cubed, Avi had said dryly to Pov as she left after dinner. Avi hadn't commented much more on her new command duties as *Isle*'s Third Sail, aside from various technical discussions that interested them both, but Pov thought that Avi enjoyed her new ranking, and took some justified pride in the recognition. Though Celka had the same number of years on Sail Deck as Avi did, Celka's raw talent had won her the second-rank post, a little early for an eighteen-year-old, but Celka, too, had taken the new rank in stride.

Pov sat in a comfortable chair in front of the living-room window, watching the Nebula perform its dance of light, Garridan asleep in his lap, Anushka sleeping in a bassinet at his feet. So much determined sleeping nearby made Pov yawn, not helped by the middle stage of a headache slowly throbbing at his temples. He rubbed the bridge of his nose irritably. Drat, he thought. I follow all of Dr. Karras's rules, take the pills, practice the relaxing, and I still get headaches. It isn't fair. Where do I file a complaint? Before they had left TriPower, Dr. Karras had run new tests on his blood pressure, chemistry panels, arterial suffi-ciency, and so forth, and pronounced herself not too concerned. Stress headaches, captain, she said. Take your pills. And *relax*.

So I'm relaxing, doctor. I hear you. He yawned again and smiled at the view outside his window. Su-perb. In his lap, Garridan snored softly inside his blan-ket, his tiny hands curled into fists on each side of his head. In the living-room corner beside the far end of the window, his gilded statue of St. Serena stood on her shrine, faintly illuminated by the Nebula glow and the small lamp at her feet. The room was dusky with tinted shadows, moving slowly with the variable Neb-ula light. Wonderful. Everything had gone so well today, so amazingly well. He smiled happily, pleased to take this moment when Fortune rode with them on the road. *BaXt,* the Rom called her, the good luck that blessed, the luck of the gypsies.

It might not last, probably wouldn't, not here at the Nebula. But he and the others would try to keep what share of the luck they could.

The outer door chimed and Kate strolled in a moment later, dressed in her red skydeck coveralls. She collapsed next to him in the other chair and pulled the barrettes out of her dark hair, letting it tumble down, then yawned. She clumped a boot on the ottoman cushion, clumped the other, then sank bonelessly into a full slouch.

" 'Lo, Pov," she said. "How's life? Avi said I should check on you because you have another headache and probably can't cope with the twins right now and would I please help you get along, if I have the time, that is." She eyed the twins, both collapsed into heaps. "I can see what she means. Tough duty, Pov."

"They're still in the sleeping stage. It gets worse later."

"As I know." She smiled and reached out her hand. He took her slender fingers in his and pressed them, then held her hand comfortably, happy she was here.

" 'Lo, Kate," he said and smiled at her. Her teeth flashed in answer.

"Isn't it beautiful?" she said.

"Gorgeous."

"I've been thinking my brother has finally been given what he's always deserved." She gestured her other hand at the window. "It's all right there. Enough for a lifetime, enough for our children. A road forever, Pov."

He nodded. "The *BaXt* won't last, probably."

"We'll get by. And it'll come back. It always does."

"How's Sergei?"

"Glued to his physics screens, naturally. I don't expect to pry him off for a few weeks. Until then I'm a Nebula widow, pottering around on skydeck, sighing for my Sergei." She demonstrated with a gusty sigh, then winked. "Until then I'm happy to keep company with Brother Wind, meaning you, of course. Do you remember the legend? O Del and the Five Kings?"

"That's Kalderash legend, not ours."

"It's still gypsy, and I like it. Don't be a Lowara bigot. You obviously need the story, will do you good."

Kate sketched a graceful blessing on the air with her hand, a *puri dai*'s gesture whenever she began a story for the children, teaching them about the Rom. Pov smiled in response, watching her.

"Hear, my dear children," Kate intoned in Romany, "of the wonders of O Del, our good God, and His servants, the Sky and the Earth, father and mother of us all. In the beginning, before men were made, the Sky and the Earth lived in harmony, devoted to each other and obedient to the Good God, O Del, the Maker of Creation. In time, as is the way of devoted couples, the Sky and Earth had five sons: King Sun, the eldest, King Moon, the second son, and the Brothers Fire, and Fog, and Wind."

Kate sketched another gesture, moving her fingers gracefully. "But O Beng the Devil, and enemy of all that is good and strong, provoked the younger brothers into jealousy of their elder brothers, and so the younger contended with the elder, wanting for themselves the greater favor of their parents. And so the Five Kings warred across the Earth and rampaged through the spaces of the Sky, spreading discord and unhappiness with their contending." Kate gestured despair and bowed her head. "And it was so," she murmured sadly.

"That sounds familiar of late," Pov said dryly. "And not with gypsy associations."

Kate blinked, as if in surprise. "Oh, we do have *four* cloudships, don't we? Almost like the *five* kings! I hadn't noticed that."

"Oh, sure you didn't, Kate."

"Hush, you. I'm telling you a story. Be polite." Kate composed her face into solemnity. "In despair, the Sky and the Earth confined their sons within a space in the Earth, angering their sons into new violence. In a fury, King Moon flung himself on his mother, the Earth, trying to separate her from the Sky. Brother Fog and Brother Fire attacked the Sky, their father, trying to enshroud him in mist, and to burn him to smoke and ashes. King Sun rushed upon his mother, making her reel; Brother Wind hurtled down upon her also, pushing her away from Father Sky. With a great outcry, she called out to O Del, the Good God, imploring his help against the Evil One."

Kate sketched another gesture, warding away O Beng and his evils that brought discord into the family, breaking the good. "And O Del was angered that sons would so attack their parents," she said solemnly, "and so He banished the rebellious sons who had attacked their mother, separating the Sun and the Moon and the Wind forever from the Earth. King Sun He placed in the day, King Moon in the night, and Brother Wind He caught between Sky and Earth, racing high in the air. But Fog and Fire, who had attacked only their father and had done no injury to the Earth, the Good God allowed to remain with the Earth, their mother. And so it is today in the world."

She leaned her chin in her palm and looked at him

with wide-eyed expectancy. "Now you're supposed to figure out how it applies, Pov."

"I am *not* Brother Wind, Kate."

"Of course you are. You're the Prince of Wands, too. I've told you this for years and years, Pov. You need to get this straight."

"You think it'll help if I tell Janofsi that he's really King Moon?"

"Actually, I think Janofsi is Brother Fog. As in naturally obscured." She grinned. "I have a bit of useful news for you. His skyriders think they're too good to hobnob with the rest of us, won't socialize at all. Their bad luck all these years, and they think they're better." Kate made a rude noise. "Not a good sign, Pov." She tsked and shook her head.

"I'll keep that bit of news high on the list," Pov informed her.

"Now I say 'which list,' right?"

"Only if you want to." He squeezed her fingers and smiled. "Thanks for coming by, Kate."

"Is your headache gone?" He opened his mouth, then closed it quickly as Kate pointed at him in triumph. "It is! You can't pretend with me. Ho-ho, and you don't believe in gypsy magic! You should listen better, Pov."

"Ho-ho."

"I'll persuade you yet." Kate leaned back comfortably and yawned. "Nice view, I think. Let's keep it awhile."

"That it is, and I agree."

"A reasonable man, is Brother Wind. We'll keep him, too."

Chapter 7

The following morning, six hours into alpha watch and twenty-three hours into the cloudship light-ranging, Pov leaned back in his interlink chair and sighed quietly, now quite bored by perfectionist photon counting and having little else to do in its place. The precision ranging required considerable computer capacity, which *Isle* had, and required considerable coordination through *Isle*'s master interlink to the other ships, which *Isle* could also do. As the light-ranging filled more and more of *Isle*'s active computer data storage, however, they had gradually found themselves running out of active memory for other things, a data sink they hadn't expected.

In late afternoon, as the light-ranging data sink ate its way steadily into *Isle*'s computer banks, Karoly had been forced to suspend Hold Deck's sort halfway through Sigrid's PAHs, to Sigrid's intense disappointment. Later in night watch the physics labs had shut down half their computer work, and this morning Helm Map had begun to reorganize itself in odd ways, as if it were a maiden aunt cornered in her kitchen by a menacing hulking shadow. Helm Map had busily hacked away with her umbrella, bonking the interlink with every blow, until Athena had realized what was happening and jumped to shut it off. Now a few telescopes were scanning various sights in the Nebula, manned by several frustrated physicists, and Karoly had put the entire Hold staff on holiday.

The glitch had utterly appalled Computer Chief Putakin, when he heard of it—as he had in spades when the data sink first started to show itself. It hadn't helped Putakin's upset to find that the fault lay with ignorant shipmasters. By an informal agreement some weeks back, the captains of the four ships had decided to delay formal analysis of the light-ranging data until the program completed itself, officially for neatness in their Nebula plan structure, informally for unstated reasons related more to upmanship than science. That delay, however, also delayed the data compression which kept the interlink from eating active computer capacity from *Isle*'s other computer programs. Putakin had never thought, in his wildest dreams, that the captains would delay analysis; the captains had assumed data delay would be a ready alternative and hadn't thought to mention it to Putakin. In the welter of Nebula plans and charts and meetings and whatall, the two data-points had never matched up at the right time.

At least we have enough computers to run the air blowers, Pov thought.

Two hours ago Putakin had finally stopped the sink and had begun rolling it backward, one slow section at a time. Helm Map was back up now, and later this afternoon Karoly could probably resume his sort on Hold Deck. By the time Putakin had recovered all the sink, almost *exactly* the same time, the interlink would finish the light-ranging. *BaXt* had her own particular sense of humor.

Outside the open doorway of *Isle*'s interlink room, he could hear the murmur of voices on Admin level, a soft musical sound punctuated by the quiet hum of the computer at his elbow. Across the room, Miska Ceverny had given up watching the light-scans some time ago and now tapped idly, playing with sail models, at a small laptop computer he had hauled in at the beginning of watch. Pov rotated his chair toward the wallscreen between their two consoles, where the Orion Nebula glowed as a wall-sized sea of colored light. Currents of gas and dust, tinted pink and green and deep violet, swirled steadily outward from the blazing Core, where the giant Trapezium stars burned white-hot among their hundreds of smaller companions. Creation. Force. Beauty. The words didn't catch it, what lay there before them.

I want to go *there,* Pov thought, looking hungrily at the light-filtered blaze of the Trapezium. And I want to go *now.* He grimaced and glanced at his wristband, wishing alpha watch were over. Let Tully watch lines wiggle. Let anybody else watch.

Where's the drama? he thought crossly, then laughed inwardly at his own impatience. Be smart, you dope. They'd just arrived from the Pleiades yesterday, after a wish-and-prayer leap across the gulf that had worked exactly by the numbers. Be smart.

Both Captain Andreos and Captain Gray had insisted on the detailed light-ranging before the cloudships dove into a dangerous unknown deeper into the Nebula. Pov and Janofsi had agreed, each cautious for a different reason—or perhaps the same one. Before the cloudships plunged ahead, they both wanted to see what might be there to bite them.

And what if the biter is invisible? Pov thought wryly. That's a wonderful thought. A few of the suspected phenomena deep within the Core, chiefly the nebula-wide gravitational and magnetic effects, were indeed invisible, even to a cloudship's sophisticated sensors. But they would see what they could see from the Nebula edge.

Could see, could see, he thought, drumming his fingers on his outship console. On the panel above, every other shipmaster's screen was empty, its former occupant finding something else to do in the last hour or so on computers that still worked. Only he, Dutiful Dope Shipmaster Janusz, sat and watched lines wiggle. He supposed it proved some point, though the point escaped him right now.

I could be reading those reports that Irisa stacked in my side room, he told himself. Get caught up—a little late, true, but I'd be caught up. Then, having noticed a little fact we missed, I could tell Putakin, hey, by the way, chief, when we start light-ranging . . .

The good chief would call the murder quite justified, Pov had no doubt at all.

Pov rocked his chair and slouched, then took his time stretching out his legs in front of his chair. He laced his fingers over his stomach and admired the embroidery on his sleeves. For *Isle*'s ship symbol, the committee had chosen a stylized wave in gold, a gleaming golden comber breaking on Siduri's island beach. Pov liked it. He looked at his boots, studying the creases, and thought of a half-dozen other things he could be doing instead of this, one notable item involving bed and Avi. He sighed.

"So go get another laptop and model some sails," Ceverny said without turning around.

"Nuts," Pov said aggressively.

Ceverny snickered at his tone. "I can't believe you're bored. Already?"

"Bored? Me?" Pov declared. "Duty's never boring. You taught me that years ago." He waved at the blank outship screens, where other cloudship captains had found better things to do elsewhere. "See the fantastic interest? It's riveting."

"At least you outlasted them," Ceverny said. "That's good for morale." He turned his chair around and squinted at Pov. "*You* agreed we wouldn't do any data analysis until everybody had a chance to look at the first full scan. *You* agreed to the data hold until we got comparison data from the cutters. You agreed to all that."

"Thanks for reminding me. Of course I agreed: you can blame Andreos just as much." He eyed Ceverny, and Ceverny eyed him back, suddenly wary under the scrutiny.

"What?" Ceverny demanded.

Pov grinned. "So why don't we steal space from the physics labs and sneak a look at the data? The labs probably won't even ask where it went, the way things have been going. I'm sure Gray is peeking with *his* computers, just to show off his advanced thought later."

"I'll bet you Janofsi is peeking, too, same reason—and I'm not that confident about *Net.*" Ceverny drew a long face and looked down his nose, then sniffed virtuously. "But it wouldn't be moral, Pov. We agreed not to peek."

"Nuts to moral."

Ceverny chuckled. "The first data capsule from *Traveler* should arrive soon," he said placatingly. "Katinka's had enough time to complete jump and start her readings. Be patient."

"Nuts to patient. I don't want to wait for the cutters. I want to peek," he insisted.

Ceverny pulled thoughtfully at his chin. "I could stare at the ceiling," he suggested. "I could even whistle a little, so you know when I'm not looking. I won't see a thing. Why are you asking me? You're the shipmaster."

"You're the witness. I need you subverted so you're as guilty as I am and can't talk about it later. It's called conspiracy."

Ceverny grinned. "Subvert away, sir." He leaned back in his chair and gazed at the ceiling, then began whistling softly.

Pov laughed and turned around to his board. All right, he thought, deciding how to do it.

He barged into the physics programs, put everything there on fast save, and snatched the available memory into his own area of the computer, with a block, save, and ward to stop the labs from stealing it back for the next few minutes. Then he erased his tracks with shipmaster's codes normally used for quite something else and smiled. Got you. He glanced at Ceverny, who was still whistling, and took a fast surreptitious copy of the Nebula sky they had partially scanned, loaded it into a side program, and pasted it with several security codes. Next he built a fence to keep it from drifting anywhere else in *Isle*'s computer banks. Chief Putakin had put in several new integrity safeguards after Talbot tried his data theft at TriPower, but Pov chose to add a prudent extra fence, then made the entire data unit invisible to random search, even from inside *Isle*.

"The data name is Adv.Tht," he said to Ceverny over his shoulder, "in case you want to look, too. I've got the top five security codes on it, so don't ring any bells."

"Got that." Ceverny thumped his chair upright and started typing at his own board. "Sneak a download copy of Helm Map from Athena, won't you, so we can do some mapping."

"Can do." They both tapped busily, starting an analysis of *Isle*'s early light-catching. It was conspiracy. It was breach of agreement. It was wrong. Pov smiled happily.

"Loading Helm Map," he said two minutes later. "You'd better close the door."

Ceverny got up and closed the door of the interlink room, then ostentatiously locked it. "I believe only you and I have the codes to get past this lock."

"Tully's got those codes," Pov said absently, hunting for the right wavelengths to load in some hydrogen lines. "Sorry."

"Oh, he does?" Ceverny said, deciding to grumble about Tully and his ever-present spies. He and Pov had this same conversation every so often, whenever the topic came up somehow: Ceverny disapproved of spies, even *Isle*'s own.

"He always gets the codes," Pov dodged. "You know that. Here comes the ultraviolet."

After the UV loaded in his area, he unblocked the active memory space and plopped it back in the labs' area, rang a bell to get their attention, then disappeared tracelessly. Mystery of the universe, never solved. Then he turned his head and looked at the wallscreen. "Beautiful!"

The screen glowed in a dozen shades of purple, superbly detailed with Helm Map's extraordinary precision when limited to a few selected wavelengths. Pov got up and paced the length of the wallscreen, looking closely at the swirls of molecules and brilliant dust in the western Nebula.

"Look," he said, pointing at a blurred disk. "There's that active protostar at LP Orionis that you liked so much."

"It'd be a good first step to the Core," Ceverny observed. "Even a full alternative."

"I haven't given up on the Core yet. Don't think so fast."

"We can try the Core next time," Ceverny persisted.

Pov gave him a genial glare. "Think slower, will you? I want to go into the Core *this* time."

Ceverny leaned back and crossed his arms, smiling at him. "Andreos will agree with me."

"No, he won't. Want to bet?"

"No. I'm afraid you're right." Ceverny looked at the wallscreen and scowled. "I don't see why Katrinya had to go out in the cutter," he complained. "*Mirror* didn't send *their* holdmaster." In the hours since Katrinya had left with *Traveler,* Ceverny had developed a few second thoughts about efficiency levels of dust studies, choosing to worry instead about Katrinya.

Pov shrugged. "Actually, I wish Thaddeus had sent Rachel. It would give her a better profile. Rachel gets to follow him around and wear shipmaster slashes on her sleeve, but everybody knows who's the real shipmaster over there. And he took charge of the light-ranging, too, something he could have delegated to her, even as a junior captain."

"A princess doesn't need expertise," Ceverny said, without much concern. "All she needs is a marriageable hand, and I understand Rachel's suitors are legion, considering the assets she'll inherit."

"It's not fair to Rachel," Pov muttered.

Ceverny shrugged, not that interested in Rachel and her inship problems. "On our side, it's called being a First-Ship Slav—or a Rom. Some of us have to try harder because of it."

"True," Pov agreed reluctantly. "Even so, what's

the point of making shipmaster rank too young if you don't get the show-off perks, get the seniors to defer to you?" He gave Ceverny a mock bow. "Speaking from my recent experience, of course. If *you* had had as much sense as Captain Gray, you'd have claimed rank as *Isle*'s shipmaster and *you'd* be sitting in my chair, not me, running the show to suit yourself."

"Even if I *were* sitting in that chair," Ceverny corrected mildly, "Katrinya would still be off in *Traveler*. Don't confuse shipmaster with spouse: the authority lines just aren't the same. Avi'll teach you. You just wait."

"With my relatives helping her along, I'm sure she will. The *romni* set up all those rules centuries ago, then probably taught them to all you gaje. Blame the Rom, Miska. It's as easy as any other reason."

Ceverny chuckled, then turned around to his inship board as it chimed for attention. Karoly appeared in one of the small screens in a link to Hold Deck. "Mister Ceverny? Pov?"

"What is it, Karoly?" Ceverny asked. "Are you ready to resume the sort?" Behind Karoly, Hold Deck was nearly empty of staff, with everything still shut down.

"No, sir, it's not that. The jump capsule just arrived from *Traveler*. It's too early but I downloaded the data into the computer, only it didn't have much to download, at least not as much as it should. So I looked at the holdmaster's real-time recording to see why." Karoly hesitated, his face very solemn.

"And?" Ceverny prompted, sitting up straighter. Pov walked over to stand by Ceverny's shoulder.

"I think it's best you see for yourself, sirs. Loading message."

The inship screen windowed another panel to show

the view of the cutter cabin, only now a reddish shimmer from the Nebula's dominant glow of hydrogen filled the transparent wallwindow, with Josef's lanky body in silhouette at the pilot controls. In the foreground Katrinya Ceverny smiled into the mirror, her white hair coiffed neatly around her lined face, looking just as she had looked hours before when *Traveler* launched.

"Here we are," she said pleasantly. She pushed a button on her console. "Starting data recording now. We've got the dust wall north of us with a density you won't believe, and Josef is cruising us alongside it. Thin plasma to east and west, slow eddies, mostly hydrogen and some drift molecules from the dust wall. I'm counting silicates and carbons as the dust base, about the percentages we expected. Sending you the initial light scans." Her hands moved over her computer board again.

"Also sending you some microwave readings," she continued, her tone easy and unhurried. "It looks to be our first close look at a water maser. Apparently there's a middle-size protostar a half light-year beyond this dust wall, still quite enshrouded in its dust shell, but it's putting out enough energy to mase a water cloud between us. The maser winks on and off with the infall flares, no predictable pattern. Here's the outside view in short radio-lengths."

The small screen filled with reddish shadows, a drifting curtain of dark gas flickering with infrared molecular frequencies. In the center, a dim sphere brightened and faded erratically, a near point-source in darker microwave. It flickered eerily, like a demon's eye winking through a smoke-hazed darkness.

Pov felt a shiver of vague dread snake up his spine and glanced at Karoly uneasily. Karoly looked back now in open anguish, his hands tight on his hold console.

"The microwave coherency is blurred," Katrinya said on the voiceover. "There could be a lot of dust mixed in the water cloud, refracting some of the light. Or maybe it's a function of the protostar flares. If the protostar is still dispersing its dust shell, not much radiation is getting out to mase the cloud. It's not a big star, anyway, maybe G-class when it settles down in a few million years. The extra readings, partial as they are, should supplement our T Tauri profile and *Spirit*'s studies at the dwarf."

The screen shifted back to Katrinya's lined face. "And some good maser data, too, though I expect we can get closer elsewhere. These maser readings are different from Earth's long-range scans of the inner Core, markedly so. Even watching for a few minutes, I can see the light curve is more diffuse, far more erratic. I can't tell if the effect comes from the dust over there at the protostar or over here in the wall." She shrugged. "The physicists can figure it out, I suppose. Tell the labs to let me know when they do."

She turned her head to look at the large wallwindow above Josef's console. "The dust is thinning now." She frowned, then chewed her lip. "That's odd. Josef, why don't you . . . Oh, never mind. Who says gravity waves have to be regular?" She tossed a quick smile back at the monitor. "If there are such things as rolling gravity waves, of course. Personally, I think Lobanov is an idiot, retooling Einstein as he does. Why do Russkis always think they—"

She stopped, frowning again as she glanced up at a light-scan screen above her monitor. "Now, that *is* odd. Josef, will you polarize the window into infrared?

Thank you." She turned her chair toward the wallwindow, obviously perplexed. "I would have thought—"

The next instant a brilliant red glare swept across her face, flashing through the pilot's window into the cabin. Josef threw his arm across his eyes and cried out, then tumbled sideways out of the pilot chair.

"Get down!" he shouted at Katrinya.

Katrinya gasped and half-stood as another red flare flashed into the cabin, then turned and hit her hand hard on her panel, launching the jump capsule. Ceverny's sidescreen went abruptly black.

Ceverny stared at its emptiness, frozen into immobility.

"We think the maser flared hard, sir," Karoly said into the silence, "just as the dust wall was thinning. The cutter's hull should protect them, of course, and the wallwindow should have polarized to opaque within another second, but the cutter's sensors have to be gone."

Karoly swallowed hard. They had all seen the red flash into Katrinya's cabin, and likely coherent microwave radiation had flashed with it. How much depended upon how well TriPower's engineers had built the cutter's wallwindow—and how much power the protostar had flared into the maser cloud at a certain instant six months ago. Given enough power at the right frequency, a water maser could flash to x-ray intensity, penetrating space like a razor.

Not out here, Pov thought in dismay. Not by the Nebula edge. The hot masers are in the Core, not out here. It's safe out here. Isn't it?

Ceverny sat numbly in his chair, staring at the blank screen where Katrinya had been, but had now vanished into the blankness, gone.

Pov stepped over to his own console and called

Captain Andreos on his private channel to *Net,* then briefed Andreos quickly.

Andreos's face tightened with worry as he listened, then grew even more solemn as he looked past Pov at Ceverny. "Water maser," he muttered and ran his fingers through his hair. "Out here? God!" He thought some more, then grasped at the same hope. "The hull would keep out most of it—if the wallwindow worked."

"Probably," Pov agreed. "But losing the sensors means they can't jump back. The ship computer wouldn't permit it, not without working sensors. It's one of the jump program's imperatives."

Ceverny stood up convulsively, startling them both with the savage abruptness of his motion. "Then we'll go get her right now!" he blurted, and took a brisk step toward the interlink door.

Pov reached and caught at his arm, stopping him from charging off to Athena's Helm Deck to give the necessary orders, as Ceverny evidently intended to do, totally forgetting he could call her on the interlink. "Not with *Isle,* Miska," Pov objected. "We're the anchor for the light-ranging. It would gut the entire program."

Ceverny shook off his hand brusquely. "So we'll start over when we get back," he snapped.

"No, we'll send *Jewel,*" Pov said, more firmly, then glanced at Andreos, who nodded his agreement. "The other cloudships can overlap to cover *Jewel*'s scanning share. *Jewel* can get there and back just as fast as *Isle.*"

Ceverny hesitated as he tried to focus on what Pov had said. "Then I'm going with *Jewel,*" he declared.

"No, I'd rather you didn't," Andreos said unexpectedly.

Pov swiveled his head at Captain Andreos in surprise. If it were Avi, he'd charge off too, in an instant, wherever it took him. "Sir!" he began in protest. "Surely he can—"

"I'm going with *Jewel*," Ceverny repeated, his own shock shifting into anger at Andreos's resistance. "Of course I'm going!" He practically danced in place, furious at the obstacle, any obstacle, that prevented him from rushing away to *Jewel*. "Goddammit, Leonidas!" he shouted. "What kind of order is that? You can't expect—"

Andreos grimaced in open regret, but looked firm. "If you'd think about it a moment, my dear old friend," he said to Ceverny, "you'd see why. If you go charging off with Janofsi to correct Pov's mistake, which is how *Jewel* would interpret it, Janofsi will pounce and blame Pov, thinking he can get *Isle* at last, get even with *Net*, maybe impress the Grays by being right all along. See?" He waved his hand, feigning Karol Janofsi's triumph. "Miska Ceverny agreed with me, he'd say. Miska Ceverny finally admitted Pov Janusz is an incompetent. Miska Ceverny—"

"The hell he'd put words in my mouth like that!" Ceverny snapped angrily. "I don't think anything of the kind!" He stopped short, then grimaced. "It wouldn't make any difference, would it? I'd yell and he'd yell . . ." He trailed off and looked at the wallscreen again, where the Nebula glittered.

Andreos nodded. "No, it wouldn't make any difference, not where it counted. It's *Dance*'s accident all over again, Miska. An error that isn't really error, only a risk we accepted—but that'll be forgotten. How we deal with this first crisis will set the tone for everything from now on. You know what's at stake, Miska, if we fail. You're too important to go with *Jewel*. It turns into a political statement."

"Janofsi can't blame me for a maser—" Pov argued when he saw the struggle begin on Ceverny's face, though he knew, as well as Ceverny knew, how it would happen, how it could unravel all over again. It was a sickness of the Slav ships, one that *Net* had been unable to heal with *Jewel,* one that still festered, fueled by Janofsi's age, *Jewel's* many disappointments, Natalya's adamant defense.

"He'd find a way to blame," Andreos said heavily. "He's proved that for months."

"He's right, Pov," Ceverny muttered. Anguish washed across Ceverny's old face, and he looked at the wallscreen where the Nebula swirled in its many colors. Somewhere out there Katrinya needed him. Somewhere out there Katrinya might be hurt, even dying. "He's right," he repeated numbly. "It's easy to blame, when you need to blame. I should know: I blamed you when *Dance* was hurt. Captain Rybak never stopped blaming and lost *Net* because of it." He closed his eyes a moment. "Easy. Especially for *Jewel.*"

"But what about you?" Pov asked. He pressed Ceverny's arm, but Miska wasn't listening, his eyes fixed on Andreos in the interlink screen.

"It's only a few extra hours, Miska," Andreos said softly, "a few extra hours until you'd know she's all right, just the time for *Jewel* to get there and send a message back. Can you give me that? I am asking."

Ceverny blinked and stared at Andreos another moment, then took a shuddering breath. He nodded, a slow agony. "Yes," he whispered, then closed his eyes in pain.

Andreos nodded, thought to say something else, then shook his head sadly and broke the connection.

From the inship panel from Hold Deck, Karoly had

watched mutely, his anguish nearly matching Ceverny's. Karoly had revered Katrinya Ceverny from his first watches on *Fan*'s Hold Deck, later following the Cevernys to *Dance,* then looking at Katrinya after his transfer to *Net* for the help she had freely offered any of Janina's staff. "Captain?" he asked Pov, lifting his chin. "Any orders?'"

"Call the hold staff, Karoly," Pov said. "Make the announcement right away before the sieve gets hold of it. I don't want this exaggerated." Ceverny made a strangled sound, but said nothing.

"Yes, sir." Karoly windowed out.

Pov turned and called *Jewel,* asking for immediate contact with Captain Janofsi.

"She's my moon and stars, Pov," Ceverny said behind him, his voice faint and old. "My moon and stars."

"We'll find her, Miska," Pov promised him. "We'll find her and bring her back."

"This is *exactly* the kind of risk," Janofsi raged, "that I've warned about since the beginning. What good are all our plans if we change them on impulse like this? Look at the result!" He waved his hand wide.

"It wasn't impulse, captain," Andreos said patiently. "It was a reasoned and considered decision. With the high dust ratios we discovered on arrival, we needed additional information. Holdmaster Ceverny has the expertise to—"

"We weren't *supposed* to study dust walls at this time!" Janofsi shouted. "We were supposed to study protostars! The plan was two cutter jumps to red dwarfs, not to a dust wall with a maser behind it!"

"We didn't know it had a maser," Pov interjected,

as calmly as he could. Behind him in *Isle*'s interlink room, Sailmaster Ceverny sat rigidly in his chair, his expression as controlled as he could make it. Pov knew that each angry word probably dripped like acid into Ceverny's soul. "Masers can be detected only in line of sight—"

"You certainly proved *that*, didn't you?" Janofsi retorted harshly. Pov tightened his lips, holding back words he shouldn't say, couldn't say.

"This is a place of hazards," Gray said calmly from *Mirror*. "It is a place of risks. We have planned for injury, for unexpected surprises."

"Stay out of this, *Arrow*!" Janofsi snapped.

Gray's eyes immediately narrowed. "I most certainly will not. I am a consortium member, just as you are. And I say you are overreacting, *Jewel*. We have contingencies, such as detaching *Jewel*. We have hospitals for treating the injured. And we have TriPower's windows. There is a good chance that the polarized window stopped most of the masered microwaves. They are likely still alive. Even if they are not—forgive me, Sailmaster Ceverny—their deaths are also within our agreed risks."

Janofsi hesitated, wanting to argue onward—but he hesitated as Andreos stared at him levelly, with a blatant warning in the look. Janofsi finally nodded reluctantly, though his face flushed with anger at doing it.

"Thank you." Andreos took a deep breath. "Please go to *Traveler*, Karol, and report back as soon as you can. In the meantime, I suggest we continue with the light-ranging and complete it on time. Is that acceptable, *Mirror*?" Gray nodded. "Then, thank you."

Janofsi immediately dropped out of the interlink, cutting contact with *Isle*. Andreos sighed heavily and laced his fingers.

"I'm going to sit with Miska until we hear from *Jewel*," Pov told them, rising from his chair. He turned toward Ceverny.

"Certainly, Pov," Andreos said. He leaned forward and looked past Pov to Ceverny. "Miska, our prayers are with you and Katrinya. I'm sure she's all right."

Ceverny nodded mutely.

Chapter 8

Pov waited with Ceverny on the conference room off skydeck, watching the old sailmaster with deepening concern as time passed. Miska sat with his hands clasped between his knees, his white-haired head bowed forward, staring unseeingly at the floor, saying nothing, waiting out each heartbeat, each minute, each half hour as if each breath were a measurement of endurance beyond limit. Pov had never seen this sudden a collapse in the grand old man. He had never seen any collapse, for that matter—he had seen Ceverny's sarcasm, humor, towering rages, abstractions, whimsy, but never this . . . blankness. Miska and Katrinya Ceverny had lived among the risks of cloudship life all through their marriage, unbowed, unafraid, the toughest of the First-Ship stock. It was as if someone had abruptly swept away Ceverny's spirit whole, collapsing him into age and loss and nothingness.

"Miska," Pov said quietly, the fifth time in the last two hours. Ceverny ignored him, as before.

Pov got up and walked around the table, then sat down in the chair facing Ceverny. He leaned his elbows on his knees to look directly into Ceverny's face. "Miska," he repeated.

Ceverny blinked and raised his head a little, then seemed to start as he saw Pov close in front of him.

He blinked again. "Did you say something?" he croaked.

"She's not dead. I don't believe that. Even if I'm wrong, we don't know it yet."

"We don't know she's *not*," Ceverny said, his voice cracking. Pov reached a hand and gripped his shoulder, and felt the wiry muscles of Ceverny's arm tense under his touch. He let his hand fall away.

"I'm sorry, Miska," Pov said sadly. "We should have let you go with *Jewel*. The people are the ship, Andreos tells me, and he's right. I'm sorry."

Ceverny blinked at him, then straightened in his chair slowly, like a swimmer ascending from deep water. "Nonsense," Ceverny said. "Nonsense to that," he repeated, more loudly. He slowly rubbed his chest with his hand, wincing, then winced again as he shifted in his chair and felt stiff muscles. "How long have I been sitting here?" he asked, a little wonderingly. He looked around at the blank conference-room walls, as if he'd awoken in a wholly strange place.

"About two hours. I was worried about you."

"And you've been here the entire time?" Ceverny blinked again.

"Yes," Pov said. "Of course."

Ceverny smiled, very faint. "The people are the ship. So is the captain, in even deeper ways. Thank you, son."

"You're welcome. Are you all right? Is there anything I can do?"

"No." Ceverny looked away, avoiding his eyes. "No, nothing."

"I can't believe that, 'nothing.' You've been my sailmaster since I was ten years old, a brand-new boy on *Fan*, and I saw you stalking across *Fan*'s companionway for the first time. You were tall and dramatic and you stalked instead of walked. I was impressed. That's who I'm going to be, I told myself. Sailmaster Pov Janusz, just like *him*. You were a lot younger then, of course."

Ceverny looked back at him.

"More handsome, too," Pov added. Ceverny's eyebrows lowered a millimeter or two. "But I was hooked. Of course, later I found out what you're *really* like, and I suffered horribly. All those trainee night watches I stood with no sympathy from you, not even a mumbled word of appreciation. One school term I got every training exercise right, did all the simulations flawlessly, my classmates were in total awe of me— and you didn't even notice. I mean, why try? Hell." Pov crossed his arms and looked away. "I'll never forgive you for that."

"I noticed it," Ceverny said mildly.

"I didn't hear about it. Later, when I was a sail tech, you blamed *me* for a drill that Tully screwed up. Tully, the zero, just let it sit. Ah, hell, Pov, he said to me, with your efficiency ratings, who'll care? So there I am: either I ruin my friendship forever with Tully by setting the facts straight, or I have this black mark on my record that'll probably ruin my ship career. I mean, what would you have done?"

Ceverny jerked up straighter and stared, as a light suddenly dawned. "It was you! You're the one that—"

"Decorated your monthly sail log with those naked Greek nymphs. Fair is square."

"I docked Tully a half-month profit's share for that!"

Pov smiled. "I know."

Ceverny sputtered a moment, then snorted in laughter. "I don't believe it. It's not true."

"It is true. A person does strange things when he's

that disappointed. Here I thought you were a hero, and you were just . . . you."

"Sorry about that."

"It's all right. I've been sitting here for two hours wondering if I had lost you. If Katrinya is—gone, that is. I wondered if you'd wander away so far I couldn't find you again. I wondered what I would do if I never again saw Miska Ceverny stalk along the companion-way, the way he does so very well, and what an emptiness it would be, losing that forever."

"We all die eventually, Pov," Ceverny said quietly. "I will. So will you."

Pov looked down at his hands and reclasped his fingers. "Usually we don't choose when it happens. Are you choosing?" He raised his head again.

Ceverny looked at Pov for a long moment. "No," he said finally. "No, I'm not choosing that."

"We should have let you go with *Jewel*," Pov said sadly.

"So I could fall apart in front of Karol Janofsi?" Ceverny asked wryly. "I wouldn't have liked that. No, not at all." He drew in a great breath, then expelled it slowly. "I'm sorry I frightened you, son. I will be stronger." His old face settled into severe lines, fierce and clear-eyed. The effort did not erase all the pain in his face, only part of it. The rest would go only with Katrinya's safe return.

Pov smiled at him fondly. "Such a disappointment," he said, shaking his head. Ceverny shrugged.

The wall comm chimed for attention, and Ceverny tensed, his eyes widening with a fear he could not conceal. They both knew what it was, in the same instant. Pov stood and walked quickly to the comm panel. "This is Captain Janusz. Go ahead."

"Sir, this is Third Helm. I am broadcasting on the

all-ship by Athena's order. We have received a message capsule from *Jewel.* Message follows: 'They are alive. First- and second-degree burns, not life-threatening.' " Ceverny moaned and covered his face with his hands. " 'Cutter is incapacitated by sensor damage, as expected. We are taking *Traveler* aboard and will transport back. Janofsi ends.' That's all, sir."

"That is good news," Pov said. "Thank you."

"Yes, sir." The comm officer paused. "Sir, please tell Sailmaster Ceverny our relief and joy at this news, from all of us on Helm Deck. I'm sure the entire ship feels the same way."

"Thank you. I'll tell him."

"Thank you, sir. Comm out." The comm clicked off.

Ceverny slowly slid his hands down his face, then dropped them to the table, clasped them together. He stared at nothing for a moment, then shifted his eyes to Pov. "I think I'll wait here," he said, "until she's safely home. Is that all right?"

"Of course. Whatever you want to do, Miska. Do you want me to stay? Send somebody down to sit with you?"

"No, that's not necessary," Ceverny said firmly. "Go back up to *Isle,* Pov. I'm all right. I'm all right now."

Pov had thought he was heading for Admin, but found himself detouring off the companionway to Medical Section. He walked into the cool soft white of the hospital and continued down the hallway past the treatment rooms, several patient rooms, and a medtech's station to the office door near the rear of the unit. *Isle*'s chief medical officer, Ariadne Karras, was a dark-haired woman in her thirties, about Pov's age, trim and efficient and quick, a good friend of

Athena. She looked up when he appeared in her office doorway.

"Did you hear the news about *Traveler*?" Pov asked.

"Yes, I did. I'm organizing the treatment plan now. It sounds like some of the burns are second-degree. We have grafts and therapy for that."

Pov nodded, then walked in and closed her door, then sat down. "I'm worried about Miska Ceverny, too. He sat for a couple of hours, just blank, not responding at all. I've never seen him that way before. I think he's okay now, but—"

"Nonresponsive?" Dr. Karras narrowed her eyes in concern. "Where is he?"

"On skydeck, waiting for Katrinya. As I said, he seemed to come out of it." Pov spread his hands. "Captain Andreos held him back from charging off with *Jewel*, and I wish we hadn't now. Katrinya is breath itself for him. He's a grand old man and I'd like you to help him, if he needs it. Miska Ceverny usually doesn't want help, so you'll get some resistance."

Dr. Karras smiled. "That sounds familiar," she said meaningfully, and gave Pov the eye. "Seems to run with the sailmaster breed. If the pills aren't working, Pov, you're supposed to tell your doctor."

"They do work—sort of," Pov objected. "And I told Avi I'd see you again, when I had time. I haven't had time." He scowled, not liking the pressure, however well meant, from either Avi or Dr. Karras. "I'm even relaxing, as you said I should. I relaxed all day yesterday after watch. Don't change the subject just because I wander into range."

"We each have our own wasteland, Pov," Dr. Karras said softly. "Yours is giving you headaches right now." She pointed her finger at him. "Make time to see me. That's an order. As Medical Officer, I'm the only person on this ship who can give you orders and make them stick. I will watch over Miska Ceverny. I am also watching over you, so stop that fidgeting and listen to me. That's an order, too."

"Tough lady," Pov said, leaning back in his chair.

"I can strut to match any of those overgrown boys on *Jewel* and *Mirror*. I have a direct request from Captain Andreos to take care of your health, you personally, and I consider that a trust. It doesn't have to be a war. You're more mature than that."

"I don't have time to have headaches," Pov muttered.

"You're also smarter than that. Athena takes care of herself, and she's a pilot. You can at least match that. What good will you be to *Isle* if you manage to neglect those headaches into something more serious?"

"So how am I supposed to stop the headaches? I follow your rules. I keep calm. I put up with all that— *idiocy* from Janofsi. I make things work. I listen to everybody. I'm perfect." He crossed his arms and looked at the documents on her walls, the diplomas, the certificates, a framed poem. Anywhere but at her.

"And frustrated."

"And irritated as hell right now. The last thing I need is nagging from you." He heard the ragged edge in his own voice and clamped his jaws shut.

There was a short silence. "I'm also a deft psychologist, captain, and I know you just heard your own voice. You're a smart man. You've got to find another way to deal with all this."

Pov looked back at her, his jaw muscles tight. "I just saw a man I love disintegrate in front of my eyes, because of something *I* permitted. I brought him to the Nebula."

"He brought himself to the Nebula. We all did."

"But I'm the shipmaster!" Pov stood up, without any idea of where he was going. "It's my responsi—"

"No, it's not," Ariadne said quietly. "Will you sit down again? Please, Pov. Sit down." She waited until he complied.

She leaned forward and laced her fingers together, her face intent. "There's one difference between you and Miska Ceverny. You reach for support. That's healthy, Pov. That's why you're here right now with me. Some people don't reach and they get ulcers or strokes or neuroses that eat them up." She unlaced her fingers and spread her hands expressively. "We're the same age, you and I. Young for the rank we hold. We both have a responsibility to our ship. Both involve very serious duties, with decisions that affect lives, happiness, success, even our destiny. That's a heavy burden."

"I always feel like a fool when I sound off at you. I'm sorry."

"Why? I don't expect you to be perfect. I'm a doctor. I decided people weren't perfect my first year in clinic. And I'm your friend. And a friend of your other friends on this ship. I've had Avi in here recently, worrying aloud about you. Last week it was Tully and Athena, both concerned. Danil dropped by a few weeks ago, too. And others. All worried about you."

"Why?" Pov asked, bewildered. "I haven't been *that* bad."

Dr. Karras laughed. "Where's the rule that you can worry yourself sick about them and they can't worry about you?"

"Well . . ."

Ariadne smiled and spread her hands again. "I'm not an oracle. I don't have a superior wisdom to offer you. But you have to protect your boundaries, by letting other people take responsibility for themselves, too. Or it'll eat you up. And I don't want to see that happen. It's not fair, it's not right, and it's up to you. That's the lecture. You've heard it before."

"Yes, ma'am."

"A little more cheerfully, please," she said, amused by his sour tone.

"So what do I do about my headaches?"

"Take your pills—I'll give you some new ones to try—and *relax*. When your brain scans and blood pressure show something ominous, I'll have worse rules, so appreciate what you've got."

Pov was silent a moment. "Do second-degree burns leave scars?" he asked.

"Pov!" she admonished.

"I just want to know, Ariadne. Be reasonable."

She tightened her lips, but relented. "Not permanent scars. Not with the tissue regeneration and surgery we can do. They'll be all right, with full recovery in due course. I can promise that." She smiled. "That's *my* responsibility."

"I hear you, Dr. Karras."

"Yes, I know you do. That's why you get my lecture only once a month or so, not more often. Routine maintenance, you might say. What I suggest now is that you not go up to Admin, where I know you were headed before this detour to me, and get yourself plunged back into the current crisis. The crisis can keep. Don't go read Nebula plans. Don't sit with Miska and wait. Do something different."

"Like what?"

"You mean you can't think of even one possibility?" She pretended shock. "This is grave."

He flipped his hand at her. "Soar off, doctor."

She chuckled. "As long as you can tell your doctor to soar off, I feel reassured. And I won't ask what that gypsy gesture just meant; I don't think I want to know." Pov grinned back at her. "See? It's already working. Listen to your doctor."

"Thanks."

"Drop by more often," she suggested. "It'd make me feel better." She wrote something on a small pad on her desk, ripped off the sheet, and handed to him. "Your new pills. Ask the front desk to fill the prescription. Take the first one now—and go find something elsewise to do."

"All right." Pov stood up and took the slip of paper.

"I'll take care, as is needed," Ariadne said, looking up at him. "Try not to worry. Reach for the support. It's your balance, and your best service to *Isle*. See? Service? I know what buttons to push."

"That you do. And I let you push them, you'll notice."

"Also an encouraging sign. I'll look in on Ceverny in a bit, maybe talk to him a while. You go relax."

Pov ended up in the skyside lounge, and sat himself down in a corner booth with a glass of Jano's best draft beer. The alcohol worked nicely at his nerves, and he kept himself to the one glass to nurse along. With one arm draped over the cushioned back of the bench, the other hand curled around the cool glass, he watched people come in and out of the lounge, not much traffic in the middle of the afternoon watch. The lights from the companionway and the more subdued lights of the lounge glinted off the array of glassware suspended over the bar, and the low talk of the crowd made a soothing murmur in his ears.

He tried to think of nothing at all, but found himself watching the faces nearby. Two techs were having a friendly argument over something or other several tables away, their lean faces animated and keen. At another table, a young mother was treating her two unruly sons to a chilled desert, but only if they behaved, she warned—which they didn't, once they'd eaten the ice cream. In despair, she had finally half-dragged the younger out of the lounge, lecturing the elder all the while. At another table near the back, an older man sat with some charts, shoveling in a late lunch he probably hardly tasted as he read single-mindedly through the report. People. His people.

What do they think of me? he wondered. The *Net* staff knew him fairly well, and the TriPower transferees were happy to take Sigrid's word about a certain general worth. The *Jewel* people remained an enigma, but he could understand the reasons. *Isle* was a ship less than three days old, in terms of this crew, thrown together at the last minute and then launched away to the unknowns of the Nebula. What did they think about that?

On *Net*, Tully had kept his ear to the sieve of gossip and personal speculation sifting through their ship, telling Pov bits of news that Tully thought might interest him. Tully liked intrigue and secrets, a little too much, but he usually read the sieve well. Did *Isle* have a sieve yet, one of *Isle*'s common run of rumor and gossip? Or was it divided into separate cycles, *Net*'s and *Jewel*'s and TriPower's? Did it matter?

I think Miska's wrong, he decided. We should have formed the crew earlier, as *Mirror* had, not anticipated a reenactment of the Slav ships' personal history.

Dance had been troubled by First-Ship politics and friction among the different nationalities of her crew, both of which had contributed in their own way to the final breach with *Net*. *Fan*'s daughter ships had always been quarrelsome, all independent and difficult ships that chose their own way, as *Jewel* had, as had *Net*. After *Net* left for the Pleiades and would not return, *Dance* had moved on to Ashkelon, another Hyades colony. Contacts between *Net* and *Dance*, even between close relatives on the two ships, had been few ever since, and likely the breach was permanent. *Dance* would never come to the Pleiades, not now, not after the way *Net* had left. She was too proud. Pov tried to imagine a circumstance where he might quarrel with Captain Andreos so seriously that he would break their bond, and couldn't think of a cause, not one.

God knew the Rom had their fights. His mother had nearly split the family over Kate's betrothal to Sergei, but had pulled back from the brink at the last moment, yielding when she could have destroyed. He knew a similar quarrel had led to his mother's original transfer aboard *Fan*, something between Margareta and their larger gypsy family on Perikles she refused to discuss. But a Rom family remained together more than apart, whatever their quarrels.

He watched a small group in tech coveralls walk in and head for *Jewel*'s designated tables, then sit down together, ignoring everyone else in the room, not even a casual glance around the lounge. No interest, no notice. We wall you out.

Like the Rom, he thought, disappointed. The Rom had survived by the walls they built between themselves and gaje society, as stubbornly persistent in their ways as other insular peoples, the Amish, the

Jews, the more fundamentalist Arabs. A few new and quite different insular peoples had sprung up on Earth's colonies, too, drawing new lines of division, new lines of in and out, yes and no. And *Jewel*'s transferees were definitely saying "no" in their actions. In *Jewel*'s special restaurant section, he saw the old problems starting again, the quarrels that had ripped *Jewel* from her mothership twenty years before, that had divided *Net* and *Dance*.

Easier to give them up, he thought, ship them back to *Jewel*, and start anew with crew borrowed from *Arrow*'s ships. Janofsi would rage, indignant at the insult to his people, probably storm out of the consortium. But Pov thought it too soon to put *Isle* partly into *Arrow*'s pocket, not that he really distrusted the Americans, merely the unknowns in a crew from different ships, a different heritage. He smiled ruefully. I'm not non-Rom enough yet for that.

Easier to give them up, only he knew he wouldn't. When *Jewel*'s people had transferred aboard *Isle,* they had become *Isle*'s people, his people, his crew. He would fight to keep every last one of them. Only how? What were they thinking?

You told Dr. Karras you'd do something else, he reminded himself. Stop thinking about staff. He was trying to think of another topic to think about when Tully appeared in the lounge doorway across the room, spotted him, and course-tracked straight for his table. "There you are," he said with a smile as he walked up. "Hiding out, shipmaster?"

"What's the crisis now?" Pov said wearily and started to get out of the booth.

"Don't get up. Stay put." Tully slid into the seat opposite him and stole Pov's beer glass without even asking. He investigated the beer, took an approving sip, and ordered the same from the table display. Then he leaned back and copied Pov's earlier arm across the seatback. Observant Tully. Pov smiled skeptically.

"Helps to be married to the shipmaster's admin aide," Tully commented when Pov didn't ask. "If you really want to hide out, Pov, you can't tell anybody where you are. That way you've got at least an hour until you're spotted and the gig's up, more if you find a really good place with no people walking through and such."

"I'm relaxing," he explained.

"Good. How can I assist?"

"Is that why you're here?" He smiled. "To help me relax?"

"Yep."

"You peached on me to Dr. Karras. She told me."

"Whatever happened to medical confidentiality?" Tully protested. The young bartender, one of Jano's three sons, brought Tully's beer and went away again. "I think I'll complain," Tully said lightly.

"I imagine there's a lot of complaining right now," Pov said dryly. "Is there?"

Tully opened his mouth, then closed it without answering. He studied Pov's face, opened his mouth again, then changed his mind a second time. Finally he pulled his arm off the seatback, dropping his teasing pose, and leaned both elbows on the table, his face intent. "So now, when I don't answer, you're supposed to ask, 'That bad, huh?' Please don't. It's not that bad, and not enough for you to worry about. Dr. Karras is right, you know. I've been watching the strain build in your face for weeks, and I don't like it. You keep it together, you keep it going, you keep being you, and everything keeps working, but the other keeps growing, too." He grimaced. "I haven't always helped as I should."

"You've been all right."

"Most of the time, I agree. I'm not beating on myself about it. I feel more frustrated that I can't hand you the answers. I'm supposed to know the answers, right? Make it easier for you."

Pov smiled. "Is that what you think your job is? Making things easy for me?"

"Absolutely." Tully took a long sip of his beer, then drew a water ring in the condensation left on the table, and put the glass neatly in the middle of his ring. "There have to be answers, after all. You get a question, there has to be an answer. It's called science."

"I'm all right, Tully. Don't frown like that. I'm just finding out what Captain Andreos always felt, back when I was ignorant and thought he always knew what he was doing, every time. It's called command." He paused. "I never really thought about trying for shipmaster, you know. I just wanted Sail Deck. Then it got mentioned to me after it had already started happening, and I went along with it. Now I wouldn't give it up for anything. It's a sense of the ship I never realized—rather like how I got surprised by the twins, being a father for real, I mean, not just thinking about it."

"Before we had our first boy, I thought being a father would be a nice event, probably. I was happy for Irisa."

"A good event," Pov agreed. "Nothing spectacular, but a nice event, especially for Avi."

"Right." They nodded sagely at each other.

"But the ship is more than that, Tully," Pov said. "Captain Andreos has tried to explain it to me a few times, but he doesn't have the words, either. It's bigger—not more important, just bigger. It's worth spending your life for her. It's worth changing yourself to be better for her. It's worth giving up other things that used to take your time. And it's worth chronic headaches." He raised his glass and toasted Tully ironically, then drank.

Pov sat the glass back down and curled his fingers around the cool glass. He slipped his fingertips over the moisture beads, watching the water sparkle and shift shape in the dim light of the lounge. As he moved his fingers, the water recombined into longer droplets and runnels, making new patterns on the glass.

"An analogy?" Tully commented, noting his preoccupation. Pov withdrew his hand and dried his fingers absently on his tunic, then glanced around the lounge at the people.

"Maybe. I'm not sure I'm the same man now. Do you think I am?"

"Absolutely," Tully declared. "What is this? Doubting yourself?" Tully frowned in concern.

"No, not really. But I'm not used to shipmaster yet," Pov added reflectively. "That's the strain, I think. It's different from the old family stuff, though that still bubbles along, as usual, and it's definitely different from worrying about Sail Deck. I'm still fitting myself in, like our new crew, finding out what *Isle* means to me. She means a great deal, of course, but I don't have it all sorted out yet. Shipmaster wasn't one of my young man's dreams. I wanted only Sail Deck. I wanted to be a sailmaster." He smiled. "Now that's a dream I want for Garridan—or maybe Anushka, if she likes the idea. I've gone on to other things."

"So how can I help you, Pov?"

"So why do you think you aren't helping? Dr. Karras said I have balance, and that the balance will see me through. You're part of that balance. Everyone that I love is." He looked around the lounge at the tables. "The ship is my balance. I am *Isle,* just like everybody else aboard her. I just have to find out who that person is, who I am now, now that she's changed me. I keep thinking about Gilgamesh and Siduri, how he left Siduri on her island, and chased off after foolish things. I intend to stay. The music and the dance and the family, she told him, the ties that bind, all that a man needs to be happy."

Tully had leaned back in his seat and listened with a half-smile on his face. "Actually, I think you explain it quite well."

Pov shook his head. "No, it's still not quite right. I don't have it all sorted yet. Maybe when the time comes to tell my children what they need to know, I'll have the right words, enough to explain what it means. I *do* know it does little good to explain it to *Jewel*: they just don't see it. They think in other terms, maybe older terms, maybe just different terms. But I think they could understand, in time, some of them. If not, we'll find a way to stay in the Nebula, by ourselves if we have to. *Isle* belongs to the Nebula: she's built for it, she deserves it. And I intend to keep her here, where she belongs."

"And I was barging about Talbot." Tully winced.

"You said you weren't beating yourself up about that." Pov frowned. "We were lucky this first time with Katrinya and Josef. We have to be more careful next time."

"We will be," Tully said confidently.

"We had better be. Another thing I intend to happen." Pov narrowed his eyes, and saw Tully's smile broaden into that odd smile that had puzzled him before. "What?" Pov demanded.

"Nothing." Tully shrugged. "You've got about twenty-seven messages upstairs, Irisa says, with everybody shocked, simply shocked, that you weren't available. Andreos wants to talk to you, so does Gray, and Kate left some weird message about Brother Wind. Who the hell is Brother Wind, Pov?"

"The Prince of Wands. Me."

"Oh, her Tarot stuff. That would have bothered me for days, wondering about that. I'm glad you told me." Tully affected intense relief, sagging all over the cushion, wiping sweat from his brow, downing his beer for strength.

"You clown," Pov said, amused.

"For you, anytime. Are you going to go up there and call them back? I really think you ought to, Pov." Now it was worried desperation, darting eyes, nervous fluttering hands, the sky could fall.

Pov laughed, loud enough to make a few nearby people turn and look. "You idiot. Cut it out, or I won't let you walk with me."

"That would be dire, I'm sure." Tully grinned and gave him a mocking salute, not repentant at all, never that. "Shall we go?"

Chapter 9

Avi switched watches with Celka to free up the evening, and she and Pov visited their Rom family for the evening meal, an occasion always treated as an event by the family, no matter how often Pov and Avi ate at the other apartment. In this case, Aunt Narilla had announced a *slava* for a minor Lowara saint, which it probably was, though calendars sometimes shifted in odd ways the farther one got from Earth. *Jewel*'s arrival was imminent, and Pov called comm to let them know where he'd be, then sat down between Uncle Damek and Sergei on the guest cushions. The littler kids were playing near the cribs in the back of the living room, and the murmur of the women's voices rose and fell pleasantly in the kitchen.

Damek had his granddaughter Shuri in his lap, a smile on his old face as Shuri prattled to him in her piping voice, her small hands waving. Usually a taciturn and often gruff man, Damek had a soft spot beneath his crusty exterior for his grandchildren, and Shuri exploited it mercilessly. Pov leaned and tugged at Shuri's ear for luck, making her golden earring dance. Shuri grinned back her urchin's grin, wide and beaming; her long dark hair was in tight curls to her waist, and she was dressed in a pretty frock for the feast tonight.

"Pov!" she announced.

"That's me," Pov agreed, and Shuri reached for him to give him a smacking kiss, then tugged his ear back.

"Me, too," Sergei said, holding out his arms, and Shuri complied, climbing across Pov to do it. Shuri kissed Pov again on her way back, and then kissed Damek soundly and rearranged herself comfortably in her grandfather's lap.

"What a heartbreaker," Sergei said, pretending to sigh.

"Wait until she's practiced more," Pov suggested. "It gets worse later." Shuri giggled.

In the corner, Cappi let out a shriek, then a loud tentative wail. Sergei glanced over mildly. "Well, Chavi finally got even. Good for her." A moment later Cappi stopped in mid-wail, newly absorbed in the toy Chavi had and he hadn't got—not yet. When he tried again, Chavi hauled off and hit him harder, and this time the wail was real.

"Be right back," Sergei said with a grin, and went over to break up the party. He brought Chavi and her toy back with him, and Cappi shifted mournfully to the other girls, Judit's little ones.

A few minutes later Bavol came out of the kitchen, hitching at his pants, and sat down with a grunt beside them. Del and Lasho joined them, too, then Karoly's two teenaged boys and Bavol's eldest son, Kem, their dark hair still damp from washing. It made a crowd on the cushions, and Damek shooed Shuri off to her mother in the kitchen.

"Where's Karoly?" Pov asked.

"Hold Deck," Damek rumbled, with only slight complaint. "Extra watch. He said he'd leave early."

"Duty around the clock?" Pov asked in surprise.

"This from you?" Damek asked pointedly. "As if you haven't yourself, from time to time—"

"Uncle, I take it back."

"—ignoring your family obligations, abandoning your family for gaje, and tiring yourself out," Damek continued inexorably. He waved his hand. "But who's complaining?"

"I say—" Bavol began, but did not get far at all.

"Bavol, my middle and most proper of sons," Damek growled, "that was not an opening for any topic at all. I was being ironic. Sometimes even I, Damek Janusz, manage to be ironic." He sniffed. "On occasion." He looked at Pov with a slight smile. "A shipmaster has many responsibilities." He leveled a different kind of glance at Bavol. "And tonight is a *slava,* an occasion to celebrate and be together in good feeling. No nagging, Bavol."

"Yes, Da," Bavol said sullenly. His father glanced at him in mild reproof for his tone, but left any other comment unsaid.

The women brought in the food and sat down with the men for the meal, dressed in bright colors and bright jewelry, their long hair tumbling on their shoulders. Avi looked especially pretty, and Pov's eyes kept wandering to his wife, an attention she noticed and shyly liked. She wrinkled her nose at him happily. Whatever Margareta had said to Damek and Damek to Bavol and Bavol to Patia, matters were easier tonight, the family openly pleased with their new home, and excited about the adventure in the Nebula.

Halfway through the meal, comm called him to report *Jewel*'s arrival, and he got up to leave, quite regretfully, but his steps quickened as he left the apartment.

He met *Jewel*'s skyrider on skydeck, and watched as Dr. Karras unloaded two stretchers and whisked

them up to Medical, where she promptly medicated
Katrinya and Josef back into unconsciousness. As she
and her team cautiously removed the plasti-strip bandages applied by *Jewel*'s medtechs, Pov caught a
glimpse of Josef's face through the crisis-room doorway, and blocked Miska Ceverny from entering the room.

"Go back to the lounge, Miska," he ordered firmly.
"No arguments."

Ceverny opened his mouth to protest, but turned
and trudged obediently down the corridor to the waiting lounge. Pov craned his head to see who else was
there and saw Irisa and Tully move forward to meet
Ceverny, then stepped into the crisis room. He felt
the faint breeze of the positive air pressure enclosing
the operating area, and stopped carefully behind the
vivid yellow line marked on the floor.

Dr. Karras sensed Pov behind her and turned, her
eyes sober above her sterile mask. "Behind the line,"
she cautioned.

"I'm behind the line. How are they?"

"Better than it looks. Burns always look like this in
the beginning. Is Miska outside?"

"I sent him back to the lounge."

Ariadne nodded her approval and turned back to
Josef's inert body. At the other table, Ariadne's chief
assistant worked on Katrinya, her hands and half her
face still swathed in plasti-strips.

Despite Dr. Karras's assurances, Pov felt a wash of
dismay as he saw the horrible damage to their faces.
The hot infrared flash had blackened and scoured
every inch of Katrinya's and Josef's exposed skin, creating a bloody dead crust that the doctors now carefully cut away, creating an open sore of exposed flesh.
They didn't look human.

Dr. Karras turned to the tray beside her and picked

up a long ribbon of artificial skin, then stretched it carefully across Josef's forehead. "They'll be all right, Pov," she said, glancing around at him.

"You're sure?" Pov asked anxiously. "What about their eyes?"

"The eyes are okay: we have procedures for those, too. It's all repairable."

"You're sure?" Pov had to ask a second time.

"I'm positive. After all, I'm the doctor. So go away, captain." Ariadne's eyes crinkled above her mask. "I'll give you a full report after surgery. It's neither worse nor better than *Jewel* reported, but they'll be all right—eventually. I promise." Pov nodded numbly. "And keep Miska out of here," she added as she turned back to Josef.

"I'll do that."

Tully looked up as Pov walked into the lounge and nodded slightly. He and Irisa had Ceverny flanked on the couch, and others from Sail Deck had come in to sit with him, too. Pov smiled at Celka and Lev as both pairs of blue eyes looked their anxious question.

"Dr. Karras says they'll be all right in time," Pov told them all, "but Sailmaster Ceverny is to stay here until she's done working on them."

Ceverny looked up, and nodded slowly. Katrinya was home and safe, and she would be all right: that was all that mattered now. Even so, Pov saw him visibly relax at the new reassurance, then give a sudden great sigh.

"We'll stay with him," Irisa said firmly.

"As long as it takes," Celka declared. Lev nodded, his eyes blinking rapidly.

Karoly was still on Hold Deck, holding down the fort, when Pov looked for him there. Karoly's compact body was uncharacteristically tense in his console chair, his dark brown eyes flicking around the room as he watched the hold staff run the continuing sort. When he saw Pov, he straightened abruptly.

"How is she?" he asked. Every head in the room turned toward them.

"She'll recover completely," Pov said, raising his voice so all could hear, "but it'll be a while until she's back on duty." A sigh sifted around the room.

Pov stopped at Karoly's chair and grasped his forearm affectionately, then saw one of the hold techs frown at them for some reason. As Pov glanced her way, she turned quickly back to her station and made herself ostentatiously busy.

"Anti-Rom Slav from *Jewel*," Karoly explained, keeping his voice low. "*Fan* First-Ship, I think. She's been restless all evening with me sitting here where I don't belong. Plus this isn't my regular shift, and they're not used to me yet."

Pov frowned. "Are you having trouble with other *Jewel* people?"

"Because I'm Rom or because I'm not *Jewel*?" Karoly smiled ironically. "It's probably both with her. Some of them are restless even with Katrinya, who's First-Ship Slav herself, so who can sort it?" He sniffed reflectively. "The bigotry was different on *Dance*: I was only a cloud chemist back then, stuck away in my lab where I could be safely ignored. Harder to ignore me now." He grimaced. "Harder to ignore it back, too. I'm out of practice." He shifted uncomfortably in his chair as she glanced again.

"You might have the deck for the duration," Pov warned. "Katrinya's in the hospital for a while." He smiled wryly. "Uncle Simen warned you about taking Second Hold."

"I never listened to Uncle Simen, anyway," Karoly retorted, "not even when it meant something."

Karoly's face was crossed by a fleeting black scowl. Usually even-tempered and calm, Karoly could be flint on certain matters, and one of those matters was Sergei and Kate. Karoly had encouraged Kate's romance with Sergei and loved them both; he would not forgive what words had been spoken, not ever, another fact Pov's mother had to consider. Karoly had made that very clear.

But for now Karoly smiled and made an act out of flexing his fingers, like a pianist intent on a fast concerto, ready to amaze the world. "Can I borrow Sigrid to help?" he asked. Karoly nodded toward the wall displays, which now shifted steadily through a complicated series of frequencies belonging to graphite dust. "I want to repeat part of the sort for a wider baseline."

He paused, and Pov and Karoly eyed the tech back until she turned around again.

"Aside from the other benefits," Karoly added, obviously not pleased with the continued scrutiny, "it'd give certain people somebody else to scowl at."

"Why would she scowl at Sigrid?" Pov asked, baffled.

"Scandi groundhogger, Pov. Another variable that adds up to 'not *Jewel,* not Slav.' There *is* a certain rationale to this, after all." Karoly grimaced again. "Apparently TriPower still counts as ground with the *Jewel* Slavs, despite all Sigrid's done for them. Katrinya actually got a complaint, in writing and logged, because she allowed Sigrid to sit on Hold Deck yesterday."

"Really?" Pov said sourly. "That's fun."

"Real fun. Just when our Greeks finally civilized

our Slavs, they get another set to start over. I pity them sincerely." Karoly snorted and crossed his arms. "Don't worry, it's nothing I can't handle. I'm a Rom. So can I borrow Sigrid?"

"That's up to Sigrid, I guess. I'm sure she'll say yes, especially if you sort the PAHs first."

Karoly nodded, glanced more comfortably around the deck, then looked back at Pov. "*Maybe* first," he said with a quiet smile. "We'll negotiate."

"You're late for the *slava*," Pov reminded him. "But they weren't fussing much, not like I'd expect. Your father said to me, quote, 'A shipmaster has many responsibilities,' with analogy to you, and then told Bavol to shut up."

Karoly nodded, looking pleased. "I'm not surprised. It'll take him a while, but I think Da's changing his mind, Pov. I couldn't believe it when I saw it starting, but I think he's really changing his mind." He shook his head, mildly amazed. "*Not* the effect Simen intended, I think."

"Calling Kate a whore didn't please my mother, either," Pov observed.

"Nor me," Karoly said, scowling again.

"They're only words, coz. And Uncle Simen's far away now, farther than he's ever been, for sure." He tugged at Karoly's arm. "Come on. Turn the deck over to Astrid before you're so late we're both in trouble, you for late and me for ineffective."

With a little more wheedling, Pov managed to detach Karoly from Hold Deck and took him home.

Late that night, Pov woke suddenly from sleep, his skin covered with a thin film of sweat from a dream he couldn't remember. He eased the covers off his chest for coolness and listened to his heart pound unpleasantly in his ears for several minutes. He sat up at last and rubbed his hand over his hair, then swung his feet over the edge of the bed, wincing as a sharp pain shot down his left leg. He bent over and rubbed his calf, then got up and nearly fell when he put weight on the leg. He caught himself on the nightstand without too much of a clatter and stood there a moment, dizzy and sweating, and decided correctly to sit down again. Avi slept onward, curled tightly on her side with her back to him.

As he sat down gingerly on the mattress, he heard Avi turn restlessly behind him and whimper low in her throat. He snapped on the bedlamp and touched her shoulder.

Avi flung her arm at him wildly, starting at the touch. "No!" she shouted. "Don't! Don't!"

"Avi..." He touched her again and shook her slightly. She rolled on her back and blinked at him, her eyes vague.

"But he said ..." she said, then recognized him. "Oh. What's the matter?"

"You were dreaming, love. Nightmares must be contagious." She shot out her hand and brushed his sweaty forehead with her fingers, then sat up quickly.

"What's wrong, Pov?" she demanded, eyes wide.

"A little dizzy. It's nothing, Avi. I woke up sweaty. Bad dreams." He lay down again and closed his eyes.

"A headache? I'll get your medicine," Avi clambered off the bed and ran into the bathroom.

Drat, he thought. He hadn't wanted to frighten her. He listened to the blood pound in his ears, easing now, then opened his eyes when she rushed back to the bedside, a pill and a sloshing glass in her hands.

"If you panic every time I have a headache," he

warned her, "I'll start dodging on admitting them. Scaring you isn't worth it."

Avi stopped abruptly, then after a moment sat down calmly on the bedside, cocked her chin, and proffered the glass. "Have a pill, dear," she said, with no fuss at all.

"Thank you, Avi." He levered himself up on an elbow and took the glass.

"You're welcome, darling," Avi said. "The hell you won't tell me!" she added indignantly.

"The hell I won't. Fact of life. You know me, the way I act about you." He looked at her challengingly and she glared back.

"I won't accept that," she said.

"Then don't get scared. Please, Avi." He swallowed the pill down with the water and put the glass on the nightstand. "What were you dreaming about?"

"Oh, old things. They're not important." She climbed back into bed, reached across him, and snapped off the light.

"What old things?" he persisted.

She hesitated. "Andreiy things, old rotten marriage things, that stuff," she said and was silent a moment. "The hell you won't, Pov."

"Is not saying an Andreiy thing?"

"Absolutely," Avi said fiercely.

"Then I take it back. Just don't fall apart like that. I get unhinged. I start acting like Andreiy."

Avi's laughter was a bare breath. "That's not possible, believe me, not for you." She laid her head on his shoulder, and he moved his arm around her. She drifted back to sleep, and Pov listened to the air shift steadily as the blood pounded in his ears.

*   *   *

When he awoke the second time, his leg was working again, a vast relief. He tested it gingerly as he got up, then stepped on it more strongly. No pain. His headache had disappeared, thanks to Dr. Karras's new pill. As he dressed and ate breakfast with Avi and the twins, he periodically checked his interior and found the equipment all working every time. Dreams, maybe, though he'd never had a nightmare get this physical.

I'm too young for a stroke, he told himself firmly, and decided that was a worry he definitely didn't need.

He left early for alpha watch and stopped by Medical. Dr. Karras examined him briefly in her office, checking his eyes, fingers, and knees, then ordered him to come back in the afternoon for repeat scans.

"I feel fine now," he told her.

"You probably are fine now. Take another pill."

"I did." She nodded, her eyebrows knitted in perplexity. "Since I feel fine," he said, eyeing her warily, "and I have a conference about LP Orionis in ten minutes—"

"You're on duty, Pov. Don't bother to wheedle."

"Thanks." Pov smiled and went on up to Admin.

Some minutes later, Pov watched his interlink screen window into sections for the conference. The operations plans had alternatives at this point, either proceeding directly to the Core or exploring a secondary star as an interim step. Pov expected they would now take the more conservative choice. The cutter accident had been a nasty surprise, and other surprises could likely track with the number of stars in the neighborhood. LP Orionis, an infant blue star to the northwest, was Ceverny's preferred choice, and his own.

LP was a singleton B-class star, isolated from other

star formation sites in the turbulent western Nebula, with several smaller siblings forming in its bipolar gas-jets. The star had already ignited and had begun to disperse its circumstellar dust shell, but was still shrouded in heavy dust that obscured light data. They needed to jump closer to scan the dust for a course into the system, but first they needed to decide officially to jump at all.

The interlink window sectioned, showing first Captain Andreos's calm face, then Captain Janofsi's wizened scowl, and finally *Mirror*'s interlink room with Captain Gray and Rachel. "How are they?" Rachel asked anxiously, as soon as Pov appeared in her screen. "We've heard it's good news."

"They'll recover completely," Pov replied, "though they'll both be in the hospital for a while. Thank you for asking, Rachel." She nodded and looked relieved.

Janofsi stared pointedly past Pov at Ceverny's empty chair. "Where is Sailmaster Ceverny?" he asked snidely.

"With his wife," Pov replied.

Janofsi harrumphed.

"This setback," Captain Gray said, briskly moving it on, "suggests extra caution at the next stop. We could have guessed a maser could flash that hard, but we still ended up surprised."

"We weren't expecting a protostar over there, Dad," Rachel said, shaking her brown hair. "And even that wouldn't have predicted the dust shock."

"We should have expected it anyway," Gray said firmly, turning his head toward her. "After all, this *is* a star nursery."

"True." Rachel looked upset.

Pov sighed, knowing he'd hear about the cutter over and over again during this discussion. When Katrinya had polarized the cutter's wallwindow to infrared seconds before the maser blast, she had saved two lives. The burst of reddish light that had burned them both had penetrated via infrared, not microwave, a product of shocked dust as the maser flashed through the nearby dust wall. It was strictly a short-range phenomenon, unsuspected in the long-range scans from Tri-Power, and a bad setback Captain Janofsi now decided to use.

"Does *Net* get to talk here?" Janofsi demanded, his old face flushed with the familiar anger. "Or is *Arrow* finally in charge? Somebody ought to be, the way *Isle* is running things." He gave Pov a look of vitriolic dislike, shocking in its intensity.

Pov tensed, startled by the sudden accusation, and on cue, his head throbbed hard and demanding as his headache rebounded with a vengeance. Dammit, he thought, and raised a shaky hand to his forehead. He squinted through the pain.

"Somebody *is* in charge," Andreos said tightly, intercepting Pov's defense before Pov could say a word, "and that shipmaster is Pov Janusz. *Isle* has the lead, as we decided long ago. *Isle* was built for it."

"You're keeping him in command?" Janofsi demanded loudly, as if the thought were unthinkable, so idiotic an idea it was. Janofsi waved his hand contemptuously, his beard jerking, as he looked again at Pov. "At what risk to my ship and crew? I never agreed—"

"You *did* agree," Gray shot back, interrupting Janofsi in mid-tirade. "I heard you agree, Janofsi. What is this? A first setback and you're going to break contract? Is that where this is going? You might do that to *Fan*, but you're not doing it to me!" Gray half-rose from his chair in outrage.

"Dad," Rachel pleaded, grabbing at his arm. "Don't—"

"Shut up, *Arrow*," Janofsi shouted at Gray. "Shut up!"

"I will *not* shut up," Gray said. His blue eyes glittered with open contempt, his head lifted with disdainful pride, as Thaddeus Gray finally had his say about *Net*'s other partner ship. "God, *Jewel*," he snarled, "you're like a old woman, thinking you're owed a living. You've always thought that, and look where it got you! The bad-luck Jonah of the Pleiades!"

Janofsi's eyes bugged and his mouth fell wide open, loosely to flap.

"Dad!" Rachel cried. "Please!" Gray looked distractedly down at Rachel as she dragged insistently at his arm.

Captain Andreos opened his mouth, but Janofsi lunged forward in his chair. "No!" he shrieked. "Not this time, Andreos! Damn you! Damn you all!" He darted his hand toward his computer keyboard, ready to slam off the linkage.

Pov sat up hard. "Don't do that, *Jewel*! Don't you *dare* do that!" Janofsi stopped short, his hand suspended in midair, and gawked at him. "No more, Karol!" Pov said desperately. "Please, no more." His headache lanced hard and he leaned on his console, wincing with the pain. "God," he muttered, then squinted up at Janofsi in the screen. "Please, Karol," he pleaded. "Whatever you think of me, don't do that."

Janofsi gawked another moment, and then, with malicious slowness, he reached out and snapped the interlink with a flourish. Janofsi's image windowed out, leaving only three ships in the link.

Pov gawked at the screen in his own turn. After all that *Net* had done for *Jewel,* after all *Isle* had offered, Janofsi could give him this ... this *insult* in front of the others. An insult based on Janofsi's blatant contempt for Pov, his Slav bias, his readiness to blame Pov for his own advantage—and contempt for *Isle.* For *Isle.* They had held back Ceverny and inflicted pain on his beloved old sailmaster, all for nothing. Because of what? *What?*

The anger began as a tightness in his scalp, followed by a wash of heat flooding through his body, as if sheeted fire had touched every nerve. He trembled with the rage, and had to hit the computer key twice to connect to the inship link and Admin.

"Irisa, will you please find Stationmaster Thorsen and ask her to come to *Isle*'s interlink room?" he asked, his voice sounding strange in his own ears. "I have a consortium matter that requires her vote."

"What matter?" Andreos asked, confused.

"To expel *Jewel* from the consortium," Pov snapped. "We certainly have cause." He tightened his hands into fists and felt himself start to shake harder with his rage. He tried hard to get control of himself. "But we should wait until Sigrid gets here, sirs," he said raggedly. "Please be patient, sirs." The words almost strangled him.

Gray swung his chair around at Rachel, whose face had blanched of color, her eyes huge, as she watched Pov. "Rachel," Gray said dryly, "call up *Jewel* and tell Janofsi that Pov is about to cut him off at the knees. He had better reconnect."

"That's not funny, Thaddeus!" Pov shouted at him, boiling.

He lunged to his feet just as Sigrid burst into the interlink room, quite out of breath. "What is it?" she panted, then stopped short and took in the faces with a single glance. "What's wrong?"

"Pov's about to commit terminal mayhem on *Jewel*," Gray said, pointing at Pov. "Maybe me, too. Look at his face!"

Sigrid's jaw dropped, her turn now. "I thought you were discussing LP!" she said. "How did this happen? Pov, sit down. Pov! Goddammit." Pov struggled as Sigrid hauled at his arm, then sat down hard in his chair when she body-blocked him. "Stars above!" she exclaimed.

"I always knew he had a temper under all that calm," Gray drawled, still too angry at Janofsi to have any sense at all. "I've anticipated the joy of a full display."

"Shove it, Thaddeus," Pov mumbled and held his head.

"What does *Jewel* say, Rachel?" Andreos's voice asked.

"Natalya is trying to talk to Janofsi now. He's ranting up and down the hallway over there."

"Does she say what set him off?" her father asked. Pov looked up at her.

Rachel grimaced. "He thought Pov's sending *Jewel* to get *Traveler* was an insult."

"What?" Pov asked, bewildered.

"Least important ship got detached, he thinks," Rachel said unhappily.

Pov's jaw dropped again. "I sent *Jewel* because she's Slav," he sputtered. "She's our sister ship, and they've known Katrinya ever since *Fan*. I don't believe this! I cannot believe this!"

Pov got up from his chair and stalked out of the interlink room and on down the hall. Sigrid was after him in an instant, and he whirled as she caught up with him, keeping a careful step away from her. "Don't touch me, Sigrid," he warned. "I'm dangerous right now."

"That I can see," she said. She put her hands on her hips and smiled broadly, not at all bothered, it seemed. "Here's my advice," she said. "Let *Jewel* come to you now. Stay stalked out. It'll help a lot."

"How?" he demanded.

"Oh, a little reminding of things they ought to think about. In fact, I'd stay disappeared for several hours again, maybe until tomorrow."

"That's juvenile, Sigrid." Pov sighed and rubbed his eyes slowly, knowing this headache was going to be a nasty one. Matched the cause, he supposed. They always seemed to.

"No, it's a tactic, sometimes quite effective. They've dumped that kind of behavior on you since the beginning. Dump it back now, show them what it really means in a crisis, when it's not just something fun to do because you're bored." She snorted. "Andreos will back you. So will Gray."

Pov squinted at her as his head throbbed in a persistent, demanding rhythm. "You really think so?" he asked uncertainly.

She nodded.

"But that makes me just like Janofsi. Stalking out, being unreasonable, refusing to talk. What kind of leading is that?"

"Once does not make you Janofsi, Pov. True?"

Pov winced and rubbed hard at his eyes as jagged light danced across his vision. His head felt like a vise. "God," he muttered in agony as the pain lanced hard enough to make him stagger into the wall. Sigrid's arms were around him in an instant, supporting him. He heard her call out sharply for Irisa, and he clutched

at her. "Sigrid!" He moaned in fright as suddenly everything narrowed to a single black point, and his ears
roared. "I can't see! Sigrid—"

"Sit down, Pov," Sigrid crooned. "Stretch out your
other leg. That's it. *Irisa!*" He heard the footsteps running, dimly through the roar.

They got him down to Medical on a gurney, and
lifted him into bed. Pov saw only the black tunnel,
heard only the roar—then felt the sharp jab of an
injector. "No!" he cried out. He had to go back to
the interlink, make it right. It was his responsibility,
his duty. His . . .

As Ariadne's drug took effect, the black tunnel ex-
panded with a rush and swallowed him whole, spinning him into nothingness.

He woke up slowly and opened his eyes, to find Dr.
Karras bending over him. "Well," she said, with a
quirk to her lips, "you finally managed a full-scan
headache, didn't you? I'm impressed."

"Don't nag," he said weakly. "Please." He squinted
at her. He could see again, with only the heavy feeling
of residual headache, nothing worse. What a blessed
relief. He sagged his head back on the pillow. "Was
it a stroke?"

"I don't think so," she said, "though I'll repeat the
scans in an hour or two. Can you move everything?
Show me." Pov obediently wiggled his toes and moved
both hands. "That's fine. Sit up for me, Pov. I want
to check your reflexes." Ariadne sat him up and swiveled his legs over the edge of the bed, then systemati-
cally tapped his knees and elbows with a small rubber
hammer. "Now give me your hands." She stepped
back and extended his arms toward her and slowly
flexed them through several ranges of motion, then

did the same with his legs. She sighed. "You've got slight weakness in your left leg. That's not too good."

"Then it *was* a stroke," he said, alarmed.

Ariadne shook her head briskly. "Not necessarily. There's a narrow borderland between severe migraine and actual arterial blockage, and migraine residuals usually clear up. The depressed reflex is probably temporary. As I said, we'll repeat the cerebral scans. Follow my finger with your eyes. That's good." She finished her neurological exam, then smiled at him. "Lie down now." She pulled up the sheet and tucked it around his chest. "Despite the problem with your leg, Pov, I think it was only severe migraine, with enough artery constriction to mimic a slight stroke. You've been heading for it, but it's not a type of consortium dramatics I recommend."

"*Only* migraine?" Pov groaned. "What happened with Janofsi afterward?" he asked.

"Well, if you must. From what I hear from Sigrid, it's called a stunned and thoughtful silence. Ceverny's handling the condolences, with help from the other captains—though *Jewel* has yet to apologize. That's not your problem right now. Duty tomorrow, maybe, but not today."

"Yes, ma'am. Where's Avi?"

"Outside in the hall, waiting to see you. You're on total bed rest, captain." She gave him a stern look. "If you behave yourself, I might let you shift to the bed in your apartment this evening. If."

"I'm not fighting," Pov said and closed his eyes.

"Good." He felt her hand press his shoulder, then lift away.

He sensed Avi in the room before he heard her and opened his eyes. She took his hand tightly and clung to him, struggling to control her expression. "Hello, love," he said and tried to smile. He shifted over in bed and spread his arms, inviting. "Lie down by me? I'd like that."

Avi lay down beside him and wrapped herself around him, then buried her face against his shoulder. When she raised her head several long breaths later, he kissed her lightly on the nose.

"That attack was something I don't want to repeat," he said fervently.

"I'll say. How do you feel now, Pov?"

"Slight headache. Other than that, I feel totally wasted. I think I'll sleep the rest of the day."

"A good idea," she agreed firmly.

"Sleep by me?"

Avi tightened her arms to bring him closer, then pressed her face against his neck, her breath warm on his skin. He closed his eyes and sighed.

"Thaddeus Gray called me to apologize to you," Avi told him. "He said he feels ashamed he made jokes when you got that mad at Janofsi. He offered to send for *Hound* and *Arrow* if Janofsi drops out. *Moon*, too, if we need her, all for free, with no claim for a larger consortium share."

"He'd commit *all* his ships?" Pov asked in surprise.

"He says he would. He says we try the Core this time. He said that's a promise." She was silent a moment. "He's a good man, despite the ego."

"I know. But I'm not going to let him overdo the regret."

"I think he knows that, but he wanted to offer." She kissed his collarbone, then nestled her head against his cheek. He sighed in response, as always, and felt her chuckle. "Go to sleep now, beloved," she murmured in Romany, hesitating as she said it right. "Go to sleep and rest."

* * *

Later that day, after Pov had been shifted home and Kate had taken the twins to the other apartment, Avi sat cross-legged at the end of the bed near his feet. While he rested, Pov watched as she rotated the top half of her Russian dolls and separated the largest doll into its halves. She lifted out the doll nested within, reassembled the larger doll, then went on to extract the third doll, eventually lining up seven brightly colored dolls on the bedspread. All seven dolls, smiles wide and joyful, were pointed to beam at Pov with high approval. He chuckled.

"A sentiment I approve," she said, winking at him. She fiddled with the dolls, getting them just right. "Why did you fall in love with me?" she asked softly, her eyes on her dolls.

"Because you're you. I wish I could persuade you, once and for all, that it was totally smart. I'm still working on it."

"That's not what I meant." She leaned an elbow on her knee and cupped her chin in her hand. "I was raised to think the universe is never friendly, that good things have to be wrested from nature and forced to exist. The wolves forever chase the sleigh through endless snows. The want, the deprivation, the millions of poor, the few rich who danced in their mansions and flattered the tsars." She quirked her lips. "Mother Russia, in an older version. On Tania's Ring, she was the collective and people mere circuits in a board. Deprivation again, the unfriendly universe."

"Tania's Ring has managed to exaggerate a few items of Russki culture, I'll agree," Pov said. "But you've said Mother Russia was more than that. I'd like the twins to know the other things, why the Rodina was worth fighting for, despite the hardships.

Something had to inspire all those millions of people, something special."

Avi smiled. "Like family for the Rom?"

"I think it was family for your people too, Avi. It's a fundamental." He pointed at the gypsy wagon on the shelf in the nursery, just visible through the doorway. "Your Rodina is like Lasho's wagon. We all make our symbols, each of our peoples. Mine is that, the road. Yours is the Rodina, the homeland. Don't you agree?"

"You haven't a clue of where I'm tracking right now," she accused. "Though I admit you're keeping up nicely."

"I like to talk with you," he said comfortably, "whatever your right-angle orbits. We aren't on the topic of 'I don't deserve Pov'?"

"No, not that one." She smiled mysteriously.

"Are we on the topic of 'Can I be Rom enough?' " he guessed.

"No."

"Maybe it's 'Can I make Pov late for work again?' I like that one, Avi. Say yes. We'll do it." Avi laughed.

"No," she said. "Or rather yes, let's do that later, maybe. Uh, I mean . . ." Avi stopped as she got herself quite confused.

"Hey, a right-angle orbit!" he crowed triumphantly. "I finally did one back. First-rate." Avi handed him a rude Romany word. "You aren't supposed to know those words yet," Pov told her mockingly. "Not until you know all the polite ones."

"Soar off," she advised him. "Soar off and take it away."

"So what are we talking about, Avi?"

"I've been thinking about what Gray offered today, committing everything, no questions. It's what you want to do, too. Our whole fortune here, in the Nebula." She paused.

"It's what I'd like," he admitted. "I'd reconsider if we had to."

"I'm not objecting," she said comfortably. "In Russki terms, you want the Nebula to be our Rodina, a place to hold and defend."

"Quite a homeland, don't you agree?"

"Yes, it would be. It is quite worth all the worrying necessary—and any effort or hardship." She sat back and hugged her knees. "I've been thinking about your mother, too. I never expected her to bend on the rules. I thought *marime* was absolute and could never be bent, not really, not if you want to be a Rom. And then Uncle Simen showed up and pasted his opinions on everything." She wrinkled her nose. "A nasty man. I knew men like him on Tania's Ring, for whom the concept is more important than the people, no matter what it did to the people, and no matter how it hurt."

"The rules are still our tradition, Avi. It makes us Rom."

"You really believe that? That rules make the Rom? Can't the Rom be something more than rules?"

"Of course they are, but right now we're in trouble with the *voivoide* because of rules." Pov frowned thoughtfully. "But it's not because of just rules, to concede your point. It's because of family. He's genuinely worried that we're being drawn away from the Rom. He cares about *us,* because being Rom is priceless and shouldn't be lost. That's been my mother's whole point, too, however she's applied it. Do you understand?"

She nodded. "I can accept that. But rules can be bent sometimes, too, if the love is there." She smiled softly to herself. "Which it is, wonders be. So I've been thinking about what I could give back, me, Avi. If family is the homeland, and Rom is the family, maybe a Russki could teach a Rom how to find the homeland, could show you the ways—if the Rom could admit a gaje knows anything worthwhile."

"Oh, this Rom could do that. I'm not lost to reason." He smiled at her. "So the topic is 'How Russki suits me.' That's a new one for us."

"I thought so." She looked around the bedroom, then turned to look behind her at the other doorways into other rooms. "The Rodina is where you find it, just like your gypsy road. Put a Russki into her true homeland and everything's secure, where it should be. Things make sense again. Things have purpose." She gestured at the apartment, all of *Isle* beyond it. "This is where we belong, you and I. With your Rom family, not with my wretched memories of Tania's Ring. This place, on *Isle,* and the future we build for her and our Rom and gaje both, whatever it is."

"I want the Nebula."

"So do I," she said firmly, "to protect our true Rodina, *Siduri's Isle.* I went wandering after I left Audreiy, wandering off to a space station, a Sail Deck, the oddness of purity rules that make no sense. It's not a natural state for a Russki, wandering like that. But now I'm suddenly home again." She looked around herself again. "I realized that the other night, when I found you sitting on the floor trying to untangle those damn strings for the twins' beds, no matter how long it took, you dote. And then your mother bent so unexpectedly, as a gift to me." She hugged her knees. "I suppose that's the only way we could have found a common ground, you and I, putting the homeland on wheels."

"It's very Rom, Avi. We call it a wagon."

"That's what makes me think it's going to work, all of it." She smiled happily. "They're the same thing, what I am and what you are, Russki and Rom. You just have to see it, and then it's so very clear. It's the two of us together, like the ships all together, something more than the parts, something special."

"I'm glad, beloved." Pov smiled at her, got a wide grin back.

"Let us hope," Avi said, "that you can bring similar clarity to other minds—including yours. Dr. Karras is going to be very tough with you now about your headaches. She told me so." She looked at him severely. "So am I. No strokes, not a single one. I won't allow it. So you just got some more rules, Povinko, and these ones don't bend, not an instant."

"Yes, dear." Pov sighed and put his hands behind his head. "I feel relaxed."

Avi grinned and blew a kiss at him. "You'll survive it."

Chapter 10

The following morning, Captain Andreos came over from *Net* to *Isle* by skyrider, and dropped by Medical while Dr. Karras was running a third set of full scans on Pov's head, a process Pov endured patiently. He felt fine today, and had told Dr. Karras so, but didn't push it. Ariadne was not in the mood. He lay half naked on his back in the scan chamber, with various filaments stuck onto himself with ice-cold gel, staring at the curving metal above his face. At least she hadn't shaved his head, and he hadn't dared to ask if she might want to. The machine whirred and mumbled to itself, clicking through its sequence of data-points.

Sort of like light-ranging, Pov thought. I am a nebula.

"Don't move," her voice said from outside, echoing in.

Pov didn't move. When the machine finally rolled him out like dinner from a food slot, Ariadne was frowning at her wall displays, Captain Andreos standing behind her.

"He says he feels fine," she told Andreos.

"He would." Andreos handed Pov a reproachful look, which wasn't exactly fair. He did feel fine. Pov handed the look right back and sat up, trailing his wires.

"Unfortunately," Ariadne said, "the scans bear him out. I can't see anything." She turned and frowned at Pov, reproaching him, too.

"I can't help it," he said involuntarily. "I feel fine."

"Then why—?" Andreos began.

"Migraine, sir," Ariadne said, "galloping along nicely into something serious, but so far without brain damage. Actually, I wouldn't expect damage: migraine can be disabling, often severely, but it doesn't damage like the other cerebral diseases." She swept one last glance over her wall displays, then turned around to Andreos, her mouth firm. "He's been pretty good about his stress levels, but *Jewel* is not helping."

"Sigrid's still over there," Andreos said. "She's got them nicely cowed." He sighed. "They think they don't need the other cloudships, not really, but they know they need Sigrid, especially if she just might get AmTel and OkiSeki to freeze out *Jewel*, too. *Jewel* has to sell her product to somebody, after all."

"Would Sigrid really do that?" Pov asked in dismay. Whatever *Jewel*'s misbehavior, she wasn't responsible for everything.

Andreos turned to him. "*Jewel* lost Sigrid as an ally yesterday, Pov." He raised a hand quickly as Pov opened his mouth again. "She knows that *Jewel* can't be wholly blamed for migraines or even shouting matches by shipmasters: the brush isn't painting quite that far. But *Jewel* just made things worse for herself—again."

"What about us, sir?" Pov asked. "What is *Net* going to do?"

"Us?" Andreos said angrily. "We're her Slav sister ships. We owe things."

"Stress levels, sir," Ariadne murmured, and started detaching the wires from Pov's body.

"Hmph. You're *his* doctor now, not mine," he reminded Ariadne dryly. "Though you're right, of course. I should be calm and carefree, every hair in place, every thought in order, relaxed, unoccupied, and bored—even when a fellow shipmaster shouts in my face."

She glanced at him in amusement. "Pov thinks destress is boring, too—and you know better than to argue wtih me, Leonidas. What *will* we do about *Jewel*?"

Andreos sighed. As he thought about *Jewel*, he ran his hand slowly through his hair, his expression harried and uncertain. "God, I don't know," he admitted. "I really don't. How long do we carry *Jewel*? We do it much longer and we'll lose *Arrow*'s group. That's obvious now. Gray thinks we're fools to put up with it."

"Rachel tried, sir," Pov said. "She—ouch!" He glared at Dr. Karras and rubbed his chest.

"Sorry," she said, not sounding sorry at all. "I think *Net* should sit and wait," she added firmly. They both looked at her. "An analog to intimate human relationships isn't that far off, considering the bonds between our ships, and waiting might be a good idea." Her hands moved smoothly to the last filament and detached it. "*Jewel*'s just had a wake-up shock, sirs, delivered solidly by Sigrid. I'd say we wait for the therapeutic effect, if it's going to have one." She turned around to face Captain Andreos squarely. "And if you stress Pov into another migraine, Captain Andreos, after I just got him out of the last one, I'll put *you* in my scan chamber and leave you there for a couple of weeks, minimum."

"Oh." Andreos blinked, then looked a little abashed.

"Yes, 'oh,'" Ariadne said mockingly. "At least I

know where he gets it from. It relieves my mind."
She pushed past Andreos and walked over to the side
counter, then brought back her penlight.

"He didn't stress me," Pov said in Andreos's defense. "I feel fine."

"Predictable," Dr. Karras sniffed, but she smiled
anyway.

The four cloudships jumped the next day to LP Orionis and reentered space a half light-year south of
the protostar complex. As he waited for the Helm
conference about their next step, Pov watched LP's
dark and turbulent dustcloud whirl in space, a cosmic
tempest lit from within by the primary's fitful reddish glare.

Although LP's primary star had ignited and had
begun to emit the heavy ultraviolet characteristic of
O- and B-stars, the system was still enshrouded in a
circumstellar dust shell a trillion kilometers deep and
a third of a light-year in diameter. It was T Tauri
again, yet not T Tauri: LP Orionis would be a blazing
beacon of a star, as short-lived as the Pleiades blues,
with its current maelstrom half fed by the turbulent
energies of the Nebula itself.

Weather, Pov thought as he watched the turbulence.
Weather of a size that dwarfed any planet's weather,
but weather all the same. In the Orion Nebula, a constant gale blew from the Trapezium to the west, built
of particles and dust flowing from the molecular interface of the Core and the vast molecular cloud behind
it. As they flowed outward, vast currents of gas and
dust combined and separated, recombined and eddied,
creating small pockets of calm eddies, dangerous
winds, and occasional jet streams. LP Orionis had
formed from an isolated turn of the gas-stream, curved

P. K. McAllister

on itself just enough to tip the balance and to collapse the local gascloud into a star.

Detailed light-ranging in infrared and longer radio lengths had defined two distinct layers of the dust shell, a hot inner shell now thinning under the primary's UV bombardment, and a colder outer shell largely opaque to everything but infrared. Even obscured by the shells of dust, the other components of the LP system were dimly visible on *Isle*'s analytic scanners, via a flickering trace of ultraviolet, a dull gleam of visible light, and the short radio waves of moving molecules. The ships' main interest lay not in the dust, but in the star components hidden within LP's dust shell.

From the central star's poles, two roiling jets of hot gas rushed half a light-year outward into the turbulent nebula, piercing the outer limits of the star's natal cocoon like twin eyes of a storm. In the northern gas-stream, the outrushing gas had condensed into two tiny stars, still little more than rotating cloudlets of gas, but each with enough mass to build a star over time with accretion of more matter from the Nebula. To the south, another tiny companion spun in place just outside the dust shell, flaring erratically in response to the magnetic pulses that climbed the jet.

At T Tauri, *Net* had discovered superheavy matter within the compressed magnetics of the young star's polar gas-jets. Under intense energy conditions, magnetic field lines tended to freeze, packing the local space with energy that could no longer expand, then imploded into the atomic structure of gas atoms locked inside the magnetic grid. LP's initial scans hinted at a similar magnetic phenomenon, raised at least another order of magnitude by the greater energies of the primary star, and complicated by the dense nebular medium surrounding the star that both added and withdrew energy and matter.

They would try the southern jet, if they could find an eddy in the maelstrom where the ships might survive LP's constant gale.

It was preeminently a Helm decision, one the ship-masters had delegated to the expertise of their pilotmasters and Captain Gray. Pov chatted with Stefania while they waited for the others, then nodded as Captain Gray and Isaac Griegman, *Mirror*'s pilotmaster, windowed into the interlink. With admirable promptness, they were joined also by *Jewel*'s Iosif Rudnick, a gray-haired older man who was often confused by Helm Map's new technicalities but seemed willing to learn.

Captain Janofsi still had not apologized to Pov, but *Jewel* was cooperating now without the former dramatics. It was enough, Pov supposed. Iosif blinked rapidly, his fingers drumming restlessly on his Helm Deck console.

"Well!" a scowling Athena said from *Isle*'s Helm Deck. "Any idea of how we go into there?" She waved at the interlink schematic. In a subsidiary interlink screen, *Isle*'s Helm Map slowly rotated its best guess of LP's realities.

"I think we should launch some scanning probes," Pov said. He tapped on his computer keyboard and highlighted the Helm Map schematic with three course-lines in a rough triangle. "We could jump the first probe over to here in the east," he suggested, brightening the jump-points with his stylus, "then skip it west perpendicular to the southern axis of the cloud. Then two other probes could slant insystem to northwest and northeast."

"Those probes might not last long," Stefania objected, shaking her blond head. "Your northeast track runs right into a water maser, Pov. We can't see it now because it's not in line of sight, but it was there earlier when we scanned from the Nebula edge."

"Close-up data is always useful," Gray argued back. "We could get some of our best maser data from suicide probes."

"Maybe," Athena said dubiously. "I suppose Isaac agrees with you."

"Naturally," Gray said, posing just a little.

Mirror's pilotmaster chuckled and shrugged. A middle-aged bearded man with alert brown eyes, Isaac was the senior pilotmaster on Gray's ships, pilotmaster of *Diana's Arrow* for many years, and one of Gray's principal right-hand people. "Worth a try," he said.

"Probes would be good," Iosif blurted, and then went silent, blinking rapidly.

"It'll be like a burglar dodging flashlight beams, I think," Athena said with a sigh. "This active a cloud probably has a dozen masers."

"All we need to do, Athena," Gray said firmly, "is ensure that our course-track avoids your flashlights. And we don't have to plot the entire system, just the southern jet. The question is *where* along the jet—and what kind of dust we might hit when we exit jump. Let's launch the probes and see."

Athena gave the necessary orders to her staff, and three of *Isle*'s jump-capacity probes lanced into the dust shell.

"Here comes a data capsule," Athena said a few minutes later. "Capturing." One of the probe response capsules, little more than an engine and a single data chip, zipped into *Isle*'s helm receptors.

"Already?" Gray asked, surprised. He automatically checked his wristband, as if the interlink clock might be off somehow.

"Something's wrong," Athena muttered, and tapped into the receptor. "Blip!" she said. "There went the northeast probe. Fried in two seconds. Yay." Stefania sighed and put her chin in her hand, not really wanting to be right.

"Did we get any data at all?" Gray asked, disappointed.

Athena tapped on her Helm console again. " 'I have jumped safely,' it says. Little do you know, friend. 'Oh, no!' it says next, ending with half the code for emergency data-launch. I think it's called robot toast, captains. Next time maybe we don't put it in direct line of sight, just as Stef and I told you we shouldn't." She raised a sardonic eyebrow.

"Isn't it fun," Gray asked Pov, "when they're right?"

"Real fun, I agree."

Athena grinned. "Here come the other capsules now. Sending recapture signal and . . . capturing." Athena accessed the new chips. "Well, we've spotted another maser," she said. "The northwest probe is twelve degrees off-line with a hydroxyl maser, sited about one hundred sixty billion kilometers above the primary star. That fits our theoretical guesses about hydroxyl. Flickering erratically, low emissions. It looks like it's about to break up."

"Gas-jet turbulence, maybe," Pov guessed, peering at Athena's data. "It's closer to the jet than the other one. The gas-jet probably disturbs the molecule alignment."

"Maybe we could jump under the masers," Iosif suggested tentatively. "Between them and the star."

Athena promptly shook her head, and Isaac answered, "That's a B-star, Iosif. We'd be inside its hard ultraviolet. And we'd still have the water masers under *us*. They form closer in, at about ten billion kilometers." Iosif looked surprised, as if he'd never heard a Nebula fact critical to their helm maneuvers, and Pov wondered what else Iosif hadn't absorbed from all the technical reports. Isaac tapped the schematic. "Ten billion is just outside LP's infall disk. Even without the UV, there's no way we can get that close to the primary's gravity well. We'd end up infall ourselves."

"I prefer other ways," Stefania said, tossing her head, "of acting out a stellar personality."

"I agree," Isaac shot back. They grinned at each other. Pilot strut, Pov thought, amused.

Gray grunted absently as he studied the probe's report, his finger tapping a slow rhythm on his console, his eyes flicking from graph to graph as he concentrated.

"What does the southern probe say, Athena?" Pov asked.

Athena loaded the data from the third probe. Everyone leaned forward to study the display. "There's the gas-jet turbulence again," Pov said, pointing at a pattern of disturbed currents of gas near the jet, clearly evident from the new vantage point. "No masers at all. It might be our exit eddy. I wonder how rough the sailing weather is."

"And how dense the dust," Gray said. "The jet's energy emission should disperse some of the dust and lower the density, but does it lower it enough?" He frowned.

"Our engine exhaust is still our best shield," Isaac said to Gray. "If we can turn ship soon enough after jump."

Gray nodded, his eyes narrowed with concentration. "We'll still get the dust impact on our aft edges."

"The wing hulls are reinforced to take it, sir. We might lose a few sensors, but not more than that."

Gray nodded again. "The problem is really jumping *out*, not in. We need a course-track of several thousand kilometers to accelerate to jump point, even with the new drive. Several thousand klicks of dust that's too heavy—" He glanced at Isaac. "How much hull metal would we lose, do you think?"

"I'm more concerned about the sail assemblies," Isaac replied. "And the forward sensors. Our hulls can take high abrasion for a short time, but the other structures can't, not in heavy dust."

"If it's too heavy," Gray agreed. "But how much is too heavy? If we shield all the forward structures with slag to jump out, we'd have to jump blind." He frowned. "Or sacrifice a series of wing sensors, one at a time." He shook his head.

"We could point ourselves first," Iosif suggested from *Jewel.* "Or maybe target ourselves with lateral stars off our wing-axis."

"Through that kind of dust?" Athena objected. "Even if we can see reference stars from inside the shell, the dust turbulence will refract the starlight. We couldn't get accurate targeting data."

"And it takes time to shield with slag," Pov said. "We might not have the time—and we don't want skyriders out in the local environment that close to the gas-jet."

They all sat and frowned at each other in perplexity. Finally Gray quirked his lips. "How many hazards have we counted so far? Is it too many?"

"No," Athena and Stefania said at the same moment. Pov chuckled as they looked at each other, again on the same tick.

"So what's our acceptable level of risk?" he asked. "We could send more probes to get the insystem data for a baseline, and not go in at all."

"Probes can't harvest the jet," Isaac objected. "I still want to practice on a B-star over *here* before we try over *there*." He nodded with his chin in the general direction of the Core. "If we try over there, that is, which depends on trying here. And we'd like some kind of harvest in the new fuel for this trip."

"We could harvest a T Tauri star instead," Iosif suggested, his voice nervous, though not as nervous as it ought to be, Pov noted. Because Janofsi had let his crew "rest" and had skipped the practice at T Tauri, *Jewel* had never actually sailed a gas-jet, only simulated course-tracks in the veils.

Had Iosif even objected to Janofsi's ploy? he wondered. Aside from Natalya, *Jewel*'s junior captains seemed content to stand in Janofsi's shadow, far too much. Pov thought about the ways that kind of automatic deference would undermine a sailmaster, and knew a pilotmaster could be just as easily impaired. The cloudship's division of command assumed five captains, not just one.

"Earth can do T Tauri," Stefania was saying aggressively. "We need something new, Iosif. It's the whole point of coming here."

Iosif nodded and didn't even argue. He should have argued, Pov thought worriedly. *Jewel* needed the experience and should ask for it now, even if it meant admitting Janofsi's error, but Pov knew all too well how it would go. Janofsi would rage that *Jewel* was just as good as *Net,* and *Net* had had zero experience her first time at T Tauri, and he would pose and stomp and shout. And Iosif would not insist, as he could insist.

Pov wondered suddenly if he should talk to Athena about Iosif. She knew him better.

"Second set of capsules incoming," Athena said, glancing to her right. "We are capturing."

Athena factored the new data into the interlink, and Gray scowled as the interlink displayed the results. The northwest probe's chip terminated in another emergency data-launch, barely a few minutes into the second chip's data recording. Gray backtracked through the chip, hunting the cause. "Dust," he grunted. "It skipped right into a dust wall and hit it at high speed."

"Wouldn't it be nicer," Athena asked ruefully, "if we had better brakes? I'd hate to ram *Isle* into a wall like that at sixty percent lightspeed. Talk about flash fry."

"*Isle* has more mass," Pov said absently as he studied the data.

Athena snickered. "Wake up, Pov, and listen to what you just said." She snickered again as he looked up and blinked, jerked out of his fog.

"Be quiet, you," he reproved. "I'm thinking."

"Hitting a dust wall with *Isle* is not thinking. In fact, I'd call it null-thought all around."

"So we don't hit a dust wall, Helm."

"I do believe that's the general idea." Athena shook her curls briskly. "So," she summarized, "we're looking for a course-track with low dust near the gas-jet, no flashlights."

"Probably near the outer end of the jet, away from the primary," Isaac added. "That small eddy transited by the southern probe looks good. We can target new light-scans and another probe or two to pick the exact spot, sirs."

"Sounds fine," Gray said. He looked around at all of them. "We're agreed?" A round of nods, even from Iosif, who should have said no. "Well, that was fast." Gray looked slightly surprised. "Maybe if we've decided by consensus, we'll get some kind of edge on the odds. Combined brains, et cetera. We'll need a good edge." He smiled grimly. "It doesn't look much like T Tauri, not with those energy levels."

"We'll find out," Athena said.

Gray nodded and windowed out, the interlink shifting steadily as the others dropped out of the link, too.

Pov sat and thought for a few minutes, thought of calling Andreos, thought of several things. Null program.

Athena was busy with the new probes, and he didn't want to interrupt. On impulse he sent a signal to *Mirror* and asked for Rachel, but she wasn't in her office, and comm's reply was rather stiff when he persisted. "Shall I route you to Captain Gray, sir?" the helm officer asked.

"I *am* asking for Captain Gray," Pov said, a little irritably. "Rachel Gray."

"Oh." The word and tone spoke volumes.

Pov paused in surprise: if *Mirror*'s staff spoke that way to another ship, what did Rachel get face to face? "Comm, let me talk to Rachel Gray, please."

He raised an eyebrow again as the *Mirror* officer skipped any reply and just put him through to Rachel's apartment.

The interlink windowed and showed Rachel as she was sitting down at her desk. Behind her were soft lights and pastels nearly identical to those in *Isle*'s own apartments. "Oh, it's you," she said. "Comm didn't exactly say." She was dressed in a casual all-body suit, her hair slicked back with clips. She looked tired and oddly defeated.

Pov promptly dumped *Jewel* off the agenda. "What's wrong, Rachel?" he asked, concerned.

Rachel twisted her mouth unhappily. "Don't ask, okay?"

"I'm asking. As in barge. If you want someone to talk to, I'm here."

"Oh, I'm just being idiotic. All this grand adventure, this wonderful new science and exploration, and I'm being busily depressed. It's not important." She shrugged, mocking herself painfully.

"Rachel."

"I'm just busy being me." Her lips tightened into a thin line.

"Anytime you want a job on my Sail Deck," he offered firmly, "you've got one."

Her eyes widened in a start of surprise, but her laugh was ugly. "That'd really solve my problems. I can't run away."

"Of course it'll solve them. Whenever a Rom runs into unreasonable gaje, he ups and leaves town for a while. Works great. Maybe later he goes back, maybe he doesn't. In the meantime, life is better."

"You're serious!" she accused. "I can't believe you're serious about that. I can't leave—"

"Sometimes it helps just knowing there's a road out of town, true?"

"Maybe." Rachel sagged back in her chair and fluttered her hands, then let them drop helplessly in her lap. "Oh, all right. I try and try, I put up with the hostility, I lose it just once, and now I'm—" She broke off and looked away, an angry muscle jerking in her jaw. "Hell, Pov, I lost my temper. That's just *not* allowed, and now I'm in Coventry again. They were *outraged* that I dared to criticize Dad about insulting Janofsi, and I got outraged back. Look what it did to Pov, I point out. Shrug." Her lips tightened again. "They *shrugged.* I couldn't believe it. And then Dad agrees with me and apologizes to you, but does that change anything with them? Hell, no."

She threw up her hands. "Where's the loyalty? I'm *Mirror,* too. I didn't politick for shipmaster—I didn't want it yet, and they know I didn't. I didn't sashay up to Dad and coo, 'Please, Daddy, give me a toy.' I'm not an incompetent. I'm not any of those things. I didn't ask to be the daughter of Thaddeus Gray. I didn't ask him to be a hero. I didn't do *any* of those things!" Her voice rose in frustration. "Everything I do gets twisted around. If I sit long watches, they're offended because I barge onto their precious turf. If I stay on watch to the tick, not infringing, they say I'm slacking off and I'm not committed. If I speak up and offer my opinions, I'm presumptuous. If I don't speak up, I'm stupid and useless. Talk, talk, talk. Rachel, Rachel, Rachel. I can't win."

"Who's doing it?" Pov asked.

"Mostly Second Helm and two of the chiefs. They're fueling the gossip, but the captains don't defend me, not even Colleen. It's easier just to sit back and watch me fail. And when I lose my temper, just once, even Isaac shouts back at me and Zachary scowls in disapproval and the others rock their chairs and watch. The sieve is hopeless: everybody's talking now behind my back, everybody's judging. Everybody—" She broke off again and twisted her hands in her lap. "I am so very angry. I shake with it. And that's wrong, too. 'She's unstable,' they say. 'She was impolite to me.' 'She didn't laugh at my joke.' Even when I don't do anything, they make something up."

Rachel's eyes glittered. "I am so angry," she whispered, and slammed her hand hard on her desk. She winced immediately, then bent and cradled her hand to her chest, grimacing in pain. "Ouch. Dammit."

"Don't break your hand, Rachel."

"I'll try to manage that. How's your headache?"

Pov ignored the diversion. "I could give you platitudes, Rachel. I could tell you everything's going to be just wonderful."

"Please don't." She rubbed her hand slowly and looked away.

"Sometimes you have to fight for your ship, even though you know you might lose. No guarantees, no payoff to count on. Is it worth it to you, Rachel? That's what counts. Not duty, not what you should do, not what's expected, not winning the point. Is fighting that hard in an unfair fight worth it? Is it worth what it will do to you if you lose?"

Rachel sighed. "I don't know." She paused and hung her head. "I really don't. I should, but I don't."

"There's no 'should' about it. I don't know, either. I've been lucky. I've usually won, eventually."

"You're different from me."

"How am I different?"

She shrugged unhappily.

Pov thumped his chest and posed. "Look at me. I try to take responsibility for everybody. I want everybody to be happy, everything to run smoothly. I worry myself sick into chronic headaches, put up with too much, forget what I should remember. I get obsessed. I hold on too long. I get angry and, just like you, think there's something wrong in the anger, some fault in myself. Me, angry? Perfect Pov? I'm not allowed to get angry. It's just not allowed."

"But you—"

"Get angry anyway, friend." He leaned forward intently, wanting her to understand. "Rachel, all that ultimately counts for me is you. Not *Mirror,* not your rank, not showing them they're wrong, but you. The hell with the consortium, the hell with alliance, the hell with politics. I wish I had answers for you, a quick solution and it's gone, but that's one of my faults, one of the bad ones. I wish it weren't so hard for you. I wish I had a magic wand. I wish you didn't have to struggle like this. But Perfect Pov doesn't have a solution, a sure deal to make everything right. Perfect Pov isn't perfect, after all."

"It's not your responsibility," Rachel muttered, not looking at him again.

"That's what Dr. Karras tells me. I think I might, just might, be one of *her* unsolvable problems." He smiled as Rachel looked up quickly.

Rachel tipped up the corners of her mouth in response. "I think you're a wise man, Pov Janusz," she said.

"No, I'm not. Otherwise I'd be perfect."

She laughed a bit, then shook her head and sighed. "Then we're a mess, the two of us."

"I'm afraid that's so. But one thing I do believe, and this isn't my wisdom at all, is that we don't have to carry the weight alone, not when we're smart enough to know we don't. And you're a smart woman. Is there anybody on *Mirror* you can talk to about this? Besides your father?"

Rachel hesitated. "Well, there's Isaac, even if he shouts at me when he shouldn't. And Moira—we knew each other on *Moon*'s Sail Deck. And a few others—I think." She grimaced sadly. "Maybe Colleen, but I don't know anymore."

"Go find out, then."

"The ship is busy. It's not the time."

"Nuts."

She looked at him rebelliously.

"Or do you think you're not that important?" he asked.

"My self-esteem is just fine, Pov," she retorted. "That's why I'm mad, after all. I'm not a martyr, no matter what self-pity I drape all over you whenever you ask."

Pov tsked. "Self-pity's just as bad as anger. Just isn't allowed."

"Oh, you!"

"Well, it's not. We have to be perfect. Perfect people never need help. Needing help is a weakness, and imposes on other people. It's not allowed. People impose on *us,* not the other way around." He smiled as she opened her mouth, then shut it tight. After a moment, she lost the mild glare and tipped up the corners of her mouth again.

"Hmm," she said.

"Indeed." He shrugged. "I don't believe it, either, but people keep arguing at me. Maybe in a decade or two, they might nudge it a little, but don't count on it. I'm too stubborn. I'm going to be perfect if it kills me, which it could, if I keep it up. So far it's only migraine, but I've had my warning."

"But what can talking do?"

"Get you some allies. Push back. Balance the sieve. Get some help from people who are maybe waiting for you to ask." He spread his hands. "The people are the ship, and the ship is the road. Anytime you want to give up and transfer to *Isle,* you've got a way out. But I don't think you're going to do that, Captain Rachel Gray, because *Mirror* is your *Isle*. She's worth fighting for."

He paused. "It's your decision, and he's your father. He's probably one of the few perfect people among us—there's likely one or two here and there—who can get along without much help. Larger than life. I'm Thaddeus Gray: I can carry it all. But he's not a princess who was handed a ship too soon, and mostly he's not you, Rachel. And he's not that perfect, whatever he thinks, and excuse me for saying so."

Rachel chuckled and made a face. "Hell, I'm in trouble for agreeing with you. I'm not going to object." She made another face. "Why are people so difficult?" she complained.

"That's an answer I don't have. I thought maybe if I were a king, I could stop all that, but your father's a king and he's still got problems. But I'm barging in, anyway, handing out my perfect wisdom and my perfect advice, and telling you to fight for *Mirror*. I'm telling you she is worth it."

Rachel looked at him intently, her eyes narrowed. "I'll talk to Isaac." She pressed her palm against the surface of her monitor, and he covered her hand's image with his. "Alliance, *Isle*," she whispered.

"Take care of Rachel Gray first. The rest comes later."

She shook her head. "Not later. Now."

He saw the determination resettle into her eyes, eyes so much like her father's that had the same look, and saw her beautiful face firm into the native strength Thaddeus Gray had given her and that Rachel had already made her own. Her father's daughter, larger than life.

"Thanks, Pov." And she did sound better.

"Got a cure for a headache?" He leaned his elbows on his desk and rubbed his temples. Rachel laughed, her voice rippling.

"You fake. Stop that."

Pov sighed dramatically. "Now I'm a fake. You can't say that; it just isn't allowed. I feel insulted. I ought to blip you off." Pov feigned Janofsi's angry flourish.

"He's an old man who doesn't know any better," Rachel said, shaking her head gently, "and I love you for guarding him as you do. That's a good thing, Pov. Don't listen to *Arrow* on this. Don't doubt what *Net* is. If you don't help *Jewel,* who's going to?"

"But they won't let us help, Rachel," he said in frustration. "They just won't."

"So why does that mean we stop trying?"

Pov looked at her for a long minute. She raised her eyebrows. "Thanks, Rachel."

"Anytime, friend." She leaned back in her chair and sighed, then gave him a rueful smile. "Well, maybe with the mutual support, we'll survive all this, you and me."

"It's a theory."

She chuckled and leaned her head in her hand. "It's a theory," she agreed.

Chapter 11

From his interlink board, Pov accessed the LP light-ranging from Sail Deck and loaded it in a side screen, then modeled the data into several graphs, first ultraviolet, then the visible spectrum, finally the longer wavelengths of infrared and short radio waves.

"Helm has proposed this course into the jet," he said.

The computer built a multifrequency database, then translated through Helm Map and put the three-dimensional result on the wallscreen. Seconds later, Helm Map highlighted the course choice, a short trajectory in a target area two-thirds up the jet. The probe data added details of composition, density, estimated energies.

Pov waited for any comment. Janofsi's eyes flicked to the Grays and Andreos, but all kept their expressions carefully neutral. There was no objection.

"Then we jump in fifteen minutes, sirs," Pov said. "As agreed, senior staff will take the watch on all ships." All the shipmasters nodded. "And all ships will remain on the interlink," Pov added, keeping his voice mild, as if it were unimportant.

Pov wanted that explicit promise from Janofsi today, whatever trouble it stirred: grandstand plays in the gas-jet could kill a ship, and Janofsi still looked rebellious, his face flushed and sour. But Janofsi had promised Sigrid, and Natalya had joined in the promise, bullying Janofsi with her own threats, and together they had him boxed. In truth, there was little Janofsi could do: Sigrid's threat promised economic death to *Jewel* in the Pleiades, and Sigrid was angry enough to do it. She had made that clear.

Janofsi opened his mouth, but shrugged casually, as if it meant nothing. "Agreed," he growled.

Pov nodded and windowed through his interlink board to Helm. "Fifteen minutes, Athena."

Athena nodded. "We'll be ready." She glanced to her left at one of her helm staff. "Brigit, latch your chair belts," she said mildly. "We are not a space station twiddling in orbit."

"Yes, ma'am," a voice muttered in total embarrassment. "I'm sorry."

"No problem. Helms, please form an insertion wedge for jump."

The other decks acknowledged and *Isle* swung in space to face jump-point. The other three cloudships moved into wedge configuration behind her, aligning on the set course. A half light-year away, LP Orionis flickered within its dusty maelstrom.

Athena studied her Helm wall displays. "Another fifty meters starboard, Stef," she asked. "Thank you. *Jewel,* will you align?"

As Athena tinkered the wedge in a precise configuration, the watch changed on all ships. Sailmaster Ceverny stepped into the interlink room and sat down at his inship console, resuming his duties after three days off watch with Katrinya in the hospital. On *Isle*'s Sail Deck, Tully sat at his console in Ceverny's inship screen, and Karoly moved smoothly into command of Hold Deck.

"We are ready," Ceverny announced. A murmur sifted through the interlink as the decks on the other ships reported.

"Course is laid," Athena said. "Activating laser bounce-pulse." The four cloudships moved into still tighter formation, linked by *Isle*'s master computer into a single unit. "Assuming slaved drive control." Then: "Prepare to launch."

Pov leaned back in his chair and gripped the chair arms. His chair vibrated as *Isle*'s engines ignited, shifting them through the first microjump. The wedge accelerated at LP Orionis, stepping up their speed, point by point.

"Three-quarters lightspeed," Athena said. The star ahead flickered, its gas-jets barely visible through the enshrouding dust. Pov tightened his hands harder on his chair, waiting, then made himself relax. "And launch!"

In a heartbeat, they leaped into the midst of LP's raging storm, hunting the eddy, and Athena braked hard after the turn. The wing sensors flared hot into infrared with dust impact, but dropped temperature rapidly. Pov blew out a breath.

"Good choice, Athena," he said.

"I'll share the credit." She smiled. "We are decelerating. Downloading pulse-link."

As they dropped speed, the wallscreen cleared into visibility, giving them a view of the hot dust that drifted in irregular patches all around them, little more than a haze in infrared reds and browns thinned by the raging energy of the jet nearby. Beneath them, obscured by more dust, the alpha star glowed in the bright ultraviolet and visible frequencies of a hot star, and had already ionized the nearby dust and gas to several solar diameters. The star shimmered in its inner cocoon of incandescent gas, a torrent of energy still escaping from both poles. A scant half million kilometers away, the southern gas-jet roiled and shifted its colors as it spun away from the primary's southern pole. A perfect insertion, on the numbers, Pov noted. *BaXt*, a favor he hoped would stay. The ships coasted backward parallel to the jet, losing the rest of their speed.

Four million kilometers wide and twenty billion kilometers long, the southern jet boiled with the shed energy of the condensing star, pulsing in cycles of x-ray and high-frequency ultraviolet. The wedge slowed and stopped, then began moving slowly forward, climbing back upward beside the jet, bringing pressure into their sails.

"Sampling dust," Karoly announced from Hold Deck.

Pov pulled in some of the Hold Deck's initial analysis of samples and studied the range of odd substances in the dust as Karoly ran his sort. Many of the molecules in the dust ranged more than a hundred atoms, with several complicated variations of PAH carbon chains. Even this close to the energetic infant star, the mix was heavy in the aromatic molecules, a constant in the wider Nebula.

"Sigrid will love this," Pov said to Ceverny. "They're even insystem."

"I do love it," Sigrid declared from Hold Deck. "A lovely soup. Catch me more, Karoly."

Ceverny turned to Pov, his face creasing in a smile. "So will Katrinya." Just the mention of his wife's name seemed to ease his abstracted expression, and Pov saw the first genuine smile on his old sailmaster's face since the cutter was nearly lost.

"So pipe some of the readings down to Medical

and let her admire," Pov suggested. "She'll like that."
Katrinya was conscious now, still on painkillers, but
healing fast with Dr. Karras's care, and already talking
about returning to duty. Bandages were irrelevant, she
declared fiercely, to whoever would listen. She and Dr.
Karras were negotiating, with Ariadne keeping it slow.

"Good idea," Ceverny said, brightening still more,
and tapped at his board. "Not that we're here to catch
carbon chains. We want some more of Janina's superheavy 'pets.' "

"We'll find them," Pov said. "I've got magnetic
pulses in Tully's scans. Launch the probes, Athena."

The chevron of cloudships turned toward the jet,
and Athena launched three dozen drones into the jet.
As the robot probes plunged into the outer swirling
edges of the jet, half blinked out, but the others survived for several seconds, sending back vital telemetry
about the titanic energies now climbing the jet.
Athena sent them the first analyses of the cycles in
the jet, larger than T Tauri, but within rough approxi-
mations of the same phenomenon. Pov relaxed a little,
reassured by the similarity, but did not let himself
relax too much.

"We're getting some tritium," Karoly told Ceverny
on the inship link. "Even in this thin dust, the hydrogen density's high enough. What should I do with it,
sir?"

"Spill it," Ceverny ordered. "We'll wait for the jet."

"That's on." Karoly smiled ruefully. "In the Hyades, sir, we'd have kept all this and thought ourselves rich."

"Times have changed," Ceverny growled. "Unfortunately." He looked regretful himself.

In Pov's interlink windows, the other three shipmasters gave quiet orders to their own crews, pacing *Isle* as she turned another ten degrees toward the jet.

"Increasing lead in front of the chevron," Athena said. "The others are dropping back."

Pov lighted a schematic in an upper corner of his interlink, then fed the schematic into his wallscreen, plotting the course of the four ships against a winding braid of the jet. *Isle* took the point, increasing the distance between herself, with *Mirror* following behind her. Bringing up the rear, *Net* and *Jewel* sailed in tandem, *Jewel* slightly in the lead. Without hurry, the cloudships arranged themselves in a staggered line, one and one and two, the distance between them increasing slowly to match the wavelength of the cycling energy in the jet.

"Launching second set of probes," Athena said.

She sent out a new array of drones, probing the roiling surface of the jet ahead. At their distance of a half million kilometers, visibility into the jet was fitful at best, like peering into a column of glowing smoke. In some places, a curling tendril of moving gas coiled around relatively empty space; in others, the gas moved as densely as a dust-laden flood, with a force and power that could tumble a cloudship like a boulder in a flash flood.

"Tougher weather," Athena commented quietly, as an enormous tsunami of dense gas rolled past them, a thousand kilometers high. "T Tauri didn't have that kind of plasma wall, just the magnetics."

"We'll have to keep to the fringes," Captain Andreos said, as the tsunami kept on rolling past them, on and on. "And hope those monsters stay farther in." He whistled in awe.

The plasma wave finally thinned, and the brilliant yellow of the hot gas acquired flashes of other colors

in brighter whites, hot blue, and the occasional flash
of oxygen's hot green. Pov watched the jet in his interlink wallscreen, mesmerized, as the cloudship phalanx
maneuvered closer to the swirling tendrils of the out-
ermost edge.

"More complicated than T Tauri," Gray said
tensely. "More coils and turbulence. The energy pattern is tighter."

"And probably more frozen in its magnetic lines,"
Pov agreed. "What kind of readings are you getting,
Tully?"

"It's got the particles," Tully replied. "I'm counting
half a dozen of the right frequencies. If we can get in
and out, we'll haul in a good catch."

Pov nodded, then watched as Athena sent a third
cascade of drones into the gas-stream ahead. Behind
them, *Mirror* launched her own drones at a canted
angle to Athena's spread, tracking the jet activity in
time as the second wave of drones plunged into the
same areas seconds behind the first. On the Helm
screens, Athena's drones vanished.

"Hit something," Athena said. "Might be a field
line."

The second wave of drones winked out. "So did
we," Gray said from *Mirror*. "Let's time the cycle."

"Starting count.... Getting some preliminary data
now," Athena said a few moments later, watching the
datascreens on her Helm console, then tapped into
Tully's console on Sail Deck. "I see a waveform, Tully.
Forty thousand kilometers, frequency ten minutes."
She fed a schematic into the interlink.

"So do I." Tully's face looked tense but elated. He
grinned broadly. "Say the word, captains," he said.
"Say the word and we'll go fishing."

Pov took a deep breath, glanced at Andreos. "Let's

try the weather, people. Increase separation to forty thousand. Port into the jet, Athena, your discretion when."

"Yes, sir!"

Isle turned toward the glowing gas-jet and plunged into the outer tendrils of the gas, her sails spread. Pov watched the monitors carefully, his eyes flicking from the hold screens to Tully's sail displays as Athena piloted a curving trajectory into the jet. A bow wave formed easily over the ship, shielding *Isle* from part of the active radiation in the jet, and her wide sails provided more protection while funneling a rich harvest of high-energy particles into her holds.

"Hold that course, Athena." Athena nodded absently, and Pov looked around at Ceverny. "Good track. How's the dust penetration?"

"Very little," Ceverny replied. "The jet is vaporizing most of it. Our risk comes from radiation, not dust." He jerked one shoulder up, let it fall, then sniffed reflectively. "A nicer choice. I prefer radiation."

"True." Pov tapped a feed to *Isle*'s rear sensors. Behind them, seen dimly through the murk of the glowing gas, *Mirror* moved on a parallel course into the jet. At this depth inside the jet, he could not see the pair of other ships beyond, but the interlink signal held through the magnetic distortion, obscured only by jagged static.

"Increase laser-pulse, comm," Pov ordered. The interlink stabilized, showing the captains intent on their ships. Janofsi's eyes darted from screen to screen, his hands tense on his console counter, as *Jewel* sailed a protostar gas-jet for the first time. On *Net,* Andreos was lounging in his interlink chair, his attention intent on Stefania's piloting, not on Janofsi.

Pov saw Janofsi swallow hard, his eyes darting in a subtle panic. We should have made *Jewel* wait outside the shell, Pov thought suddenly. We should have sent her home, or never brought her at all. A protostar doesn't give second chances.

"Magnetics ahead," Athena called. "God, it looks like another plasma wall, too."

"It *is* a plasma wall," Ceverny growled.

"Take us out, Athena," Pov said quickly, his attention jerked away from *Jewel.* "Line approaching, *Mirror.*"

"Acknowledged," Gray said.

"Reversing course," Athena said.

Isle turned through a wide curve and accelerated out of the jet, *Mirror* only a few seconds behind in an identical maneuver. Their ships burst through the outlying tendrils and sailed outward several hundred kilometers, escaping the invisible edges of the field-form. Two minutes later, *Net* and *Jewel* emerged on parallel course, tracking the maneuver. Janofsi gave a visible sigh of relief and ran his hand over his forehead.

"No problems at all, *Isle,*" Gray declared with satisfaction. "How's your catch, *Net*?"

"Decent," Andreos said, sounding just as satisfied. "Shall we do it again, captains?" he asked.

Pov opened his mouth and hesitated, then glanced again at Janofsi. If he spoke now, he knew what kind of firestorm he'd start—because of what? Worry about the panic he thought he saw in Karol Janofsi's eyes? Janofsi would deny it and rage. He wavered, caught between his fear for *Jewel* and wanting LP Orionis and the Core and all of it. When he didn't answer, Andreos raised an eyebrow.

"Pov?" he prompted. "Your lead."

Pov tightened his hands on his chair. "On the mark, sirs. Athena?"

"We are turning," Athena replied.

The cloudships turned and plunged back into the jet, then exited as neatly ten minutes later, like beads on a string, including *Jewel. Isle*'s hold counters read nearly full, all of it high-weight product.

"One more trip," Gray exulted, "and we've proved the venue! On the mark, *Net*?"

"Let's do it," Andreos agreed, his face wreathed in a smile. "Stefania, back into the jet!"

Captain Janofsi scowled uncertainly. Pov saw the older captain wanted to say something, but stopped it by clamping his lips tight. The cloudships turned back toward the jet for another run.

Janofsi abruptly put his interlink connection on single-feed to *Isle,* doubling his angry face in Pov's screen. "We don't need a third run. Don't listen to Gray."

"Drop out if you want to, Karol," Pov suggested. "It's all right."

Janofsi ignored it. "He's *always* pushing and niggling and stepping in on you." Janofsi slammed his fist on his chair arm, his black eyes flashing with a new rage. "You shouldn't let him do it, Pov! He'll take over everything, just as he's always done, and then we'll end up owned! And I'm not getting owned by *Arrow*!"

"Karol," Pov said patiently, "this isn't about being owned. If you think it best to—" But he could not get through to the man, not even now.

"You're letting them take over!" Janofsi's voice was a shout now. "I didn't agree to extra runs we don't need." The bellow was audible enough to carry over the outship link, and Pov saw Andreos sit up sharply.

"What's going on, Pov?" he asked. *Net* and *Jewel* plunged into the outer edge of the jet, quickly enclosed by the shimmering gas.

"I knew this would happen," Janofsi was raging, his face flushed with a fear he could not admit. "You're too green at this. You don't know how a little nudge here, a little nudge there, works for him. It's how he took over the Pleiades! And now he's taking over the Nebula!"

"Captain Janofsi," Pov said desperately, "please pay attention to your ship. We don't have time for this."

Janofsi shouted incoherently and slammed his hand on *Jewel*'s interlink feed. Pov swore as his face windowed out. "Goddammit!" he swore again. He punched at his keyboard, trying to reestablish the link to *Jewel.*

"*Jewel,* break off your run," Andreos ordered. "Karol!"

"He's going ahead," Stefania's voice said over Andreos's inship channel. "I'm following in his draft."

"Entering the jet," Athena announced on *Isle.* "I am launching new drones."

"Thank you, Helm." Pov looked around at Ceverny. "He won't listen," he said angrily.

"That's nothing new," Ceverny replied sourly. "Ask Captain Janda. Ask Sigrid. Let's just hope that *Jewel* holds up her end of her slip-course with *Net,* or we'll have two ships at risk."

Pov tapped into Athena's laser-pulse controls and built a comm-beam to *Jewel* on the frequency, then smashed in and overrode *Jewel*'s interlink controls. Janofsi plopped back into view, sitting there in his interlink chair. When Pov's face dropped into view again, he started in surprise.

"Don't you dare," Pov warned him solemnly.

Janofsi hesitated, as if he might, then decided to lounge back in his chair. He put on a smirk, gloating about himself. I'll show you, his smile said, and while Janofsi was busy gloating, Pov pasted *Isle*'s slaving code on the link and showed him. Janofsi couldn't blip out now even if he wanted to.

The phalanx plunged again into the jet. Behind *Mirror, Net* and *Jewel* sailed in a tight trajectory, the two ships nearly touching the outlying edges of their sails. Though the run parameters required that one ship give slip-course to the other, Pov could see on his schematic that *Jewel* was refusing to take the point, slowing her speed to force *Net* into the lead.

"He won't yield slip-course to me, sir," Stefania told Andreos over her Helm link. In the interlink screen, Captain Janofsi smiled.

It was *Net*'s turn to take slip-course from *Jewel*, but Janofsi would not yield the course. The two ships entered the jet nearly even with each other, *Jewel* gaining ahead as Stefania slowed speed to catch *Jewel*'s draft. Janofsi promptly compensated by slowing his ship's own speed, bringing them parallel again. Andreos pounded his console with his fist.

"Yield course, *Jewel*," he demanded.

"No," Janofsi said, and grinned. "You take the point, *Net*. You always want the point. Here it is."

Andreos ground his teeth, and stared resentfully at Janofsi for a moment. "Making full entry into the jet," Stefania's voice said.

"Take the point, Stef," Andreos muttered in fury. Janofsi's smile got wider.

On *Mirror*'s interlink deck, Thaddeus Gray threw a glance at Rachel, but didn't comment.

The two dreadnoughts launched their drones, angling them ahead of the ships into the ascending whorls of luminescent gas. The drones vanished into the semiopaque glowing gas, their course tracking on a Helm schematic from Athena's monitors.

"Magnetics approaching," Athena said and turned *Isle* outward. Tully adjusted the cant of *Isle*'s large sails smoothly to match the turn, keeping the catch flowing steadily into the holds as *Isle* tacked around to her exit course.

"Turning," Athena said.

"Acknowledged," Gray replied as *Mirror* copied her turn.

Jewel was drafting starboard of *Net* and had to turn first as the ship upstream, but *Jewel* sailed onward on the same trajectory, moving deeper into the gas-jet. "Start your turn, *Jewel*," Andreos prompted sharply. *"Jewel!"*

But Captain Janofsi did not hear him. He was sitting blankly in his chair, scowling in perplexity as he rubbed his left arm. He looked down at his arm and rubbed it harder, still perplexed, then gasped aloud as the pain abruptly crushed him. "Uhhhh," he said as he clutched at his chest. "Uhhhh," he said again. He gaped, his mouth flapping, his face filling with terror and pain, but then, abruptly, his fierce black eyes emptied, leaving nothing of the anger and the pride and the outrage that had made him Karol Janofsi of *Jewel,* only a lingering mild bewilderment, the slightest of protests, and then nothing at all. Stunned, Pov and Captain Andreos watched him slump forward.

"Jewel!" Stefania was shouting on *Net.* "God-dammit, Iosif. *Turn!* Comm, link me through his Helm Map channel." Pov's interlink windowed quickly, and he saw a raging Stefania in her command chair on *Net*'s Helm Deck. "Iosif, dammit! Wake up!"

"But Captain Janofsi said—" Iosif's voice blurted in surprise.

"I don't care what he said!" Stefania declared. "I'm going to climb you like a tree, Iosif, if you don't start your turn right now!"

Pov tried desperately to interlink into *Jewel*'s Sail Deck through his own link to *Jewel,* but smashed into *Jewel*'s ship codes when he tried, blocking the invasion. "I can't get through to Natalya," he told Andreos frantically.

"Stefania," Andreos said. "Tell Iosif to get Natalya down to the interlink. It's urgent."

"But he won't turn, sir!"

"Tell him!"

Stefania did, and Iosif still wanted to sputter. "Captain Janofsi—"

"—isn't there, Iosif," Andreos shouted back. "Get Natalya down there! Why isn't she monitoring? Blast it! Now, now, *now!*" Andreos was standing on his feet, his fists clenching. "Turn, *Jewel!*"

Isle swept free of the last tendrils of the jet and climbed, and *Mirror* emerged seconds later. The magnetic front shuddered past *Mirror*'s position and headed straight for *Jewel* and *Net.*

Iosif began the belated turn, but turned too fast for the roiled gas all around them. As *Jewel*'s sails compressed to danger point, he instinctively slowed speed, wallowing in *Net*'s path. Turning more swiftly, *Net* nearly ran over her as they struggled out of the jet. Iosif gasped audibly when he saw the collision coming and wrenched *Jewel* upward just as she shot into safety out of the jet.

"Down and over!" Stefania shouted at her staff. "Dive under her!"

Then she looked back at the interlink monitor and

the large Helm window beneath it, and froze. She stared a moment longer, then shakily reached for a button on her Helm console and pushed it. When Pov saw what button she had pushed, he cried out in sudden terror.

"Sir," a voice shouted on *Net*. "*Jewel*'s lost a sensor array! It's heading right for us!"

"Yes," Stefania said faintly, her face very pale, as the vacuum barriers whined down behind her. "It's going to hit us somewhere, captain," she told Andreos. "It's too close. We can't avoid." She paused. "I choose it to be Helm Deck, sir." An immense sadness swept over Stefania's face. Then she looked at her Helm staff for the instant that was left, before the maelstrom consumed her.

Chapter 12

Several hours later, Pov sat in the darkness of his office, the only illumination a muted green and blue from his computer watchtales, a ghost's gleam.

He laid his head wearily on his arms, blocking out even that flickering light, wanting oblivion now, but finding himself haunted by memories. Stefania at her side station on Helm Deck, turning to report to Athena in her light voice, her blond hair shining. Stefania, nervous and unsure, sitting in Athena's command chair, carrying on after Athena was stricken. Stefania laughing on skydeck with her skyriders, Stefania sparring with Bjorn on TriPower, Stefania wry, angry, happy, exulting. There were other figures, too, not as clear, but all faces on Helm Deck known to him, skyriders all, their eyes questioning as they watched him from the shadows of the room.

The hull breach had killed them all, the entire Helm Deck staff on alpha watch, with all the grisly consequences of vacuum. Eight dead. It might have been more, but Stefania had put down the vacuum barriers in time, the necessary instant before *Jewel*'s sensor array smashed through the Helm Deck wallwindow. As Katrinya had thought first of the ship, launching her message before she even thought of herself. As Stefania had thought first.

Stefania was timeless now.

She and Pov had not known each other that well, blocked by a difference in personality that had inhibited the deeper intimacy he shared with Tully and Athena, and now, increasingly, with Rachel. But they had made their peace in time and found it easier, and she was a part of him, as everyone on *Net* was part of him.

He felt a dull sickness of grief for Stefania and the others, pricked by the belief it somehow was his fault, his fault. He had managed to carry on afterward, numbly offering help to *Net* and *Jewel,* coordinating with the Grays on *Mirror,* doing what had to be done. And finally it was over and he could leave the interlink, to sit in his office and shudder with the reaction.

I could have spoken, he told himself. In all the months we coddled *Jewel,* clinging to the past she represented, for love, for binding, for patience, I could have spoken. I could have insisted, I could have spoken.

That Andreos no doubt felt the same brought no comfort. The blame was large enough to share.

Iosif had turned too fast and weakened the grips on *Jewel*'s under-array, then had slowed too much as his sails compressed, bringing *Net* too close behind, then dodged away again in too sudden a panic, spinning the array loose. Link upon link, each error compounded by a pilotmaster who had never sailed a gasjet. Natalya, sharing Janofsi's disdain for the interlink, had not monitored her own ship operations and never knew until it was over. Janofsi, in his disdain for doctors, had raged and stamped and ignored his health until it killed him. Error. Error. I could have spoken.

From the room corners, the newborn ghosts of Stefania and the others watched him, hidden in the shad-

ows, their eyes bewildered and strange. Where are we?
the voices sifted in confusion. What is this place?

Ghosts, haunting him.

The Rom believed that ghosts could wander after
sudden death, lingering by the roads and graveyards,
sometimes visiting their kinsmen in this restless confusion, hunting a life suddenly gone, unaware they were
dead. In time, they wandered away, and found peace.
A ghost brought luck to the living, good or ill, but the
Rom avoided such encounters, if they could, and
urged their departed to wander still farther, away from
life to whatever waited beyond. Stefania had a Nebula
to wander now: could she eventually find the peace of
a grave, so far from humanity's native earth?

He shifted in his chair and sighed deeply, then lifted
his head and looked into Stefania's bewildered eyes,
shadowed eyes, as she drifted uneasily in the corner.
My fault, Stef, my blasted fault, he told himself. We
think we're invulnerable, in our proud cloudships. We
think we can challenge a nebula, even this one, and
we talk of the future and our bright, bright success,
so sure to come. So assured, so certain. And we never
really believe death could be as certain, when you dare
too much. Athena got better. Ceverny saved *Dance*
single-handedly. Nobody has to die. We win, every
time. We're owed it.

He pushed himself upright with his hands, but the
effort faded and he sagged back in his chair to stare
again at the room corners.

He heard the chime of his office door, and ignored
it. It sounded again, insisting at him.

"Leave me alone," he called out in a croaking voice.
"I'm off duty." The door opened an instant later, and
a trim figure highlighted by the corridor lights stepped

in, then turned and shut the door behind her. "I don't want you here, Mother," he said angrily. "Go away."

"The Rom do not grieve alone," she said, then marched the few steps to his desk and sat down in a chair across from him.

"I'm not grieving as a Rom. I'm grieving as a gaje, and you don't want to be here to see it. You don't want the confirmation. I'm not supposed to care, remember? They were all gaje, and we just don't care when they die."

"You separate yourself even from Avi? She grieves, too."

"Avi understands."

"So, my son, do I." She laced her fingers on her knee and lifted her chin. "Why do you think it was your fault? I assume that's why you sit here with the dead." She hadn't even looked at the room corners, and took care not to look, but she knew.

"It was my fault. I'm lead ship. I could have pulled *Jewel* out of the maneuver."

"I cannot believe it was wholly up to you."

"I'm lead," Pov said dully and looked at Stefania in the corner, admitting it again to her. "I saw Janofsi's panic and didn't say. It's my fault."

His mother took a deep breath, then expelled it in a deep sigh. "I know I can't persuade you to think otherwise, because what you say has some truth. A leader is responsible for more than himself. But ghosts, my son, are confused. Their words are not good guidance."

"She's there in the corner," he muttered.

"Yes, I know." Margareta did not look around. "My son, a leader always has some of the responsibility, whatever happens to his people, whatever the facts might be. But leading has even more: dealing with that pain, and continuing to lead. And allowing the dead to leave, my son."

Pov said nothing. He had misunderstood his mother's intention, thinking her there to gloat—or had he thought that? He didn't know what he had thought. He wasn't thinking, was as confused as poor Stefania. He looked down at his hands in his lap and sighed.

After another minute of silence, his mother rose and bowed solemnly to him, her hands at her waist, her bow graceful, offering him Rom respect.

"What's that for?" Pov asked, surprised.

She straightened. "I see the leader," she said firmly, "a good man I am proud to follow, in those areas in which he is leader. I am proud he is my son." Her voice was stripped of its usual mockery and sly games: she meant this. For some reason, his mother had come to sit with him, as the Rom always sat with each other to mourn. For Stefania? She didn't care about Stefania or any of the gaje who shared their cloudship, or so she had always pretended. Death was unfortunate, she would say, waving her hand dismissively, but gaje death meant little to a Rom. It is part of our walls. It is part of the division. It is necessary.

"His father would be proud, too," Margareta said, just as firmly. She sat down again. "You should ask me, not ghosts, what you should do, my son, and then consider my advice. I am *puri dai*; I am part of your strength."

"What I do is gaje," he shot back. "You've always opposed it. You always have, in the essentials. You gave in only because Tawnie defied you, too, not because of Kate and me. Now you're probably just waiting for the next crisis, and the *voivoide* will probably hand it to you. But I tell you, Mother," he said, raising his voice, "even if *he* told me to give up the cloudships, I would still say no." He sagged back, exhausted by the effort, and dropped his hands limply in his lap again. His eyes drifted to Stefania. "Even after this," he said stubbornly.

His mother clucked her tongue at him. "You doubt me still, I can see, and I agree I have let you wonder about it." Her face was a shadow in the darkness. "Serious choices are best considered at length, and the *voivoide* has given me other facts to consider since, but I am not unrelenting." She shrugged slightly. "I've lost Tawnie and Karoly to you and your cloudship life, and Kate was always yours, not mine, from the beginning. Both of my children, and the two strongest of my younger kinsmen: all tell me, as *puri dai*, that there is a road they see, over there in the distance, beyond those trees and that river, a road worth following, and they will follow it, whatever my wishes, and whatever I do with myself. I may rant, I may order, I may cry to tradition, but they will go. They tell me that road is the best of the Rom, what Rom are in the essentials, as you say, and tell me I am wrong to doubt it. Matters are turned upside down, when the young tell such to the elders, but even elders should listen, when the young have clearer eyes."

She pointed at him. "The Rom do not grieve alone. You tell me you can be both Rom and captain: show me now. Lead as a Rom, my son. Go out to your ship and accept the blame if you insist, but go out to your ship. I know you are tired and grieving, but so are others. Avi needs you, and so do others, Rom and gaje alike. I know you are sick with the grief, when you prefer ghosts to the living. But you are leader." She folded her hands again.

He hesitated.

"You doubt me still?" she demanded.

"Yes, I do," he said slowly. "How could you expect otherwise? What I've chosen *is* a threat to what we are as Rom. I've never denied that. I've always understood you had your reasons."

"I know. And that, above all, is why I've decided to support you."

He looked at her incredulously. She hissed softly and got to her feet, then stepped around the desk and reached to caress him. He felt her fingers tease with his hair, then the firm pressing of her palm in blessing.

"Do as you will, Pov," she said mildly, dropping her hand. "Disbelieve me for a while yet, if you must. I am good at waiting." Her lips turned up in a roguish smile as she looked down at him. "I outwaited your grandmother, and I tried to outwait you: one out of two isn't bad, if we are counting failures—if it is a failure. We will always fight in some ways, you and I: you are your father's son, and I loved him and fought with him and loved him nonetheless." Her mouth twisted in pain, suddenly vulnerable as his mother was never vulnerable. "I miss him, Pov," she whispered, and glanced at the room corners as if in hope that another might be there, then looked quickly away. "I will always miss him, even though his ghost is long at rest now. I can see him now only in memory, and that fades more with each new year. Soon he will be gone altogether, and I will wander a long time when I am a ghost, to find him again, if I can."

Pov rose from his chair and pulled her close. She sighed and laid her head on his shoulder.

After several moments, she pushed him back firmly. "You trust too much," she reproved. "This could all be an act." She sighed, disappointed in him, which made him smile.

"I agree it usually is." He lifted her hand to his

mouth and pressed his lips against it, and felt her other
hand caress his face. "But it doesn't matter, in the
essentials. Are you really going to support me? Defy
the *voivode*?"

"We will try to keep it short of defiance," she said
archly, and disengaged herself from him, took a step
away. "There are ways to do that, and the best way
is success. As in money, which the Rom have always
revered. If we succeed on your new road, other Rom
might come to share it, and a problem multipled sometimes stops being a problem, when it's multiplied
enough. The Rom have always been flexible." She
smiled craftily. "I have decided to prove Simen is
wrong and you are right. I expect you to help."

"Revenge," he accused mildly. This was more the
mother he knew. "You want to get even for what he
said to Kate."

Margareta tossed her head. "Revenge, I agree. And
love. The one doesn't cancel the other." She turned
and walked toward the doorway, looked back a moment, then left him.

Pov stood in the darkness by his desk, watching the
doorway as it closed behind her, and felt half inclined
to think his mother as much a ghost as the others. He
felt astonished, but she had always surprised him,
again and again, usually for the worse, true, but not
always. *Puri dai,* the wise and intuitive female elders
of the Rom, the older women who understood limita-
tion and family from a lifetime of experience, who
oversaw the seeding of the new, the harvest of the
present, who might see even into the future, when
they were gifted with the art.

And he had always loved her, whatever her tricks.
An often perilous love, to be son to Margareta Janusz,
but it was part of him, as other things were part.

From the room corners, Stefania watched him in the shadows, her pretty face vague, her eyes confused as they hunted answers she couldn't find, not yet.

"Don't wander long, Helm," he told her sadly. He sighed and left her behind in the shadows, to rejoin his ship.

Net and *Jewel* made temporary repairs, then jumped with the other cloudships into the safety of the open Nebula. There, drifting slowly in tandem, the cloudships sorted their catch, storing the higher-energy fuel in special mag-shielded canisters and sampling the other atoms caught in the jet. Pov listened to Karoly's hold report with quiet satisfaction, though the price had been far more than they had hoped to pay.

As the day passed, the Hold Decks finished their final sorting and started the computer on the summary analyses. Normal routine helped *Isle*'s people, gave them something to do, a preoccupation as they grieved. In his office on *Isle*'s Admin level, Pov found distraction too, but wondered what *Jewel* would do next. He understood the crew's bond to their tempestuous captain: through thick and thin, chance and desperation, Captain Janofsi had kept his ship together, stubbornly refusing any other fortune than the cloudship life *Jewel* gave to them.

He had seen the glint of fanaticism in Natalya's own eyes as she supported Janofsi on every point; even *Jewel*'s chaffer, Ludek Ziolka, had set aside logic and his best judgment to follow Karol Janofsi wherever Janofsi had chosen to go. The loss of Janofsi had to be devastating to *Jewel*'s morale. Would she continue onward? Had Pov and Andreos built enough of a bridge to their fellow Slav ship to bring *Jewel* through this most horrible of her crises? He suspected not, but couldn't put a reason to his suspicion—except the look in Natalya's eyes when she stumbled into the interlink room and found Karol dead.

Though *Jewel* would vote later who among her junior captains would succeed Janofsi, Janofsi's designatory order had given Natalya the temporary rank. In this crisis, Natalya would decide, and her ship would follow her as fanatically as *Jewel*'s crew had followed Janofsi, whatever the judgment otherwise, whatever the sense. What would Natalya do?

He had the first part of his answer an hour later in a peremptory summons to the skyside lounge by *Jewel*'s transferees. Antos Dobry, their spokesman, was contemptuous and succinct.

"You will come to the skyside lounge," the bearded man said on Pov's comm channel. "Now." The link snapped off, a habit of *Jewel*'s people that made Pov's teeth grate.

He decided to go alone, though Danil strongly advised against it.

"Staff demands are a chaffer matter," Danil argued. "It's got to be some kind of demand. I should be there."

"The demands won't be about contract, Danil," Pov said tiredly. "This is between me and them on quite another issue." Pov left Admin and walked downship, his mood grim.

At Dobry's insistence, Jano had opened the skyside lounge in midafternoon to accommodate *Jewel*'s transferees. When Pov walked in, he found the room crowded to its uncomfortable limits, every table filled, extra chairs crammed into each niche and cranny available. It looked as if every *Jewel* transferee had shown up, a full third of *Isle*'s crew. He felt chilled by the low mutter, almost a growl, that swept through the room as he was seen. Dobry was seated on the bar, his legs dangling, and motioned casually for Pov to join him at the front of the room. Behind him, Jano stood with his arms crossed, his face thunderous.

"Here's Janusz," Dobry called loudly to the crowd, and Pov nearly hesitated in midstride at the calculated disrespect, but managed to keep his walk smooth and controlled. When he reached Dobry, the man patted the bar beside him. "Hop on up."

"Thank you, no," Pov said coldly. He turned slowly to face the watching crowd. "You wished to speak to me as a group, according to Mr. Dobry. I am here to listen."

"*I'm* our spokesman," Dobry said angrily. "You will talk to me."

Pov swiveled. "You will call me 'sir.' "

"When it's deserved," Dobry sneered.

Their eyes locked for a moment before Pov deliberately broke the stare. Pov looked around at the faces at the tables. "Does he speak for you? All of you?" He saw a dozen heads nod promptly, but others hesitated, glanced doubtfully at each other.

"He speaks for us!" one of the certain ones called out. More nods.

"All right." Pov put his hands in his pockets and turned back to Dobry. "What do you want to say, Mr. Dobry?"

Dobry hammered his palm on the bar with a resounding impact. Pov did not react, only looked at him. "*Isle* will return with *Jewel* to the Pleiades. Captain Tesar has decided, and that's what we say. When we get there, we are all transferring back to *Jewel.* And *Isle* will pay reparations for Captain Janofsi's death, too."

"*Isle* is not returning to the Pleiades," Pov said quietly. "And *Isle* is not responsible for the captain's death."

"You paired *Jewel* with *Net!*" Dobry accused, leaning forward aggressively. "I'd say that's *fault.*" Dobry did not elaborate why; Natalya probably hadn't, either, Pov thought. "You insulted Janofsi, you and Thaddeus Gray, and it killed him! You didn't protect *Jewel,* and now he's dead because of you, *Captain* Janusz!" The title came out as a snarl.

Pov looked at him for several moments, then turned back to the crowd. "Does he speak for you in these statements? All of you?" Again, the dozen sure and quick nods, the series of more reluctant nods from the others. But no one objected to clarify, to demur. *Jewel's* people still had their rock-solid unity.

Pov tightened his lips. "A veto of the captains' decisions requires a two-thirds vote of all the crew. I assume that you are taking *this* action because you know you don't have the votes. Reparations, if any, are a chaffer's matter. This is not the forum to decide—" He was interrupted by jeers scattered through the crowd. He raised his voice, kept his tone clear, calm. "—such matters as are defined in ship's contract. But it does not mean matters cannot be decided." The jeers stopped abruptly, and he heard a rustling through the room as people shifted position in anticipation. Pov turned to Dobry.

"Please get down from the bar and take a seat, Mr. Dobry. I wish to talk to all of you as a group."

"There's been enough talk. We go with *Jewel!*"

"Then stay where you are," Pov snapped. He walked away from the bar to the center of the cleared space before the tables, then looked slowly from face to face. Some faces were angry, some half ashamed, others confused. The people are the ship, Pov thought: my people. These.

"I grieve with you," he said softly, looking at the faces, and those in the back leaned forward to hear. "Whatever his faults, Karol Janofsi was loyal to his ship. His ship was his life—and now, as might come to others of us in time, if we are unlucky, it was his death. It was an honorable death, though not the kind we usually associate with heroes—saving another's life, attempting some horrible peril—but it was honorable. Janofsi served *Jewel* with all his heart. Most of us try to give that kind of faith to our ship, that kind of commitment. So do I. The people *are* the ship, and the ship is her people."

He paused. "If I were the kind of captain you thought me, I would walk over to that comm in the corner, tell *Jewel* she was welcome to come get you, and borrow replacement crew from the other ships. Gray would lend to me; so would *Net.* I could tell them that none of you matter to me. I could say that anybody they send could replace each and every one of you. And I'd let you go." The room was deathly quiet. "But a crucial fact happened when you came aboard this ship: you became *Isle,* and I will not surrender any part of her."

"It's not your choice!" Dobry shouted. "Whatever you think!"

Pov ignored him, intent on the faces at the tables. "I do not give you up. My ship is my life, and you are my ship, and nothing will ever change that as long as I am captain, as long as I still breathe and live among you."

"Very touching, I'm—" Dobry began sarcastically.

"Shut up, Antos!" a man shouted back. "We listened to you. It's his turn now." A rumble of agreement sifted through the room. Pov relaxed slightly. Careful now. One chance: use it well.

Lead as a Rom, his mother had told him, a man for whom family is the one essential, no matter what.

Family. He looked at the faces a long moment, then cleared his throat and talked to them as his own, as if walls had never existed.

"We haven't had much time to know each other," he said quietly, but loud enough to carry through the room. "Barely a few days as one crew, then this jump to the Nebula. You're aware of the disagreements among the ships—the strains of outside danger have worsened the quarrels. We're used to being independent, and never to being owned—nor dependent on each other. But that has nothing to do with you and me, not in the essentials. We haven't had time enough for me to ask for your trust. We haven't had time enough for me to know I can trust you. But now is not the time to talk of trust and its breach. Now is not the time. There will be time later, when we can talk until all is said that needs to be said. I will listen. I hope you will listen to me. But, for now, I am asking for a trust I haven't earned." He spread his hands. "I offer a trust you haven't earned, either. It could be a beginning of something later, perhaps not." He lowered his hands. "*Jewel,* stay with us. Find a new home here, if it pleases you. Find a new future here, if you wish to share it. Be one with us, this ship, if you choose to be. I will try never to fail you."

He stood before them, looking at them squarely, and waited. The silence grew until, finally, a woman stood up at a table in the back of the room.

"I will stay with *Isle,*" she declared. "Until we have our time to talk later, captain, when all things can be said." She tapped her heels together softly and nodded in respect. "Sir," she murmured, and began walking toward the door, wending gracefully through the tables. A dozen others stood and bowed, then followed, then a dozen more. The others, more than half the transferees, sat frozen at their tables, staring at Pov.

"And who will return with me to *Jewel*?" Dobry demanded. "Stand and declare yourself."

"That's not fair, Antos!" another woman said. "Some of us want to think about this."

Dobry's finger stabbed at her. "Think about what? Your loyalty? I thought you'd be the last, Marya, to betray *Jewel*."

"Betray?" Marya said back angrily. "To betray *Jewel*, by your terms, is to betray *Isle*. It is not a decision made instantly, even if it *is* betrayal. I don't agree with Natalya about the fault here—*Net* protected *Jewel* in the jet, and the captain would not yield the course. *Net* could have let *Jewel* die, then shrugged afterward. Too bad, what a tragedy." Her voice roughened with the sarcasm. "It doesn't make sense to me, Antos. I want to think about it."

"There is no rush," Pov said first as Antos opened his mouth. "We can talk later, and if you decide it is needed, we will respect your wish to retransfer back to *Jewel*." He smiled ruefully. "When we get back to TriPower, Marya. When the present need has ended, all can be said."

Marya thought about it, then nodded. "Thank you, captain." She stood and glanced at the nearby tables. "I believe this meeting is concluded. Isn't that so, Antos?"

Dobry levered himself off the bar with a jerk and stalked toward the door, every stride hard with rage. Pov sighed and looked at his boots, suddenly exhausted through and through. He listened to the rus-

tling, the quiet murmur of voices, as the rest of the
transferees stood and slowly left the room. Jano
stopped and hesitated by his side, then slowly followed
the others. When the room had cleared, Pov raised
his head and looked around bleakly at the empty tables. The lingering anger seemed to drift on the air,
an emotion almost palpable as a scent, a cold draft.
He had not convinced all of them, he knew. He had
not won them.

He tried to move and had to try again when his feet
stuck somehow to the floor. Then, picking up his
stride, he left the lounge and walked out onto the
companionway. He was barely halfway up its length,
heading vaguely toward the prow elevators, when people began spilling into the companionway from the
side corridors in front of him—the other crewpeople
of *Isle.* He saw Axel, Ariadne and Irisa and the
Greeks, Danil and Celka and the Slavs, Avi, Kate,
Sergei. He stopped abruptly in surprise. Had everyone
left his station? Who was minding the decks? Silently
the people in the companionway, swiftly joined by still
others, lined up along the windows, four or five deep
on either side, making a narrow pathway between
them. He looked at them stupidly, not understanding
this odd and silent ceremony.

"Avi?" he asked, his own voice high in his ears.
"What's going on?"

Danil smiled and walked forward and grasped his
elbow. "We put the skyside lounge on the all-ship,"
he explained. "They heard it all." Then he drew himself up and bowed as only a First-Ship Slav could bow.
"*Isle,* at attention!"

Heels tapped smartly and heads snapped up, every
spine ramrod-straight. And the eyes as they looked at
him: he saw the eyes. Fierce. Proud.

His.

Danil tugged on Pov's sleeve, got him into motion. Together they walked between the silent rows, and Pov looked at the faces in wonderment. When had he done this? When?

As they reached the elevator, Pov thought of something else and stopped abruptly. "But who's watching the ship?" he asked Danil plaintively.

A soft chuckle filtered through the companionway as they laughed at him, pleased that he was pleased, though no one moved a muscle. Pov turned back to them. "Thank you," he said. "Thank you all. Please return to your duty."

"Yes, sir," they said, nearly as one, and began to vanish back into the side corridors as quickly as they had assembled, even Avi, though she waved as she left, her smile wide and proud. When the companionway had cleared, Pov looked at Danil again. His chaffer was smiling ear to ear.

"Your idea?" Pov asked.

"It was a shared idea, I'd say."

"Thanks, Danil. More than you know."

"*Jewel* is blaming us," Danil said quietly. "We're going to lose her."

Pov nodded. "I know."

"Let *Jewel* go, Pov. Even with family, sometimes you have to let go."

"But—"

"Sometimes you do," Danil repeated and walked away.

Jewel kept her silence another day as her crew prepared for Captain Janofsi's funeral. On *Net*, the skyriders made their preparations for *Net*'s own dead. In the afternoon, with sad and muted ceremony, eight bodies were given to the depths of space, to wander the Nebula until the chance of course and gravity drew them into a newborn star, creating each anew in another form.

Pov stood silently with Captain Andreos and the Grays on *Net*'s skydeck as each silvery container rolled forward and impelled itself forward through the lock, launching into the deep. Natalya Tesar of *Jewel*, claiming the press of her own funeral preparations, did not attend. *Jewel* would never forget her grievance, Natalya declared with her dramatic absence; now, neither would *Net*. Captain Andreos's mouth was set, his eyes flinty with an anger he had rarely showed. The breach was complete, by *Jewel*'s own doing. It wasn't fair, Pov supposed—but *Jewel* had been not rational for years, not after her run of harsh fortune. And they were past fairness now. They were past everything.

A few hours later, they assembled again for the second funeral, one with full captain's honors. Natalya Tesar's severe face appeared in the general broadcast to all ships. She had dressed in full uniform, and the other officers of *Jewel* stood in ranks behind her, as stiffly drawn to attention, their expressions almost as grim. As one, gathered in *Isle*'s captains' meeting room, Pov and his captains rose to their feet.

Pov had considered the obvious retaliation of not attending at all, not even by broadcast, but they stood to honor Captain Janofsi, and for his memory they had attended.

"We are gathered," Natalya intoned solemnly, "to bid farewell to our beloved captain, Karol Janofsi. Let us remember him with honor."

Natalya stood silent, her spine unbending, as soft music rose, the national anthem of Janofsi's ancient

Poland, skirling quietly from the ship speakers. The music ended and Natalya kept another long pause of silence, then firmed her chin.

"As the stars rise in all quadrants," she said in a low voice, "so shall we all rise with the Resurrection." She nodded slightly, and the screen divided to an exterior shot of *Jewel,* taken from her starboard monitor, as *Jewel* ejected the funeral casket containing Janofsi's body into space. "Fare you well, captain. Take with you our respect, our honor of you, and our love." The casket arrowed outward, glinting in the distant light of the Nebula's blazing Core. "Light to light," Natalya said, her voice rising strongly, "rebirth to rebirth, until the end of the ages, we will be with you, Karol Janofsi." Natalya gestured choppily and the casket exploded, blasted to scintillating atoms by the explosive charge.

"Lord, have mercy," she intoned, her face like granite.

Pov blinked in shock. "They blew him up," Athena gasped. "Oh, great God. Why'd they do that?"

"Lord, have mercy," *Jewel* chanted in measured response.

Pov jumped toward the wall-comm, but Athena was there an instant before him and hit the all-ship control. "Helm, starboard and down! Full power! *Jewel*'s going to self-destruct!"

Pov grabbed her shoulders and shouted past her into the comm. "Drop the barriers! Everyone down on deck!" He felt the surge in the ship's gravity as Helm Deck took *Isle* into a panic dive, down and away from *Jewel.* The gravity slipped, and Pov and Athena staggered, clutching at each other, then fell hard against the nearby chairs. The other captains dived to the floor.

"Christ, have mercy," Natalya said.

"Christ, have mercy," *Jewel* chanted remorselessly.

"Warn *Net!*" Pov shouted at the comm as he sprawled, his arms around Athena. "Call *Mirror!*"

"*Mirror* is already diving, sir," the helm officer replied, his voice loud but eerily calm. "*Net,* too," he added in relief. "Sirs, we have ten thousand kilometers separation, and increasing." The gravity surged again as *Isle* spun harder away from *Jewel,* increasing speed. Athena tightened her grip on Pov, her chest heaving with sobs.

"Lord, have mercy," Natalya intoned with finality from the wallscreen. And *Jewel* exploded.

The roar of sound burst through *Isle*'s wallscreen, and a brilliant flash of painful light, and then, abruptly, nothing at all. Pov raised his head and stared in horror at the blank wallscreen. The computer sequenced null-signal and spun *Isle*'s stylized wave into the screen, awaiting its next command.

"Brace for possible impacts," Helm said, his voice hoarse with shock. "Sirs, I am preparing for micro-jump." A moment later, *Isle* skipped through a micro-jump, leaping far ahead of the hurting debris of *Jewel*'s self-immolation.

"Level course," Helm continued, half strangling with the effort. "We are decelerating." His voice broke in a racking sob.

Pov helped Athena to her feet, then held her as she cried. He saw Ceverny get up, his eyes filled with horror, joined by Danil and Tully.

"*Net?*" Tully whispered, his face stark white.

"Go find out," Pov said. "Get their course-track from Helm. We can send a message capsule, say we're all right. Maybe they'll do the same."

Tully nodded and hurried out of the room. Pov

tightened his arms harder on Athena, who was still sobbing wildly, and kissed her forehead, her hair, her face. "We're okay, Athena," he said, trying to comfort her. "We're okay."

"Why did they do it?" she said in a choking voice and hit his shoulders hard with her fists. "Why?" She pushed him away abruptly, breathing hard, then threw up her head. "I never wanted revenge for Stef!" she shouted in his face. "I didn't ask this!"

She choked back another sob and strode out of the room, then broke into a run in the corridor, running for the elevator.

Ceverny sat down with a thud in one of the chairs, then slowly rubbed his face up and down. A moment later Pov stepped off balance as his head felt too light, and he reached for a chair himself. Danil was white as chalk.

"Sit down, Danil," Ceverny ordered. "I think we'll all need to sit for awhile."

"Why'd she do it?" Danil said. "Why choose *that*?" Danil's face flushed red, then stark white again. "Why?" he demanded furiously, as if Ceverny had an answer.

"We'll never know now," Ceverny said, and gave a shuddering sigh. "You had better talk to our *Jewel* people, Pov. If they knew of this and didn't warn us—"

Pov shook his head. "They didn't know, Miska. Why ask for a meeting, if they knew? What would be the point? Natalya didn't trust them to tell, didn't ask if they agreed. She just did it."

"Lord forgive her," Ceverny said, and looked very old.

Chapter 13

They rendezvoused four light-years south of LP Orionis, and drifted slowly in the local gas-stream for the next two days while *Net* rebuilt her shattered Helm Deck. Pov spent the time largely with the *Jewel* transferees, visiting with them informally in small groups or in their apartments, with Miska Ceverny and Janina Svoboda beside him, both elder Slavs they knew from *Jewel*'s earlier days at Aldebaran with *Fan*. Theirs was a different kind of grief, a shock of a ruptured loyalty they had considered unassailable. That *Jewel* had chosen death for them without asking, some could accept, but that *Jewel* would try to murder three other ships in her suicide shook them to the core.

Why? they asked in despair, asking a question no one could answer except the dead. Pov found among them the strongest and asked for their help, which they gave willingly. And the weakest, when they spun into hysteria, Dr. Karras gently took into Medical and medicated into a needed oblivion, not for long, but long enough. On the third day, Katrinya Ceverny joined Pov in the visits, angrily refusing any cautions, even from an anxious Miska, and wobbled from apartment to apartment on her husband's arm, her face and hands encased in bandages, to talk softly and cry and comfort. Other Slavs came over from *Net,* and several

Greeks, to join with *Isle*'s crew in the healing that had begun.

And when *Isle* voted for the Core, after the captains had recommended it, the choice was unanimous.

The captains had had some reservations, partly fueled by a renewed sense of personal mortality. Had Natalya not allowed her anger to keep her away from *Net*'s funeral, thus refusing *Net* the customary respect of her personal presence and inviting retaliation by the others, all four shipmasters would have been standing on *Jewel*'s deck when Natalya blew her ship to kingdom come. The Rom believed a ghost brought luck to the living, good or ill: Stefania's luck had been very good, indeed.

And the cloudships had usually been lucky, despite *Fan*'s long financial troubles and *Jewel*'s years of bad fortune. *Dance* had survived her dust accident, though it had cost her a daughter ship, and now had a new and better contract at another Hyades colony. *Arrow* had decades of unblemished success, and *Net* had discovered her secret at T Tauri. The new ship-drive worked well, and Katrinya and Josef were recovering rapidly. When the cloudship captains calculated their luck, they called it a reasoned balance of risk and benefit, an economic science of measuring chances. *BaXt* called it gambling, and would likely have the last word on the matter, as she usually did.

Luck. A mixed luck, enough to trouble them.

They met on *Isle*, Captain Andreos, the Grays and Colleen, Pov and Miska Ceverny, to consider their choices. The wallscreen of the Admin lounge showed a schematic map of the Core, overlain by a dim telescopic shot of the stars and turbulent gases swirling outward from the Trapezium.

"Can we do it with three ships?" Pov asked soberly. "We assumed we'd have four."

"I could still send for *Arrow*," Gray offered.

"*Hound* could come, too," Colleen added firmly.

Captain Andreos smiled. "I appreciate the offer, but three should be enough. We modeled for four because we had four ships, but four is not an essential. With our windows shuttered and certain points reinforced with slag armor, we should have sufficient ship integrity to transit the Core. The ship maneuvers would have to be perfect, of course, our scanning within a small range of error."

"I can't model less than a class six risk," Gray said unhappily. Gray was a sobered man, quite aware of his contribution to the tragedy, though it was a topic none had discussed, not yet. He spoke more hesitantly now, without the usual proud confidence and the unquestioned assumption *Arrow* always knew best.

"Even with four ships," Captain Andreos noted, "it was class five. I don't think one degree of risk is worth the delay, nor the hazard to your other ships, Thaddeus."

"Class six," Gray said, looking at the wallscreen. Then he turned his head to Andreos and smiled ruefully. "We've already paid a high cost, with the brunt on you, *Net*."

"And another cost we could pay later," Colleen said decisively, shaking her red head, "when the tritium prices dry up. Let's try it, sirs. If anyone can challenge this venue, it's a cloudship. If we give up and go home, we might all face *Jewel*'s troubles in a few years."

"I agree," Gray said firmly, glancing at her with a smile. "But I yield to *Net* on the choice."

Andreos nodded his thanks. "We think we should try it, too. My skyriders are adamant about that, as their honor to Stefania. But we must be cautious, yet not so cautious that we hesitate at the wrong time and wreak the very disaster our caution is meant to prevent." He smiled ironically. "But that's a familiar problem, isn't it, captains?" They all responded with a wry chuckle. Andreos leaned back in his chair and sighed. "But for the life of me, I cannot think of what I should have done instead with *Jewel*."

"*Jewel* made her own destiny," Colleen said impatiently.

"It's not that simple, Colleen," Andreos reproved. "A few others helped in making her destiny, including *Arrow*. To be frank, my principal concern is not our technical expertise, nor the scientific challenge of the Core. Either we are equal to that or we aren't. As you say, if anyone can do it, we can. My concern is that one ship cannot do it alone."

"We have tried to cooperate," Gray said stiffly.

"Yes, you have," Andreos agreed, nodding. "And I'm not casting blame that's not deserved. We both may have contributed, but *Jewel* did most of it to herself. People make choices, and most of them have nothing to do with science. Our consortium begins a new choice, Thaddeus, and it may end up as radical a change for our cloudships as the new markets we're hoping to discover here. You don't understand why we struggled for *Jewel*; that has been obvious." He shrugged. "It's not something we totally understood ourselves, except to know it was important. If we had understood better, perhaps we would have been wiser. But you've criticized us for the personnel problems in our mixed crews, not often to our faces, true, but we know you feel *Arrow* would have done it differently. *Arrow* would have done it better."

Gray and Colleen shifted uncomfortably, obviously

preferring not to hear any of this, but Andreos was relentless.

"We have mixed crews," Colleen countered.

"Mixed Americans aren't the same, and you know it," Andreos retorted. "And if you want to be defensive, *Hound,* we can talk about the Core now instead of later in this meeting." Colleen sat back and crossed her arms, struggling to control her expression. "Better than that, please," Andreos said with some asperity.

Colleen's eyes widened at the reproof, and she glanced indignantly at Gray.

"See, Thaddeus?" Andreos said, shaking his head. "I speak to one of your captains as I'd speak to one of mine, and the walls go up. We're *Arrow.* We're better. With your successes, you have some grounds to think so, but ask any Greek on our ships about First-Ship Slavs, and then ask what those pretensions meant ultimately for *Jewel.* I don't intend the process to recycle, and end up handing us another suicide ship in the future. I do *not* intend that at all." His mouth was a tight line as he glared at them.

"So what are you suggesting?" Gray asked mildly, his eyes fixed on Andreos's face. "Single ownership? A corporate board to run all six cloudships?"

"No, not that radical. I'm talking about arrogance. Everybody's arrogance." Andreos glanced aside at Pov. "I'm talking about family, I think," he said more slowly.

"Family?" Colleen blurted, and looked totally confused.

"Or the gypsy road." Andreos leaned forward intently, his eyes fixed on Gray and Colleen. "Pov and Rachel have already built it between themselves, but you and I need it, too, we senior captains. We can't wait a half-generation for the change. We need alliance, in its truest sense, Thaddeus. An alliance that can conquer this Nebula. That alliance will change us: we'll lose some things we've always considered an essential. And we'll hear unaccustomed and outrageous things, like another cloudship daring to call us arrogant and insisting we change." He leaned back. "I am not claiming *Net* had no fault in this. I am not claiming that at all. I am just starting a process." He smiled icily.

Gray opened his mouth, then shut it, and decided to look at Colleen instead. "I think we've been insulted," he suggested, and Andreos moved in disgust, but stopped as Gray jerked his hand. "Not yet, Leonidas. Wait a minute. As I said, I think we've been insulted." He looked at Colleen again.

"You have," Rachel said loudly.

"It happens," Colleen replied to Gray, starting to smile. "He's very good," she said. "I'm glad he's on our side."

"So am I," Gray said solemnly, and looked back at Andreos. "All right, we'll talk about all that, over time."

"It's important," Andreos insisted.

"It's important," Gray conceded, though *Net* would obviously have to bring it up again, maybe several times. One step at a time, Pov thought, and saw Rachel grimace, then wink vastly so her father caught it.

"I'm outnumbered," Gray said irritably, not playacting now.

"You always were," Colleen murmured, then laughed a silvery laugh, high and lovely. He looked at her with baffled frustration.

But the tension had eased with Gray's concession, and all the captains sat back farther in their chairs. They looked silently at each other.

Rachel took a data disk out of her uniform pocket and handed it to Pov, taking the lead. "Speaking of alliance *and* the Core," she said firmly, "here are the recommendations from our technical staffs."

Pov turned to the console computer inset into the table and loaded the disk into the computer. "We'll add it to the recommendation of *Isle*'s staff, which are primarily Sailmaster Ceverny's ideas." Pov smiled at the older man seated across the table. "Mr. Ceverny, if you will," Pov invited, gesturing at the wallscreen.

Ceverny stood up and walked over to the wall-screen. With painstaking care, he sketched a course across the map with a stylus, creating a glowing track in bright green.

"As you know, captains, the Core promises us wealth, challenges, and risk. Based on our light-ranging from the edge, we have defined some of the closer structure behind the Trapezium, but most of the data is still lost in the blaze of the O-cluster. Here, at Theta Two, we have a dust ridge bisecting the Trapezium core tangent to the alpha star of Theta Two." Ceverny pointed with his stylus at a wide shadow on the glowing green track, a structure that had appeared as only an ambiguous thin line in the long-range scans. "It's probably the perimeter of a partial circumstellar dust shell, either the remnant of Theta Two's original shell colliding with a supersonic gas stream, or a remnant that's been pushed from elsewhere in the Trapezium. The gas-stream shaped it; light pressure keeps it where it is." He scowled at the shadow. "Maybe."

"Shocked dust," Gray commented. "There to protect us, not immolate. A suitable irony, Mr. Ceverny." He glanced at Rachel. "That's our first objective. It could shield us from the O-star radiation."

"If it's thick enough," Ceverny agreed. "Most of

the dust in the Core is highly attenuated, destroyed by ultraviolet or blown away into the outer Nebula." Ceverny turned back to the screen. "But a dust wall still exists there. If we could jump into a trajectory behind it . . ."

"If," Gray agreed.

Ceverny nodded. "An interesting venue my wife wants to sample, and a possible screen for us, if we can weather the turbulence from the Trapezium cluster. Besides the sixteen high-mass stars, the Trapezium contains over two hundred other stars, many of them protostars shrouded in dust, but with a number of lesser-mass stars adding their UV emission to the glare. As we pass behind the dust wall, we can angle our combined sail coverage to manipulate the dust as a shield."

"Use sails to catch dust?" Colleen objected, then paused. She scowled. "I can't believe that dust wall is coherent. It could shed dust at high concentrations, right in our faces."

"According to our light readings, most of the dust is ionized, probably close to ninety percent." Ceverny turned around to raise an eyebrow. "I despise dust, too, Colleen," he said, sniffing reflectively, "but I appreciate the irony of *using* dust rather than suffering its existence. It's a new technology that might be useful here and give us some better shielding, given the high gas/dust ratio in the Nebula. If it works *here,*" he said, tapping the dust bar in the Trapezium, "it'll work even better in the outer reaches. It might even be adaptable for TriPower's shielding, given Sigrid's larger power reserves, if EuroCom agrees to let Sigrid move her station here."

"Sails on a mobile station," Rachel said in delight. "I like it."

Ceverny frowned as people got far too enthusiastic.

Andreos didn't help him. "If we cloudships are nimble in advancing our own technology," he said musingly, "eventually we may sail mobile stations instead of cloudships." Ceverny cleared his throat, and Andreos leaned back in his chair and lounged. "But I leave that item of future ship design to a future generation, where it belongs." He waved his hand negligently at Rachel.

"_If_ we can transit the bar," Ceverny said determinedly, "we'll reach this outer extension of the molecular cloud behind the Trapezium." His stylus sketched a short curving line on the map. "The molecular cloud extends in a bowl around the O-cluster, with a shock-front in the interphase between the cloud and the ionized space the O-cluster is busily burning into the cloud. That shock-front compresses gas and raises temperatures. Hold Deck wants to watch the chemistry."

"With what application?" Gray asked with interest.

Ceverny shrugged. "If the gas is dense enough and the UV shed by the cluster tolerable, we could sail this shock-front for decades. It extends entirely around the cluster's ionized sphere bordering the molecular cloud and draws from the cloud behind it all those cold molecules that might survive long enough in the light for us to catch them. Some of the molecules exist only in these dark clouds, little fragments of this and that we'd like pure for certain chemical processes."

"PAHs," Pov said helpfully.

"Our main interest, however," Ceverny rolled on, "might be the larger molecules, the aromatics and carbon chains. I was getting to PAHs, you young pup, and I'd like to remind you I'm giving this presentation." He gave Pov a mild glare. "We can manufacture most of those in null-gee mobile stations, but why spend the energy when we can just scoop them up out there?" He gestured grandly at the entire screen.

Pov got up and borrowed Ceverny's stylus, gave him a smile, then scooted his projected course a little farther around the back of the bowl. "If we keep on going this way, we can look at the *next* Trapezium busily forming inside the molecular cloud."

"We don't need *two* O-clusters in our life, Pov." Ceverny scowled at him.

"Basic science research, then," Pov said. "Earth has been trying to peer at those protostars for three centuries, getting light-blinded all the while."

"Nuts to research," Ceverny said aggressively, "when the risk is class six. We have only three cloudships."

"Three's enough," Andreos said confidently. "Because when we come *back* to the Nebula, Miska, with TriPower cruising along behind us to buy anything we catch and to cook up wonderful things in its processors, we are going *there*." He pointed at the map. "To the K-L Nebula."

Ceverny's mouth dropped open, but he recovered quickly. "And I thought I was the dreamer," he said sourly. "Not with three ships, Leonidas."

"Six," Gray said quietly. Every head swiveled toward him.

"But—" Ceverny began.

"We're not going there *this* time," Pov said, "just next time, and maybe not next year or the year after, but we *are* going." Pov nodded at Andreos. "So we need basic data on what's there in the K-L, and we have to get close enough to look. You can help model."

"You want more protostars," Ceverny accused.

"Why not?"

Ceverny glared at them all. "Am I the only voice of reason in this room? It's too dangerous. You saw what happened to us at *one* protostar with masers we could thankfully find pointed in another direction. In the K-L—"

"It's a convention of lighthouses," Rachel said gleefully. "I'm going, too." Rachel turned to her father and nudged him hard with an elbow. "Chime in, Dad."

"Actually, I agree with Mr. Ceverny," Gray said, frowning at the wallscreen. "At least for this trip."

"Dad!"

"Thaddeus," Colleen murmured unexpectedly.

Gray looked at them both and hesitated, then shrugged. "Maybe a scan of the K-L, if you can talk Miska into it, too. How far would we have to go along the curve, Pov?"

Pov turned back to the map and frowned. "I'm not sure. Right now we can see the protostars in infrared, but I'd like to get close enough—and out of the O-cluster's glare—to look with other frequencies. If we could pick up visible light and ultraviolet, we could get a composition, paste it all into the picture."

"Lots of smog in between," Ceverny said, still resistant. "The K-L's embedded in the dark molecular cloud."

"Not too far in." Pov shrugged. "I won't be unreasonable. If we can't get a good look from a safe distance, we'll use probes later. But surely we can get *some* data worth getting. What do you think?" He looked at Ceverny and watched the struggle on the old man's face.

"Open a tritium container, Miska," Captain Gray said dryly, "and you get protons in your face."

"You're a proton," Ceverny told Pov irritably.

"Gray's got the right of that." He walked back to the table and sat down with a dignified thump. Pov laughed.

"Katrinya will agree with me," he warned. "And if she abstains because she's on sick list, our Second Hold is my cousin. If Karoly fails me, I'll sic Sigrid on them both."

Ceverny sighed. "I object. My own shipmaster conspires with my *wife* to outvote me."

"I haven't talked to Katrinya yet," Pov said virtuously. "Though I will." He leaned on the table to look at Ceverny's face. "Real objections, Miska?"

"Oh ... I suppose not. But not *too* far along the bowl. Use some prudence."

"Absolutely," Gray echoed and pretended to flinch as Rachel and Colleen swiveled their heads toward him. "What *did* happen to objective decision?"

"We're past that, I'm afraid," Captain Andreos said, but did not look very disturbed. "We're going to the Core. We've paid too high a price not to try." He looked around at the faces. "I suggest we put our various staffs to modeling parameters. We have the short-range data now; we have some practical experience. I want our physicists and holdmasters to review the original plans and make suggestions for changes if they're needed. Likewise our Sail Decks and other technical people. We're in no particular hurry, and a few days of thinking about class six is likely wise."

"Can we jump from here?" Rachel asked.

"I think so," Pov replied, "but Athena and Isaac think we should shift a light-year or so for a better entry angle. What do you think, Thaddeus?"

"I agree," Gray said, "but let's *think* about it." There was a brief silence as three ships found themselves in accord: they would go to the Core.

"Then we're agreed," Andreos said, looking around the room.

"We're agreed," the rumble of voices replied. Andreos nodded and got to his feet, and chairs shifted as the others stood as well.

After the murmuring of goodbyes, when they had left him alone, Pov turned to look at the wallscreen, looking at the challenge before them—more than a physical challenge, more than just ships against the elements that raged in the Core. In the older days, a sailing ship might survive alone in a storm, battling against the waves with the power of her own sails, the strength of her hull, the courage of her crew. Here they needed each other, in the hope of a new road.

May the roads be never ending, he thought and closed his eyes. May the roads wind forever, for their sake. *BaXt*, guide us. Give us luck. Keep us safe.

Three days later, the cloudships jumped two light-years outward into the Nebula fringe for a better insertion angle into the Core, then aligned their ships into a close wedge, *Isle*'s and *Mirror*'s sails overlapping on the edges, with *Net* sheltered behind the two dreadnoughts. Athena and Isaac lined up the ships on their target, a short entry-course just east of the Theta Two bar, then fidgeted the ships some more to get a tight-beam alignment.

"Are we ready?" Pov asked Athena on the interlink.

"Say the word, captain. We are ready."

"Let's go, Helm."

"Lock down," Athena said quietly. Over the interlink, Pov heard the triumphant replies from *Mirror* and *Net*.

"We are locked down!"

"Trim the ships," Athena continued, her voice ringing over the interlink.

"Ships are trimmed," the voices responded.

"Launch!" Scarcely a picosecond apart, the cloudships' engines flared, driving them forward in formation toward the Core.

Ahead of them, the Core was a brilliant glare, a blurred sun-heart that pulsed with a single beat, beckoning to the voyagers. They left the screens at full intensity as long as possible, watching the light grow to a supernova, a blaze of light.

"And jump!" Athena cried.

As one, *Siduri's Isle* and her two cloudship companions jumped deep into the Core, daring the tempest.

Chapter 14

In tight formation, the three cloudships decelerated quickly, wary of the dusty medium in the bar and the perils that awaited them when they slowed to real-time speed. *Isle* and *Mirror* took lightning-quick readings through the distortion of their speed within seconds after jump, checking the accuracy of their insertion next to the dust bar. Athena turned the ships quickly, using the slaved drive, and the ships' three engines blasted at their entry path, clearing the way. This close to the O-stars, the dust would be thinned, even in the bar, but isolated dust drifts could become a wall at their exit speed.

"Eighty percent lightspeed," Athena reported. The static cleared, reconnecting *Isle*'s direct visual contact with the other two ships. In their interlink room, Pov and Ceverny watched the dust bombardment carefully on the exposed aft sections of the ship, each wincing at the scouring of *Isle*'s forward hull from the ship's plowing at near lightspeed into the dust.

"Fold the touring sails, Tully," Pov ordered. "Give us a smoother profile."

"Will do." The other two ships promptly copied the order, and Athena edged the ships closer together with side-jets as the sails were retracted.

"Thousand-meter separation," Athena reported. "Do you want us tighter, sirs?"

"Bring it to eight hundred," Gray said. "Then I suggest nobody exhale for a while." He grimaced, his face tight with concentration on the screens. The cloudships edged closer.

"Not too close, Athena," Gray warned.

"At eight hundred." In the tight formation, *Net*'s wingtips nearly brushed the engine assemblies of *Isle* and *Mirror* on either side.

A moment later Ceverny clucked his tongue in dismay, and Pov swiveled, so keyed up that any dismay racheted him around like a string pull. "What?" he demanded, then saw the screen on the inship board that had caught Ceverny's attention and relaxed a little. Two of *Isle*'s aft wing sensors had blipped out, destroyed by dust impact. The other sensors registered high in infrared, too high, heated by the pulverized dust. "We're going to lose half that array," Pov predicted, then sighed as three other sensors vanished.

"I've lost most of mine already," Andreos said gloomily. "And I've got four hundred degrees on my wing points. Next time somebody else be in the middle." He crossed his arms and scowled. "I sincerely hope we're right."

Pov chuckled. "So do I, sir." Andreos grinned at him, wired too.

"Braking," Athena said. "Seventy percent lightspeed."

"I'm wondering, sirs," Pov said, "if we could do microjumps backward after exit, maybe find a way to stop instantaneously."

Gray shook his head. "Not with our current hull structure," he snorted. "Talk to Sigrid."

"Just an idea."

Gray snorted again. "Actually, you should talk to God. He's the fellow who thought up inertia."

"And dust," Ceverny growled. Rachel rolled her eyes at Pov.

"Sixty percent." As the minutes passed, the hull temperature rose steadily, testing Sigrid's new alloys to a temperature no one welcomed. They had modeled for high temperature and tested the alloys across a broad scale, but had hoped to avoid the extremes. *Isle*'s aft sensor array on its exposed wings had collapsed, and enough dust escaped the engine flares to compromise other assemblies, including the aft sail points. Without secure points, Isle's entire sail integrity could be damaged.

"How're your sail points, *Net*?" Pov asked.

"I can't tell," Andreos said tiredly. He looked resigned, his mouth quirked in a rueful smile. "Sensors are gone."

Pov drummed his fingers on his console, his eyes flicking from screen to screen as he waited for the speed to drop.

"We have x-ray leakage," Tully reported suddenly from *Isle*'s Sail Deck. "Portside hull, section sixty-two." It was one of the smaller hold containers, close to the exposed aft wing.

"Karoly?" Ceverny asked urgently.

Karoly glanced behind him at the hold displays. "Yes, I see it. Minor hull breach, with two percent loss in pressure. It looks like the dust ate into one of the exposed welds. Sealing off the section." He paused. "Or should I eject the container altogether?"

Pov pulled Tully's display from the Sail Deck monitors and frowned at it. The x-ray leakage was beyond safety limits, but not severe, not yet. "Is your staff at a safe distance?" Ceverny asked.

"At least a hundred meters except for two, whom I am moving now," Karoly replied. He gave a crisp order, then turned back to the interlink. "There's enough lead alloy in between to block most of the leakage—if we can keep the leak at one."

Ceverny nodded. "Don't eject yet," he decided. "We'll want to look at the weld later."

"Yes, sir."

"Forty percent lightspeed," Athena said.

"Wonderful," Ceverny grumbled. "Now we'll have to slag our welds."

"We'll slag everything," Gray agreed. He leaned back in his chair and flicked his eyes over the displays, then turned to look at Rachel's board. "In twenty years, nothing has tested our ship design like this. I'd say we did some good predicting. Not quite enough, true, but I'll take the minor damage."

I've lost all my sensors," Andreos said, looking resigned. "Every single one. Are we still going backward, people?"

Gray chuckled. "I'll lend you a few sensors later, Leonidas."

"I need them."

"Thirty percent lightspeed," Athena reported.

Gray blew out a breath. "Let's coast in backward, Athena. Keep us close."

"Yes, sir."

"I've got an irradiated hold and sail point damage," Pov said. "We can't send out skyrider for the repairs, not inside the Core. Robots will take longer."

"Let's hope it's not too hot for robots, too," Gray said. "The dust has to be drifting here for a reason. Let's hope it's temperature."

"True."

When their speed fell below twenty percent

lightspeed, Pov accessed the exterior scans, then filtered quickly as a blaze struck into the ship, then hastily filtered again. Against the glare of the Core stars,
the dust ahead scintillated in the firestorm of golden
sparks, each grain trembling on the edge of immola-
tion as heavy ultraviolet beat at the curtain of dust
from both sides. On starboard, nearest to the ships,
lay the lesser of the two major star groups of the inner
Trapezium, Theta Two, two massive O-star systems.
On the other side of the dust bar from *Isle,* now barely
shielding the cloudships from the dominant illumination that powered an entire nebula, blazed Theta One,
a tightly packed cluster of a dozen O- and B-stars
surrounded by hundreds of smaller protostars. The sky
swarmed with stars, obscured only slightly by a drift
of smoke.

"We have more x-ray penetrating the ship," Tully
hurriedly reported to Ceverny. "Not at danger levels,
but above safety minimums."

"What about the shielded sections?" Ceverny
asked. All the children had been moved to *Isle*'s inner-
most residential sections and would remain there until
the cloudships left the Core.

"None, sir," Pov said quickly. "The kids are safe,
but I recommend caution in keeping staff in the
outer sections."

"Thank you," Ceverny rumbled.

"How long until a grade one exposure, Tully?"
Pov asked.

Tully looked over at the tech on the x-ray sail
board, and Pov heard the murmur of the response.
"Maybe twenty hours, sir," Tully repeated to Pov.
"Less in the exterior sections."

"That's our parameter for repairs," Gray said. "I'm
getting the same reports. And that's behind dust."

"It's rather thin dust," Andreos said. All around the ships, a glowing ash drifted in swirling patterns, pulsing with the radiation pressure of the Core.

"I'm surprised it survives here at all," Gray said, frowning thoughtfully. "I wonder the hell why. Let's take a sample." He turned toward Rachel, ready to give the command.

Janina windowed in from *Net*'s Hold Deck, her plain face amused. "Do we drop a bucket off the stern, Thaddeus?" she asked. "Please note our sails are still retracted—*and* we're going backward."

Gray's face flushed quickly at his mistake. "Details, details," he said, waving his hand. "Write that down, Pov, for the new talks on ship design. We need a bucket for *Net* to drop off her stern."

Gray's sarcasm did not sit well with Holdmaster Janina Svoboda, no, not at all. She looked startled, and then got mad. "Or maybe I can open a window," she shot back, "and let some dust blow in, catch it that way."

"Also a window with a crank," Gray riposted. "Just for Janina."

Rachel gasped softly, and probably would have kicked him if she could have reached him. We are *Arrow,* Pov thought dryly, and we know best—even when we don't. Andreos sat back and tightened his mouth.

"You do that, Thaddeus," Janina drawled, as only a First-Ship Slav could drawl. We are *Net.* Shove it, *Arrow.*

Gray opened his mouth.

"Goddammit, Dad!" Rachel hissed. Gray looked around at her, startled. "You were wrong, not her!"

Gray hesitated, then looked back at Janina's angry

face. His expression changed completely. "I sound like Janofsi, don't I?" he asked, looking shaken.

"That's how it starts, I think," Andreos said, nodding. "I don't claim to have all the answers."

Gray sighed and ran his fingers through his hair. "Unfortunately, I often do. Janina, I apologize. Please forgive me." Then he quirked his mouth at Andreos. "You'll probably have to repeat this lesson a few times, Leonidas. I've got too many years of winning it all." Gray looked around at his daughter. "But for her, never what happened to *Jewel*," he said softly. "Never."

The three ships coasted backward to a near stop, then separated slightly to give *Net* a bit more room. "Inverting ships," Athena said from *Isle*'s Helm Deck. "On the mark, sirs. And turn." At the tick, Athena began the ship turn, with Tully smoothly extending the sails as *Isle* rotated in space. Pov and Tully watched the weakened sail points carefully through the shifting torsion, but none came loose—yet. Tully let out a breath of relief when it was done.

"Let's keep our speed at slow tour," Tully suggested. "We've got red flashing on four of our sail point sensors."

"Keep it slow, Athena," Pov said promptly. "Just enough to fill the sails."

"Yes, sir."

"Here comes your sample, Karoly," Ceverny rumbled.

"We're ready," Karoly answered. On Ceverny's in-ship screen, Karoly turned his head toward his wall displays as dust spun into the sails and spiraled into Hold's catching chamber. "Irradiating sample for dust. It looks like a nice distribution, sirs. Those stars must be ionizing the dust surfaces; we're catching more grains than we did at LP or the Nebula edge." He watched the hold displays skip through several dozen frequencies in millimeter range. "Low on even-ringed PAHs. They're definitely avoiding our electrical fields. Hmm. The effect goes up with ion potential, Sigrid," he said, looking to the side. "Interesting."

"Turn the field effect down," Sigrid's voice advised from offscreen. "I want them all." Karoly chuckled.

"How are our radiation levels, Tully?" Ceverny asked.

"Some minor fluctuations," Tully answered, "apparently tracking to local dust density. Still within acceptable ranges, at least inside the ship. I wouldn't want to go outside, sir. One of the chiefs says we've got metal busily ionizing on a few exposed filaments. They've already lost ten percent of mass."

"We slag those, too," Ceverny said wearily. "Hell, let's just put ourselves inside a meteor and be a rock."

"Put it on the list, Pov," Gray said lightly. "*Isle* wants to be a rock."

"Now, Thaddeus," Andreos reproved.

"Be sour as you want, *Net*," Gray said, but toned it down. "I won't. I like a class six risk—it's better than nine any day. We can't stay here long, but we weren't fried on entry and we'll leave only mildly baked. Not bad, not bad at all." Gray leaned back in his chair, then glanced at Rachel at the other console. Rachel gave him a tight smile in response, but not much more.

The repair chiefs maneuvered robots outside and began their repairs to *Net*'s sensors and *Isle*'s sail points. Pov watched as the three ships' Helm and Sail Decks began a coordinated scan of the neighborhood, adding to their mapping data and seeking the next destination deeper into the Core.

Less than two light-years away, the nearest binary of Theta Two displayed visible disks; beyond it, the multiple stars of its sister system glittered like brilliant diamonds on a jeweler's cloth against the massive darkness of Orion's molecular cloud. They scanned the two star systems of Theta Two, identifying the distant edges of another dust bubble on the far side, and took quick readings of the local gas density and its thinning dust. Pov raised an eyebrow when *Mirror*'s readings confirmed a black hole orbiting on the far side of the A component, busily eating away at its nearest companion and shedding hard x-rays as it did.

"Can we get a close-up scan?" Pov asked.

"Zooming the telescopic scan," Rachel said. In the interlink wallscreen, the farther sister stars jumped closer, moving apart to fill the screen frame. Gas streaming from the dying O-star flickered eerily as it fell into the cannibalizing hole, an invisible point identified only by the spiraling gas of the accretion disk. Rachel filtered to ultraviolet, then x-ray: the screen glowed in eerie greens and yellows in an otherworldly shimmer of inexorable destruction. Black holes allowed no argument: in time, the entire star system would be consumed by the first of the sisters to die.

"Well," Andreos said, "we thought it was there, and it duly indeed is. With smaller B-stars, we get neutron stars like Lucifer's Deep; with these O-stars, and larger B-stars, we'll get a colony of black holes in another million years or so. Imagine, over twenty black holes in a sphere a couple of lights across. If those other baby stars don't migrate out fast, they'll have a short life."

"We keep our distance from those x-rays," Ceverny declared.

"I wonder if we could harvest a black hole," Pov

said, just to make Ceverny swivel around. "Now *that*'s a gas-jet!"

"I didn't hear that," Ceverny growled and turned back pointedly to his own console. Pov chuckled.

In the interlink screen, Rachel waved her hands in excitement. "First close-ups of a black hole, guys! Not even that probe into Cygnus got this close."

Gray tsked at her. "If we'd jumped to the *other* end of the dust bar instead of this one, Rachel, that monster would have us rather busy right now."

Rachel shrugged. "We knew it was there. No worries, Dad." She wrinkled her nose at him.

"I intend to continue backing up Sailmaster Ceverny," Gray advised her firmly. "If only to restrain the enthusiasm of the young. Ceverny's got Pov to cope with; I've got you. We both consider it a trust."

"Good luck," she tossed back with a sudden grin. "God, what a view."

Beyond the dust bar, hundreds of stars glittered in a swarm surrounding Theta One, most of them very young and glowing brightly in infrared from within their dust cocoons. In the center, several of the twelve O-stars of Theta One overlapped their brilliant disks, massive stars nearly touching in stellar distances and undoubtedly sharing a single gravity well. Two of the smaller protostars had migrated too close to the O-stars and had been caught in their common gravity well, spiraling inward under the invisible pull of the giant stars. Both now lost matter in great translucent curves as Theta One stars slowly dismembered them, adding to their own mass. Cannibal stars, Pov thought, a little awed.

Pov stepped down the screen intensity to take some scans from the light-ranging program and probed deeper into the swarm of protostars of the inner Core.

It would be priceless data, another thousandfold to add to the knowledge they had gained at the Nebula edge.

"We should give this data to Earth, without any fee," Andreos said, echoing his own thoughts. "This kind of new knowledge is beyond commercialism."

"Some of it," Gray said. "But we need prudence, I think. After all—" He stopped and frowned. "God, where do you draw the line?"

"I don't think we should draw lines," Andreos replied. "I think we should let Earth have it all. Either this is a cloudship environment and our future, or it's not."

"All for one, and one for all," Gray said dryly. "I've read that somewhere."

"So have I," Andreos retorted, matching his tone. They grinned at each other.

The three cloudships cruised along the inner curve of a thicker dust wall, and *Isle* collected more samples of the medium, looking at everything possible in several dozen frequencies. When the view ahead cleared to better visibility, Pov ordered the detailed light-ranging of the interface along the molecular cloud.

"Focus anywhere, Tully," Pov said. "But close enough to get a good look at the K-L, either to scan or jump again."

"Pov, we haven't agreed to the K-L yet," Gray reminded him quickly. Ceverny made a growling noise from his own chair, reminding him too.

"No reason not to think about it," Pov said easily.

"No reason at all," Rachel chimed in.

Captain Andreos laughed.

"You're supposed to help on this," Gray accused him.

Andreos just smiled and rocked his chair. He

looked at the firestorm of dust swirling around the ships, and at the inky blackness of the massive molecular cloud bordering the interface far in the distance. "Beautiful!" Andreos breathed, then gave a great sigh. "Sorry, Thaddeus. You'll have to carry on alone." He winked at Pov. "I'm too busy watching the road."

As the light-ranging continued with a close and careful scan of the dark borderline edging the Trapezium, Pov listened to Ceverny taking several reports from the chiefs on ship repairs, then monitored the radiation penetrating the outer hull. Another foot of lead plate would have shielded *Isle* completely: they would remember that fact for next time, and add another twenty percent safety factor. In the meantime, most of the exposed areas were related to Hold Deck functions, and Karoly shifted his staff inship to better safety. Ceverny also evacuated several outer residential apartments on portside and arranged with Jano to wine and dine the evacuees in the skyside lounge, a decision made even more popular when Jano himself picked up the tab.

Near the end of alpha watch, Pov's head had begun a slow warning ache, and he prudently turned the interlink over to Ceverny for the next few hours of the light-ranging. It was absurd to leave, but so were his headaches. He went down to his apartment and found a pill, checked on the twins in the secure sections amidships, then got called to Medical by the all-ship. When he walked into Katrinya's hospital room, Ariadne turned and looked, then sighed.

"I'm missing it," Katrinya complained, waving her bandaged hands. On the room wallscreen, the Core blazed with its brilliant stars.

Pov looked at Ariadne, feeling confused. "Missing what?"

"If you want company, Katrinya," Ariadne said soothingly, "I can put you and Josef in the lounge. You can watch together."

"More than company. Pov, I want to sit on Hold Deck," Katrinya insisted in her muffled voice, not articulating completely as she struggled to talk past the bandages around her mouth, a problem complicated even more by mild sedation. She was groggy, but adamant. "I want to see. More than screen. Want to be there. Want to help."

Pov looked at Dr. Karras. "Can she?"

Ariadne crossed her arms and sighed, then looked down at her feet, then slowly shook her head. "She needs rest, not more excitement. You don't have that much strength to use up, Katrinya. You need to rest and get better."

"Please," Katrinya pleaded, turning to Pov, and her voice choked in a sob as she waved her hands again. Pov saw the shine of tears through the eye slits, two blue eyes pleading with him. All her life, Katrinya Ceverny had stood proudly beside her husband, strong and self-reliant, asking no favors from a hard life. Until now.

He knew Ariadne expected him to back her up, but he hesitated. "Maybe we could move her hospital bed down to Hold Deck," he suggested to Ariadne. "You could give her orders about what she can do and can't. Sigrid'll make them stick."

Ariadne sighed. "It's not wise, Pov. It'll exhaust her, and she doesn't have the strength to waste."

"This isn't about wise, I think," Pov said. "Would it be dangerous?" Katrinya's eyes moved hopefully from Pov to Ariadne.

"No, not dangerous," Ariadne said slowly, then shrugged and gave in. "I'm not stopping your medication, Katrinya," she said, giving Katrinya a firm look. "I won't have you in excessive pain. You'll have to take the buzz along with it. Is that all right?"

Katrinya sank back on her pillow with a gust of relief. She waved her hand resignedly. "Blitzo is fine. Want to see."

"And only four hours." Ariadne was inexorable.

"Pictures rest of watch," Katrinya countered. "Sleep, then Hold Deck second time."

"It's a deal," Ariadne said. She smiled at them both, then walked out to call the medtech.

Katrinya reached out her hand groggily to him, and he gently caught her bandaged fingers. "You fine?" she mumbled. "Not sick?"

"I'm fine." He leaned closer and smiled at the two blue eyes. "It's beautiful out there." Her fingers tightened, though it must be hurting her. "It's wonderful. Sparks everywhere, suns blazing, and a black hole. Even Miska stopped complaining about the dust—well, not entirely," he added wryly. "You know him."

"New kind dust? Want to see scans."

"You'll see them. I promise."

"Thank you," she mumbled. Pov raised her bandaged hand to his lips, saluting her courage.

When Pov walked into his apartment a while later, he found that Katrinya wasn't the only person who wanted to see something. He hesitated in midstep, startled, as he heard a sudden clatter in his office, then the murmur of voices inside. He walked over to the doorway and looked in, and saw his mother holding up a technical diagram of *Isle*'s sailset assembly, peering at it in silhouette against the ceiling light. Avi was seated on the floor, various papers from his Nebula plans scattered around her.

" 'Lo, Pov," she said and waved casually. Margareta glanced at Avi, then turned around to look at Pov, long skirts swirling. His mother looked at him a moment, then sniffed judiciously and held her diagram back up to the light, her bracelets clinking against each other.

"What's going on?" Pov asked, bewildered, and looked at Avi.

"I am being educated," Margareta replied, her diagram still in the air. "By my daughter-in-law, who understands such things."

"Not *all* of that." Avi drew up her knees and wrapped her arms around them, then hunched her shoulders comfortably. "She wanted to read the Nebula plans, Pov. I figured you wouldn't mind."

Pov couldn't think of a single thing to say, and stared at his mother, then at Avi. After a few more moments, his mother lowered the sail schematic and hummphed in soft disappointment, then looked at Avi. "Perhaps another one will make more sense?"

"If you'd only explain, Margareta, what it is you want to know—" Avi began.

"Everything. Why we go, how, where, other facts."

"Mother," Pov blurted, finding his voice again, "you've worked on Hold Deck for twenty years. You voted in the ship votes. You aren't ignorant."

Margareta turned around and smiled at him benevolently. "Of course not, but my attention has not been the best. For example, what is this?" She held out the schematic, and he walked over to her and took it from her hand.

"*Isle*'s gaje sails. What I've been in love with all these years."

"We are not contending about that anymore," she said and bent over to rummage in his box for something else. "I conceded all that." Pov took her by the shoulders and gently moved her aside.

"Let's load them up and go out to the table," he said.

Avi helped him put the papers back in the box, and he toted it out to the dining table, then snapped on the overhead table light. Margareta sat down and arranged her skirts, then leaned her elbows on the table and watched as he brought out all the papers and arranged them in piles. Avi was watching it all from another chair, a delighted smile on her face, though she was obviously as much in the dark as he was.

"Why do you want to know this stuff?" Pov asked finally, when his mother only watched him as he sorted, saying nothing.

Her hand shot out suddenly and caught another diagram, this one the intermix diagrams of the new fuel. She pulled it over and looked at it carefully with a frown. "Stop goggling, my son," she said mildly as she looked. "In the end, you'll have only yourself to blame. Remember I said so when it happens."

Avi laughed out loud.

Pov put his hands on his hips, amused and touched. His mother's gifts, when she gave them, were always unique. "Mother, most of this stuff is too technical for you. You don't have the math."

Margareta looked at him crossly. "I know that, and I am too old for more math. I will perhaps ask my son-in-law on some points. He is a physicist," she added, as if Pov didn't know. "But I decided I should look at these at least once, so that when you explain matters to me, I'll have some basis of reference. For instance, what is this?" she demanded, holding out the schematic.

"The future. What are you wanting to know, Mother? Why are you here?"

Margareta sat back in her chair and propped the schematic in front of her with her hands, then frowned at it. "I agree I overcompensate." She huffed a little. "After twenty years of disdaining your science, I find my wagon floundering in a river. You are right to laugh at me."

"We weren't laughing at—" Avi started, but stopped short when Margareta gave her a perfectly loving look, soft-eyed and smiling, with a shared amusement, a willingness for more, a perfect satisfaction in the other. It was the look she had given a younger Kate, a very young Pov—before her Garridan had died and the cloudships had stolen her children. Avi drew in a soft breath and seemed hardly to breathe afterward, as they looked at each other a long minute.

"Avi, you apologize too much for yourself," Margareta said firmly. "This must change." She looked back at the diagram, then set it aside. "I will insist."

"Yes, Mother," Avi said softly, her face luminous.

Margareta noticed what Avi had called her, and smiled. "I like how you listen, my daughter," she said, nodding, then looked at Pov with less approval. "He will learn from you, as is proper. It is what *romni* do, teaching their husbands how to behave."

Avi gasped softly, and she covered her mouth with her hands, her eyes dancing as she looked at Pov's face. "Oh, my."

"You had better not," Pov threatened her.

"And *romni* listen to husbands," his mother finished with an air of satisfaction, "as is proper for the Rom."

She looked up at Pov and cocked her head. "Have you ever heard the story of the camel and the tent? First the nose, then the hump, then the camel inside and the Arab outside? It is an old Rom story, told since the beginnings of the people." Her smile was utterly wicked.

Pov sat down and crossed his legs comfortably. "You're dangerous, Mother. You really are."

"Only to gaje who are not our gaje," Margareta said, tossing her head. "All the rest is education." She picked up the intermix diagram again and studied it. "You trust too much," she said absently.

"That's not going to change," he retorted. "I'm what I am."

"But you will listen to advice," Margareta insisted, "even if you do what you want later."

"I will listen." He smiled at her. "After all, it's what a good Rom does." She nodded, greatly pleased.

Chapter 15

Late in the night watch, the helm officers had completed their light-ranging and called the captains into an interlink conference. Yawning until his jaw creaked, Pov pulled on his uniform in the dark, then managed to get himself up to Admin level and installed in his chair. Onscreen, Captain Gray and Rachel lounged back comfortably, looking a little more alert, hands folded in front of them.

"Good night," Pov said meaningfully.

"The purity of science," Gray said easily. "It's all for science."

"It's been too many years since I worked swing." Pov laced his fingers over his stomach and copied their slouch.

Pov the Grump on night watch. He'd forgotten how it had always been. It could even diminish a nebula.

While they waited for Ceverny and Andreos, Pov tapped into the ship reports to check on the x-ray leakage and the completed repairs, then sneaked a look at Athena's Helm Map plotting. Athena, sitting in her chair on *Isle*'s Helm Deck, caught him at it and blanked his channel.

"Not yet," she said firmly. "Watch out, Isaac. He's foraging."

"I hear you," Isaac said from *Mirror*. "I'm prepared."

"Have a heart, Athena," Pov protested.

"It's *my* Helm Map. No." Athena was a grump on night watch, too, he remembered, worse than anybody.

"I'll get even," he promised.

"Do try," she invited. "We can have a war, feint and counterfeint, charge and recharge, retrench and slam, I win. It'll be fun." She shook her curls.

Pov laughed. He settled back in his chair and tried to stay awake. It was harder when it was all you had to do. In the interlink screen, Captain Andreos strolled in and sat down, then closed his eyes. Pov yawned and decided to stand up.

After a few more minutes, Miska Ceverny walked in, his uniform rumpled and his hair only half combed. He dropped himself into the other interlink chair. "What time is it?" he complained.

"Time to get out of here," Gray answered. "Athena?"

"Two items, sirs," Athena said briskly, sitting up straighter. "The first is shielding ourselves from the dust as we accelerate. The chiefs propose more shielding over our forward stress points, full shutdown of forward sensors, maybe slag across our entire impact hull. The dust is heavy here, but not a wall, particularly in this part of the dust bar. Or we can jump and arrive with hull damage."

"I'd rather arrive as spaceworthy as possible," Gray said.

"It would take another four hours to refit," Isaac said. "X-ray leakage is still within tolerable limits, but we have continuing metal damage in some delicate structures, mostly portside toward Theta One." He grimaced. "Another reason to slag: as we accelerate, the dust could obliterate those weakened points. All the damage is repairable, but two of the weakened structures on *Mirror* are close to hull seams, and I'd rather not allow the crack to start."

"We could put explosive covers over the hull sensors," Ceverny suggested. "Then blow off the slag as soon as we need to see. We could slag the aft wing sensors, too, to avoid repeating our earlier dust damage on entry."

"A good idea, Miska," Gray said. "Sirs?" he asked formally. Pov and Andreos nodded.

"It seems prudent," Andreos said. Gray glanced courteously at Rachel, and she nodded, too. It was a deference that seemed promising, if Gray's crew would follow their captain's lead.

Athena loaded Helm Map into the interlink, and Pov and Ceverny immediately turned their chairs toward the wallscreen display. To one side, Theta One blazed in filtered ultraviolet in its multiple stars; directly ahead lay the impenetrable blackness of Orion's molecular cloud, its surface roiling subtly in a dozen shades of dusky infrared. "The second point to decide," Athena said, "is choosing our place of entry into the shock-front between the ionized bubble and the molecular cloud. That kind of shock-front is a medium we've never even approximated in our plasma runs. We can guess about its nature from light-readings, but enough of the readings are anomalous to hint at some unknown processes." Athena pointed with the computer at several whorls of dark gas visible against the black cloud behind it. "These are probably circular dust storms. The mass of each storm is insufficient to be prestellar, at least according to our theories of stellar formation, but we've never actually seen a star get started."

"The K-L Nebula is forming much deeper in the cloud," Gray said. "I doubt if those cloudlets survive long under that kind of light pressure. The effect might be magnetic." He got up from his chair and walked offscreen to look closer at his own interlink display.

"Another possibility," Isaac acknowledged from *Mirror*. "We know very little about magnetic phenomena in clouds this large, much less a shock-front powered by an O-star cluster. The cloudlets definitely radiate in infrared, but so does everything else over there. Dust, we think." Athena shrugged at him. "We could be wrong," Isaac admitted. "We can't tell from this angle: it's all blurred by the general infrared from the molecular cloud behind the shock-front."

"Maybe from the side—" Pov said.

"Exactly," Isaac said. "So Athena and I are suggesting one of these interim spaces between the cloudlets. The spaces appear turbulent and might be dusty, though I doubt it. After all, the whole point of a shock-front is cloud destruction."

"But we're largely jumping blind," Rachel said soberly, speaking up.

"In part," Athena admitted. "We can see where to jump, but we can't fully analyze what's there to jump into. It's probably not dust. It might be shocked gas. It's probably not a whirlwind or a jet, but it might be rough weather, probably outflow from those cloudlets. There's a definite flux in the infrared, probably a gas phase of some kind."

"Where's the K-L on this plot?" Pov asked.

"At this angle," Athena said, "in line of sight behind Theta One. Personally, I'd rather not trust the

theorists that we really do fold space when we jump,
no matter what's in the way. If we try to jump *through*
Theta One, it might have other ideas about getting
folded, with that kind of accumulated gravity." She
frowned. "In our light-ranging from the outer Nebula,
this shock-front effect, whatever it is, is mostly blurred
by the glare of the Core: it might be worse directly
above the K-L."

"I'd rather see where I'm going," Andreos suggested mildly from *Net*.

"I totally agree, sir." Athena sat back and crossed
her arms.

Gray came back to his chair and sat down, then
stretched out his legs and frowned a moment. "I prefer an intermediate jump myself," he decided. "Pov?"

"It seems prudent," Pov said reluctantly.

"Distancing is obviously a problem on the cloud-
edge," Rachel said, "and I think it will remain a problem." She spread her fingers expressively. "How far
away is it, whatever it is? Everything's infrared from
the dust emissions, with line intensity not telling us
much for distance-ranging. Line intensity could mean
too many things besides relative distance." She nodded at Athena's Helm Map plot on the interlink
screen. "There's the first example, I think. Are we
sure of the distance from here to that shock-front,
Athena?"

Athena nodded. "With our readings from the edge,
we have enough triangulation—just. We don't know
how deep it is, a half light-year, a third, a few solar-
system diameters, but by comparison our ships are
peas floating in the sea. We'll fit, wherever we land."

Rachel frowned thoughtfully. "We need some new
ideas for distance-ranging, I think. Triangulating and
Helm Map won't be enough, not in the inner Core."

"What heresy," Isaac grumbled genially from *Mirror*'s Helm Deck. "Helm Map is always enough. It's a rule."

"Whose rule?" Rachel challenged.

"My rule. But I could be wrong, another heresy you didn't hear me say, Rachel." He rocked his chair and smiled at her. "I agree we need some new ideas."

"But we can jump *there*," Pov said, pointing to the shock-front. "We can go at least there."

"Yes," Isaac said. "We can go there."

Andreos glanced at all of them again, got back a round of nods. "Then, sirs, we jump in four hours."

Pov went back to bed and lay awake for an hour, trying not to toss and turn for Avi's sake. It's always like this, he thought resentfully, deciding to complain. I get to sleep and then they wake me up and tell me things, and then I go back to bed and think about the things. He tried to imagine a soft darkness, then himself drifting in space with it ... and decorated it with protostars and started a mental scan of the Nebula geography. Stop. He tried a long fall into velvety darkness, counting slowly as he fell, spinning slowly around. ... The Nebula Core reformed around him, its protostars whirling in place, flickering redly among a brilliant golden glow. Stop. Desperately, he thought about making love to Avi, how it started yesterday and got more interesting and then continued on. ... He turned his head and looked at Avi sleeping beside him as he woke up more, not less. Well? he asked himself.

It's inconsiderate, he told himself back. Go to sleep. I can't.

He stirred restlessly, then realized he had a second problem, getting rapidly worse, as other images of

Avi's naked body flickered across his mind, the touch of her hands, the sweet surge of her hips against his. Stop.

How?

He squirmed again, then froze as he felt Avi's hand slide onto his hip. God, he'd woken her up. He lay still as her hand slipped upward, exploring his chest muscles through the fabric of his pajama top, then finding the center seam and trailing a finger along the close, unzipping it upward in a slow, tantalizing movement. Up to his collar, then down, slowly, slowly. His flesh tingled with the slow caress; as her hand moved lower and brushed lightly over his erection, he closed his eyes and sighed.

"Still want to sleep?" she murmured, her laugh a low breath of sound.

"Sleep was number three on my list. You're fondling the current number one. I didn't mean to wake you up."

"Didn't you? I'm annoyed you didn't. We need to practice, get this right." She moved her hand more firmly.

He turned his head to look at her, startled. "Isn't it right already?" he asked.

Avi laughed. "Now who's insecure? Of course it's all right. I'm talking about timing. In a couple of weeks, if the timing's right on the hormones when we get home, let's make another sibling." She sat up and whispered her gown over her head. "First stage, Povinko. Get prepared."

"I am prepared, as you already know. Are you sure about the other?"

"Positive." She flipped back the bedcover, tumbling it off the end of the bed, then pushed him down as he reached for her. "Russki choice," she growled. "Lie back."

Afterward, they lay nested against each other, Avi lean and soft against his body as heartbeats slowed, body warmth dissipated into the cool conditioned air of their bedroom. Pov moved his face against her hair, breathing deeply of her scents. "You are the Nebula," he murmured. "It's all here, every important part."

"I've noticed you make that connection rather regularly," she said, sounding amused. "I used to be the Pleiades."

"You're both," he said huskily and kissed her.

She caressed him slowly, smiling at him in the darkness. "And you are the Rodina, the homeland," she said after a while. "People will think we're odd, what we say."

"So don't tell them." His lips moved down her neck. "I'm not thinking about Admin level at all. I just noticed that." She tugged on his hair gently, pulling his lips to hers.

"I wish the windows weren't plated over," she said when she released him. "Then we could go into the living room and do another Russki choice, with the golden glow and red lamps shining in, the fireflies dancing and rippling, moving the light across your body. I'd like to see that, how it moves." She slipped her fingers over his ribs and hip, lingeringly. "There must be music outside that we can't hear, some kind of airy melody, made up of fire and creation and love. Has to be."

"But dangerous." He frowned. "I'm not sure we're noticing that as we should."

"Beautiful and dangerous."

"There's x-ray loose in the ship, and we're only at

the first jump-point. What's going to happen at the
next one?"

"You are beautiful." She caressed him. "Can you
be dangerous?"

"Not much. I could try harder, I suppose."

"I'm sure you're dangerous already," she said lazily,
her hands moving. "You are the Nebula." She moved
still closer. "Show me dangerous, Pov," she whispered.
"Show me fire and creation and love, the Prince of
Wands in all his passion. Show me again, beloved."

He kissed her fiercely.

An hour later, after Avi had fallen asleep, Pov got
up quietly and showered, then dressed and left the
apartment. His footsteps quickened as he reached the
companionway, and he made himself slow down to a
brisk walk. The shuttered windows of the long companionway counted themselves one by one as he
walked to the elevators, a line of tall panels that kept
out the dangerous light of the Core. They had missed
something, he thought. Something in the scans. He
was sure of it. As the cage door opened, Axel Bergstrom began to step out and gave him a smile of
surprise.

"Good morning, sir," he said affably and moved to
one side as they stepped past each other.

"How're the gnomes, Axel?" Pov asked as the
doors began to close.

"Busy!" Axel called back and waved. Then he was
gone. As Pov rode the elevator upward, he tapped an
impatient rhythm on his leg, trying to catch the elusive
fact. What is it? What fact?

After another hour, he still hadn't found it. He went
step by step through Athena's scans, checking the distance-ranging, the infrared readings, the Helm Map

course, the jump sequence. Nothing. Finally he leaned an elbow on his console and rubbed his eyes slowly. What was it?

"Headache, Pov?" Ceverny's voice rumbled behind him as Ceverny came into the interlink room for alpha watch. The older man sounded concerned.

"Uh, no." Pov straightened and looked around with a quick smile. "Not at all, Miska." Because of—he thought, suddenly realizing it was true. He blinked, a little startled, as a pattern he hadn't noticed clicked into place. He never had a headache afterward, even if he'd had one when they—

"What?" Miska asked, staring at him curiously.

"Nothing," Pov muttered hastily, and turned back to his interlink board. So explain *that* to Ariadne, he thought, amused. What a prescription. No, it can't be that easy. Probably isn't. Behind him, Ceverny gave a little snort and sat down, his chair creaking. Avi will laugh, Pov thought.

"What *are* you smiling about?" Ceverny demanded.

Pov whirled his chair. "Don't ask me. I'm warning you."

"I insist on at least a hint." Ceverny lowered his eyebrows fiercely, threatening him.

"Okay, I'll give you two," Pov said. "Sex and Avi."

"Oh." Ceverny turned around to his inship board. "I told you not to ask."

"Next time I won't."

"I don't see why you mumble and get bashful," Pov commented. "Don't you and Katrinya still—" Ceverny silenced him with a glare. Pov laughed. Got you.

With masterful dignity, Miska Ceverny turned back to his own board. A minute passed, broken only by a quiet tapping on two keyboards. Pov windowed back into Helm Map and frowned at the displays.

"Actually, we do," Ceverny announced to no one in particular. Pov chuckled.

Ten minutes later, the Grays windowed into the interlink, followed by Captain Andreos. "Are we ready, Athena?" Andreos asked pleasantly. "Berka? Isaac?"

Pov opened his mouth, then realized he had nothing specific against the jump. No fact, whatever it was. "Ready, sir," the others answered.

"Prepare for launch," Andreos ordered.

Isle and her companions jumped again, decelerating into the heated plasma of the shock-front. As the two pilotmasters had predicted, the steady beating of ultraviolet had destroyed most of the dust, and the ships made a smooth entry into the hot plasma. The temperature of the atoms rose to several thousand degrees, a hot plasma busily winding itself into currents. As they smoothly inverted after jump, the highly ionized atoms spun into their sails, flowing smoothly into the holds and helped by the high temperature of the gas. Karoly sampled steadily from the flow, bottling the higher-energy ions. The weather was rough, as Athena had predicted, but not unmanageable. The three ships turned down-current and increased speed, reducing the gas impact on the ships for a smoother sail.

On one side of the ships, the Trapezium stars blazed hotly in ultraviolet, slowly burning into the heart of the molecular cloud that had given them birth. On the other side, a roiling boundary of dark gas marked the other side of the shock-front, a ragged and shifting edge of the molecular cloud now under attack. The boundary between the Trapezium's ultraviolet impact and the molecular cloud was not a smooth boundary, but pitted and bulging across a narrow band a half light-year across. Beneath that front another two light-years ahead, the K-L Nebula glowed in deep infrared, with definable infrared point-sources counting in the dozens. Protostars, younger, maybe hotter, the next-Trapezium still embedded in its dark-cloud nursery.

"Let's try light-ranging—" Pov began.

"Pov," Tully interrupted, his voice urgent as he windowed directly into the outship link. "X-ray is rising. It's gone up two percent in the last three minutes."

"From where?" Andreos asked in alarm. "From the O-stars?"

Pov looked at the white blaze in the wall display, his neck hairs prickling. A supernova could start that fast, a bare minute or two as the star collapsed inward, beginning the explosion that would rebound outward, obliterating everything in its path. One of the other Trapezium O-stars might be old enough, he realized, the second star to die.

"No," Tully said, shaking his head hard. "It's coming at us laterally across the shock-front. From that cloudlet at forty degrees west, it seems. The entire structure is lighting up in x-ray. Or maybe the whole shock-front." He glanced down at his sail displays and grimaced. "Another one percent, sir. It's definitely a wave propagating directly at us. The curve is climbing fast. It could go asymptotic."

"What could it be?" Rachel asked, her eyes wide.

Pov and Gray stared at each blankly, each waiting for the other to explain.

"In Jewish legend," Isaac offered dryly from *Mirror*'s Helm Deck, "it is said that the city of Paradise is guarded by a great hollow wall." Pov looked at him, just as blankly as he had looked at Gray. "To enter Paradise," Isaac continued soberly, "one must enter the wall, a dark emptiness inhabited by an Angel of Destruction, a great and powerful being that travels as a storm of dust and lightning, and who knows when any have entered the wall. And when it comes upon souls within the wall, it destroys all who are unworthy of Paradise." Isaac looked at the bright blur of x-ray in the wallscreen. "I am not so sure of my inner righteousness. I suggest we get out of the wall, sirs."

"Angels?" Gray asked, confused. "What the hell, Isaac?"

"Hell is definitely relevant," Isaac replied, without smiling. "Seriously, sir, as in what's coming toward us right now. Let us get *out* of the way."

"Six percent, sirs," Tully prompted, obviously in total agreement. "We have x-ray leakage starting in the forward hull."

"Could we jump over it?" Athena asked. "Get into the next trough of whatever wave that is?"

"We can't see through it," Andreos objected. "It's too bright. And we don't know the wavelength. How far is enough, Athena? Where's the other side of the cloudlet? Rachel was right. We can't see enough here." Gray frowned distractedly. "We can't go closer to the Trapezium. The light's too hard."

Tully's eyes were now wide with alarm, fixed on Pov's face. "Sir," he said earnestly.

"Another choice is jumping back to the dust bar," Gray said, "but that effect is slanting across our return track. We might accelerate right into it." He shook his head.

"Then the other way?" Pov suggested. He gestured at the dark cloud on the other side of the shock-front. "Into the molecular cloud?"

"That's a dust wall, Pov," Ceverny objected.

"It's thinner on the edge," Athena said. "Maybe it's thin enough. We can blast our way in with our engines. And we have slag to spare now."

"Twelve percent!" Tully called, his voice strained.

Whatever the phenomenon might be, it was climbing fast.

"We must jump, Thaddeus," Andreos said urgently to Gray. "We must jump *now*."

"Pov?" Gray asked, frowning.

"Lay the course, Athena. Quickly."

"Yes, sir."

Athena hurriedly plotted the course as the three ships maneuvered closer together, forming a wedge. The ships retraced their sails hurriedly, forming the tight cone of the touring sails used for every jump. As Athena took control of the other ships' Helm Decks through the slaved drive, the three ships pivoted neatly in space, aligning on the boiling dark edge of the molecular cloud.

"Warn the crew," Pov told Ceverny. "Everyone not sitting down goes flat on the deck. Now! Drop the interior barriers, too."

"Emergency launch!" Ceverny said into the inship channel. His voice boomed through the corridor outside, bouncing off the walls and floor. "On the floor, everyone!" Over the interlink to *Mirror* and *Net,* Pov heard the same command echo through the other ships.

"Are the barriers secure?" Pov asked.

"Secure," Ceverny answered promptly. *Isle* had just become a series of nested boxes, each environmentally complete, protected from hull breach in any of the others. Pov thought wildly of the twins and Kate and Chavi, safe in the ship's protected amidships. The barriers were tripled there. Oh, keep them safe, he prayed, not knowing Whom he asked. Anyone. Any god with the power to keep them safe.

And Avi, please God Avi.

"*Launch!*" Athena shouted. The engines flared,

skipping the wedge faster and faster with each micro-jump. Athena pushed the drive to the limit, far beyond any of their tests, forcing the intervals shorter and shorter as she compressed an hour's time into scant minutes.

"It's flaring behind us!" Tully shouted. "Thirty percent! Pov!"

"And jump!" Athena called harshly. The linked ships leaped madly into darkness, an inferno at their heels.

"Inverting *now*," Athena cried an instant later. She turned the ships neatly and threw all power to the drive. "Hold on, everyone! I'm braking hard." Pov grabbed at his chair as he felt *Isle*'s gravity field falter under the strain and weight surged through his body at wrong angles. The ship shuddered again, followed by another wild surge, and another. "Hold on!" Athena called again.

"Hull breach!" Ceverny shouted into the inship link. "Prow level six!" Pov waited tensely as the reports chattered back from the level above chaffer Deck. Level evacuated. Decompression crew in. Seal made. Pressure restored.

Then: minor injuries, suffered in the scramble off the level. Wing sensors gone in a blast of impact heat. Half the sail assembly torn away in the turn. Structural damage portside. More damage starboard. Hull damage, but intact. He closed his eyes. Engine damage, not severe. Wing damage, moderate. Hold damage, not severe.

"*Net?*" he asked. "*Mirror?*"

Gray grimaced. "Moderate damage. My hull is a little thinner," he said grimly.

"Mine, too," Andreos said soberly. "The slag

melted *into* my sensors. It's all slag now." He gestured in despair.

"Can we see?" Gray demanded. "Where are we?"

"What's our speed, Athena?" Pov asked.

"Sixty percent lightspeed," she said. "I am easing back on engine power." She hesitated, then bit her lip unhappily. "We ought to model that speed-up decision-making, sirs," she said soberly. "I just realized we didn't have to jump into the cloud-edge, only far enough ahead to get some time. Even x-ray doesn't go faster than lightspeed." She scowled.

"*If* that was x-ray," Gray said. "Let me see your readings, Tully." He bent forward and studied the graph displays as Tully fed his full data into the interlink. "Well, the sail computer calls it x-ray, though I think it's mostly a convenient label for 'very bright.' I doubt if it was x-ray at all."

"A magnetic field line?" Pov asked, catching his drift. "The lines at T Tauri looked like x-ray on a few scans." My fact, he thought abruptly. The flux on the scans. It sure the hell helps to know it now.

Gray leaned back and scowled. "I can't see a single resemblance in the waveform," he said. He tightened his jaw into a rigid line, his anger barely under control. "We nearly destroyed our ships by panicking, sirs. If Athena weren't a hot pilot and Helm Map's distancing weren't just adequate enough, we'd be dead now. I suggest we think about that."

Andreos shook his head. "The field line might have bisected the shock-front edge to edge, Thaddeus. We didn't know how wide it was."

"So we could have jumped ahead of it," Gray countered, "as Athena said."

"And jump into the next field line? If that was the

shock-front's version of T Tauri's frozen magnetic field lines, there's more than one."

Gray shrugged, still scowling.

"I prefer to call them angels of destruction," Isaac said, sounding subdued. "It's as good a label as any— and aptly cosmic."

"Angels whom we almost joined." Gray thudded his fist on his console. "Dammit! We're better captains than that!" Gray was obviously angry at himself the most. He abruptly got up from his chair and walked out of the room.

Rachel sighed and looked down at her hands, then turned around to her inship board and talked to her chiefs, asking for more reports on *Mirror*'s ship damage. Behind him, Pov heard Ceverny asking the same questions, more urgently.

"It was the right decision," Andreos said softly. "We had nowhere else to go that could be safe. Sensors can be replaced." He raised his hand as Pov opened his mouth. "But we can't see what we need to see here," Andreos added, looking worried. "We have to solve it—but how?"

"Probes?"

"They can't range across a wide enough arc," Andreos said. "We'd need thousands of them to get the detail we need." He waved at the wallscreen. "We looked there and saw a window. Nothing waiting for us, so we jumped."

"And jumped fast again. We didn't even know we could do it in a few minutes."

Andreos scowled at him. "The problem with nimble, son, is that sometimes you're not nimble enough. True? And the intermix of the fuel could have exploded on us if our engineers had modeled their parameters a little too short. At least *Jewel* chose her fate. Right?"

"Yes, sir," Pov agreed, more mutedly.

"Damn!" Andreos said to no one in particular, and turned around to the needs of his own ship.

"Forty percent lightspeed," Athena said glumly to Pov.

"Thank you, Athena," Pov said. They traded a bleak look.

Chapter 16

Isle and her two sister ships drifted backward within a haze of dark smoke that obscured the stars. In Pov's Admin office, Pov and Sigrid watched the exterior scans while the labs hunted out the frequency of the shock-front pulses, counting one by one the succession of Isaac's angels of destruction as they patrolled the interface. The count was frequent enough to prove Isaac right in their wild dash to safety: the shock-front pulsed like a beating heart, thundering in response to the Trapezium's steady assault on the dark cloud that had given it birth. A new phenomenon, another unsuspected force, the warning flicker on a light scan they had all missed. Through the drifting dark molecules of the molecular cloud's tattered edge, the interface flickered like distant lightning in a thunderhead, a dim and ominous glow.

On *Isle*'s hull, the robots were again crawling from point to point, repairing the ravages of the dust impact. It would take longer this time, a lot longer. Had the hull specs been ten percent less, a slightly weaker alloy than the alloy they had thought ridiculously strong when they chose it, *Isle* could have split apart like a fan. Avi had called from amidships. All were safe. When the watch changed, Pov had retreated to his office, and Sigrid had joined him unexpectedly, bringing a bottle of wine with her.

Well, they had survived again. Pov supposed it was cause for celebration, if a somewhat muted one.

Pov poured the wine, offered her a tall glass. Together they watched the darkness outside the ship move like a living thing.

"I didn't know it looked like this," he said after a while, his voice sounding strange to himself.

"Nobody did—though we've all speculated some scenarios." Sigrid took a small swallow of her glass of wine, then angled another chair to prop a foot. "A few wrong ones, I might add. I can quote you a theorist or two that just got proved utterly wrong."

Pov smiled. "Including cloudship opinions about dust. We have to change those." Though the dust had wreaked its damage, *BaXt* had then given them an unexpected harbor—here, in the sheltering dust of the dark cloud. In the distance, the shock-front roared, blanketed by the heavy mass of organic molecules it sought steadily to destroy. All around the ships, a flowing sea of dark dust sifted against the hull, a quiet ash, a damped fire, gentle and soothing, stirred only gently by the cloudships' slow passage.

Sigrid shook her blond head wonderingly at the dark cloud which enclosed them like a womb. "The light absorption here must rival some dark asteroids. Nearly total absorption—and we're only a hundred thousand kilometers behind the edge. A blaze like the Trapezium reduced to fireflies." She shook her head again.

"Well, they say it's a war, O-stars and a dark cloud."

"I think the molecular cloud is still winning, angels or no." Sigrid sipped at her wineglass.

The smoke between them and the interface visibly shifted in a slow pressure wave as another shock-pulse moved along the shock-front. The swell propagated slowly toward them, then subtly shifted *Isle*'s artificial gravity as the ship compensated for the swell. "Are we losing rivets when it does that?" she asked idly, pretending a casualness neither of them felt. It had been too close. It had been too damned close.

"Not much," he said, "but your engineers get to think about another design item when we get back. We'll have a long list, Sigrid."

"It'll be worth the work." The tiny stationmaster smiled wryly at the wallscreen. "PAHs," she sighed.

"You and your PAHs."

"The stuff of the future," she said back more vigorously than he expected. "There's more to life than sails: get alert. It'll be an entirely new chemistry. All of it in zero-gee, where chemistry works nicest, and an unending sea to distill and experiment with forever." Her blue eyes were intent on his face.

"I feel that way about sails." Pov poured more wine into his glass and propped his feet on his desk. "Endless and endless sails."

"Don't get drunk," she advised him severely. "It won't impress the other shipmasters."

"Thanks, Mom," he said.

Sigrid chuckled and saluted him with her own glass. "Somehow I don't think I've converted you. I'll keep working on it. You're still mired in tritium and ions: but chemistry can take us farther. Put an electric field around molecules and you can sort them by shape, get absolutely pure samples—and in bulk. Start a crystal growing and feed it suitable atoms, and you end up with a perfect crystal, absolutely uniform. Imagine a perfect crystal the size of this ship, one computer chip of a superbrain—or a transmitter than can pierce the light barrier and finally give us translight communication, light with a jump." She paused and sipped at her glass, then gestured expansively. "We can make carbon rings and keep them cycling, step by step, and you can create the entire series of possible hydrocarbons, each with different properties, different uses. New pharmaceuticals, catalysts, piezoelectrics. High-tensile fabrics and artificial steels, new plastics and gels and new everything. I can do some of this in my station processors, but the energies I have to invest usually aren't worth the minuscule result or the development costs. But here," she said, gesturing at the wallscreen, "Nature has already invested the energy, little packets of profitable energy wrapped into bits of matter I can use. Most of them are PAHs. I have reason behind my madness."

"A treasure trove," he agreed indulgently. "Sigrid, I'm a sailmaster. I always will be. I like waveforms and energy states and grid-lines: I don't think like a chemist." He saluted her with his glass. "But I'll concede the worth of PAHs. I trust your opinion."

She harrumphed to herself and didn't say anything.

"What's the matter, Sigrid? What are you worrying about?"

"Oh, I don't know." Sigrid leaned back and crossed her arms. "I just feel I don't get through. You all think my PAHs are funny, a joke. You just don't see it. If anyone could see it, it'd be you, the cloudships, but you don't."

She looked down at her small boots, crossed neatly on the chair. "Access to the molecular clouds," she said firmly, "will revolutionize chemistry as much as basic atomic theory. Right now, as future generations will look back at us, we're still busily hunting the philosopher's stone, dressed up in our alchemist's pointed hat and flowing robes, talking about bile and quicksilver and phlegm and etheric essences, peering in amazement at the odd substances in our flasks without a clue about why." She waved at the drifting smoke again. "Why is it cold? Why is it dark? What are the cloud-size phenomena, the phases of chemical interaction propagating through a cloud like this that we can see only as random events—or not see at all? Is gravity a particle? Does the etheric essence really exist? Is matter different from what we understand it to be? Or does matter not exist at all? I propose to you that, in subatomic reality, it really doesn't."

"I agree," Pov said, studying her face. She frowned at him.

"It does make one uneasy." She waved her small hand at the screen again. "Why do PAHs avoid electric fields, and what could we do with that? Why does carbon-60 pack itself in little balls—and could it do it bigger? Could we build a dust grain that's ship-size and manufacture molecules a trillionfold? Are there other chemical systems just as elaborate as hydrocarbon, a parallel chemistry we don't even suspect? Silicon has possibilities, and these clouds are rife with silicon. Chlorine is another. Or maybe the key isn't even whole atoms, but quarks. Maybe even quarks are too big, and there's something smaller, a single perfect essence that runs the universe. Maybe there's a fundamental that explains everything. Maybe gold is the perfection of matter, and those old alchemists were right." She smiled softly, looking at the screen. "Maybe, too, the fundamental is beauty."

"You belong on Sail Deck, Sigrid."

"I do not. Be polite. Though I do admit we might see an evolution, a blending of you and me. At least

I hope so. Right now we're cloudship and station."
She pointed at Pov, then herself. "In the future, we
might find an intermediate form, a ship-station, a mobile city, a ship-home as big as we wish to build it. In
the future, we might wander so far that we leave the
planets behind us forever. Imagine that: exploring the
Orion arm clear to the galaxy's heart. No product to
sell to stupid groundhoggers, just the going to see
whatever's there." She shrugged her small shoulders.
"Not in our generation, probably, maybe not for several to come, but someday. Someday we may all be
gypsies wandering your road, a mobile humanity in
the ways that count, the next great wave of explorers."

The ship surged gently on the swell as another angel
rattled down the interface.

"Sounds more Viking than gypsy to me," Pov said.
He refilled his glass and settled back. "All that exploring and what-all."

"I admit the heritage. All I've heard from you for
the past year has been the Core, the Core, the Core.
There's more to life than O-stars, Pov. We're sitting
in the better part you choose to ignore. You pretend
this vast indifference, this indulgent tolerance for a
Scandi stationmaster's chemical preoccupations, this
judgment and assessment and—"

"Who's judging?"

"I have many forms of revenge." Pov eyed her, and
Sigrid bared her teeth. "After all, as you point out, I
come from Viking stock, all that rampaging along the
English coast with sword and fire and general lusty
behavior."

"The gypsies didn't get to England until all that was
over." Pov shrugged.

"We got as far as Sicily."

"We got to Sicily later, too. You missed us, Sigrid."

He tsked. "The threat just doesn't work—Rom just don't have a racial memory for Viking terror."

"Personal mayhem, Thorsen to Janusz?"

"Now *that* might have an impact."

"So get alert, Pov."

"Yes, ma'am." Sigrid chuckled.

"I hear you, Sigrid," he said quietly. "So does Andreos. We came here to find a future, whatever it is. You'll have a say in it. Hell, you might end up running it. I wouldn't mind." He saw Sigrid relax. As the lone stationmaster among cloudship captains, Sigrid had a delicate dance in promoting her station's interests. Sigrid wanted the K-L, too. She wanted it all. Angels or not.

They sat in a comfortable silence, watching sheet lightning flicker through the interface, a night horizon with roiling clouds. *Isle* and her companion ships drifted easily on the swell, still coasting steadily backward on the momentum of their hard entry, sheltered from the distant storm by an enshrouding night.

"Shion nevo ankliste, tal aminghe bachtalo," Pov murmured after a while. Sigrid turned her head. "It's a Rom prayer to Shion, the New Moon, the ever-changing Mother who drifts unseen in darkness. *Alaclame bivolengo, Te mukel ame bachtasa, Ai sastimasa, Ai lovensa.* That means 'The New Moon has come out, may she be lucky for us. She has found us penniless; may she leave us with fortune, and with good health, and with money.' One of the gypsy icons for luck, Sigrid. Shion measures time and shapes the universe, a Mother much larger than us but benevolent and aware." He pointed at the dark drifts of matter in the wallscreen. "Shion. She is the luck that brings destiny." With his other hand, he toasted Sigrid with his wineglass in a gentle salute. "See? I can listen.

You find endless PAHs for the collecting; I see the
Dark Lady Shion, the New Moon robed in the night."

"Lady Chemistry, you mean."

"More than that."

"There's *nothing* more than chemistry." Sigrid affected a reproving look, then lost it in a sigh as she
looked back at the wallscreen. "Lady Beauty." She
sighed again. "Your Lady is very lovely, Pov. I think
I'll become her devotee, swing a censer of incense,
chant in a procession, build a temple or two."

"Gypsies don't do that stuff."

She smiled. "You just compose poetry."

"And follow the luck."

"Always the luck. Some of it seems to have shed
itself on me. There I was, lusting for only *one*
cloudship to partner with TriPower, one little advantage to get out of my second-station status with Euro-
Com, and you bring me destiny. I'm too practical for
destiny, whatever my chemist's wishes. It doesn't fit."

"Nuts." But Sigrid wasn't listening. She sighed and
watched the wine shimmer in her glass, and seemed
to speak more to herself than to him.

"I'm a tough executive, alone and liking it," she
said softly. "When Ralf announced he wouldn't move
to the Pleiades, the hell with me and Lang and whatever I wanted, I told him to get lost. So he told me I
could occupy myself better by giving Lang a brother—
he wanted a spare son to carry on the family name,
he said, just for insurance. I told him he could keep
his family name, too, and his insurance, the hell with
him, and I advised him what to do with both. It was
a nasty fight. I've never missed him." She shrugged
unconvincingly.

"Why haven't you ever remarried, Sigrid?"

"Is that your business?" Sigrid asked aggressively.

"Sure it is. Captain Andreos is alone, too. Why don't you marry him? He likes you."

Sigrid looked away, and a slight pink flush crept up her neck from her collar. "You need more than 'like.' "

"That's because you haven't worked on it yet. He doesn't think he'll ever remarry, either, but it's been ten years since Sophia died and he shouldn't be alone. Neither should you. I think you two should get married. I'll bring the wine for the wedding."

"Stop matchmaking," she sputtered.

"Absolutely not." He pointed his finger at her, delighted, as Sigrid got pinker. "Look at the blush," he teased. "I didn't know you could blush, Sigrid. I'm amazed."

"I remind you, sir," Sigrid retorted with spirit, "that some of the molecules in this cloud are cyanide. I'll make you some vodka from the alcohols and lace it nice."

"Sounds good to me."

"Back off, Pov, will you?" she said in a low voice, then looked away again, at the wallscreen, at the door, at anything but him. "It's not . . ."

"I think I'll tell Katrinya," he said gently. "She'd love to help."

"Oh, don't tell Katrinya," Sigrid insisted, with obvious horror.

"Why the hell not? She'll be delighted."

Sigrid opened her mouth, then shut it. After a moment, she opened it again, shut it again. I'll definitely tell Katrinya, Pov thought. Deft guile and brains could hide a lot of loneliness, when you've practiced hiding it well. He looked at Sigrid fondly, wishing she didn't feel apart. She wasn't.

Sigrid laughed. "I can't think of a damned thing to say. Not one."

"This is new," Pov agreed. "But love is like that, don't you think?"

"Maybe. If it is love."

"So go find out if it is. You're good at finding things out. You're a chemist. So is he. Sort it. That's what holdmasters do, after all."

"Maybe." Sigrid propped her other foot on the chair and sipped at her wine, her eyes on the drifting darkness in the wallscreen. "Maybe," she repeated softly to herself. "PAHs first."

"Angels first. We've still got to get out."

"We will," Sigrid said confidently. "Shion has spoken. It's our destiny."

The next day Pov ordered the ships to full stop. In twenty-four hours, the three ships had penetrated a quarter million kilometers into the molecular cloud, and the shock-front was now a bare flicker in the distance, the swells from the interface subsided to a nearly imperceptible stirring of the black dust. After checking radiation levels outside, minimal this deep in the molecular cloud, Pov sent out two skyriders to begin repair of *Isle*'s sail assembly, using spare webbing and axial supports from the ship's hold stores. Another skyrider assisted the robots in replacing the damaged sensors in the hull, and during the night the engineering chiefs had evacuated the breached prow section and replaced an entire segment of hull plate.

Another twenty-four hours to complete repairs, the chiefs reported during alpha watch, plus twelve more for a full-ship integrity check, with a stressed lateral hull support still doubtful no matter what the skyrider repairs. They had no spares for the largest structural beams: the damaged lateral support could be replaced only at TriPower.

Isle had the worst damage, the luck of the draw when the wedge smashed into a tendril of heavier dust at the edge. Sheltered between and behind the two dreadnoughts on entry, *Net* had lost only her sensors and an inch of hull plate. *Isle* and *Mirror* had lent freely from their sensor stores to rebuild *Net*'s entire aft wing array.

As the work continued, the captains considered what next to do, throwing open the question to the entire assembly of ship chiefs not directly involved in the outship repairs. As the chiefs talked in several conference rooms in their various sections of the ship, Pov spent an hour in Sergei's physics lab, listening to the ongoing analysis by his brother-in-law and Sergei's fellow physicists about the shock-front pulses, then met with the repair chiefs and Tully for another two hours to consult about *Isle*'s damaged sailset. At mid-watch, he and Tully went outboard in Kate's skyrider to inspect the sail assembly at close range. Near the end of that morning's alpha watch, as the repairs continued, Thaddeus Gray asked Pov and Andreos to an interlink conference.

Pov excused Tully to supervise the sails, then watched as Athena and Berka windowed in from their Helm Decks, then Isaac Griegman from *Mirror*. Rachel sat tensely behind Gray in *Mirror*'s interlink room.

"The chiefs' recommendations are mixed over here," Gray said as a preamble. "I imagine yours are the same, both of you." He nodded toward his daughter seated at the other console. "But Rachel has an item of good news, we think."

Rachel lifted her chin. "Isaac and I think we've

found a solution to our distancing problem," she said. "We practiced with our LP maser data from the edge, and the distance-ranging matches up." She loaded a Helm Map projection looking from the Nebula edge to LP Orionis. "With our cutter triangulation, we estimated 6.4223 light-years from our Nebula entry at the edge to our first entry at LP. From that view, we saw this maser." The map highlighted a small point on the blurry disk of LP Orionis, then zoomed forward to show the maser winking in the left quadrant of LP's dust shell. "Masers are near point-sources in space, little more than a half-dozen solar-system diameters wide, and we can determine their precise relative position respecting other masers in their area. We can also determine the radial velocity of the rotating cloudlet toward or away from us with redshift readings. If we assume that the maser molecules have a range of random motion that is identical from one maser to another, which we've confirmed in each maser we've examined, we can measure lateral drift. It gives us three dimensions. The maser can triangulate for us."

"Excellent, *Mirror,*" Andreos said in delight.

Rachel gave him a tight smile. "We matched the LP maser calculation to our proven distance from the edge of LP. The range of error was less than twenty thousand kilometers."

"*That* precise?" Athena asked in surprise, raising an eyebrow. "That's better than what Helm Map does now."

"What heresy," Isaac joked, looking pleased, too. "We've never thought of using maser-ranging in Helm Map—masers have never been a relevant part of our local space. The K-L has over two dozen masers facing Earth; likely we'll find another two or three dozen from other angles of view. With a little more jumping around the Nebula to confirm some of the subtler cloud rotations, we can use the K-L masers as beacons for the entire Nebula."

They all sat silently for a minute, somewhat stunned as each mentally raced through the possibilities. Cubic mapping had become an art for the cloudships: with this one precise measure of distance, the risks of any jump declined a hundredfold. TriPower's freighter traffic used mechanical beacons to pilot a set narrow course-track from point to point into the Pleiades: the cloudships had needed more flexibility to hunt the drifts of ions they harvested. Beacons, Pov thought. Maser beacons to help us see—and to see better than we've ever seen before. For Katrinya Ceverny, it would be a quiet satisfaction, a suitable revenge.

"It would help," Isaac added, "to confirm with actual on-site readings in the K-L."

Thaddeus Gray scowled. "What about your angels?" he asked. "The shock-front—"

"Before we get to that," Ceverny rumbled, "our Hold Deck has another datum that is very relevant."

He shifted his inship screen from *Isle*'s Hold Deck to the interlink. Katrinya tried to sit up straighter in her reclining bed as they tapped in, but Sigrid promptly pushed her back again. Katrinya instantly relented, though it was obvious any excess by Sigrid promised trouble later. Sigrid grinned, undented, and perched on the edge of Katrinya's bed

"A very relevant datum," Sigrid said, nodding.

Katrinya poked her playfully in the hip, and Sigrid shut up. "It's *my* announcement, Sigrid, though you can share. During the initial sort in the shock-front before we had to jump, Karoly found three of our superheavy particles in the plasma. They were highly degenerated, less than twenty percent of full shell packing, but they were definitely superheavy decay products."

"Well, similar magnetics create—" Gray began.

Katrinya shook her head. "The shock-front pulsing is not the same phenomenon. According to Sergei and the other physicists, the pulse is a plasma resonance, shock-front-wide, not frozen magnetics. The field lines are not frozen." She gestured ironically. "They're too busy singing."

Andreos smiled wryly. "Singing?"

"Not my word," Katrinya replied. "Go lecture Sergei." Then she sniffed judiciously and waved her bandaged hand again. "Actually, Isaac started it. Choirs of angels and all that."

"So where did the particles come from, Katrinya?" Pov asked.

Katrinya glanced up at Sigrid. "Oh, Sigrid had some ideas. Obsession can be occasionally useful. At her suggestion, we tracked the plasma drift from the interface directly over the K-L against the proven degeneration curve of those three particles. With a little energy support from the plasma resonance, a dab here and there of direct UV impact, a curve around a cloudlet's magnetic field, and so forth, a given particle might still exist at twenty percent this distance from the K-L. Might. It assumes about forty variables Sigrid's way, but it might."

Andreos narrowed his eyes thoughtfully. "But the K-L protostars are several light-years below the interface. We've never found superheavy particles outside a gas-jet environment. The shells unpack almost immediately once they drift."

"Not in the K-L, apparently," Katrinya said. "I think we've found King Solomon's mines, sir." Her voice was triumphant. "We wanted something only we could do, but Earth can harvest at T Tauri, once they have the ships and the technique. But they have to harvest a gas-jet. What if the particles are free-float in the K-L? What if all we have to do is sail a strong breeze to catch them?"

"It's tritium all over again," Andreos said slowly. "It'll be cheaper to let us—"

"Harvest," Katrinya said. She looked up at Sigrid again. "And what if we combine it all with Sigrid's PAHs, do some real manufacturing—in zero-gee, with nearly unlimited energy nearby, new phenomena for processes, a genuine control of magnetics on a wide scale?"

"That would take more than TriPower," Andreos commented.

"Oh, I'll share," Sigrid said with a big smile. "So long as I'm richest." She spread her hands. "We'll all be rich, rich enough to build a city station, enough to build an entire colony in space, without a planet. Finally it'll be cost-effective, here in the Nebula. What the drive couldn't give us because time ran out, Leonidas, the Nebula can."

There was a silence, as they all looked at her, stunned, then looked at each other.

"You *think* it's K-L drift," Gray said slowly.

"The three particles *are* decay products," Katrinya said. "There is no doubt. And those three were in our sort."

"It's not a function of the interface?" Gray persisted.

"Minor shell support at most. Sergei is positive."

Gray and Andreos leaned back in their chairs at the same time. "Hmmph," Gray said, then looked around at Rachel. "And exact distancing, you said."

"I vote yes," she said firmly. "Let's go see, Dad."

Her face lit with enthusiasm, and Gray hesitated. "Oh, let's go see!" Rachel leaned forward eagerly.

"We model it a dozen different ways," Gray declared, pointing at her. "No fast decisions in the middle, not again."

"It's a deal, Dad," Rachel said. "After all, we'll be back next time."

"And the times after," Pov addded.

"Hell, we'll move here," Andreos finished for them happily. "I think it's time we talk about angels. Our Paradise in the K-L seems well-guarded. How do we elude our angels to get in?"

"Any ideas?" Pov asked, looking around at the faces.

The answer was Shion's enveloping night, and the safety she provided for the cloudships in her sheltering dust whenever the latest angel rumbled by. The plasma resonance of the shock-front had a complicated frequency, apparently self-modifying over time and never truly predictable, but they had acceptable parameters on the wavelength: at worst, the brightening sky ahead gave enough warning if they were quick. By a series of a dozen short jumps along the edge, the three cloudships skipped along the interface border to the massive interface storm directly over the K-L, then ducked under the turbulent outflow. They could not jump deep inside the molecular cloud, not this time, but they could escape the angels' wall long enough to look safely elsewhere.

In infrared, the protostars of the K-L Nebula glowed like brilliant rubies in a suffused sunset, dominated by one principal jewel in the center of the cluster, an infant O-star. Discovered in the twentieth century with other protostars in the K-L, the star had

remained nameless ever since, denominated only by a
star catalog reference and a radio-ranging beam coor-
dinate, an infrared object called only by the names of
the two radio astronomers who had first discovered it.
Thaddeus Gray named it Cedalion, after the staunch
pilgrim who had guided the blinded Orion to the island of Helios, the Sun. A brilliant infrared point even
in Earth's skies, Cedalion dominated the new star cluster, a ready reference point for all other mapping,
their first sure beacon.

"We can name them all," Pov mused, as the infrared scans continued, probing into the swirls of condensing dust and gas several light-years beneath them,
a hundred future stars and others still to form, the
future powerhouse of an even greater Nebula.

"Why not?" Gray asked, looking up at the interlink
from a report in his lap. "We can use up the rest of
the names in the Orion myths."

"We'll run out of names fairly fast, Thaddeus. Orion
wasn't Hercules, and even with Hercules and all his
labors, we'd run out of names here."

Gray chuckled. "So we'll add Theseus and a few
other suitable heroes. Or we'll name the others after
ourselves. Why not? I think I'll look over the choices
for 'Gray's Star.' You pick one, too."

"As in 'Pov-Was-Here'? Oh, sure. Remember hu-
bris, Thaddeus."

Gray snorted and went back to his report. After a
while, Pov left him to it, turned over the interlink
watch to Miska Ceverny, and went looking for Avi.

He found her amidships with the twins in the large
and comfortable shielded section that sheltered *Isle*'s
children. Along one long wall were a ranked series
of doors, brightly painted with flowers and child-sized
animals, which led to the dormitories and nursery. At

the far end of the section, behind a clear divider, the older kids sat at school. At the nearer end, several arrangements of comfortable couches framed a large play area where the younger kids could play and parents could watch. By the couches, a large wallscreen showed the drifting black dust of the molecular cloud surrounding them, and K-L stars far beneath them glowing dimly in their infrared wavelengths. Avi had arranged herself and the twins to face the view as she nursed Anushka, with Garridan asleep beside her in his warm blanket. Pov sat down on her other side and put his arm around her shoulders.

"The homeland," Avi said, nodding at the wallscreen.

"The road," he responded. Avi smiled, then looked down at Anushka, her face soft in its expression, at peace. She smoothed the baby's wispy hair as Anushka suckled busily on her nipple, her long fingers graceful and delicate as they moved.

Grace. He smiled at Avi's downturned face, in love with her all over again.

Avi looked up at him suddenly and caught him looking at her, all his heart in how he looked. Her eyes widened slightly, then filled with tears that she quickly blinked away. She cleared her throat and looked down at the baby again.

"Have we found the source of the particles?" she asked, her voice husky.

"Not yet. We're still mapping the K-L, and we may not get our answer this trip. We'll probably have to explore directly inside the cluster, maybe track the magnetics to find out why and where. Right now the magnetic picture is mostly a hash. I suspect it's going to stay that way until we've got some new theories.

More for Sergei to think about. Good thing he likes to think."

He reached out and unfolded Anushka's fingers, splaying them on his forefinger. Anushka's fingers moved in response, tightening as she held on to him. "Do you think she'll choose Sail Deck," he asked softly, "when it's her time?"

"It's in her blood," Avi said. "Of course she will. So will her brother, before he becomes shipmaster." She looked up and smiled. "My prophecy this time, a little Rom in the inspiration, a lot more Russki. Do you think I'll be right?"

"I never argue with a *romni* about that stuff. There's no way to win. Ask my mother."

Avi chuckled.

They stayed a week, mapping the K-L point to point, before they turned for home. Karoly and Katrinya had caught more superheavy particles as part of the random drift floating by the cloudships as they hovered, then more, borne on the drifting dust currents that flowed over and around the ships. The new catch suggested a much larger source below, perhaps a river of such particles a cloudship might catch, an easy fortune confined by the rigid magnetics of the developing cluster, perhaps a function of the pressing molecular cloud itself. We'll find out, Pov promised to himself, as *Isle* readied herself for launch at the interface edge, ready to leap into the outer Nebula and, from there, to home—to their Pleiades home. Home for only a short time, soon to change, as all times changed.

Ad Orionem. To the Nebula. The new homeland. The road.

Pov looked at the blaze of the Core stars ahead,

the glimmering of the glowing Nebula beyond it, the sea of light.

"Prepare for launch," Athena said from Helm Deck.

"Acknowledged," *Mirror* and *Net* replied. "We are ready."

"And launch!" Athena cried.

The Roc Frequent Readers Club
BUY TWO ROC BOOKS AND GET
ONE SF/FANTASY NOVEL FREE!

Check the free title you wish to receive (subject to availability):